About the Author

Graham was born in Derby, England, in 1948. He completed an engineering apprenticeship with Rolls Royce, but the company went into voluntary liquidation in 1970, which caused a change in his career path. He married Ann in 1972, and they set up a home in Buckinghamshire, then Farnborough, Hants, handy commuting distances from London. They raised their two children there, Julie and David, and eventually, Graham set up his own air conditioning company. This was very successful, but as retirement approached, he spent time writing the novel he always thought he had in him. *Blood of Your Hero* is the result.

Blood of Your Hero

Graham Hart

Blood of Your Hero

Vanguard Press

VANGUARD PAPERBACK

© Copyright 2025
Graham Hart

The right of Graham Hart to be identified as author of
this work has been asserted by him in accordance with the
Copyright, Designs and Patents Act 1988.

All Rights Reserved

No reproduction, copy or transmission of this publication
may be made without written permission.
No paragraph of this publication may be reproduced,
copied or transmitted save with the written permission of the publisher, or in
accordance with the provisions
of the Copyright Act 1956 (as amended).

Any person who commits any unauthorised act in relation to this publication
may be liable to criminal prosecution and civil claims for damages.

A CIP catalogue record for this title is available from the British Library.

ISBN 978-1-83794-347-0

This is a work of fiction. Names, characters, businesses, places, events and
incidents are either the products of the author's imagination or used in a
fictitious manner. .

Vanguard Press is an imprint of
Pegasus Elliot Mackenzie Publishers Ltd.
www.pegasuspublishers.com

First Published in 2025

Vanguard Press
Sheraton House Castle Park
Cambridge England

Printed & Bound in Great Britain

Acknowledgements

The many history books that provide the backdrop to this story.

Also, my sister Pat who proof-read my original manuscript and gave some pointers. Unfortunately she passed away before she could see it published.

Dedication

To Ann. Thank you for fifty years of marriage and two lovely children, Julie and David, who all supported me in my projects.

Preface

These were anxious days for England. The year? 1796. The problem? Napoleon Bonaparte. The detested "little corporal" was shown in cartoons astride the English Channel, one boot in Paris, the other in London.

Worried faces in the taverns and village greens of England muttered the same questions: 'Will he invade?' 'Will we stand a chance?'

There was never a reply, just the sad shaking of bewildered heads. Mothers of unruly children would threaten that "Boney" would get them if they didn't behave, which seemed to bring instant capitulation. Napoleon had his army massed and ready in Boulogne. His problem? The confounded British Navy blockaded the English Channel. "Wooden walls," Englishmen called them, and everyone knew that Britannia ruled the waves.

Amongst the common sailors in the English crews were scoundrels forcibly enlisted from prisons and other unfortunates grabbed drunk and helpless by the infamous press gangs. Some were never meant to be heroes, but sometimes ordinary people do extraordinary things. With heroic leaders goading them on, they hurl themselves at screaming protagonists. They hear for the first time the sound of scything steel cutlass and the sight and smell of freshly spilt blood. They don't have time for fear or thought.

The grey-faced Napoleon Bonaparte stared narrow-eyed at the blockading British ships. He sucked saliva from inside his cheeks and spat hard. 'Damned English rosbifs!' he muttered.

'How do we ever get across? Unless we learn to fly!' His generals chortled politely.

'Or perhaps get the Spanish to join us,' one of them ventured, 'and outnumber the bastards.'

Napoleon grimaced and spat again.

Chapter 1

A shadow drifted, purple, into Harry Smith's dream. He watched it unfurl and hoped it would transform into a nubile young woman, but it wouldn't play his game. It was on a mission, some kind of warning. It looked dark and sinister now, like rippling waves, and beneath the water, the terrified face of a drowning man. Harry plunged his hands into the freezing brine and felt icy fingers reach up and grab the back of his head, pulling him down, down into suffocating darkness.

'Wake up!' screamed a voice in his head.

'It's a dream! You don't have to die!' His blue eyes flickered open, staring madly, heart thumping at his chest. He sat up, sweating and bewildered by the clarity of the dream. Then, a new horror. Smoke! A thick, black pall of it invaded his sky. He shook his blond head hard, trying to separate truth from fiction.

'Where the hell's that coming from?' he demanded of himself, but in his heart he already knew. 'The house! Oh my God! It's the bloody house!'

He hauled himself up from the wheat sheaf that had been the venue of his post-lunch snooze, grabbed his sickle and ran. He clambered madly over the fence into the lane, feet pounding on the hardened mud. The smell of fire reached him now, the smoke thickening, voices shrieking. His arms and legs pumped harder. His mother! His father! 'My God!' He rounded the last bend and the heat of the inferno hit his face: silhouettes of people with buckets, hopelessly hurling water at the raging flames. Blackened faces with horror in their eyes turned towards him. His legs were unstoppable; men had to catch him and drag him to a halt.

'It's no use!' they were saying.

'We can't get near it! They've had it, I'm afraid.'

'Christ, no!' yelled Harry, but it was true. His whole life was being destroyed before his eyes. The farm was all he knew. His mother and father had been his teachers. They were simple people, reclusive and quiet.

Harry turned his anger onto God. 'How the hell could you let this happen?' he demanded of the sky and then sank to his knees and cried.

It began to rain. Heavy drops hissing as they hit the dying flames and ashes. It seemed as if God had made a mistake and had sent the storm too late. Harry lifted his head and cursed Him again, letting the rain wash the tears from his face. The black, twisted wreckage of his home began to emerge from the mix of smoke and vapour. Harry stood again and stared.

'They had worked long and hard all their lives,' came a voice. He assumed it was one of the neighbours attempting consolation, but then. 'They are with me now, at peace.'

Harry's eyes opened wide. 'God! Is that you?' he demanded.

The voice went on in his head. 'You are right to be angry, but you are twenty-one years old and a man. It's a terrible thing to have happened, but now you must make your own way in life.'

Harry looked all around, startled and afraid, seeking out the prankster who could be so cruel as to trick him in this time of despair, but there was nobody there. He began to kick around the ashes and remains, wondering which were his parents, which were the walls and roof. He couldn't decide but mechanically dug shallow graves, spread unknown ashes into them and covered them with soil. He made rough crosses out of twigs and stabbed them into the ground, finding the humility to say a little prayer. He stood there and stared, tears streaming and feeling horribly sick. The man watching him grimly from the gate was Hugo Burrows, landlord of the local inn.

'You're going to need somewhere to stay,' said the man, almost weeping at the tragic scene. Harry wondered if it was the voice in his head again and spun around. He had not been aware that he was being watched.

'I suppose,' he muttered.

Hugo was of portly build, in his forties, with dark thinning hair, compensated by thick sideburns. His ruddy face wore a kindly grin now. 'There's rooms to spare at the inn.'

Harry, of course, had never been near the inn. "Den of iniquity", his parents used to call it. He didn't know what that meant, but it sounded awful.

'Can I stay there?' Harry mumbled needlessly.

''Course you can,' replied Hugo. 'Won't charge you anything, but I'd expect a few jobs done.'

This sounded all right to Harry. 'I'll come down in a bit,' he managed.

'See you in a while then,' responded the kind fellow, who turned away to put a foot into a stirrup and clamber back onto his horse. The more Harry stared at the wreckage, the more his life seemed to pass before his eyes. He'd never been to school. Couldn't read or write. Farming was all he knew, but then, people always said that the present king, George the Third, loved farmers. They'd always be needed. He'd never draught them into the army, even if "Boney" did invade.

At last, Harry turned away from the devastation. All of his homely belongings were gone except for what he wore and his sickle. He hurriedly felt his pocket to check that the small leather pouch was still there. It was, and his treasured "lucky" shilling was still inside, as was the chip of blue john stone that his father had hacked from the wall of a cave in his native Derbyshire. He made his way down the lane to the village, his mind still reeling at the horror of events, tears in his eyes.

If only I hadn't been at the neighbour's farm helping with the harvest. If only I'd been at home. How the hell did that damned fire start, anyway?

He looked up at the inn sign, swinging gently in the breeze. The "Plough and Horses" didn't seem too threatening, quite pleasant, in fact. Harry wondered what awful "iniquities" lurked within. He pushed the door open and stepped inside. A log fire roared in the hearth, which should have been cosy but made him recoil, too reminiscent of the horror he had just faced. There was nobody about. The room was full of rough-looking tables, chairs and benches and an overpowering smell of stale ale and tobacco smoke, which he had never experienced before. Harry stood and stared at the ever-changing reflections of the fire, flickering in numerous artefacts of brass and pewter that adorned the bar and beams.

'Pleased you made it,' came a voice from a back room. Hugo's ample figure emerged at the doorway.

'So sorry about your awful losses.'

The comment made those realities rear up again in Harry's mind. He would have to get used to people saying such things. He suddenly felt very weak and had to sit down.

'Yes, you make yourself at home,' said Hugo. 'You must be starving. I'll get you some of my famous stew.'

Life soon settled into some semblance of normality. Harry was well looked after by the landlord and, in return, worked hard on general repairs, gardening and care of the horses. He could occasionally be seen leaning on a hoe or broom, just staring into space, his mind reliving the torture of his parents' deaths. He spoke less and less, becoming more reclusive in the prison of his thoughts. It would take something special to rouse him from this insular world and in the tap room of the inn one night, it finally happened. The girl they called Molly Elizabeth came into view. Her eyes were a striking blue, bluer than his own. They seemed to radiate light. Her blonde hair was piled on top of her head, her face and body a picture of loveliness; the long, blue gown, cut low at the front. She laughed and chatted with the customers as she wielded the jug of ale, refilling mugs and collecting coins. Up until now, the most exciting moment of his life had been his brilliant diving catch that had ended the innings of the Reverend Crocket in the annual cricket match between Villagers and Farmers.

'We've won! We've won!' shouted ecstatic, white-flannelled teammates as they ran towards him, arms outspread. He hadn't noticed Molly in the host of cheering onlookers, but at that moment, he was the centre of everyone's attention, especially Molly's. The elation he was feeling then was immense. It was about to be surpassed. His heart gave a powerful thud as she turned and stared into the gloomy corner where she knew he'd be sitting. She looked at him with big eyes, the colour of forget-me-nots.

'More ale?' she enquired.

She might just as well have said, 'Do you want to sleep with me tonight?'

'Yes, please,' returned Harry and everyone in the room turned around to stare.

'He spoke!' somebody said.

'You spoke!' confirmed Molly, making him blush.

'Say something else,' she demanded, and although she already knew it, asked, 'What's your name?'

'Harry Smith,' he responded and there was some mild cheering to be heard.

'Well, I'm very pleased to meet you, Harry Smith,' she said, smiling and holding out her hand in mock politeness for kissing. Harry was pleased to oblige and perhaps lingered just a little too long over the act. She bent forward to pour the ale. This was more bosom than he had ever seen on a girl, and he felt his cheeks redden even more.

So, said an excited voice in his head. *This is what's meant by* iniquity.

Next morning, Hugo told Harry that farm hands were needed at Westhouse Farm, just down the next lane. He had never heard of it, even though he had lived quite nearby. He had not realised that Molly was the landlord's darling and that he had seen last night's hand-kissing episode, the excited little blushes on both faces as they pulled apart. Harry had outstayed his welcome and he knew it. He shook hands with Hugo and thanked him for setting him back on his feet. He slung the small bundle of newly acquired clothes over his shoulder and set off down the lane. He knew Molly would be watching him go, but he didn't look back. He strolled off, muttering and blaming God again for putting impossible temptation in his way. Molly Elizabeth peered from behind her bedroom curtain, trying to pretend her heart wasn't breaking. It was.

Chapter 2

Harry looked hard at the gate of Westhouse Farm. Should he go in? He wasn't sure. At that moment, he didn't have any better ideas. He did what he always did at times of uncertainty and took the lucky shilling out of its leather pouch.

'Heads I do, tails I don't,' he muttered and tossed it in the air. Having caught it and slapped it onto the back of his left hand, he saw the picture of King George.

'Heads I do,' he said with a sigh and pushed the gate open. He wandered around to the back of the building. He knew his place in life; it would always be the tradesmen's entrance. Chickens scuttled out of his way as he made for the door, and he knocked bare-knuckled on the black-painted oak. A cheerful, round-faced maid appeared and greeted him in an accent he had never heard before. He explained that he was applying for work and the Irish lady disappeared to find the master of the house. Richard Westhouse was a gentleman farmer, which meant that he owned the place and knew everything there was to be known about farming, but he would prefer others to do the hard work. It didn't matter that Harry could only stumble out a few simple words. One look at his sturdy physique convinced the man that he was perfect for the job. He could start right away. There was hay to be shifted into the barn.

A pitchfork was a wonderful friend to Harry. It felt so comfortable in his hands. It didn't want to talk, just get on with the work. It slammed into the hay, hoisted it up and dumped it into the barn. He hardly felt the exertion of his muscles as he settled into a rhythm. This was child's play for him, although the sun was rising well up into the sky, causing him to perspire and discard his shirt.

***

It was a morning like any other for a gentleman farmer's daughter as Helen Westhouse woke up. She had slept deeply and rubbed at her bleary eyes as she tugged the curtain open. The scene was familiar enough, but there was a surprising exception. A handsome fellow with a mop of fair hair was applying his body to the task of shifting hay into the barn. His bare torso was tanned and sparkled somewhat with sweat. Helen rubbed her eyes again in disbelief, but he was real. She felt her heart kick a little message of approval. Harry was in a world of his own. His head was full of the blonde-haired girl at the inn, but he gradually became aware that he was being watched. He turned towards the house and saw a curtain flicker back into place.

'Oh God. I wonder if he saw me!' muttered Helen. She waited a few seconds for him to return to his task, then peeked again. Again, he felt the weight of her stare and wheeled around, this time catching a glimpse of auburn hair and a white giggling smile as she dodged back behind the curtain.

'Oh my God!' murmured Harry. 'The lucky shilling may well have done me a favour. Or is it you again, God, playing another of your tricks?'

It was not Richard Westhouse's fault that life was so dour on the farm. He had tried his best since the death of his wife four years ago.

'There must be more to life than this,' Helen would grumble to her attentive brother as they sat by the roaring fire in the evenings, and he would agree. The farm was three miles from Fernhills village in splendid isolation. Old Harris used to drive them to school there in the pony and trap and they laughed at the way they slid around on the polished wooden seats. They were too old for all that now: Helen, twenty and Bart, nineteen. They were forbidden to go near the sinful inn. Church on Sunday was their only escape.

'At least Papa has found a rich suitor for you,' groused Bart, but Helen just made a face.

'Hmmm. Boring, Matthew Stokes,' she grumbled back.

'Lots of money,' Bart continued. 'He'll inherit his father's shipping business someday. All I get is this rotten farm.' They both stared forlornly into the fire. It was true that Matthew seemed a boring character for all his expensive education, but as Bart had said, he would inherit untold wealth one day and make her a lady of leisure. She had almost resigned herself to this bitter-sweet fate. She had not accounted for Harry Smith!

The new farm hand continued with his work, the pitchfork getting slippery now with sweat. He stood and straightened his back, wiping his glistening brow with the back of his hand. He looked up when the back door of the house opened. The auburn-haired girl stepped out, flat basket over one shoulder, nonchalantly beginning her first task of the day, which was to feed the chickens. It had been her mother's domain but had been passed to Helen when the effects of tuberculosis were starting to take their toll. The girl copied her mother's arm-swinging style as she distributed the morsels amongst her adoring flock, stepping rhythmically around the yard, oblivious to anything else, or so it seemed. She had half an eye on the muscular fellow who was now leaning on the pitchfork, mesmerised and watching the operation transpire. She tipped the basket upside-down and tapped the bottom of it to remove any lingering scraps and to demonstrate to the birds that their treat was over. Harry's treat was over, too. The girl stepped back into the house. He had never so much as spoken to a girl before those few utterances with Molly Elizabeth. His teammates at cricket had bragged about their conquests and he had pretended to have had moments of his own. Now, the possibility was becoming more real. He would love to get to know this auburn beauty but was guessing now that she was the owner's daughter and that the landed gentry had higher plans for their daughters than marriage to farm hands.

'Face it, Harry,' he muttered to himself. 'She's out of your reach.'

Out of your reach? groaned his brain. *She's the same as any other created since Eve! If you think she's out of reach, you'll just have to reach a bit further, my friend, won't you?* He really didn't know where such thoughts came from. Was it the Lord God talking to him, or was it his own inventive mind? One way or the other, he liked this idea. What did he have to lose?

The next day, when Helen stepped out with her basket of scraps, he was waiting in the barn. He had a fine view of her from the window in the hay loft. She swaggered about as before, driving her flock wild with the scattering of the food. She wore a tight-bodied dress of red flannel that billowed out from the hips due to ample layers of underskirt. She looked all around hoping, almost expecting, to see the handsome new man but was disappointed. He looked on from above. He would love to go down there and talk to the girl, but what would he say? This was Harry Smith. He barely knew how to string a sentence together. *Go on!* urged a voice in his head, but he dithered and held back. Then it happened. He didn't know how or why, but some unseen object beneath her feet made her stumble. She lost her balance and toppled to the ground in an undignified flurry of red flannel and lace. He was down the ladder at impossible speed and into the yard where the chickens had seized their chance and were attacking the basket still in her hand. He grabbed it and flung it away, the flock marauding after it.

'Are you all right?' he managed.

'I think so,' came the stunned reply. 'You must think me very stupid.'

'Oh no,' said Harry. 'I think you're very b...' He wanted to say "beautiful", but settled for '...brave.'

'Thank you so much for saving me,' went on Helen, her hazel eyes magnified by a welling of tears. 'I must go and get cleaned up.'

She turned and made for the door, brushing at her clothes with her hands. Harry watched her go. At the scullery window, he caught a glimpse of a retreating Irish smile.

Chapter 3

'So, d'you think we'll be invaded?' groaned one of the farm hands in the barn. Harry had been listening to their conversation and had almost joined in, but you had to be quick-tongued to do that.

'I hear they've got huge balloons that can carry men over the Channel,' muttered one man. 'Or maybe they could dig a tunnel underneath!'

'Not possible,' said another. 'The only way is to sail straight across, and they'd never get past our "wooden walls". God bless the good old navy!'

There followed some boisterous cheering, and as it died down, Harry grabbed his chance. 'King George loves us farmers,' he managed. 'They call him Farmer George. He'd never draught us into the army.'

'Good thinking!' said one of the men, impressed with Harry's remark. 'Let's hope this Pitt fellow thinks the same.'

Harry didn't know who the Pitt fellow was but agreed. It became clearer when the man went on, 'It's prime minister's what makes the last decision.'

None of them wanted to "take the king's shilling" as they called it and join the army. They all agreed that the country needed farmers, and that was why they should stay.

Harry lay in his bunk that night, his head full of thoughts of war: those dreadful French who were taking over most of Europe in the wake of their revolution and certainly had designs on invading our island. Blue eyes and hazel eyes stared into his dream, then a strange drifting shadow, purple and menacing.

'Christ, no!' he mumbled. He'd seen it before. It wouldn't do what he asked. It had a task of its own. It formed into rippling water and the horrified face beneath it. A drowning man that Harry tried to grab, but he felt fingers, icy cold on the back of his head, dragging him down, down into murky darkness.

'Wake up, you fool! You don't have to drown! It's a dream!' His eyes flickered open, his heart beating fast.

'You all right, Harry?' came a fellow worker's voice from a neighbouring bed.

'Yes,' he replied but couldn't disguise his heaving breath. 'Just a bad dream. I'm fine.'

The next thing he knew, the cockerel was crowing and men were grumbling their way out of bed. Harry followed on and squinted into the sunlight of a crisp autumn morning. The sky was big and blue and nothing seemed wrong with the world. Helen would soon be out with her chickens, a thought that made him stir and make sure he was in place when she came out of the door. Eventually, she was there with her basket, looking lovelier than ever. She seemed to have taken extra care to have her hair in ringlets dangling onto bare shoulders; her dress pulled a little lower at the front. Harry watched the whole procedure. She stood there, tapping the upturned basket, signalling the end and casting her eye around.

'Reach a little further,' Harry urged himself. 'Go on!' He stepped out of the barn and smiled at the girl, but no words would come to his lips. She saved him by talking first.

'Thank you so much for saving me yesterday,' she said coyly. 'Those birds would have pecked me to pieces.'

'It's a dangerous job you have there,' Harry managed and was quite impressed by the confident sound of his voice. So was she.

'Were you hurt at all?' he went on.

'No, no, just a couple of bruises.'

'My name's Harry. What's yours?'

'Helen.'

'Pleased to meet you, Helen.'

'Likewise. We should be friends.'

'Yes. Of course, we should.'

'See you later then.'

'Yes.'

The conversation had been stilted and shy but had gone exactly where both had wanted it to go. They were to be friends. In their hearts, they both knew exactly what they really meant. It was "lovers".

***

'You know it's all arranged for her to marry some rich fellow, don't you, Mr Smith?' the voice was a confidential whisper with an Irish lilt.

Harry stopped in mid-swing of the pitchfork and wheeled around to see Beatrice O'Malley wearing a serious face. She had been maid and housekeeper at the farm for about five years, brought in to assist Sarah Westhouse when the effects of her tuberculosis took a firmer grip, and of course, she had stayed on after the dear lady's death to deal with the domestic mayhem that inevitably followed. She had never lost her brogue or her uncanny ability to read people's minds, but she had never used the latter to affect anyone's life until now.

It was obvious that her words were news to Harry. His lips dithered as though unable to respond. He didn't know whether to chastise the lady or to thank her. She stared at him with sincere eyes that could read his mixed emotions.

'Just thought you should be aware,' she went on. 'Don't let her know that I told you.' She accompanied the last words with the gesture of tapping the side of her nose with her forefinger to signify confidentiality. Harry just nodded and Beatrice walked away. He thrust the pitchfork vehemently into the pile and hoisted the biggest load of hay he had ever gathered angrily into the barn. An even more shocked expression engulfed his face. The fork load uncovered a bevy of rats, blinded by the sudden daylight. They scampered aimlessly, terrified, squealing. Harry's vision was filled with awful images of gnashing yellow teeth, staring eyes and whiskers, horrible squirming tails.

Since he was a boy, he'd been terrified of the things. He'd woken up in the hayloft one day to find himself surrounded by them, one biting at his hand, one very close to his face. He had stood up and kicked them away, but it left him with an inbuilt dread of them. A phobia he could never ignore.

***

'Is it true that you're to marry some rich fellow?' muttered Harry.

'How do you know about that?' demanded Helen, indignant.

'People talk. Just something I heard.'

'It's what Papa wants.'

'Do you have to do what *Papa* wants?'

'No.' Her eyes widened with a touch of anger. 'I'll do what I want with my life. I just don't know what that is yet. I don't really like the man. He's dull and boring, but he can take me away from this *bloody* farm!'

Harry's eyes rounded in surprise at her language and at her sentiment.

'You'd marry him just to get away from here?'

'Stupid, isn't it? I just don't know. I've only got my brother and father here for company and an Irish maid. Never had any friends since school.' She looked him straight in the eye and finished the sentence, 'Until you.'

Harry was smitten. He watched the tears welling up in her eyes. She looked beautiful and so troubled. He wanted to hold her in his arms and the voice in his head repeated,

Reach a little further. He saw his hands move forward and perch on her waist.

She looked him in the eyes again. 'What are you doing?' she asked softly.

'Giving in to my instincts.'

'You have instincts to put your hands on my waist?'

Harry's eyes were working their magic. They roamed her body, devouring every sumptuous curve.

'Much more,' he admitted.

'Are you going to give in to all of them?' queried Helen.

'That depends.'

Helen's mother had told her that her body was her gift from God, for her to give to the man she loved. She had felt no great desire to give it to Matthew. At this moment in time, her desperate wish was to give everything to the lovely man who held her so gently, who was drinking her in, whose lips were struggling to find the next words.

'You want to unbutton me, don't you?' She breathed, surprising even herself.

Harry was flustered by her unexpected remark and stuttered, 'You can read my mind, can't you?'

'Your mind? No, I can read your eyes. They're sparkling, a little bit wild. A little bit hungry.'

Her hand moved to her top button and it became undone. He followed her lead and, trembling, undid number two, number three. The excitement was unbearable, such a thudding in his chest, and Helen loved the effect she was having on the captivated male. He couldn't believe it was really happening. Was this lovely girl about to share the secrets of her body with him? The back of his hand brushed the soft warmth of her cleavage. Was he about to see the most beautiful sight on God's earth?

No... He wasn't! A voice from outside came, penetrating their ecstasy. Someone was calling Helen's name. A youthful male voice. Her eyes changed instantly from seductive warmth to startled wide, her hand quickly darting to her dress to reverse the unbuttoning process.

'I'm here!' she shouted. 'What do you want?' She made for the door of the barn and squinted out into the sunlight.

'There you are!' grumbled Bart. 'I've been looking for you everywhere. Are you all right? You look very red.'

'I'm fine,' she retorted. 'What's the matter, anyway?'

'It's Matthew. He's here to see you.' Her heart sank and he could see the clouds forming in his sister's eyes.

'Oh Christ,' she mumbled and walked slowly to the house, her head a mess of swirling thoughts. She caught her reflection in the mirror and Christ! She *was* so flushed with excitement. She took a few moments to compose herself, then walked serenely into the drawing room, apologising for her appearance and sat with Matthew Stokes. Beatrice, as chaperone, sat nearby with her knitting, and they listened to his plans to build a beautiful house where he could raise a lovely family. Helen responded in all the right places but was hardly listening. Her head was full of the wonderful fellow in the barn, his excited, manly charm. When Matthew got up to leave, she looked into his eyes. They were blue like Harry's, but they didn't sparkle.

Harry paced around the backyard, frustrated and annoyed. 'How can she waste her life on some rich bastard she doesn't even like?'

He didn't know what he would do, but he grabbed a hoe and went around to the front of the house. The polished oak carriage stood in the driveway with its two immaculate black horses and blue-cloaked driver with a tricorn hat. Harry began hoeing the flower bed with one eye on the front door of the house. Eventually, it opened and Beatrice saw the man out. He grinned and tapped his top hat onto his head. His self-satisfied expression made Harry squirm. He began to shake with anger. The door closed and the visitor strode towards his carriage. Harry moved to the edge of the drive and leant on the hoe. As the man drew near, Harry found the words. 'Why don't you leave the lady alone?'

Matthew Stokes stopped in his tracks. He had never been so affronted. His mouth gaped in astonishment.

'She doesn't want you,' Harry went on, not knowing where the courage was coming from.

Matthew stared. He knew he was being watched from the house and dared not remonstrate with the fellow. He touched the brim of his hat in mock bonhomie and gritted his teeth.

'You insolent peasant!' he muttered. 'Consider yourself already dead!' He marched on to the carriage, both men bursting to hit the other, both knowing this was not the time or place, but the time and place would eventually come. Both knew it.

'Mr Stokes is such a gentleman.' Observed Beatrice, but Helen couldn't help wondering what on earth Harry was doing. He watched the carriage go before stabbing the hoe angrily into the ground and returning to the back of the house.

Helen found him sitting in the barn, head in hands.

'Harry?' she enquired. 'Are you all right? I saw you meet my Mr Stokes.'

Harry raised his head; his face was a picture of concern. 'Told him to leave you alone,' he muttered. 'Said you didn't want him.'

She could hardly believe it, gasping, 'You did what?'

'He called me an insolent peasant. Told me to consider myself already dead.'

'My God! I'm not surprised! How dare you interfere like that?'

Harry looked up to see the girl stepping quickly towards the door. He heard her sob as she disappeared from view. She almost knocked poor Beatrice over as she ran up the stairs and threw herself onto the bed. It didn't take much Irish intuition to understand what had happened.

'I'm sorry, Miss Helen,' came the lilting voice.

Helen raised a tearful face to the intruder.

'I'm afraid it was me who told Harry about you and Matthew.'

Helen sat up and dabbed at her face. She didn't feel the need to answer.

'What a mess, Beaty,' she muttered, and Beatrice sat beside her on the bed, extending a comforting arm.

'You're not the first to have such troubles, my girl, and I'm certain you'll not be the last. Fellahs, eh?' She heard a sigh of agreement from her ward.

'What would your dear mother have said, eh? I bet I know what she'd say.'

'What?'

'I think you know, too. She'd say life's too short to be dutiful. Dead and buried, she was at forty-two. If you love Harry, let him be the one.'

'But Papa expects me to marry Matthew. He's got it all arranged.'

'It's your life, Miss Helen. Your father just wants you to be safe and looked after. He doesn't understand the workings of a young girl's heart. You need to tell him.'

'You're right, Beaty,' she muttered.

Soon, she was standing and stepped out of the door. She hurried down the stairs and caught her reflection in the mirror, a dishevelled mess, but she didn't care. She was unstoppable now. She opened her father's study door, where she would always have knocked and waited for his consent to enter. Richard Westhouse, startled by the intrusion, dropped his pipe and had to hurriedly stamp on smouldering tobacco before raising an angry eye to his daughter.

'What's the meaning of this?' he demanded. Not the best of introductions for what was to follow.

'I need to talk to you, Papa.'

'Well? What about?'

'About Matthew, Papa. I don't want to see him any more!'

'What? Why ever not? He's a wonderful man. What's he done?'

'Nothing, Papa. He's done nothing. I just don't like him that much. I certainly don't want to marry him!'

'But he'd make a perfect husband for you! He's a rich man, Helen. He'd make you more than happy!'

'No, he wouldn't. I don't like him. I want you to stop him coming here!'

'This is ridiculous. I thought you were getting on so well together.'

'Not well enough, Papa. And there's something else.'

'What? Well? Out with it, girl!'

'I'm in love with somebody else. Harry Smith.'

'You're what? Are you out of your damned mind? The farm hand? You're crazy!'

'Maybe, Papa. That's what love does. Makes you crazy. Do crazy things.'

'You keep away from that, Harry Smith! It won't be hard. I'll sack the bastard! Go to your room and stay there till I tell you to move. And you'd better give some careful consideration to what you've said about Matthew Stokes!'

'You horror! You mean, horrible monster!' she yelled, totally out of control.

Richard had no answer. He felt like hitting the girl and she even saw the involuntary movement of his hand before he managed to contain it. He couldn't hurt the girl who possessed the shining eyes of his dear departed wife.

'Get out!' he yelled, and she was gone, stamping heavily on every stair accompanied by loud sobs. She stormed past the horrified Beatrice, who had heard most of it and slammed the door shut.

'Get me, Smith!' demanded the devastated father. 'Get him here! Now!'

It didn't take long. Richard Westhouse had his temper under control and was perfectly civil with the man, if a little flustered.

'I'm sorry,' he said. 'We no longer require your services.' Harry stared at the man in astonishment, but he knew what he'd done. Exactly the same as he'd done at the Plough and Horses, shown an interest in the wrong girl. When would he learn?

***

The voice was a hushed whisper, 'Harry!'

He looked around as he crossed the yard.

'Harry!' the voice came again. He raised his face, whitened in what was by now moonlight, and saw Helen leaning from her bedroom window.

'Wait there!' she called.

'Your father's sacked me,' he grumbled. 'I've got to go.'

'Get your things. I'm coming with you!'

Harry was stunned. The girl disappeared from her window before he could speak and by the time, he had gathered his few belongings together, she was down there in the yard beside him.

'Are you sure you know what you're doing?' asked Harry and Helen replied that she had never been surer in her life. He took her bundle in one hand and put the other around her shoulder. They made for the gate.

The gravel was noisy, too noisy, beneath their feet. They stumbled and tiptoed on, hoping and praying they would not be noticed. It was too much to ask. Footfalls in the stones behind them made them wheel around, their faces horrified and milk-white in the moonlight.

A figure lumbered forward from the shadow of the house. 'Papa?' Helen gasped and thought she could see the silhouette of a shotgun in his hands.

'Oh God! Don't shoot!' she stammered, expecting his angry roar and the blast from the gun that would end her life, but it didn't happen. The figure emerged into the half-light.

'Thank god!' she swooned. It wasn't her father.

'What the hell are you doing?' demanded a youthful voice.

'Bart! Thank God it's you!'

'Where are you going?' he persisted.

'It's no use, Bart. We have to go.' Helen was breathing heavily as she spoke. 'Harry and I just want to be together. Papa won't allow it. I can't end up with Matthew Stokes; I just can't!'

There was a sob in her voice now and Bart could do nothing other than hold out his arms and hug the girl he had grown up with. Their past lives raced through both minds as they hugged their final embrace. The games, the arguments, the crazy night when Bart had gone into her room wanting to experiment with sex. She had told him not to be so stupid and he had settled for a look at her breasts. The brother and sister parted with tears flowing freely.

'Look after her!' Bart demanded of the farm hand, turned and was gone. Helen and Harry closed the gate carefully behind them and stepped into the shadows of the lane. Mud and puddles from recent rain made for difficult progress. They needed to be quick but staggered and stumbled through the mire, continually checking behind them that they were not pursued. No plan, no thoughts in their heads other than escape, they blundered on. Clouds enveloped the moon and rain began to spit in their faces. It couldn't weaken their resolve. Soon, the lights of the Plough and Horses "den of iniquity" loomed before them. It was their obvious shelter for the night, although Helen was reticent to enter the forbidden place where Harry had formerly taken refuge. She gritted her teeth. She had forsaken her cossetted life. She would have to accept the outside world as it was. Harry pushed the door open and ushered her in. The log fire roared its cosy welcome.

'Harry Smith! Upon my soul!' enthused Hugo Burrows. 'Didn't expect to see you again so soon!'

He also recognised Helen, the apparently bashful daughter of Richard Westhouse, who he saw regularly at church but never spoke to. Richard was one of many who thought him some kind of devil for the sinful work of running the inn and would have more than most people to repent about. He eyed the girl cautiously but held out a hand for shaking, which she accepted.

Harry took the man to one side. 'Have you got anywhere we could, er, sleep tonight?' he enquired. 'How about my old room?'

'I'm sorry, my friend. It's taken. All my rooms are. Market Day, see. Have you forgotten? It's always like this.'

Harry's heart sank. 'Best I can do is the old settee in the back room.'

Harry knew it well. It stank of the dogs. He made a forlorn face before muttering, 'Well, if that's the best you can do.'

'Fraid so,' went on Hugo. 'Pleased to see you've got a new lady friend.' An obvious reference to ending his interest in Molly Elizabeth, who had by now been pushed to the back of Harry's mind. He looked around nervously at the thought of seeing her again and was relieved to note that she was not around.

Hugo saw his concern but went on, 'There won't be any charge, Harry, but look, I don't want any trouble from her old man, who I'm sure has not consented to this, wanting to know how I could let such things carry on under my roof! He thinks badly enough of me as it is. I think you should be gone pretty early in the morning, just in case he's on your tracks! I'll deny all knowledge, of course.'

'Quite right, Hugo. Fact is, as you've guessed, we're running off together. Her father hates me. We've no idea where we're headed.'

'Young Joseph is taking the horse and cart down to Portsmouth in the morning. You could do worse than grabbing a lift. You can get anywhere from there.'

Harry showed Helen into the back room and she nearly vomited at the stench of the dogs. Harry shooed them off the settee and turned and rearranged the cushions to lessen the effect. Helen sank into the antique piece of furniture. Had she really given up her comfortable, clean home for this? She looked at Harry. He was somewhat dishevelled due to the rain, but his eyes sparkled clear and blue. She knew that she had made the right choice. She'd go through hell to be with this man. A soaking and a few stinking dogs in the den of iniquity were not going to deter her now.

The next thing Harry knew, he was waking up with his head uncomfortably perched on the settee arm, pins and needles in both legs and a fairly uncomfortable bladder. He looked across at Helen, who had passed out as a book-end version of himself, head balanced on the well-worn arm, her legs curled up beneath her. His requirement for the toilet was his most pressing thought. He stood and shifted his feet about until they felt normal enough to take him, then made for the backyard where he knew the facility was. He stood in the dim place, a look of relief on his face in the rising vapour. There was no roof, which gave the desired ventilation and allowed the slight penetration of the pre-dawn light. His task was complete; he began to readjust his clothing when he became aware that he was not alone. The rough old door clanged shut and someone was leaning on the inside of it. Trapped! The dread coursed through him. Which of the people who wanted his blood would it be? Matthew Stokes? Richard Westhouse? What the hell was happening? How the hell could he be so stupid? Caught like a rat in a trap! He gazed at the figure, heart thumping, and began to discern the shape. Thank God! It wasn't a man! The soft curves of a womanly frame glimmered in the half-light.

Then, a whisper, 'Got you, at last, Harry Smith; come here, darling, and take me. Our time's come at last.'

'God, Helen. You scared me to death.'

She played with the single fastener on the front of her cloak, the hood still over her head. The fastener came undone, revealing her beautiful naked body beneath, lovelier than he had dared to imagine.

'Take me,' she murmured again and Harry's heart pounded harder. He pressed her against the door and their bodies merged. Both breathed heavily in ecstasy.

'Got you at last,' she whispered again and pushed the hood back off her head. She looked up at her man for the first time and he gazed down into her seductive eyes. Oh my God! They weren't hazel! They were blue! The shock went right through the man. He wanted to stop, but it was too late. His passion exploded in an uncontrollable climax. Both stood there gasping hard on the precious air, hearts thudding accompaniment to their reeling emotions. It seemed to take forever for their bodies to calm. Harry's eyes roamed the girl's face, incredulous, wild with questions, silently demanding answers.

'Don't you ever forget me, Harry Smith,' whispered Molly. The man could only stare in stunned disbelief.

'Keep this to remind you of me.' She wrapped her purple scarf gently around his neck and murmured, 'It'll save the blood of your hero.' She refastened her cloak, turned and was gone.

Harry stood in the doorway, the mixture of images and her whispered words befuddling his brain. His first sexual encounter had been incredible, but it had been with the wrong girl, or was it? He felt dizzy and looked flushed and bewildered when the back door of the house opened.

'There you are,' remarked Helen. 'I thought you'd run off without me!'

'Never,' replied the man.

'Are you all right?' she went on, concerned by his appearance.

'Just a bit of a stomach upset. I'll be fine,' he muttered. He had quickly learned the art of forsaking the truth to suit the situation.

Chapter 4

Richard Westhouse looked blankly at his maid. He had heard her words, but they seemed incomprehensible. 'Gone?' he repeated. 'Gone?'

She nodded nervously. 'Bed not slept in, sir. No sign of her in the yard nor any of the outhouses. Looked in the barn and the stables. She's gone, sir. Disappeared.' She added the last word because his face still showed an unwillingness to understand, but the truth was sinking in and he knew exactly what had transpired.

'Bloody fool,' he muttered and then *yelled* the same words as his anger exploded. Beatrice didn't know whether he was berating her or his daughter. It was neither; his bile was directed at himself. 'What the hell have I done?' He cursed and thumped the arm of his chair. 'She's gone off with that Smith fellow, hasn't she? Bloody little fool!'

He became aware through his blearing vision that Beatrice was sobbing into her handkerchief. 'Oh, sir,' she muttered, 'it's not your fault. It's mine. She was so confused, poor girl about how she was feeling about the two men. I told her what I thought her dear mother would have said. If you love Harry, let him be the one.'

Richard felt his anger redirect itself to the stupid woman. How dare she evoke the sentiment of his darling wife? How dare she encourage such a ridiculous idea? But he held it inside. His arms opened, accompanied by a sigh, and she stepped forward to accept the invitation. It was the first time he had ever touched her. She felt soft and warm. She loved the feeling of security in the man's strong arms.

'Made a bloody mess of things, didn't we,' Richard mumbled, and she agreed, but her practical mind was already rising above her emotions.

She muttered, 'So, we should act quickly, shouldn't we? Go looking in all the likely places?'

Richard's face was a furrowed picture of anguish and thought.

'Get the men in here,' he said suddenly. 'And get Bart here too.'

The men assembled in the drawing room. It was the first time some of them had been in there. They looked around nervously, shifted their feet about, studied the floor. They were all waiting for Bart. At last, the young man appeared at the door, struggling with the top button of his shirt as he entered the room.

'Right,' said Richard. 'You're all aware by now what's happened. Miss Helen has run off with Harry Smith. She's done it to spite me for meddling in her affairs. Like all young women of that age, she thinks she knows what's best but is not thinking carefully enough about her future. So, we have to get her back. Does anyone know if they made any plan whatsoever, or did they just take off in the heat of the moment?' The men exchanged glances, but all expressions were blank. 'What about you, Bart? She confided more in you than anyone.'

Bart had given up with the top button and fidgeted awkwardly with imaginary cuff links instead. He felt his face flushing and couldn't control it. He almost spat out the truth that he had seen them go but thought better of it.

'She didn't say anything to me,' he lied, and there was a slight quiver in his voice that he knew he had to control.

'But I knew she was keen on Smith and found Mr Stokes a bit too boring.'

Richard responded with a thoughtful grunt and a look of disappointment. He didn't have much faith in his son's abilities generally and this bumbling reply did little to improve matters.

Bart was at least trying to think his way around the situation and added, 'Has anyone checked to see if any horses have gone?'

This was the first positive thought Richard had heard on the matter, and he shook his head in reply. His son darted out of the room and across the yard. He was pleased to get away from the stifling atmosphere of the room and give himself time to think.

'If I go after them, I don't have to catch them, do I?' He went into the stables and breathed in the familiar smells of hay and manure.

'It's what they both want, isn't it? Just to get away and start a new life together. What's the point of dragging Helen back here?' He went through the procedure of checking all around, and, as he was well aware, the full collection of horses was there.

'Papa would chastise her. Try to make her do what she desperately doesn't want to do. Everyone will be miserable. Even Matthew Stokes, with an unwilling wife. No, they should be left to get on with their lives. I just need to make a show of going off after them and failing. I'll volunteer!'

'None have gone, Papa,' was his breathless announcement as he re-entered the room. 'They can't have got far on foot. I'll go and rig the trap and see if I can catch them up.'

'Right,' said Richard. 'Well, I don't think there's any point in us all marauding after them. Get to it, Bart, and let's hope you can catch them quickly.'

Bart was out of the door again and began the nimble task of harnessing his favourite mare, Venus, to the buggy. The dear horse was going to have to get used to being the substitute listener to his problems now that his sister was gone. They made for the gate, where Beatrice intercepted with a hastily prepared bundle of bread rolls and apples. It was all that she could lay her hands on quickly.

'Don't go trying too hard,' she whispered as she handed the food to him. He smiled and gave an almost imperceptible wink, then slapped the reins on the horse's rump and they slithered out into the mud of sodden Fernhills Lane.

Chapter 5

'I wonder if they're up yet,' muttered Helen.

'I expect so,' replied Harry, who was roused from the depths of his thoughts.

The cart rumbled on. It swayed about and the pair held on to the sides for stability.

'I'm sorry,' he went on, 'this ride is not helping my lousy stomach.' He had a good excuse now for his unwillingness to speak, his head still reeling from Molly Elizabeth's ploy.

Helen ignored his complaint, thinking how much worse it would be without the cushion of straw beneath them. Then she noticed it. The purple scarf around his neck. He was fingering it from time to time as his thoughts rambled on.

'I hadn't noticed that before,' she muttered.

'What?'

'That scarf. You didn't have it on last night.'

Harry swallowed hard. 'It was my mother's,' he lied. 'It was in my pocket before. I thought I should wear it.'

Helen gave him a look which said, *That doesn't sound very convincing,* but it didn't seem to matter very much. The cart trundled on. Harry put his arm around her, and she nuzzled into his chest.

'Can you imagine their faces?' said Helen at length. 'The panic when they find I've gone.'

'Do you think they'll come after us?'

'Well, we've got a good start on them,' responded Harry.

'And what will poor Matthew Stokes do when he finds I've run off with a farm hand instead of marrying him? He was going to propose to me soon. Can you imagine him down on one knee with a beautiful jewelled ring?'

'He said to consider myself already dead. That was just for speaking to him about you. God knows what the hell he'll do.'

Harry reached for the leather pouch in his pocket. 'Talking of jewels,' he said, and he took the chip of blue john between his fingers, 'I'll get this made into a ring for you.'

'Ooh, how pretty!' she enthused. 'Is it a sapphire?'

'Yes,' Harry joked. 'It's worth a fortune.'

She could see the smirk on the man's face and knew he was playing with her. She giggled her appreciation, adding, 'I'll be so proud to wear it. Have you got any more treasure in there that you haven't told me about?'

'Just my lucky shilling.'

'Has it really brought you any luck?'

'Nothing,' he grumbled and then thoughtfully added, 'Until it told me to knock on the door of Westhouse Farm.'

***

Bart halted Venus at the Plough and Horses Inn, tied the rein loosely to a rail and ventured in. There were a few customers clustered around the fire and the jolly-faced Hugo Burrows behind the bar with cloth and pewter mug in his hands. His expression fell slightly when he recognised the brother of the Westhouse girl, again from fleeting glances at church, but raised himself to a smile and a cheery professional welcome.

'Young Master Westhouse, isn't it?' he enthused.

'That's right,' offered Bart.

'Seen you with the family on Sundays. Didn't think I'd ever see you in here!'

'Didn't think I'd ever venture in,' was the young man's reply, 'but I'm looking for my sister.'

'Your sister? What makes you think she'd be here?'

'She's playing some sort of game with us. Pretending she's run away. I just wondered if you'd seen her.'

'Not been near this place,' said Hugo with sincere eyes. 'Not her sort of place, is it?'

'No, but I just don't know where to look. I've tried the church.'

'She'll turn up when she's good and ready,' said the landlord. 'Now, would you like some of my best ale?'

Bart grimaced, but Hugo insisted. He sipped at the stuff and immediately wanted to spit it out. It was more bitter than the concoction his mother used to give him when he complained of an ailing stomach. He swallowed and forced a grin. He devoured the full half pint as Hugo watched. 'More?' he enquired, but Bart shook his head.

'No. Must get on,' he mumbled, 'I've got a sister to smash, I mean cadge.' The alcohol obvious in the novice drinker's brain and tongue.

'Cheerio then,' blustered the landlord. 'Hope you find her soon!'

Bart paid the man and made somewhat uncertainly for the door.

He untied the reins and gave Venus the required slap. 'Come on then, girl. Let's see if we can find this damned pair of runaways. '

***

The main route to Portsmouth was of far better construction. The horse's hooves clopped rhythmically on stone and the cart had far less propensity to jolting and rolling. Even so, Helen and Harry were pleased to hear Joseph yell, 'Whoa there.' To the horse. They raised their heads from the straw and winced at the weird smell that invaded their senses.

'The sea,' said Joseph in response to their puzzled looks. 'Don't suppose you've ever smelt it before.'

'You're right,' said Helen. It was just one more "first" in the girl's new life. It was new to Harry, too. This was the furthest either had ever ventured from home.

'Is this Portsmouth?' he asked.

'Norport,' said Joseph. 'They call it Portsmouth's little sister. You can get anywhere from here. Stagecoach, ships. It's got it all.'

'Wonderful,' said Harry. Helen had a small bag of coins that she had collected over the years and they paid the man the agreed fare, struggled to their feet and looked around. The Half Moon Tavern looked a welcoming sort of place where they could eat and drink and maybe even negotiate for a room. Their first real room together, with a proper bed. They swallowed hard and wandered in.

'There'll be a room vacant later,' responded the landlord. 'The fellow in there is refusing to budge at the moment, but he hasn't paid for another night.'

'That's fine,' said Harry. 'We'll wait.'

The place was beginning to fill with people. Street vendors were coming in for their evening drinks, the boys from the blacksmiths, some farm hands, some whores. One of the street girls whispered something to her friends about Helen and they all giggled. Harry bought ale and watched Helen sipping away at it for the first time ever. She hated the taste but began to like the uplifting effect of the alcohol. Harry drank more quickly than Helen and found his mug topped up more often by the attentive maid, who smiled cutely at him and reminded him hurtfully of Molly Elizabeth. His hand moved unintentionally to touch the purple scarf.

It was beginning to rain and Bart's head was beginning to clear itself from the effects of his first experience of intoxicating drink. He was beginning to wonder why on earth he was continuing along the Portsmouth road.

'Don't try too hard,' dear Beaty had said, and he had never intended to. His sympathy lay with his sister, although he was struggling with the idea of life on the farm without her. He reckoned that to make a real show of his efforts, he should be away for two or three days before returning home with a tale of woe. He began to nibble at one of Beatrice's bread rolls and wondered where he might stay.

The Half Moon Tavern was getting rowdier. Another group of men had turned up intent on quaffing the maximum amount of ale in the shortest possible time. The whores were infiltrating their group; voices were getting jollier and louder, pot and pewter were clanking, ale was spilling. Helen and Harry found themselves just staring at the scene. They had never seen such behaviour. Bawdy, drunken happiness surrounded them. The alcohol was lifting them to similar heights, the thought of that bedroom looming into their minds. They couldn't help but look longingly into each other's eyes, emotion building, excitement, desire, an increasing thud of beats in the heart. Suddenly, cutting through it all, a terrible voice. A screech from the door.

'Press Gang! Quick! Get out!' The whole room fell silent, then realisation, gasps and shrieks of panic. Drinks were abandoned, coats grabbed, and stools overturned as the human wave made for the door, muttering, cursing, fear on their faces. Helen watched. She didn't understand. Harry slumped into his chair, his brain awash with ale.

'My God!' Helen grumbled. 'What the hell's happening?'

Bart struggled on, the rain now lashing into his face, both arms aching with exertion as he fought to keep Venus on the road. Her hooves slipped around on wet stones; the wheels of the buggy skidded out of control. Now, a new problem. People were blocking the road. They were spilling out of the tavern, drunk and in a panic.

'Bloody press gang!' they were cursing. 'Get out of here!' Venus shied and slithered; the buggy slewed off the road into the shallow ditch. Bart cracked the reins hard, but the fretting horse couldn't move.

Helen was shaking Harry, but his eyes were rolling, arms hanging limp at his sides.

'We've got to get out,' she shrieked. "Press gang" But the words meant nothing to his semi-conscious brain.

'Help me!' she gasped to the stragglers in the crowd, but they were all intent on saving themselves. She stood and ran into the street. Rain was driving hard. People were disappearing into houses and alleys. Doors were thumping shut, bolts clanking home. Up the hill, some unfortunate fellow was trying to push a toppling buggy back onto the road behind a terrified horse. The distinct, white blaze on the horse's face was what made her heart leap. Her eyes widened in disbelief as she studied the man.

'Bart?' she muttered, the name barely a whisper on her lips. Then, 'Bart!' The name screeched from her throat.

He didn't hear. He had just about managed to shove the crippled vehicle back onto the road when the thin wailing voice penetrated. Someone was calling his name.

'Bart!' shrieked out again. He knew that voice, but he had never heard such terror in it. He looked up to see the rain-soaked figure stumbling towards him, her wet, straightened hair plastered hard on her head and face. Her wild hazel eyes shone through at him.

'Helen? My God! It's you!' He stood upright just in time for her to slam into his startled embrace. They hugged hard in the pouring rain, vapour rising from their heaving bodies, expressions of pleasure and disbelief.

Then, the alarm returned to Helen's face. 'You've got to help me,' the girl panted, her eyes searching his face for a response. 'It's Harry. He's out cold. The press gang will get him!'

Bart didn't understand either but followed as she turned and began to run down the hill. He had just about caught her when she turned into the tavern door. Harry was still in the chair, oblivion on his face. The landlord and maid were yelling at him, shaking and cajoling, but were getting no response. Bart grabbed poor Harry, pulling him forward onto his feet, shoving his shoulder under the lifeless arm for support. Helen propped the other side and the three of them made for the door. Their timing could not have been worse.

'Him!' yelled the voice of an important-looking man in naval officer's garb. Blue chequered shirts filled Bart's vision, grim-looking faces and heads of hair slicked down with tar and rain. Rum and tobacco were breathed close to his face. Rough hands grabbed and held on tight. Harry almost collapsed as his support was hauled away. He heard Helen scream. He saw the melee in front of him, Bart disappearing. He swung his fist at the nearest sun-baked face but missed.

'Him too!' yelled the voice. Harry was swamped by the mob. He felt a sailor's fist land squarely on his mouth. Stars and then emptiness filled his brain. Two more men were suddenly in His Majesty's Britannic Navy, whether they liked it or not, and their lives would never be the same again.

'And get the whore!' yelled the man. Helen gasped, her hand going instinctively to her mouth. She had never been called such a thing. She saw hands reaching out to grab her, leering faces and salivating mouths. Then, a strange sensation. A strong arm grabbed her from behind, pulling her back. She toppled into the safety of the tavern as the door thudded shut, bolts clanking into place. Angry sailors thumped and kicked at the door, but their prize was gone. Their lieutenant ordered them away. They had more men to ensnare that night.

Helen felt the sting of smelling salts in her head. 'She's coming round,' someone was saying. Her eyes fluttered open to a blur of anxious faces.

She was lying on a bed. Candles flickered uncomfortably close as people examined her face. 'She'll be all right,' said a reassuring voice. It was Susie, common-law wife of landlord Tom Yarker. She put a comforting hand on Helen's brow and stroked her fingers into wet hair. 'What happened?' the patient groaned.

'Press gang, dear. I'm afraid they got your two fellahs.'

'Who are they? What'll happen to them?'

'They have to get more men for the navy. It's not nice, I know. They go to the prisons to grab a few poor wretches. They stop ships coming into port till they give up some men. Then they go for the taverns and grab a few unwitting, drunken souls. They've even been said to raid church congregations and carry off the befuddled men and groom!' Helen's grimace worsened as the young woman spoke.

'I'm afraid your two were just unlucky. They're in for a spell at sea while we fight off them damned Frenchies.'

'Oh God! They'll be killed! They can't fight or anything! They're farmers!'

'They'll be all right, dear. They just get them doing work around the ship while the real sailors get on with the fighting. Trust me. I get to meet lots of seamen in this profession. They tell me all about it.'

'When will they get back?'

Helen saw the worried glance that passed between Tom and Susie.

'Nobody knows, right? Could be weeks, months, never!'

'C'mon dear,' said Susie. 'There's lots like you, gets left, just waiting. You'll be fine. At least we managed to stop them from grabbing you! God knows where you'd be now.' Helen felt the hand give one more gentle caress of her head and returned to a feeling of drowsiness. The onlookers were drifting out of the room.

'You get some sleep now,' said Susie. 'We'll talk about it in the morning.' She blew out the last candle and was gone.

When Helen turned her head, a tear spilt from the corner of her eye. 'I've given everything up for this,' she grumbled and stared at the adjacent pillow where Harry's head should be.

'You said you'd look after me,' she groaned to the absent man. 'You said you'd always be there. You never even got around to bedding me! God, I hate you for leaving me like this!' She needed to give vent to her frustration, felt strength in her arm and swung a punch into the innocent pillow, raising a small cloud of dust. Sobbing angrily, the words escaped from her lips. 'God damn you, Harry Smith!'

Harry reeled in pain. The punch that had landed the night before suddenly hurt again. He ran his tongue between his lips, feeling the swelling and tasting the blood. 'Damned press gang!' he murmured as memories pulsed in his brain. He felt his head swim as the ship pitched up and down, and the stench! It was as bad as the farm. Vomit welled in his throat, but he managed to swallow it down, wincing at the half-digested taste of old ale. He propped himself up against a damp wooden wall and stared hopelessly into darkness. Bewildered and hurt, his mind felt numb as he slumped back into the relative warmth and comfort of the straw. He surrendered and closed his eyes.

Bells rang into his dreams. He thought for a wonderful moment that it was the church, but it wasn't. Men were marauding past his door, greeting one another, cursing, haranguing. It was the end of morning watch, the start of the forenoon. A key turned in the lock and the handle turned. The door flung open, pushing straw across the room and letting eye-bursting light stream in. Harry winced and just caught sight of the lieutenant's silhouette before his eyes slammed shut.

'Get this man out!' he demanded, and Harry forced his lids open into narrow slits. Burley figures strode towards him. Blue chequered shirts engulfed him and the unholy stink of tar, sweat and tobacco. He floated out of the room in the grasp of strong arms and was dumped in a passageway, only now realising that his hands were tied together behind his back.

'Untie the fellow!' the lieutenant demanded. 'Can't have him thinking he's a prisoner, can we?'

Nimble, strong fingers grappled with the knot. Harry was relieved to feel the free movement of his arms. 'This must be yours,' said the sailor, holding up the restraint they'd removed and dangled it in front of his eyes. It unmistakably was… a purple scarf.

Chapter 6

Seagulls cawed and squabbled outside Helen's window. Her eyes opened to a fluttering curtain that sent blades of sunlight stabbing across the ceiling. It wasn't her own bedroom. It wasn't the usual cockerel's crow. The feather pillow next to her still bore the hollow where she had punched it in frustration last night. This was dreadful. She didn't want to be alone in a strange place, but that was what she had been dealt. She cursed and struggled out of the bed. She wiped condensation from the window and peered out over rooftops and between church spires to the glittering sea. She thought that, just maybe, she could see white sails on the horizon, but by the time she had rubbed her smeary eyes, they were gone. She looked down into the street, half hoping that it had all been a bad dream and that Harry would be down there looking up at her window. He wasn't. Two dogs were tussling over a bone and a man with a horse and cart was delivering bread. Life in Norport trundled on as normal. Nobody would care about a couple of strangers who had been coerced into the navy; nobody, that is, but the girl whose life had just been ruined.

She washed in the cold water from the jug as she would at home. She dragged a comb through her tousled hair and squinted at her distorted image in the cheap, rippling mirror. Satisfied as she could be with her appearance, she ventured out of the room and down the narrow stairs. Tom Yarker was polishing away at a table.

'Good morning,' he tried, but Helen could only manage a sort of groan in response.

'Breakfast?' he enquired, then turned away from her when he saw her sickly expression, continuing with his work. There followed several heartbeats of silence as Tom thought carefully about his next few words. 'Have you thought about what you're going to do?' he enquired. She clearly had not. He gave up and wandered out of the room. Helen could hear him in mumbled conversation with a female, and eventually, Susie appeared wearing far too bright an expression.

'You sleep well?' she enquired.

Helen managed a grumbling, 'Not bad.'

'You going to stay here for a while?' went on Susie.

'Don't know,' responded Helen truthfully, then shook her head a little sadly. 'Just don't know what I'll do.'

Harry tried to stand upright, but the pitch and roll of the ship made it virtually impossible. He leant against an oaken wall for support as two sailors slid an enormous wicker basket past him into what had been his bedroom for the night. The familiar farmyard stink and clucking of closely packed chickens reminded him cruelly of his former life. The basket was tipped unceremoniously onto the straw to release the frenzy of wings, beaks and claws competing wildly for space. 'Any dead'ns take straight to the galley,' said the lieutenant.

Harry made his way along the corridor to a dazzling source of light, which turned out to be a stairway towards the blue sky. His eyes became painful slits as he peered upwards. He lurched and staggered his way up, grabbing at the rail, up, up into an incredible new world. Huge white sails filled their bellies in the gale. Masts reached up to the sky, topped with trailing pennants. Ropes angled everywhere, dotted with wooden pulleys and netting. Everything screeched and groaned in its battle with the wind. Waves smashed into the bows as they dipped and sent spray crashing like gunshot across the deck. Harry's head span in dizzy contemplation of the scene. Someone was pushing him from behind.

'Keep moving!' moaned the unsympathetic voice. Once on deck, his feet slipped and tumbled on the brine-slicked planks. The crazy rocking motion sent him staggering forward. He grabbed at a rail for support. Through a cloud of spray, he could see the pale needles of rock that tapered away from The Isle of Wight, his last tantalising glimpse of the country he called home, the country that had called up his services in its time of need. He reached out madly as if he thought he could grab hold of the disappearing land.

'Swim for it!' yelled a crazy voice in his head, and his foot had begun to clamber onto the ropes before his senses returned and cursed his stupidity.

'You're stuck here!' moaned his voice of reason. 'There's no escape!'

'God, I'm sorry, Helen,' he muttered. His head was buzzing harder and his stomach gave a violent heave. He knew he would have to be sick but was scared of making a mess of the sparkling deck and looking ridiculous. He leant over the side and gave in to the horrendous feeling, sending the vile contents of his stomach spewing away in the wind.

'Having fun?' laughed a mocking sailor. The grim response was lost in the screech of the wind.

***

'You could stay here if you're prepared to work,' said Susie.

Helen looked up at her, her eyes a quiver of questions.

'You can serve ale, can't you? You're pretty enough to please the boys, take money for their drink, or anything else they want to give you!'

Helen looked hard at the woman. Her words were slowly sinking in. She had seen her at work the previous evening, filling the tankards, taking the cash, her bosom spilling over her low-cut dress, men grabbing or pinching her bottom, lewd suggestions on their lips. She had seen one girl drop money into her cleavage before grabbing a sailor's hand and hauling him up the stairs.

'My God!' Helen exploded, hands to her face to frame her horrified gape. She visibly shook and turned away, making for the stairs and storming on up. She slammed the door behind her and glared at her distorted expression in the glass.

'Oh, mother!' she expounded. 'Can you hear what they're saying? They want me as a whore!' She thumped her angry fist down on the dressing table, picked up a brush and flung it at the glass, making a huge star in the corner, adding cracks to her awful image. She bundled her few belongings together and pounded her indignant fury down the stairs.

'You go steady!' warned Susie. 'You don't want to go adding a broken leg to your troubles!' Helen didn't reply. She swept out of the door and into the street. The harbour breeze stank of seaweed and blew a chilly sort of welcome as she buttoned up her cloak.

Harry shivered as more spray plastered his shirt onto his soaking back. He looked along the rail and saw another poor soul clinging on tight and vomiting into the waves. He looked hard and 'yes!' he could almost be sure. It was the brother of the girl he loved. The girl he should now be huddled in bed with, sharing the warmth and splendour of her body. Instead, he was captured, powerless to move from this horrendous prison of canvas, wood and rope. He felt nothing but hatred for the lad who had got him into this mess!

'You, stupid bastard!' were his words of greeting as he slipped and staggered towards the cowering figure.

'What's up with you?' responded Bart.

'You are, you idiot!' yelled Harry through the din of the rigging. 'I tried to rescue you from this lot!'

'What? It was *me* trying to save *you*!' countered Bart. 'You were pissed out of your brains! They'd have got you anyway! It's all *your* fault that *I'm* here!' The two glared at each other. Both wanted to land a frustrated punch on the other, but both succumbed to nausea once again, turned and vomited in unison over the side.

Helen thumped the frustrated knuckles of her black-gloved hand on a green-painted door. The sign, which read "Port Admiral", looked very grand, and she hoped someone there could talk sensibly about her plight. She imagined a smartly dressed clerk getting down from a lofty desk and making for the door. Instead, it was retired seaman Enoch Hoskins who had looked up in surprise at the intrusive knock and was now dragging his wounded leg across the floor. He opened the door enough to show an inquisitive eye to the stranger. He was pleased to see the attractive young woman. He was not so pleased by her anxious look. He opened the door a little further, revealing his broken nose, scarred cheek and full set of rather straggly moustache and beard. She winced a little at his appearance, but his eyes seemed to have a warmth that shone through from the leathery face. 'Yes?' enquired the man's husky voice, which betrayed years of smoking since leaving active service. 'Can I be of help?'

'I hope so,' said Helen. 'I'm looking for my husband and my brother.' For some reason, she thought it safer to lie about her marital status. She looked over the man's shoulder through tobacco smoke from the pipe he had secreted behind his back. There sat the clerk, less young than she had imagined, probably in his late teens, scribbling with quill in his ledger.

'What's their names?' asked Enoch.

'Smith and Westhouse,' she replied, and he turned with raised eyebrows to the clerk.

'We had a Smith or Westhouse through here?' he enquired.

The clerk ran his finger down a list of pressed men. 'Yes, sir,' he responded. 'Harold Smith and Bartholomew Westhouse.'

Helen was nodding from the doorway, although somewhat bemused by the formal use of their proper names. 'Both pressed into service last night, sir. Sailed with His Majesty's Ship *Adventurer* on this morning's tide.'

The involuntary gasp from Helen's mouth was accompanied by her look of horror. 'They've gone already? My God!'

'Fraid so, my dear,' said Enoch. 'Hot pressed. That's what it's called when they goes straight on board a ship instead of getting some training.'

'My God,' repeated Helen. She grabbed the door frame for support as dizziness overcame her. She felt horribly sick. Now, she had to admit the truth to herself. 'They're stuck in the bloody navy, whether they like it or not.' Her head gave a forlorn shake as she spoke. 'What the hell can I do about it?'

Enoch stuttered for words. There was nothing anyone could do. Especially now they had set sail. 'I'm afraid they're in for a spell at sea,' was his familiar-sounding reply, although spoken more sympathetically than Susie's earlier appraisal. 'They'll be joining up with Admiral Jervis,' he went on with a knowledgeable air. 'They're down in the Med blockading the Frogs in their port, or is it the Spanish?' His voice faltered. 'I'm never quite sure.'

The detail was of little interest to Helen. Her head was full of visions of battle, of Harry, of Bart, of cannon and blood. She winced and felt a shiver in her spine, finding it hard to form her thoughts into anything worthwhile to say. At last, Enoch punctured the silence.

'You can write to them,' he said and watched her eyes widen in surprise.

'Really?'

'Oh yes. Little cutters go out from here to the fleet and back quite a lot. Take sacks full of letters they do, to and from wives and sweethearts and the like. Just bring me your letter, mark the fellow's name on the outside and his ship, and I'll get it sent out with the next lot.'

This sounded wonderful to Helen. At last, something positive that she could do. She said her thanks and goodbyes to Enoch and the clerk and set off towards the town. Enoch watched her go for perhaps just a little too long.

'You fancy her, don't you, Mr Hoskins?' said the clerk, with a grin, then ducked as his master threw something imaginary at his head.

When Helen reached the shops, she caught the whiff of freshly baked bread and recognised the delivery cart from her earlier sighting in the street. She saw "Browns the Bakers" above a quaint green door and a bottle glass window sporting loaves and cakes and currant buns. The pang of hunger told her that she had missed breakfast. There had been no smiling Beatrice with her porridge, her lovely fresh bread and homemade strawberry jam. She took out her purse and opened it up. The awful truth hit her. 'Oh my God!' she muttered, attracting the disgusted stare of a bonneted lady passing by, 'The money! All gone!' It was true. No matter how she twisted and shook the purse, there was nothing there. 'How the hell do I carry on with no money? I can't even get damned paper and ink to write my letter to Harry!' She didn't know why, but she walked into the shop. She had never set foot in one before. Perhaps she thought some kind person would give her some bread. She stood and surveyed the loaves and cakes.

'Can I help?' chirped a cheery voice with a Hampshire brogue.

Helen turned to see a short, portly lady, white aproned and hatted, flour liberally dusted on her hands and face. 'Er, my young son wants to feed the seagulls,' Helen managed, quite proud of her improvisation. 'I wondered if you had any scraps or stale bits I could have.'

The woman maintained her smile. 'No, dear,' she went on. 'All our spare bits go straight to the orphanage. You could buy a few fresh rolls. They're only a farthing.'

Helen blushed with embarrassment. 'Er, no. I'm afraid I've stupidly left my purse at home. I'll come back later.' She turned to walk out of the shop when she became aware of another person behind a counter.

'Sorry we couldn't be of assistance,' he seemed obliged to add. A thin beanpole of a man, he looked the exact opposite of his ruddy-faced wife; the only splash of colour was his pale blue eyes.

Another thought struck Helen. 'I don't suppose you have any jobs going for young boys, I mean, delivering or anything?'

'No dear,' came his weary reply. 'Hardly enough work for the two of us, let alone taking on any helpers of any age. You might try some of the other shops.'

The man was obviously trying to be helpful, but she really didn't feel that there was much use in pursuing this strategy. All the shops had family names. There wouldn't be any jobs for outsiders and right now, she felt like a foreigner in a strange land. The people had a distinct accent. Her hours of practising correct pronunciation with her mother seemed such a waste of time now. She sounded haughty and too well-bred. She walked forlornly out of the shop. She stood and stared at the delivery horse and cart, which sparked another thought in her mind. 'Why have I not thought of this before? Venus! She must still be out there somewhere! Find her and I can get out of this dreadful place. She'd take me home. I could tell Papa that Harry had made me go with him. Bart tried to rescue me, but the two of them got taken by the press gang, leaving me all alone. What else could I do but come home?'

She headed back to the place where she had been reunited with her brother, but there was no horse and trap. No whinnying Venus to stroke on the nose and make for home. There were wheel marks in the mud where she had slid off the road. There were hoof marks; there was dung, but no Venus. She looked all around and called the horse's name. She walked up and down the street. She shook her head with disgust as she passed the Half Moon Tavern. She searched everywhere, her desperation mounting. There was no sign of the damned horse. Someone would be her new proud owner, or maybe she had wandered off back home on her own. Whatever had happened, Helen felt defeated. She stared at her reflection in the baker's window. The face that stared back looked more like her mother. She looked worried and wrinkled, hungry and alone. Nobody here cared about her, the haughty stranger. Nobody would offer her lodgings, food or work. Nobody… except one.

Chapter 7

Harry and Bart glared at each other, both thinking the other was to blame. Both felt overbearing anger, but both felt too weak to fight. They felt disorientated, stupid and sick.

'So, what the hell happened to Helen?' groaned Harry.

'Don't know. They're not stupid enough to grab women for the navy yet, are they?'

'No, but those bastards might have grabbed her for something else.'

'Christ! They might have raped and killed her for all we know!'

'Nah! I think she must have ducked back into the tavern. Hopefully, she'd be safe in there. I reckon she'll somehow manage to get back home.'

'Bloody hell,' cursed Harry. 'I'll never be allowed near Westhouse Farm again, will I? I've lost her for good!'

Both stared blankly at billowing sails, at straining ropes, at pounding waves. 'Don't think I can stand much more of this,' mumbled Bart. Both leant on the rail, taking in the truth, hating the pitch and roll, not knowing what had happened to Helen, shivering with the plastering effect of the freezing cold spray.

'Ah, there you are!' came a youthful voice. The reluctant recruits turned grimly to see a grinning lad, maybe sixteen years of age, in smart jacket and trousers, straw boater hat.

'Midshipman Lawrence,' the lad introduced himself, 'and you two must be Westhouse and Smith.'

'How do you know our names?' grumbled Harry.

'I told them last night,' said Bart. '*You* couldn't. You were out cold. I told the people at Norport, too, for their ledger. I told them it was all a mistake, that we'd been practically kidnapped. They said they'd see what they could do.'

'What they could do?' moaned Harry. 'There's nothing they can do! We're stuck here in the bloody navy till they kick us out again. Isn't that right, Lawrence?'

'I'm afraid it's *Mister* Lawrence to you now, or *sir*, if you prefer it, but yes, it's right. Usually, if you have some sort of reason not to serve, there's some kind of induction board with top brass, but there has to be a damned good reason to be pardoned. You're in His Majesty's Britannic Navy for a while, whether you like it or not. This dear ship was desperately short of men. You'll get paid, although only half of the regular seaman's wage. You'll be well looked after, though, with food and grog and the like. You'll be all right!'

'Oh no!' went on Bart. 'We want out! We're farmers doing vital work at home. Who feeds the nation if we're out here?'

'The nation needs you here! Who defends the people from invasion if not the navy? Half the crew were farmers once, or blacksmiths or shopkeepers! Admittedly, some were jailbirds, but we've got to stop those Frenchies from invading. We'll all be murdered if they do! C'mon down below. We'll get some food in your bellies and some grog, then you might feel a bit less obnoxious!'

'What the hell's this grog?' grumbled Harry.

'Oh, you'll find out!' said Lawrence. 'Along with a lot of other new stuff you've never heard of, but you'll be fine. You'll see!'

***

It was a sorry dawdle that carried Helen back to the Half Moon Tavern. She knocked on the rough old door that had been her salvation the night before.

'Oh, it's you,' uttered Tom Yarker, surprised. 'Did you leave something behind?'

'My self-respect,' mumbled Helen, and walked past him into hell.

She was now an employee of the Half Moon Tavern whether she liked it or not, and her life would never be the same again.

Chapter 8

Matthew Stokes' face was distorted in disbelief. 'Did you say *not here*?'

'Yes, sir. I'm afraid I did,' continued Beatrice. 'Just upped and left. Mr Westhouse is going out of his mind.'

'But this is preposterous!' moaned Matthew. 'I must see Mr Westhouse now. Immediately!' He added the last word because Beatrice had folded her arms somewhat defiantly as though she had no intention of succumbing to his demands but then saw Matthew look quizzically over her shoulder. She didn't need to turn around. She could detect the unwashed smell of the man she served.

'It's all right,' murmured Richard Westhouse. 'Show Matthew in while I go and smarten up.'

Matthew Stokes was outraged. He flung cloak, hat and cane onto a chair in the drawing room along with a splendid bouquet of flowers. He paced up and down, heart thumping harder, his anger uncontrollable. 'At last!' he groaned when Richard Westhouse appeared at the door, hair combed, shaved, and generally cleaner looking than before.

'I'm sorry I took so long,' mumbled Richard. 'I overslept this morning. Couldn't sleep last night. Sick with worry, I'm afraid. Don't know what's become of her, or Bart, for that matter. He went off to find her.'

'My God!' Stokes exploded. 'I can't believe it! I'm here to propose marriage to the girl!'

Richard's face furrowed deeper and he slumped into a chair, saying, 'I'm afraid that's what this is all about, Matthew.'

The young man continued to pace the floor, hands clasped together behind his back, sweating. He wore the incredulous look of a man grappling to accept the truth, shaking his head.

'She doesn't want to marry me?' he demanded at last.

'It's worse than that, Matthew,' grouched the would-be father-in-law. 'She's gone off with one of the farm hands. Harry Smith. You met him, in fact. We saw him greet you as you walked to your carriage.'

Matthew gaped, astonished. 'That was no greeting!' He spat the words out. 'That bloody peasant tried to warn me off! Said I should leave her alone! I told him he was as good as dead for such insolence! Miserable bastard!'

'Oh dear, dear,' muttered Richard. His head was in his hands now. He looked up at Matthew's reddening face, the young man obviously envisioning beating poor Harry to a pulp. 'It's all my fault,' went on Richard. 'I sacked the fellow when she said she was in love with him. Just wanted him out of my sight. I told her you would make a wonderful husband, but she wouldn't listen. I thought she'd run off to spite me.'

'No, no. It's not your fault; it's mine. Too staid and boring, I'm afraid. I just didn't appeal to her. At least I've been spared the ignominy of her refusal. But I promise you this, Mr Westhouse, I'll get that girl home to you and I'll have that fellow's guts for trinkets!'

He picked up his belongings and the bouquet of flowers and made for the door. 'Good day, sir!' were his parting words. At the front door, Beatrice stood, holding it open. She wore the twinkling smile of someone who knew far too much for her station. It hurt him deeply, and he thrust the bouquet into her arms, saying, 'Find some water for these!'

'Hey! Matthew!' yelled Richard. 'Come back and apologise to my maid!' But the man was unstoppable. He strode on, grim-faced, towards his carriage and came to the spot where Harry had stood. The hoe was still stuck there in the ground like some kind of trophy of the peasant's victory. Matthew was livid. He grabbed the hoe and smashed it onto the path, scattering gravel and imagining Harry's head splitting in two. He hurled it into the garden and imagined it spearing Helen in the guts. 'Marry you, Miss Westhouse? I must have been out of my mind!'

Richard and Beatrice looked on, horrified at the man's anger. He pounded on towards the carriage, shouted something at the driver and climbed on board. The carriage ground its way out of the gate and out of sight. Maid and master stared at each other, their astonishment leaving them speechless. Beatrice began to brush petals and leaves from her clothing. Richard helped and she smiled coyly as he dithered to touch debris that had adhered to her bosom.

'Don't worry, sir,' she murmured, and just a hint of a blush caressed her cheeks. 'I wouldn't scream; I mean, if you were to accidentally touch me there, sir. I promise. I wouldn't scream.'

***

Matthew Stokes banged his cane hard on the ceiling of his carriage. 'You all right, sir?' came the driver's response.

'No, I'm bloody not!' snapped the passenger. 'Pull up at the inn!'

'Wait there!' was his next command as they ground to a halt at the den of iniquity. He clambered out and pushed his way into the place, nearly dislodging a startled drinker's mug from his hands. 'You the landlord?' he demanded of flustered Hugo Burrows.

'That's correct.'

'I'm looking for Miss Westhouse. Do you know her?'

Hugo swallowed hard and wondered how many more people would be on her trail. He didn't know this fellow and certainly didn't like his brusque manner. He decided to play innocent, saying, 'She lives at the farm down the lane.'

'Yes, yes. I know that!' grumbled Stokes. 'She's run off or something. Mr Westhouse has asked me to track her down. Have you seen her recently?'

'No, sir,' he lied. 'Have you tried the church? That's more to her liking than this place.'

Chapter 9

Harry and Bart were led down the stairs, which Midshipman Lawrence told them they would "henceforth know as companion ways".

'This here's the gun deck,' the lad went on. 'So-called 'cos we fire the guns from here.' He was smiling as he delivered the oversimplification to the "land lubbers". The confusing thing was there were men sitting at tables scoffing beef stew and bread. The mass of blue and white chequered shirts equalised them into camaraderie. Their faces were animated by chewing and conversation; all shades of coloured faces, pale, brown and black, evidence of the navy's recruitment policy around the world. Some joked together, not minding if sometimes the contents of their mouths were ejected with their words and laughter. Some were more morose, complaining, grumbling about their lot. All had tar-slicked hair. All had promised allegiance to God and the king and would die to save their fellow man.

'Of course, you also eat here,' went on their guide, 'and sleep here too.' The lubbers looked around for beds. 'In hammocks,' sneered the lad. The low beams and suffocating atmosphere made Harry wince. He was used to a big open sky. Here, at nearly six feet tall, he would have to duck his head every time he moved.

They sat at a table between two tethered cannons. They couldn't help but stare at things. Huge, black and deadly. They couldn't even imagine the terrifying explosion and recoil they could perform, the smoke, the deafening roar. Stout ropes held them in place on wooden trolleys; cannon balls sat neatly in rows on nearby shelves.

'Thirty-two pounder,' said Lawrence, seeing their curiosity. 'The beast herself is nearly three tons, *more* than three if you count the trolley. Seventy-four cannons on this dear ship. Beats anything the army can muster, eh?'

The recruits nodded, amazed by Lawrence's enthusiasm. A twelve-year-old boy wandered in and introduced himself as 'John Gun'. Sandy-haired and freckly, he looked a little too gaunt to be healthy but wore a huge smile. He'd brought them stew on peculiar square wooden plates and chunks of bread. 'So-called 'cos I was born right here on this very ship, in between two guns,' the lad went on. 'Never knew my father, nor my mother. Brought up in the orphanage I was, till they were desperate enough to give me this job here. How about you men?'

Harry adopted a pained expression. 'My mother and father died in a fire,' he mumbled. 'At least I knew them.'

'Me and Bart here got caught by a press gang. Farmers really. I hear there's plenty more like us.'

'Oh, yeah. Half the crew is pressed men, or else they come from navy families and just follow on. It's a good life, though. We get to fight the Frogs!' He made a gleeful jabbing gesture with a knife.

'Food's not bad,' commented Bart, wanting to change the subject.

'That's 'cos it's nice and fresh,' said John Gun. 'You wait till we've been at sea for a bit and we get down to the salted stuff and biscuit and ships rat! That ain't so good!'

'He's kidding,' whispered one of the men and the lubbers gave a sigh of relief, until he added, 'Ain't so good? It's bloody delicious!' and laughed as he got up to leave.

The mention of rats made Harry wince. 'There's rats on the ship?' he groaned. Bart shrugged, but Harry imagined once again the gnashing yellow teeth, staring eyes and whiskers, the slithering tails. He glanced furtively around, expecting to see them and gasped in a lungful of air to try and stave off the dizziness that his phobia always produced. He wiped at the sweat on his brow, backed away from the imaginary animals and hit his head painfully on the low beam. 'Bloody hell!' he groused, but the hurt shook away the vision and he walked away rubbing the throbbing wound.

***

Helen looked at herself in the mirror. 'I can't possibly wear this,' she groaned. 'It's far too low at the front!'

'Nonsense!' replied Susie. 'The fellahs will love it!'

'I don't want them to love it.'

'Course you do! The more they're ogling your bosom, the less they can concentrate on how much ale you're giving them or how little change.' Susie winked hard. 'And put the extra money in this inside pocket. It's called 'Naught to do with the landlord. Understand?'

Helen nodded but continued to stare at the incredible shape the corset and dress had given her. What would her mother say? 'God, I hope she can't see this,' she muttered.

'Hey, lads! Look at the new girl!' said one of the customers. Helen blushed profusely as she approached with a jug of ale in hand. She saw all eyes focus on her neckline and smiled. 'Naught to do with the landlord, eh? I'll have my fare home in no time!'

Matthew Stokes looked inside the church. He knew there would be no sign of the runaways in there, but wanted to be sure. He asked the rector and others if the pair had been seen, but blank faces and sadly shaking heads were the only response. He returned to the carriage and made for home. 'Ridiculous to blunder around on your own,' he told himself. 'Be better to use the resources of Father's office.'

'Write this down!' he demanded of a cowering clerk an hour's frustrating journey later.

'I am seeking the whereabouts of an absconding couple. Helen Westhouse, twenty years of age, hazel eyes and auburn hair, and Harry Smith, twenty-one, tall, blue eyes, fair hair.' The young man scribbled hopelessly with his quill. 'For God's sake, keep up!' Matthew yelled. The clerk finished the sentence, plunged the quill into the ink well again and sat poised, ready to continue. 'There will be a reward for information leading me to them. Regards, Matthew Stokes. I want that sent out to all Stokes depots in all harbours.'

'All of them, sir?'

'Yes! Bloody well, all of them! And get it done quick!'

'Yes sir,' mumbled the clerk and he grudgingly reached for more paper.

***

'So, what exactly is your grievance?' asked Lieutenant Strater.

'We were kidnapped,' replied Bart. 'We're not sailors or even dockworkers or fishermen. We've never been to sea in our lives. Basically, sir, we're farmers. We just don't know what's going on.'

Strater had steely blue eyes. They bored into the reluctant recruits as they dithered before him in the wardroom. 'Have you got protection papers?' he asked, drawing blank looks from the men. 'Are you in some protected trade?' he went on. 'Shipwrights or the like?'

'No, sir,' managed Bart. Strater gave them his resigned expression.

'Then I'm afraid you can have no complaint.' There was a moment of silence as the finality of his comment sank in. 'Dismissed,' said Strater with a casual wave of his hand.

'Just a minute!' weighed in Harry, and Strater's stare became more aggressive. 'We've got people depending on us back home.'

'You're needed in the navy,' went on the lieutenant. 'We have every right to recruit as we think fit. This ship was seriously short of men and you've been selected to serve your country in time of need. Now, I don't expect to hear another moan out of you two and I certainly don't expect insubordination of the type you have just exhibited, Smith. The navy has plenty of reasons for dishing out a flogging and that's one of them! Take them away, Lawrence, and I suggest a little introduction to the holy stone and junk axe to get them into the swing of things.' The young midshipman signalled to the pair with his eyes.

They were angry and frustrated but powerless to argue. They followed on. Whipped dogs.

'Told you it was no use,' said the lad as they cleared the doorway. 'At least you had your say and you've got your answer. There's no way out of this. You may as well get used to the idea and knuckle down to it. The holy stone's what he suggested. A bit of that soon calms you down.'

'So, what the hell is it?' muttered Bart. 'Sounds weird.'

'Take a look,' said Lawrence. He opened up the storage box and produced two flat stones, each about the size of a book. 'Looks like a bible, doesn't it,' he went on. Harry and Bart wore quizzical expressions. 'That's why we call it holy. It's for scrubbing the decks. You'll soon get the hang of it.'

'And the junk axe?' mumbled Bart.

'Even more tedious,' smirked Lawrence. He grabbed one from the chest, its well-worn handle testimony to hours of usage. 'It's a bit blunt.' He ran his finger along the cutting edge to prove the point. 'You chops up old rope with it to use as cannon wadding and next time you visits the heads or toilets, as you might say, you'll find a bag full of the stuff for wiping your backside!'

'Bloody great,' moaned Bart. 'We've been dragged into the navy so we can spent hours scrubbing decks and chopping bum wipers! Couldn't the boys do that?'

'Yeah, of course, but when the real action starts, that's when we need the likes of you. Cannon drill. That's what they'll get you doing. You'll love it. And you'll love giving those Frenchies a blast or two of gunpowder and shot!'

Bart and Harry listened wide-eyed to the lad's enthusiasm. They almost began to think there was enjoyment to be had in this patriotic chore.

Eight chimes of the bell rang out. 'Grog up!' declared a voice and men moved excitedly towards the barrel on the deck where a man stood with a ladle guarded by two red-coated marines. Bart and Harry joined the shambling queue and were eventually doled out a measure of the golden-brown liquid. Both sipped at it experimentally. Both winced. Even though it was well watered down, it was worse than the ale they had only recently been introduced to. Others were quaffing the stuff with enthusiasm and they turned to watch the new men's response. They thought it advisable to swallow and force a smile. 'Numbs the brain a bit,' said one of the tars. 'Makes the world seem a happier place.'

Harry looked out at the misty horizon. He couldn't understand the curvature. It had never been noticeable among Hampshire's rolling hills.

'Why don't things slip off the edge?' he pondered out loud.

Bart gave him a quizzical glance. 'Didn't you learn at school about Christopher Columbus, and the world being round?'

'Never went to school,' replied Harry, causing deeper furrows on his companion's brow.

'So, didn't your parents teach you?'

'Only about farming. And God.'

'So, you don't know all about gravity keeping things down on the ground or the earth being held by the sun and the moon by the earth?'

Harry pulled a face which said, *What the hell does all that matter?*

Bart raised his eyes skyward and proclaimed, 'One day, men will find a way to fly off this world and go exploring whatever's beyond,' causing laughter amongst the nearby men.

'The only thing beyond is heaven,' said Harry. 'My parents taught me that much. I think that man's right. The grog is definitely numbing your brain!'

As days wore on, Harry and Bart were beginning to look more and more like sailors. They were issued with blue chequered shirts and white trousers, woollen stockings and black deck shoes. 'Wear 'em with pride,' muttered the purser. 'And 'ere. Take these neck scarves.'

Bart took a red spotted one, but Harry declined. He already had his own ill-gotten purple scarf. 'It'll save the blood of your hero,' Molly Elizabeth had said. The words had left him even more dumbfounded as she slid away from him, his brain and energy sapped.

'What hero?' he muttered out loud, causing a quizzical look on the purser's face.

Harry's physical strength meant that he adapted far more quickly to naval life than Bart. While Harry was to be seen hauling on ropes, lifting and carrying, even encouraged to clamber about in the rigging of the masts, Bart was assigned the more mundane tasks with holy stone and junk axe. He thought this a fairly simple thing until, one day, he received a thump around the head and shoulders with a knotted rope by a particularly officious midshipman. 'No, bloody slacking!' the man had yelled, and from then on, he worked a little more diligently and with occasional furtive glances over his shoulder. Both he and Harry were equally exhausted at the end of the day and had learned by watching others how to sling the hammocks and even how to get into the things. They were so closely packed that you jostled with your neighbours as they swung about to the vagaries of the sea. Even so, it was your one period of respite. Nobody barking orders in your ear.

Your chance to let your thoughts wander to the life you left behind. The *girl* you left behind. God, this was tough.

'I'm sorry, Helen,' Harry kept muttering to himself. 'Should have been starting a new life with you, but instead, I've been landed with this lot. God, I hope you're coping out there somewhere on your own.'

The shrill notes of the boson's call screeched out all too soon. 'Get up! Get out!' was being yelled. You cursed yourself for falling asleep and letting the morning come too soon. Your movements were instinctive. Get up, get out! Your feet hit the deck. You grabbed your clothes from the bottom of your hammock. They felt damp. You struggled them on. The powder monkeys would be there soon with their buckets of freezing water. Sluicing the deck. Laughing and swilling the feet of any straggler. Get the hammock down. Roll it up. Slide it through the hoop and get up on deck. Stand to attention. Don't you dare give in to the biting gale and shiver? Harry remembered the words from his father's mouth. How stoic and strong that man had been. He'd instilled such manly qualities in his son.

'Don't let them know you're hurt,' he would say. 'Push on till the job's complete. Then you can rest.' He hadn't deserved to die that terrible death. Probably collapsed trying to save his dear wife. 'Take it. Bear it. Stand there erect, and take it like a man!' A hard-enough task on a windswept farm, almost impossible in the biting gale on a wallowing ship. Chest out, chin up till you heard 'stand at ease!' Then, you could plant your feet further apart for stability and slide your hands behind your back. Till then, it was 'attention!' and don't you dare waver.

***

The moment Helen had been dreading finally arrived.

'Your turn upstairs,' said Susie with a sincere look. Helen handed over the jug and made her way up the narrow stairs. She gazed for a moment at her rippling reflection in the damaged glass and dared not even think about her mother's scorn.

She recalled the story she had read from the bible about the sinful woman who was about to be stoned by the crowd when Jesus intervened and said, 'Let he who is without sin cast the first stone.' She remembered how she had sneered at that woman, an adulteress; surely a whore was even worse. Now, that was her. The lowest of the low. She sat on the bed and waited. Her heart thumped with derision. She began to feel sick.

Luckily, she didn't have to wait long. The door opened and an ale-swilled sailor staggered in. He put money into the box on the wall and supported himself against the dressing table, staring at his reflection in the crazy mirror. 'God, you're ugly,' he muttered to himself, hardly the first words Helen was expecting to hear.

'Thanks,' she said out loud and the man turned towards her. His eyes opened wide as he took in the beauty of his quarry. His stare dwelt on her ringlets and hazel eyes before plunging into her cleavage, his excitement tangible as he moved towards her.

'God, you're an angel,' he muttered.

'Hardly,' returned Helen. 'Not in this bloody profession.'

He put his hands on her shoulders and felt her tremble. His calloused palms scratched her white, virginal skin as they pushed the dress across her shoulders and down her arms, revealing more curvaceous cleavage. This was going to be hell for the novice whore. How she wished she and Harry had not been disturbed that day in the barn. He would have been so loving, so gentle. This man was a brute. He pushed the dress down to her waist and dribbled yellow tobacco saliva onto her breasts. He grabbed them roughly, rubbing the slime into her nipples. Helen winced; she couldn't bear it. 'Take it right off!' he growled.

She wanted to slap him or to run away. She couldn't stop tears welling up in her eyes. The man glared at her, his steely eyes demanding that she obeyed. She stood and let the dress fall to the ground, naked, inspected like some slave girl at the market. He pulled off his shirt, revealing scars of many a battle and the reddened welts on his back from some distant flogging. Then he revealed his full nakedness. A shock ran through her. She had seen the full glory of the bull at Westhouse Farm and her mother had said it was just like a man's, only much larger. He loved the audible gasp that the sight of him brought from her lips. He toppled her onto the bed and she felt the full weight of his body on top of her. He was into her in a flash, his movements rough and painful. He interpreted her yelp as pure pleasure, but it was the painful loss of her virginity. She remembered what Susie had told her and moaned with mock delight at his throbbing climax. The well-rehearsed words came back to her and she breathed them softly in his ear. 'You're the best... I ever had.'

Chapter 10

'Letter arrived from Portsmouth office, sir!'

Matthew Stokes looked up from his desk. There was excitement in the young clerk's voice as he crossed the room and placed the sealed, folded paper in front of his employer. 'Do you think it's a reply, sir? To the letters I sent out?'

'Very probably,' said Stokes, in matter-of-fact tone, but his heart was beginning to thump its anticipation. He broke the seal, his eyes quickly scanning the page and then looking up at the young man. 'Have they found them, sir?' his chirpy response.

'Yes and no,' said Stokes cryptically. 'They knew nothing but contacted the neighbouring little harbour at Norport. The man Smith is in their ledger as having been pressed into the navy. Bloody fool! They have no knowledge of Miss Westhouse.'

'Gosh, sir! If he's been nabbed for the navy, what do you reckons become of *her*?'

'No idea. She might head straight back home. I'm sure Mr Westhouse will let me know.'

In his mind, Matthew could see her in some stagecoach, dabbing at her tears with a lacy handkerchief. 'That's where it gets you, Miss Westhouse,' he gloated.

'Jilting me for some no-good peasant. I *told* your father you'd get home. As for that bastard Smith?' He stroked his chin, pensive, then, as logical thought took over again from anger, uttered, 'Stuck in the navy, are you, Smith? Another letter, I think.'

Harry had been asked to fetch a couple of pulleys from the carpenter's quarters. He didn't know exactly where that was except that it was on the orlop deck, somewhere near the purser's office, where he had been issued with his seaman's garb. He went down two companionways into the dingiest part of the ship. This was well beneath the water line and the smell of mould was stronger than anywhere else on the ship. The place was dotted with dim, swinging lanterns. The oak walls were speckled with condensation and the thick roots of the masts creaked in their eternal battle with the spine of the ship. He looked around for some helpful signage but found nothing. As he approached the rear of the vessel, he heard muffled squealing.

Oh, God! Not rats! he thought, visions of that boyhood nightmare soaring in his mind. *No.* It sounded more like high-pitched human voices, the playful tones of off-duty powder monkeys perhaps, but it was neither of these things. He peered around a canvas partition that had been nailed to the floor and ceiling, with the words 'Is this the carpenter's quarters?' on his lips. It obviously was not.

His mouth gaped at the sight of four young women sitting or half lying on bales of hay. They stopped their chatter abruptly when they saw him. After several heartbeats of silence, one of them ventured, 'You looking for us, sunshine?'

It seemed odd. It was what his mother used to call him. 'Er, no,' he managed. 'I'm looking for the carpenter.'

'Well, he was in here five minutes ago, darling, having his chisel sharpened!' They all sniggered then gave in to full bellied laughter. Harry reddened. It was not their ribald behaviour that shocked him; girls at the market were often just as bad. It was their very presence.

'I just didn't know there were any women on this ship,' he confessed.

'You ain't been in the navy long then?' quipped the one with red hair. She was the most attractive of all of them, her green eyes shining from a freckly face.

'No. Only a couple of days. Press gang got me stone drunk in Norport.'

'Oh dear!' she responded. 'Now, where've I heard that before?' The others laughed again, and she went on.

'You need someone to show you around.' She took him by the arm and, to an accompaniment of "oohs" from her colleagues, ushered him behind another canvas partition. 'You got any cash?' she whispered. 'Or grog, or food, or French perfume? I'll do it for anything like that.'

'Do what?' he managed naively.

'You know,' she replied and pushed her dress down off one shoulder. Harry swallowed hard. She pushed the dress off the other shoulder and it slipped down to the top of her bosom. Visions of Helen and then Molly Elizabeth against that rough old door flashed crazily in his mind and his fingers went automatically to the purple scarf around his neck. His head whirled in confusion. He found himself succumbing to the redhead's charm and the unknown waft of her perfume excited him.

'So,' she went on. 'You got anything?'

'Just my lucky shilling,' he croaked.

The dress slipped down to the ground and she whispered, 'That'll do.'

***

Helen rapped on Enoch Hoskin's door. The ex-seaman dragged his game leg across the floor once again to open it inquisitively. His eyes widened when he recognised the attractive young woman, and he opened the door wider to invite her in. 'Been wondering where you'd got to,' he greeted her. 'Thought you'd be around within the hour with the letter you wanted me to send.'

'It wasn't that easy,' she replied with an air of genuine understatement. 'But I've got it here.' She opened her bag to produce the folded paper, '*Harry Smith, Adventurer*,' scrawled on the top.

'That'll do fine,' said Hoskins. 'Starfish cutter's setting off tomorrow. I'll see to it that it's in his sack.'

'That's very kind of you, Mr, er.'

'Hoskins,' responded the man.

'Well. Pleased to have met you, Mr Hoskins. How long do you think before I might get a reply?'

'Be a week, I'd imagine. You never really know.'

She made for the door. 'Well, I'll drop in and check from time to time.'

'Yes, you do that, Mrs Smith. Look forward to seeing you again.'

They said their goodbyes and Hoskins watched till she disappeared from sight. He closed the door and looked at the clerk still scribbling with his quill. The young man couldn't disguise the cheeky smirk on his face.

***

'So, do you understand this *bells* thing?' Harry asked Bart.

'Oh yes. That young Lawrence fellow explained it to me. Apparently, there's a man with a half-hour glass. It takes just half an hour for the sand in it to drop from one bulb to the other, then he turns it over and it starts again.' Bart watched Harry's face for signs of understanding or mystery. So far, so good.

'Each time he turns it over, he rings the bell and adds one more chime. So, you get one bell, two bells, three and so on up to eight.'

'Why eight?'

'Cos that means four hours have passed and that's the end of a watch.'

'So what?'

'So, the men who were on duty get to rest, and those who were resting go back on.'

Harry was nodding; Bart was definitely getting through and thought he might as well continue.

'We're just learning stuff at the moment, but eventually we'll get put into one of the groups. First watch of the night is from eight o'clock to midnight. Middle watch is from then till four. Morning watch is four till eight.' Bart could see Harry's eyes beginning to cloud, so he just added, 'and so on.'

'Why can't they have a damn big clock like on the church?' queried Harry.

'I think it's something to do with pendulums not working on a rocking ship. They're trying to come up with some kind of clever timepiece that a rough sea doesn't affect, but for the time being, we have to go along with the bells.'

'Good job you're around to explain this stuff to me, Bart,' muttered Harry, but then, with a twinkle in his eye, added, 'I bet there's something I know that you don't.'

'What's that?'

There were a few moments of silence as Harry looked furtively over each shoulder, in turn, to build up the suspense. Then, when he was sure nobody could overhear, he added in a half-whisper.

'There are women on board.'

'What?' Bart's eyes widened in disbelief.

'Honest, there are. Down on the orlop deck. They'll do it for almost anything.'

'You mean…?'

'Yep!'

'Blimey,' mumbled Bart.

'You ever been with a woman?' asked Harry.

'What, on Westhouse farm? You must be joking. More chance with a bloody sheep!'

Chapter 11

Black plumes nodded on horse's heads as they turned into the churchyard. The little congregation sat huddled on uncomfortable pews, sheltering from the rain, and Reverend Crocket signalled them all to stand. Pallbearers came ponderously into the church, their heavy burden wobbling on their shoulders on their way to the altar. The men were relieved to rest it on the metal stand. Chief mourner Richard Westhouse said a silent prayer, remembering the good times and bad he had shared with this dear brother. Cedric was younger than him and nobody believed that he would be the first to go; the whole village was shocked by his sudden collapse whilst working in the field. Unmarried and childless, his adjacent farm would pass to Richard, doubling his area of land, doubling his responsibilities. He had grimaced at the thought. He stared at the coffin, dripping wet and bedecked with flowers. He imagined his brother at peace inside.

The service was short and solemn. The black-clad little group trailed out behind the polished elm casket and clustered around the freshly dug grave at the end of the Westhouse plot. Richard stared at the latest headstones: Uncle William, Aunt Mary and his dear wife Sarah. He hardly heard the words that Reverend Crocket used. He couldn't take his eyes off Sarah's headstone. Rain dripped rhythmically onto the brim of his top hat from an overhanging branch and dribbled down the inscription he was staring at like tears. He envisaged the sorrowful face of his wife. 'Where are my children?' she seemed to ask. Her eyes were scornful as they rested on her widower. 'You've lost them, Richard,' she uttered and tears welled in the man's eyes.

He couldn't stand her wrath. He had let her down badly. 'You're right, my dear,' he mouthed. 'It's all my fault.' He bowed his head. 'I've been so stupid. Caused dear Helen to run away. Let Bart go off after her. God knows what's become of them. You're right, my dear. I must go and find them. I must get them back.'

'Are you all right, sir?' whispered a worried voice beside him. Richard stared blankly at Beatrice as she linked her arm to his, images of Sarah still clear in his brain.

'Do you want to throw some of the soil that the vicar has blessed?' the voice lilted on.

Richard still didn't respond. Beatrice took a handful and scattered it onto the coffin on his behalf. 'Ashes to ashes.' Crocket's voice wavered as he saw the chief mourner turn his head, but he continued with the rhetoric. Richard and Beatrice walked solemnly away, causing knowing nods and glances amongst the villagers. 'I must find them,' he muttered to his attentive escort. 'I have to bring them back.'

***

'One for you, Smith,' said Midshipman Lawrence. He held out the folded paper with its blob of red sealing wax. Harry stared. He had never received a letter in his life.

'Take it then!' insisted Lawrence and Harry held out a hand.

'It must be from *her*!' said Bart, excited. 'Open it, for God's sake!'

'But how would she know where to send it?'

'God knows! But she's a resourceful girl, and she is my sister. She probably explains in the letter. For Christ's sake, open the damned thing!'

'What does that say?' asked Harry, still staring at the outside.

'It says *Harry Smith, Adventurer*! Don't tell me you can't even read your own name and that of your ship!'

'I told you!' returned Harry. 'I never went to school! My mother and father couldn't read or write. I never learned how!'

'For God's sake, give it to me!' groaned Bart, exasperated, and he grabbed the thing from Harry's tentative grasp.

'My darling, Harry,' he read out. 'What a dreadful thing to have happened. I do so hope that you were not injured too severely and that you are now being treated with some respect. I checked with the Port Admiral, who told me that you and Bart had been taken by the press gang onto His Majesty's Ship *Adventurer*. So that's where I addressed it. I just hope that you have received it. You must be sick with worry about me, but I'm fine. I don't know, though, whether to wait for you here or go home. If you can possibly reply to this note and give me some idea of how long you'll be away, it would help and reassure me greatly. The one thing you can be sure of is,' and Bart blushed a little here before continuing with the lover's private vow, 'that I will always love you.' He said the words quickly. 'I so look forward to hearing from you. All my love and affection. Helen.'

'She's a wonderful girl,' muttered Harry and he felt huge pangs of guilt about his improprieties with Molly and the redhead on the orlop deck, physically splendid as they had been. When Bart and Harry's eyes met again, they were both welling with tears, both men blissfully unaware of how she had even been able to afford to buy the paper and ink.

***

'Good grief!' Hugo Burrows dropped the tankard he was drying. 'Mr Westhouse!' he proclaimed. The gentleman farmer doffed his hat as he came through the door and stood there awkwardly, shifting his weight from foot to foot and glancing inquisitively around. The landlord's brain slowly recovered from the shock and he recovered the pewter tankard from the floor, examining it for damage. There was a difficult silence. It was Richard who spoke first.

'I'm sorry to have given you such a start,' he mumbled. 'It's a matter of great importance to me. It's my daughter, Miss Helen. She's been very stupid and run off with one of my farm hands. I... I need to find her, and I just wondered if she had called in here. Or Bart, for that matter, my son. He's been looking for her too.'

Hugo's mind was working as the man spoke. What should he tell him? He cleared his throat thoughtfully. 'Well. I've seen your son, Mr Westhouse. He came in a few days ago looking, as you say, for Miss Helen. I thought it more likely that she'd have hidden in the church, but he said he'd already looked. He seemed to think she was playing some kind of game.'

'It's no game, I can assure you. She's making a stupid mistake going off with that fellow and now I'm afraid for Bart's safety, too.'

Hugo reddened as the visitor spoke. He didn't want to let him know that the couple had spent the night under his roof or that he knew where they were heading. He had sworn that he wouldn't tell.

'I told the other fellow you sent the same thing,' continued Hugo, but saw Richard's eyes widen as he spoke, his expression finally becoming fully quizzical, his confusion confirmed by the words 'What other fellow?'

'Smartly dressed man. A real gentleman, you might say. Top hat, cloak, walking cane.'

Richard needed no further clue. His feelings were mixed. Matthew Stokes had sworn to get Helen back home, which could only help his cause, but his violent feelings towards Harry Smith may well put his daughter in danger, too. He stroked at his chin, pensive.

'Why don't you tell him,' interrupted a voice, which made both men wheel around. They both thought that the place had been empty, but Molly Elizabeth had been listening from the back room. Hugo's mouth gaped at the girl's intrusion.

'It's obvious the man's sick with worry about his daughter,' she went on. 'Why don't you tell him what happened? He'll find out eventually. It'd save a lot of time!'

'Get back to your work!' exploded Hugo, an authoritative finger pointing to the back room, but the girl remained in place, her blue eyes glaring venom at the man's response.

'Let her speak!' demanded Richard. 'What is it you're keeping from me?'

'Well?' spat Molly. She was holding a broom very tightly and seemed to shake it slightly as her eyes demanded that Hugo spoke.

'They were here,' confessed Hugo. 'They spent the night here on my old settee. They disappeared the next morning. I'm sorry, Westhouse. They swore me to secrecy.'

'And they got a lift down to Portsmouth,' Molly added, and it was Hugo's turn to glare.

'Anything else you think I ought to know?'

Molly, of course, had a wonderful secret memory, but she wasn't about to let either man know about that. She just added, 'Only that he swiped my purple neck scarf, presumably as a present for his girl.'

'I'll get it back,' whispered Richard. 'I'll get them all back, one way or another. Thank you for your help,' he added pointedly. 'Especially you, Miss, er.'

'Miss Molly Elizabeth,' the girl replied, and he saw sincerity in those luminous eyes.

He waved his hat briefly above his head by way of cheerio and departed, a new spring in his step. As the door closed, Hugo turned towards the girl with a look of utter disgust.

'You, miserable little bitch!' he exploded. 'You made me look a complete fool! And a liar!' He moved towards her and she held out the broom as if it had some magical power of defence. He grabbed it and shoved her hard. She staggered back, glaring defiance. 'You still fancy that Smith fellow, don't you? That's what this is all about! You want them caught and separated so that you can pick up the pieces. I saw the way you looked at him before. You're *my* woman. Understand? I took you in, a homeless waif. I made you what you are!'

'Yes! A bloody serving wench at some pox-ridden village inn! It's hardly anything to be proud of!'

'You're an ungrateful little witch!' he spat the words and Molly swung the broom wildly in retaliation. He parried it, anger pulsating in his brain, picked up a stool and swung it violently. Somehow, Molly dodged it and the momentum of the man's swing made him stumble to the ground at her feet.

Chapter 12

Harry thought Gun Captain Parker was probably the most fearsome-looking fellow on the ship. He still wasn't sure how the hierarchy worked. There was a baffling array of men called lieutenants, bosons, masters and mates, midshipmen, and various ratings of seamen. He only needed to know that everyone was superior to the "landsmen", as the pressed men were officially called, except perhaps the boys. Parker stood about four inches shorter than Harry and was probably no more muscular, but his face bore the scars of a dozen battles and his dark eyes demanded respect.

He stood at the rear of his beloved cannon and glared at the novice crew he'd been given. They felt his contempt. 'Any of you men done this before?' he rasped but was met by a row of blank faces. 'Well, let me tell you, my friends, that we will very soon meet up with the enemy. French or Spanish, it doesn't make much difference. His Majesty's Britannic Navy has the fastest rate of gunfire known to man. That's because we practice and practice, and then, while they're all swilling their wine at the harbour, we practice some more!'

There were grins and a couple of sniggers amongst the group, but Parker had not intended the remark to be funny.

His glare silenced the humour. Men stared as he began to caress the black iron monster as though it was a beautiful girl. He ran his fingers along the full ten feet of her from breech to mouth, then bent and kissed her, sighing with pleasure and delivering a playful slap on its side. 'She's a beauty, ain't she?' he muttered. 'Thirty-two-pound shot; she fires. She weighs more than three tons. Sits on her lovely trolley of English elm 'cos elm's tough and don't splinter like oak. Needs her hefty breeching ropes to stop her flying back to smash the opposite walls when she's fired and recoils.'

He had the men's full attention. His love for the monster was obvious to all. 'Treat her with respect, eh?' he went on, eyes boring earnestly into them all, 'and she'll smash the enemy and save our souls.' Some couldn't hold his stare. Others could. Those who could be beckoned to the front, Harry and Bart amongst them. Parker set about the task of allocating jobs to each man. Harry was to be a rammer, Bart a sponger. They were handed the requisite tools from the rack.

'Right,' went on Parker, 'let's make a start. When I say *load the cartridge*, this man hands the bag of highly explosive gunpowder to the loader, who puts it in the barrel. Smith, my rammer, then shoves it as far as it'll go with his ramrod. I then say *load the shot* and then *wad the gun*. After the loader has obliged with each, Mr Smith gives another ram so it's all nice and tight. We then run out the gun, which means get it into firing position at the gun port, then you all stand clear. It's up to me for a while. When I get the order to fire, I do my bit. *Boom!*'

His sudden yell made the men jump and Parker laughed. 'Wait till you hear the real thing! And for God's sake, keep well out of her way. Three tons of hefty metal becomes more like twelve. She flies back till the ropes stop her. I've seen men crippled and killed who've been too slow to get clear! Then I give the order to *sponge out*. Westhouse! That's where you come in! You dip the sheep skin rod in the bucket of water and you shoves it into the barrel, just like the rammer, only now it's red hot in there. It'll steam and hiss like fury, but you'll put out any nasty embers left and cool it down for the next shot. Any questions? No!'

He responded himself before anyone could find their voice. 'Let's do it!'

They did it. They did it again. This was going to be a regular part of the daily routine. While the French and Spaniards were swilling their wine at the harbour, His Majesty's Britannic Navy was going to be the fastest. Bart and Harry were going to be a vital part of that well-drilled team.

'Can we get a letter back to Helen?' Harry asked as they went off duty.

Bart said that he'd be happy to write it for him if he told him what to say. 'Trouble is, she wants some idea how long we might be away and we haven't got a clue. Just tell her that we're both fine and that we're working hard and hope it'll all be over soon. Say you're getting plenty of food and drink. Anything you want. Just not perhaps about your women downstairs!'

Bart got paper and ink and a quill from the Purser and they struggled through, Harry floundering for words, Bart forming his ramblings into meaningful sentences and contending with the pitch and roll of the ship as he scratched away with the quill. After what must have been a couple of hours and three or four screwed-up failed efforts, they were happy with the result and gave the folded paper to Midshipman Lawrence, *Miss Westhouse, care of The Port Admiral, Norport* scrawled on the outside.

'I'll have to read it,' he muttered. 'In case you put anything that may be useful to the enemy if they grab it, I'll have to censor it and blot bits out.'

He scanned the page as the author and scribe looked on with worried expressions. 'No, you're all right!' he concluded. 'You've not put anything about where we are or where we're heading.'

'Ha!' said Bart. 'That would only be possible if we *knew* those things!'

'You mean you don't recognise the famous rock of Gibraltar?' said Lawrence, waving a hand in the general direction of the thing. Bart swivelled around, his eyes widening at the looming sight. He'd seen a drawing of it in one of his father's books. It looked like some kind of magical kingdom with its pinnacle in the clouds. Now, it seemed to be rising out of a mist, the top quite clear and distinct against uninterrupted blue. He remembered reading a little about its strategic importance. It hadn't meant much to him. He certainly never dreamt he would see it in reality. Harry, unfortunately, had never heard of the place, but he stared at it wondrously.

'You'll be back on duty soon,' Lawrence's voice interrupted their musings. They had both been allocated places of work or *stations,* as the navy liked to call them. They were both to be on *larboard* watch, a name, they were told, for the left of the ship, although most people preferred the newer term "port", which was less easily confused with "starboard" when orders were shouted in difficult conditions. For the time being, the navy decreed that it would keep the old term and Bart and Harry's so-named watch would recommence at the next ringing of the bell. Both men had been suffixed with the letter 'B' on the listings, which they discovered meant that they would form part of any boarding party should the need arise.

'Nothing to worry about,' Lawrence had reassured them. 'You'll get plenty of practice with the cutlass before that happens!'

Susie only needed to glance at Helen and motion with her eyes for her to understand that it was her turn again upstairs. She gave a little sigh before passing on the jug of ale and heading off to that dreaded place. She gave the sticking door an extra shove and was surprised to see a fellow already sitting on the bed. Even more surprised to realise that it was landlord Tom Yarker.

'Sit down,' he greeted her and indicated the place on the bed beside him. She obliged but was already perceiving an admonishing tone in his voice. 'Empty it out,' he went on and she blushed, knowing exactly what he meant.

'How did you know?' she mumbled.

'Landlords are a lot smarter than you girls think,' he responded. 'Just empty it out.'

She reached into the folds of her petticoats and pulled out the bag of coins. "Naught to do with the landlord" had become very much to do with him. She tipped the contents onto the bed, mostly farthings and ha'pennies. He gave her his disappointed look, scooped them up and pocketed the lot.

'I don't expect this to happen again,' he murmured. He was on his feet and out of the door. She sat there dejected.

'How the hell do I get out of this now?' she mouthed, but as usual, there was no reply. No consoling mother, no Beaty, no understanding words from God who would by now have certainly consigned her to hell. She somehow had to be strong and bear this tawdry existence. Alone.

'Sails to starboard!' yelled a remote voice high in the rigging.

'Where to starboard?' returned Lawrence.

'Nor nor west!' yelled the dismembered voice.

The Midshipman pulled out his telescope and trained it on the creamy white apparition that was climbing over the horizon. Harry could still not understand how things didn't slip off the edge of the world. 'This rock is where the dear ancients used to think ships fell off the edge,' one of the seamen was saying. 'When they were sailing out of the Med,' he went on. 'Course, we know better now, don't we? We know that you have the pleasure of sailing away to dear old England!'

'Hope so,' added Harry. 'And let's hope it's bloody soon!'

'It's one of ours!' proclaimed Lieutenant Strater, who had also pulled his telescope. 'It's the cutter *Starfish*! She's flying flag thirty-nine. No need to look that one up in the book, eh? It means she's got mail. I'll let the captain know. He'll probably want to change course to meet her.'

Captain Griffiths had already seen it. He sat in the huge stern window that stretched in half a dozen panes across the width of the ship in his cabin and wondered how long it would be before he was consulted. He didn't have to wait long.

'Enter!' he yelled in response to a respectful knock on his door. A red-coated marine strode in, his white cross belts and breeches dazzling in the low beams of the sun, the captain's personal guard.

'Lieutenant Strater would like a word, sir,' he announced. Griffiths nodded and the man was shown in. He was met by the sight of the captain sitting in the long window seat, staring out at the little ship that was approaching.

Any comment that Strater could make would be superfluous, so he just added, 'I'll bring the mail directly to you, sir.' Even that was unnecessary. It was the usual procedure.

As the Starfish approached, Bart could see how small the neat cutter was. 'Glad I'm not on that little thing,' he muttered to Harry. 'It's getting tossed about horribly by the waves. I get sick enough on this sturdy old tub!'

Harry just nodded and watched the careful hoisting of the mailbag up onto the ship. 'Can you imagine if they dropped the lot!' he observed. 'God, they'd be in trouble! Ah, and hopefully my letter to Helen's amongst the lot that's going back,' he said, as the procedure was reversed and the outgoing sack landed softly on the little rolling deck.

'Wish it luck,' said Bart, who then planted a kiss on his palm before blowing it forward.

'I know Helen said she was all right and that we shouldn't worry,' mused Harry. 'But she didn't have much money left, if any, after our drinking spree at the Half Moon. How's she managing, Bart? She'd bloody well better be all right.'

Lieutenant Strater took the sack directly to Griffith's cabin. There was a clutch of letters marked for the captain's attention, the top one of which was red velum, which meant it was a communication from the Admiral.

'What now?' he wondered as he spread the letters on his polished oak desk and was tempted to open the one from home first. 'I suppose I have to open this one first,' he grumbled and picked up the red one. He could see that the lieutenant was trying to read it upside down. 'What a joy it must be, sir, to have a clerk to put your demands so neatly onto the page.' Griffiths didn't respond and could sense Strater's growing frustration.

'Is the content as wonderful as the script, sir?' asked the lieutenant at last. Griffiths waited a full minute before replying.

'It seems we're to have a spell ashore, lieutenant,' said the captain. 'We're to put into Lisbon and join the rest of the fleet there. It seems that the Spanish have been persuaded to join up with the Frogs, the only way Bonaparte can muster a big enough fleet to invade, although I'm sure he's cursing the fact that they can't do it alone. They're in the Med, so they will have to come this way. When they do, we come out of port and give them hell.'

Griffiths could tell without looking that the lieutenant was smiling. 'I'll let them all know, sir,' he said as he turned to leave the room. 'I take it we're to turn straight away?'

Griffiths smiled and nodded before adding, 'Go to it, lieutenant!'

Chapter 13

Helen gazed out of her window at another glistening autumn morning. She stared long and hard at the sea, her head filling with thoughts of Harry, thoughts of guilt and disgust at what she had become. 'If he knew, he'd bloody kill me!' she told herself. 'And what about Papa? He would too! I wonder if he sent anybody else out to look for me. Look for Bart, more like it. And what about Matthew? He wants to kill me for deserting him for some farm hand! What a bloody, bloody mess! Oh God! Please, God. I know I don't deserve anything from you, but can you please, please help me. Do I have to keep on with this living hell just to end up in the hell you consign me to when life ends? None of this was my fault, was it? I love Harry so much. I just wanted to be with him. I'm sure Jesus would have saved me from the mob who want to stone me to death.'

Silence. She turned away from the window, a tear in her eye and a shake of her head. Not even God would deign to speak to her. Sinful little whore! She dressed and went out into the chilly sea breeze. Life was going on much as usual. People were going about their business, horses clomping on the cobbles, seagulls cawing overhead. Some sounded as if they were laughing at her. Their mad, flapping wings made her suddenly think about her adoring flock of chickens back home. 'I expect poor Beaty's got the job of feeding them now!'

Her wandering feet took her past the shops and she caught a whiff of the newly baked bread. She glanced in at Mr and Mrs Brown, standing cross-armed behind the counter.

Still not much work for the two of you, she thought. She carried on. She thought that, just maybe, Harry would have received her letter and have written back but knew in her heart that it was too soon to enquire. Even so, as she was so close to the Port Admiral's office, she might just look in. She turned the last bend and, 'Oh my God!' Her hand shot to her mouth.

She stared at the two men in the doorway; the thump of her heart gave its warning. One was undoubtedly Hoskins, who was pointing away to the left and waving his hand as though giving directions. The other, although his back was turned towards her, was also unmistakable. His height, his build, his so familiar bearing. This was the man she'd grown up with, the man who had smacked her legs when she misbehaved, who'd smiled and told her it would soon be better when she grazed her knees or cut her hand. How could she have been so rude to him that night? Why could he not understand her? She was lost. She wanted to run and hug him, but that was impossible now. That was all in the past. She was a whore now! A nasty, despicable whore! He should hate her, should want to beat her to a pulp for such a dreadful misuse of her life. The sickening betrayal of her mother's aspirations. She trembled. She waited. She stood in the shadows, trying to control the tears and the thumping of her heart. Both over-ruled her. She leant against the wall and almost collapsed. She saw her dear Papa walk away in the direction Hoskins had pointed. She mopped at her tears with her handkerchief and took some minutes to convince herself that she could walk and conduct herself with some serenity. Composed, she crossed the street, glancing cautiously to confirm that he wasn't looking back. She knocked hurriedly on the green-painted door. After the customary wait, Hoskins opened it. His eyes betrayed his pleasure at seeing her.

'Ah, Mrs Smith!' he greeted her. It felt odd, but he was still under the illusion that she was married to her Harry. At least, that was what she thought. In fact, he had just learned otherwise but was playing her game. 'Come in,' he went on, the door opening wider. 'You'll never guess who I've just met.'

'Oh, I think I will, Mr Hoskins,' she replied, getting a raised eyebrow look from the man. 'My guess is that it was my dear Papa.' The eyebrows dropped again and he gave an understanding nod. 'You saw him,' he confirmed, and she gave him a thin smile.

'What did he say?'

'Just that he'd travelled from Fernhills; that he was looking for his son and daughter, name of Bart and Helen *Westhouse*.' She blushed. He went on, 'That they might be with a fair-haired fellow, name of Harry Smith. Either you got married in a hurry, or it's Miss Westhouse I'm addressing now, isn't it not Mrs Smith?'

'All right,' she returned, impatient. 'It's bad enough being a woman alone in a strange place, let alone admitting that you're single! I didn't mean any harm!'

Hoskins was chuckling under his breath. 'No harm done, Miss Westhouse.'

'Anyway,' the visitor went on. 'What did you tell him?'

'Only what I know, which is that the two men were pressed into the navy. God knows how many people I've told that now.'

'Who?' she demanded, troubled. Hoskins stroked at his beard; his brow furrowed.

'You,' he started, and she sighed impatiently. 'Your father,' which drew a rolling upwards of her eyes. 'And a man from Stokes Shipping Company.'

Her mouth gaped involuntarily at the last words. 'Stokes?' she muttered. 'Oh my God! They're on to me too! What did you tell them?'

Hoskins's expression regressed to slight guilt, but he added, 'Only that the two men were in the navy. Nobody knows *their* whereabouts. They'd never find them.' He didn't like the scornful look Helen was giving him but somehow could only see beauty in her face, no matter what her expression.

'And what did you tell them about me?' she went on.

'Nothing,' he managed, although his mouth was drying. 'I *know* nothing about your arrangements.'

'Good,' she responded. 'But I suppose they'll still keep looking for me. I just haven't decided yet what I'm going to do. I'm waiting to hear from my Harry.' There were a few moments of silence. 'I don't suppose there's a letter back from him?'

Hoskins was shaking his head. 'Perhaps if you were to let me know where you're staying, I could deliver it to you, soon as it comes.'

'No,' she replied. 'I think it would be better to leave things as they are. I'll check from time to time.'

'Very good. Just as you wish.'

He watched her walk away, his eyes appreciating the loveliness of her form and his brain wondering about the strange emotion she was arousing in him.

Harry was dejected. He had spent too long leaning on the rail, staring out to sea and thinking about Helen. He couldn't help but imagine her surrounded by rough sailors, leering at her while she smiled naively back, unaware of her charm and their lewd intentions. The sun was baking hot, far hotter than at home. The sea was a dazzling blue with small white crested waves, the sky perfectly clear. He wondered why those ancient mariners would have wanted to leave this idyllic place for the mad, butting swirl of the Atlantic Ocean, the grey pitch and roll of the seas around England. His hair had slowly bleached to almost white and his face had attained ever-deepening shades of reddish bronze. Both he and Bart had been to the "Barber's Shop", as they called it, to have their lengthening hair plastered into place with a smear of tar. They looked even more like real sailors; felt it too.

The heat was making Harry's head swim. He turned away from the rail and found himself wandering down towards the orlop deck. He pretended to himself that he was seeking a cooler place, but in his heart, he knew there was a different reason, and he didn't like himself for it. It took a while for his eyes to adjust to the gloom and his sinuses to become accustomed to the stale smell of mould and dross. He peered around a canvas screen that he knew, and she was there.

'Hello, sunshine!' she exploded with far too much vigour for his sour mood.

'Hi,' he returned.

'Oh dear!' exclaimed the redhead, catching his solemnity. 'That's a grumpy-sounding fellow if ever I heard one!' Harry managed the hint of a smile.

'What's up?' she went on. 'Missing home?' There was no reply.

'I get that a lot,' she continued. 'I bet there's some girlie back there just waiting for you to get back.' She searched his face for some response. She thought she saw a sparkle in his eyes. Her hand slid unashamedly to his groin and sensed his excitement. She pushed her dress off one shoulder and watched the man tremble. She pushed it from the other, letting it fall to the ground. To Harry, at that moment, she was the loveliest sight on God's earth, and she pulled him down onto the hay. He looked into the soft green eyes and wished to heaven that it was Helen. Helen looked into another damned sailor's lusting eyes and wished to hell that it was Harry. The would-be lovers rose and fell together, both feeling the ecstasy of each other's embrace, the powerful climax bringing a fusion of their minds. Harry was lost in Helen's soul, Helen in Harry's. Both lay spent and exhausted, gasping on the precious air. Some kind of magic filled their heads. Two young women whispered, and for the first time in their lives, they meant it, 'You're the best I ever had.'

'That girl of yours back home is very lucky,' uttered the redhead. 'What's your name?'

'Harry Smith.'

'Pleased to meet you, Harry Smith,' said the redhead, and held out her hand in mock politeness for kissing.

Oh, God! he thought. *This has all happened before!* He obliged with the kiss and couldn't help glancing anxiously around in case someone was watching who might take offence. Nobody was.

'Mine's Jelzina,' said the girl. 'What have you brought me?'

Harry had not thought about it. He felt guilty and embarrassed. He took out his leather pouch and felt inside. She watched, intrigued. 'Ooh!' She sighed as he brought out the tooth of blue stone. 'Is it a sapphire?'

'Yes,' he lied. 'It's really valuable. Keep it.'

Jelzina looked impressed. She took the stone and placed it carefully in her purse. 'It matches your lovely eyes,' she said. 'We don't call each other by our proper names down here, my love. From now on, I'll call you Johnny Sapphire.' They both laughed.

Chapter 14

Richard Westhouse paced the floor. The inn that Hoskins had recommended was just to the west of Norport seafront, and he had procured a room for a week. 'If I can't find her in that time, I may as well go home,' he muttered, hands clasped behind his back.

He stopped his pacing, stood and stared wistfully out of the window, thinking, *Young Barty in the bloody navy! Whatever next?*

He shook his head. 'Why the hell did I let him go off like that? Still. Can't change things. I must get a letter off to him like that Port Admiral fellow said. Tell him about his poor Uncle Cedric. Tell him when he gets home, there'll be another farm to run. God help us! Perhaps this spell in the navy will make a proper man of him. Miracles do happen!' He settled down at the table in his room with paper, quill and ink and scrawled, 'Dear Bart.'

When Bart opened it, he could hardly believe his eyes. 'It's from Papa!' he gasped to Harry. 'How the hell has he tracked us down?'

'Christ! He must have gone looking for you when neither you nor Helen showed up. He'll have found out from that Port Admiral fellow, same as Helen did. God! D'you think he and Helen have met up?'

'Goodness knows!' Bart's eyes were already flicking down the page for clues. 'Read it to me!' said Harry, impatient.

He says, 'Dear Bart, I've received news that you and Smith,' Bart omitted the words "that bastard", 'have been coerced into the navy. Hardly the career I ever thought you'd pursue. Neither did you, I imagine.' Harry sniggered, but Bart read on, becoming more sombre. 'Unfortunately, I have some bad news to convey. Your dear Uncle Cedric collapsed while working in the fields and has died.'

'Christ, no!' groaned Bart, conjuring up pictures of the jovial man he had known most of his life. He almost preferred him to his own father.

'That's terrible!' Bart took a few moments to compose himself and Harry didn't rush him. He knew how awful it felt to have lost someone dear. Bleary-eyed, Bart read on:

'This means Westhouse Farm will double in size. I sincerely hope that when you have finished with your duties in His Majesty's Britannic Navy, you will come home and help me run the place. You will, of course, inherit the lot when I pass away. In the meantime, I wish you luck and hope that you are being well treated. I also hope that you play your part in defeating this dreadful Bonaparte and that we may all live without the continuous fear of invasion. As yet, I have not discovered the whereabouts of Helen, but I will continue to search. If you have any news about her, I would be glad to hear it. The Port Admiral here, who was the one who told me of your fate, says you can send letters to me marked '*In the care of the Port Admiral*'. I'll check with him from time to time. Be brave, my son. Your loving Papa.'

Bart looked up at Harry, who was looking no less worried than usual. 'Can't find Helen, eh?' he muttered. Then, as he looked to the sky, 'Dear God, I hope you're looking after her.'

'Papa will find her,' said Bart, but with little confidence, and both gave each other an unfounded assuring grin. The relentless bell rang out its eight chimes and they were both back on watch. They had found it strange when the order had come to turn the ship around. Now, instead of entering the alluring blue Mediterranean, they were heading into Lisbon harbour, where the friendly Portuguese would welcome them and their support against their dominant neighbours, Spain. It was hard to know, now, who your enemies were and who were your friends. Just follow orders, they were told. Practice, practice, practice at cannon drill and with cutlass. One day, it will all be over, or you'll die trying. God, life was hell; tomorrow is no longer guaranteed.

'At least you've got a home to go back to,' muttered Harry.

'Oh, don't you worry,' he replied. 'If and when we get through this lot, you're coming back with me. There'll be work aplenty and a roof over our heads. And my dear sister will be there waiting for you, I know it.'

'That's if that bastard Stokes hasn't got back in there and re-staked his claim,' moaned Harry. 'She might well think I'm never coming home and go back to that awful idea of becoming his dutiful wife. It's what your father would want!'

'God, I don't know,' grumbled Bart.

There was a tentative knock on Helen's door. 'Come in if you're 'andsome!' she called out in her newfound professional drawl. The handle turned and the hinges creaked. She looked up from the dressing table stool where she was brushing her hair, naked from the waist up, to see a young man's face peering from beneath a wide-brimmed hat and above an upturned collar. There was not much face to see, but his eyes looked oddly familiar and they were widening in disbelief. He wanted to turn around and run, but he was transfixed by the sight of her naked breasts.

Helen smiled at his frightened expression. He stuttered when he tried to speak and eventually managed, 'M-Miss Westhouse!'

Helen's mouth gaped as she understood the young man's dilemma and the familiarity of his face. It was Hoskins' clerk. The youth who was usually scribbling away with quill and ink during her conversations with the man. 'I-I don't believe it!' he gasped.

Helen couldn't believe it either. Her cover was blown. The last person she wanted to know of her whereabouts was Hoskins. He would tell all who asked about her where the despicable little whore could be found, especially her father. This was dreadful. The end!

'You're not the one they call *Helen of Troy,* are you?' he gabbled.

She wanted to deny it, but how could she? It was the professional name she'd been dubbed by the men. It was a compliment. They didn't know her name was really Helen. They called her that after the beautiful Trojan queen whose abduction had sparked off the Greek-Trojan war. She undoubtedly had the most beautiful face they had ever seen possessed by a woman of her profession. The name had been scrawled on her door by an impatient, aspiring consort. She sat there in her half-naked splendour, not knowing how to react. The clerk spoke first.

'You *are* Miss Westhouse,' he managed.

'And you are Mr Hoskins' clerk,' she confirmed. 'What a small world, isn't it?'

'Y-Yes,' he stuttered. 'I don't know what to say. I mean, I c-came here expecting…'

'Expecting what?' interjected Helen. 'Some old whore you could lose your virginity on?'

'Pretty well,' he trembled. 'I'm sorry. I can't believe it's you. You're too…'

'Too what?' she interrupted again, but he soldiered on.

'…*Respectable*,' he said in a steadier voice. 'Respectable and beautiful. That's what I think.'

Helen was stunned. She had not expected such compliments. She covered her breasts with her hands, suddenly self-conscious, dithering and not knowing how to proceed. He was a lovely young fellow. None of this was his fault. She looked sincerely into his eyes, which had now been robbed of their magnetic distraction. 'So, what are we going to do?' she asked.

'I can't... I mean, I can't,' he struggled. 'You're too... damned nice!'

She was wrapping a shawl around her in modesty to spare him his embarrassment. 'I'm not really nice,' she said. 'I was respectable... once. I was forced into this way of life. It wasn't my idea.'

He was looking awkward now. He couldn't cope with her honesty. 'Mr Hoskins likes you too,' he babbled.

Helen looked up at him, surprised.

'He wasn't half pleased when he found out you weren't married,' he went on. 'He'll be right upset when he finds out what you do.'

'He mustn't find out,' she muttered. 'You mustn't tell anyone. I've got to get out of here somehow and get back to my proper life. I can't bear this!'

She was close to tears now, and the young man felt so confused. He put a consoling hand on her shoulder. A shoulder that felt soft and warm through the shawl. He shivered and she looked into his eyes again. His legs felt weak and he sat down abruptly on the bed. She needed this fellow to be her ally. 'Do you really think I'm too nice to do it?' she asked.

'I saved up my money,' he quivered. 'To do this.'

'None of this is your fault,' she said. 'Keep the money in your pocket. Just please don't tell Mr Hoskins, nor anybody else.'

She let the shawl drop as she spoke and moved closer to him. She picked up one of his hands and pressed it into the soft loveliness of her breast. She heard the gasp of breath and the whispered words.

'I won't tell.'

Chapter 15

'Lisbon?' queried Matthew Stokes. 'Are you sure?'

He had come to his office early. He couldn't sleep.

'That's what it says, sir.'

'I thought they'd be way down in the Med by now. Let me see!'

Stokes grabbed the letter from the young man and stared hard at the writing. He could hardly believe it. 'His Majesty's Navy is amassing in the harbour, here at Lisbon.' The letter was from the office manager of Stokes Shipping Corporation in the Portuguese capital. It was in response to the request that had been sent out to all of Stokes' branches offering substantial reward for good information.

'Found you, Harry Smith!' snarled Matthew, his hatred for the "peasant" overbearing as ever. 'You're going to wish you'd never been born, you bastard!' He crumpled the paper by clenching his fist around it and accompanied the words with a fierce thump of the table.

'Get me, Wainwright!' he demanded through gritted teeth, his face reddening and his brow showing traces of sweat. 'And find out when our next ship is heading out to Lisbon or anywhere near it!'

The clerk was rooted to the spot, dismayed by the show of passion and anger.

'Get to it!' demanded Stokes.

***

It was the last day of Richard Westhouse's tenure of the room at the Mermaid Inn, Norport. He had not received a reply from Bart as he had hoped, and there was still no sign of his daughter. Could he really go home to Beatrice and say that he had failed? Could he ever look upon his wife's tear-stained tombstone again? His troubles were etched on his face as he left the inn for the last time and set off with faded hope to Hoskins' hut. His knock on the green-painted door was tentative. He tapped his foot impatiently as he waited for it to open.

Helen donned her black cloak and set off down the road. She rolled her eyes dismissively at another laughing seagull and passed the familiar row of shops. The baker's smelled divine and Mr and Mrs Brown stood as usual, arms crossed, behind their counter.

'Wasn't that…?' queried Mr Brown.

'Who?' said his wife.

'Wasn't that the young woman with the fine accent who came in here wanting scrap bread to feed the seagulls?'

'Can't say that I recognised her particularly.' Both shrugged their shoulders dismissively.

Helen walked on, thinking, *Surely there'll be a letter for me today.* It was the hope that kept her alive.

Enoch Hoskins had made it to the door and opened it a cautious crack. He saw the hopeful face of the deserted father and knew that he had to disappoint the man. He opened the door further to beckon him in.

'I can see from your face there's no news,' said Richard, and Hoskins confirmed the fact. 'The fleet could be miles away by now,' he added. 'Probably in the Med! It could take quite a few days for letters to travel backwards and forwards. I'd wait around for a few more days if I was you.'

'And not a trace of my daughter?' queried Richard, without any hope whatsoever.

The young clerk at his desk shifted uncomfortably. Warm thoughts of Helen had filled his mind since his wonderful encounter with her, and he felt his pulse race on again.

'No, sir,' said Hoskins. 'Do you think she might have gone off home?'

Richard Westhouse was shaking his head in response when 'Oh my God!' The clerk looked over the man's shoulder and out of the window. A young woman was approaching. 'Helen of Troy!'

'Er… I'm sorry, sir,' he muttered to his employer. 'I feel horribly sick!'

Both men watched in astonishment as the youth made for the door.

'I think he's been sampling the demon drink!' said Hoskins with a look that could have been either amusement or disgust.

Mark Williamson was out of the door in a flash. He had promised that he wouldn't tell and he'd been true to his word. He had sat at his desk dreaming of her, his face flushed, hands shaking and falsely blaming some rotten ale to account for his unusual countenance. A disaster had to be averted. He pushed the door shut behind him and dashed across the street. Helen saw him coming and his desperate signals to turn around. She obeyed. 'It's your father!' he gasped as he reached her.

She pulled the hood up over her head and walked briskly away, uttering, 'Thank you, my dear. Oh, thank you so much!'

'Perhaps that'll put him off for life,' said Richard Westhouse with a grin. 'Never touched the stuff myself. Neither have my son and daughter.'

'Oh well, that might change now,' replied Hoskins. 'At least for your son. He'll be getting rations of rum and beer every day in the navy. It's what keeps the lads going!'

Richard looked disdainfully at the man. 'God, if he ever gets back to me, he'll be a drunken lout. God knows what'll become of the farm! God help us all!'

He turned and was gone. 'Feeling better?' he enquired of the clerk who was making his way back.

'Much better,' was the reply. 'Much better by far.'

***

Jelzina looked scornfully into Harry's eyes.

'What?' she demanded. 'You want it back? You must be joking!'

'I was really stupid to give it away. Here, I've brought you some perfume to replace it. One of the men swapped it for my rum ration.'

'You've got a bloody cheek! It's *my* bloody sapphire now! I earned it!'

'It isn't really a sapphire!'

'What?'

'It's Blue John. Just cheap stuff you find in Derbyshire caves. It isn't worth a jot!'

'You bloody swindler! So why d'you want it back?'

'I promised it to someone.' Harry's voice was wavering. 'I said I'd make it into a ring for her. She said she'd be proud to wear it.'

'What? Even though it's only rotten Blue John?'

'Even so, yes.'

'That bloody girlie back home! She's all you think about!'

'Yes. She is.'

'You promised her this lovely jewel in a ring, and you've gone and given it to the ship's whore! Shame on you, you bastard!'

'Can I have it back?'

'I wouldn't be able to call you Johnny Sapphire no more. I'd have to call you Johnny Bloody Blue John!'

She saw a pleading sparkle in Harry's eyes. She couldn't help herself. She was a hardened professional, but somehow, she was melting inside. 'Tell you what,' she muttered. 'Give me the perfume and if you're real good this time, I'll let you have your lousy rock back.' She began her routine of pushing the dress from her shoulders. Harry's heart thumped hard. He lost the capacity for logical thought. The deal she had offered was damn good. He sank down beside her and obeyed.

Chapter 16

Richard had all but given up. His thoughts began to turn to Beatrice back at Westhouse Farm, the soft feel of her when he gave her that hug, the warm look she had given him when she told him that she wouldn't scream. He imagined Helen running home to her embrace, the tears, the comforting Irish voice. 'She *must* have gone back,' he mused and wandered on up the hill. He came to a row of shops and was attracted by the whiff of newly baked bread. Again, he was reminded of Beatrice, sleeves rolled up in the kitchen and smothered in flour. There was a warm feeling inside.

He stopped and stared at the loaves and cakes in the window. He thought he should buy some for the journey home. He stepped inside the dingy shop.

'Yes, sir,' came the rotund lady's voice. 'Can I help you?'

Richard pointed out the bread rolls in the window and handed over the necessary cash.

'Thank you, sir. Will there be anything else?'

Richard pondered. He had asked the question so many times around the place. He was weary of it now. Should he ask just one more time?

'I'm looking for my daughter,' he mumbled. 'I'm a deserted father. The silly girl ran off after a quarrel and I haven't seen her since. I just wondered if you might have seen her.'

Mr Brown was giving a more sympathetic look than his wife. Richard thought it was worth continuing.

'She was here somewhere with a man she had run off with. One of my farm hands. Her brother must have found them, but both he and the farm hand were nabbed by one of those confounded navy press gangs.'

The story was beginning to ring a bell in Mr Brown's mind.

'You know, there was a big press gang swoop a month or so ago,' he said. 'One of our ships was setting off in a hurry without nearly enough men. They had to "recruit" real quick.'

'Yes, well, I understand what happened, dreadful as it was for the men involved, my son included. At least I *know* what has become of *them*. My daughter, though, was left alone in a strange place. I dread to think what's become of her.'

Both of the Browns were looking worried.

'You don't suppose…?' said Mr Brown. He looked hard at his wife and seemed to be turning things over in his mind. 'That young woman who came into the shop the day after the press gang thing, asking for spare bread. How old would she be?'

'About twenty?' she guessed and saw Richard's eyes widen in hope.

'Well, yes, that fits,' he confirmed.

'She came in here,' continued Mr Brown, 'saying her son wanted to feed the gulls. Did we have any spare bread? Never been asked that before. She wasn't from around here.'

'Well, no.' responded Richard. 'She doesn't have the Hampshire brogue, but she also doesn't have a son.'

'Don't think *she* did, really,' said Mrs Brown. 'She was making up an excuse 'cos she didn't have any money. She asked if there was work to be had here, too.'

Richard was beginning to see credence in this story. He described his daughter to them and this seemed about right. 'Have you seen her since?' he asked.

'I think so,' said Mr Brown. 'She walks past here sometimes. I *think* it's her. She wears a black cloak, you know, with a hood. It's hard to say.'

Richard stared thoughtfully at the pair. 'I'm supposed to be going home today,' he uttered. 'But this has given me a glimmer of hope. Perhaps I'll stick around for a while.'

'Well, if we see her again, or anything, we'll let you know,' said Mrs Brown. 'That's if you let us know how to get in touch.'

'Oh, I'll come back to see you again. This is the best lead I've had all week. I hope to God it's her.'

Richard left the shop and looked up and down the street. He took a deep breath and realised that the smell of the sea had taken over once again from the newly baked bread. Even so, there was a freshness about the breeze, a little more optimism in his face.

***

There was a loud knock on Matthew Stokes' office door.

'Come in!' he yelled, and the tall figure of Poplar Wainwright appeared. This was a man who Stokes trusted implicitly. He was the one he turned to when some shady deal was required; debt collecting his speciality. He also acted as his personal bodyguard and carriage driver. There weren't many excursions Matthew made without this man watching his back. His mother told him that he was given his strange first name after the tree where she gave birth to him as she worked in the fields. As he grew older and more able to understand these things, he suspected it was more likely that this was where he was conceived. He and his mother never discussed the matter further.

'Sit down.' Matthew ushered him to an armchair and he knew this was going to be a lengthy discourse. He braced himself for some arduous task. He was particularly well qualified for this one. His mother was Portuguese.

***

'Miss Helen Westhouse, In the Care of the Port Admiral.' Mark Williamson was reading out the addressees on the newly arrived batch of letters. Enoch Hoskins looked suddenly interested, saying, 'Give me that,' and he stared hard at the folded paper. The master of the little cutter that had docked that morning with the mail had told him that the fleet was gathering at Lisbon. 'This'll have to wait till dear Miss Westhouse comes to collect it,' he mumbled in the clerk's direction, who was then disturbed by a flood of thoughts about the young woman. Uppermost was the soft warmth of her body as she initiated him into the wonders of manhood. This took some time to shift from his mind and Hoskins was just beginning to wonder if the youth was going to be sick again. Then, the awkwardness of the situation kicked into Mark's brain. She wouldn't dare come back to their office, knowing that her father was around.

'If I knew where she was, I could deliver this,' said Enoch. 'I know she's aching for news of this Smith fellow, though I know for a fact he's got no idea when he'll be back, which is what she wants to know.'

Mark squirmed.

'Are you all right?' demanded his employer.

'Yes. I mean…'

'I don't know what's wrong with you, boy. You're acting mighty strange.'

What could Mark say? He knew exactly where Helen was.

'I promised… oh drat!' the words were out. He knew Enoch Hoskins too well. There was no way he could keep the secret now.

'Promised what?' the man demanded.

Mark dithered. Hoskins gave him his strict employer's stare. 'Do you want paying this week?' he growled. Of course, Mark did. He also knew that this was no empty threat. His wages had been docked in the past for spelling mistakes in the ledger, lateness or untidy appearance. He began to sweat and Hoskins took hold of the lad's shoulders and gave him a reproving shake. 'Well?' he demanded.

'I know where she is, sir. You won't like it. You think she's sweet and respectable. Well, she ain't. She's a tart, sir. She works at the Half Moon Tavern!'

Hoskins couldn't believe it. He stared at his clerk, who was perilously close to tears. 'I promised I wouldn't tell, sir. I know how much you like her. She didn't want you to know!'

Hoskins was lost for words; he wanted to hit out at him for such stupidity and even felt the involuntary forming of a fist, but he could see the anguish in the lad's face. He had been forced to renege on his word. Hoskins picked up the letter, stared hard at the name on it, stared hard at Mark Williamson for a while, shook his head, then turned, straightened, and walked out of the door.

Richard Westhouse walked on, his eyes catching onto every female passerby in renewed hope that it might be her. 'What you staring at?' said one indignant young woman of similar appearance to his daughter. He dodged away as her burly male escort glared at his annoyance. Another head of auburn hair passed by, then another. Then suddenly, a thump of his heart. He stood rooted to the spot and stared incredulously at the black-cloaked young woman at the door of the Half Moon Tavern.

'Helen?' he silently gasped the name. Her ringlets swirled as she turned and went in through the door. His heart pounded hard. *Could it really be her?*

He forced his feet into movement again, his pace quickening as he reached the door and peered in. The place was crowded and the din of drunken voices hit like a solid wall. He hated the stink of old ale and the inevitable smoke of the tobacco habit bleared his eyes. He pushed on into the crowd, veering away from tankards and smouldering cigarettes in cavorting hands, catching mere glimpses of the retreating girl. Then, she was lost from sight; she was rushing up the stairs. She met Susie at the top, her face contorted with fear. 'It's Papa!' she gasped. 'He mustn't find me here.' She cast a worried glance back down the stairs. 'What the hell do I do?'

Richard pushed on, his head a conflicting mess of thoughts. 'Is this my lovely daughter? Has she really fallen so low as to inhabit a place like this?'

'Can I help you, sir?' interrupted a concerned Tom Yarker.

'I'm looking for someone.' Richard was breathing hard. 'Her name's Helen.'

Tom smiled at the distorted face. 'She's free, sir. First door on the right.' He put his hand on the visitor's shoulder.

'And take yer time, eh? Don't want to be worn out before y'even get there!'

Richard tried to calm himself, smiled thinly at the landlord and breathed deeply. He looked up the narrow staircase to a gloomy landing with a cracked ceiling. He had never done such a thing as this. Bawdy laughter rang out all around him. Women and men drank and cajoled. Rough hands slapped bottoms. Women slithered onto men's laps. He felt his feet carry him slowly, relentlessly up, visions of the girl's childhood invading his mind. His dear wife held her proudly in the birthing bed. The pretty lace dress she wore on her fifth birthday. How sweet her wobbling curtseys.

The top stair creaked under his foot and he turned to the green-painted door. '*I love Helen of Troy,*' someone had scribbled on it.

'*So do I,*' wrote another.

'*Get in the queue,*' wrote a third. He now envisaged her as he had last seen her. Angry and cursing him, storming out of the room. He had no idea what he was going to say to the girl. No idea how she would react to seeing him. He knocked awkwardly on the door and heard. 'Come in if you're 'andsome!' He turned the handle and the hinges creaked. The girl sat at her dressing table, her back towards him, naked from the waist up, brushing her auburn hair. Her reflection was a rippling mess in the cheap, distorted mirror with its pattern of cracks.

'Are you the one they call Helen of Troy?' he asked.

She put the brush down, cupped her hands playfully over her breasts and turned towards him.

'That's what they call me,' purred Susie, and she slid her hands provocatively down to her waist. His eyes couldn't help but follow but then darted back to the stranger's face.

'Thank God,' he murmured and turned to walk out.

'*Oi*!' she yelled after him. 'You have to pay to see this lot!'

He looked to his left and saw the money box on the wall. He slipped some coins into it before allowing himself a backward glance at her indignant, half-naked pose and then walked out of the door. The top stair creaked under his foot and then another sound from behind. The click of another door opening. It was Helen. She couldn't resist a final look to see if the deception had worked. The auburn wig, the same height and build. Without looking back, Richard knew it. She had played a careful trick. Who else but his daughter would now be taking this final reassuring look? He kept on walking. He didn't want to look. Disgust for what she had become was overwhelming, yet he pitied her. He didn't want her to see the falter in his steps. He kept on going, his gaze fixed ahead. He tried to pretend that his heart wasn't breaking. It was.

He heard ribald comments from the crowd as he reached the foot of the stairs. 'That was quick!' and 'She must have told him he was too old!' Laughter rang amongst the clanking of pot and pewter. Richard made his way to the door and breathed deep on the smoke-free air.

The man limping up the hill towards him looked familiar.

Susie went back to her own room where Helen was hiding.

'Did he fall for it?' she asked.

'Oh yes,' confirmed Susie. 'I was just an auburn-haired stranger he'd mistaken for you. What do you think he'd do if he found you?'

'Kill me,' replied Helen with a shake of her head and a resigned, worried look. 'Just kill me.'

Enoch Hoskins reached the front door where Richard was standing.

'Have you found her then?' he asked.

'Yes,' replied Richard. 'She doesn't know it, but I have. And you've been telling me lies, saying you didn't know where she was!'

'Oh no, sir! I've only just found out myself! I've got to deliver this letter to her. It's from her man in the navy. What do you mean by she doesn't *know* that you've found her?'

'Exactly what I said, Hoskins. I've seen her, but she hasn't seen me, and I want to keep it that way. I don't want her to realise that I know what she's become. Look, deliver your letter, try to find out what it says, then I'll walk back to your office with you. There must be some way we can get her out of this!'

Enoch nodded and walked in. Tom Yarker offered to take the letter to Helen himself, but the Port Admiral insisted that he should do it. He was directed up the stairs and to turn to the right. He knocked on the door and heard Helen's welcoming cry. The gasp that issued from her mouth when she saw who it was could be heard downstairs.

'How on earth have you found me here?' she demanded.

'Just a little detecting on my part,' he returned. 'People talk. I overhear things.'

'Hmm. Nothing to do with that clerk of yours, I hope.'

'No, no. Not him. Other people.'

'Who?'

'Never mind,' said Enoch. He had the perfect way of changing the subject. 'There's a letter for you!'

Her eyes widened with delight when she saw the folded paper in his outstretched hand, the name Helen Westhouse written across it, but her heart sank slightly when she recognised that it was her brother's handwriting.

She opened it up and saw. *My darling Helen.*

That's odd, she thought; *Bart would never call me that.*

She glanced down the page and saw that it was signed *All my love, Harry,* which made her heart leap again, but she realised for the first time that her intended lover couldn't write, probably couldn't read, would most likely have got Bart to read her letter to him. She read aloud, excited. 'Thank you greatly for your letter. It was clever of you to find out where I was. We are being treated very well. We protested like mad about being taken but don't have any choice now. We have to help defend our country, so we will do what we can till it's all over and we can come back home. We have no idea how long that will be. Please don't put yourself in danger. Go home and wait for me there. All my love, Harry.'

She looked up at Enoch. 'I can't go home!' she groaned. 'Papa would kill me! When Harry comes home and finds out about me, he'll want to kill me too! Then there's bloody Matthew Stokes. He's got cronies looking out for me. He hates me for jilting him. What the hell do I do?' Enoch touched her for the first time. He put his hand on hers. She didn't flinch. He felt encouraged. He put a comforting arm around her shoulders and she put her head against the secure feel of his chest. He could tell that she was sobbing.

'We'll think of something,' he mumbled, and she looked up at him with big eyes, saying, 'There must be more to life than this.'

Chapter 17

Lisbon was a majestic sight from the sea. Domes and spires loomed above red-tiled houses that had sprung up in recovery from the latest earthquake. A defensive wall spanned the approaches with cannons strategically placed to deter the invader. 'Act of God,' one of the sailors remarked. 'That earthquake. It doesn't just happen for no reason.' But this was the capital city, not only of a proud nation but an empire that took in Brazil and African territories. It was recovering. It had powerful trading links with the rest of the world. Right now, it was central to the power struggle that Napoleon Bonaparte had initiated. Spain and France had attempted invasion in the north, but an allied force, including Britain, had driven them back, the Duke of Wellington rising in reputation, detested by the outwitted French. Lisbon was a safe harbour now for His Majesty's Britannic Navy. Harry and Bart watched it loom closer as they leant on the larboard rail of *Adventurer*.

'Bet you never dreamt you'd see places like this,' remarked Bart.

'Never knew they existed,' said Harry. 'Never thought there was much at all outside Smith Farm or the cricket team. Never knew the world was round.'

Bart shook his head. At least *he'd* had the benefit of the village school and his father's books. At least *he* could read and write.

'Do you think we'll be able to step off this old tub onto solid ground?' mused Harry.

'Don't suppose so,' replied Bart. 'They'd be too scared of us all running off.' But the thought of it conjured up pictures of freedom in both minds. Bart imagined the newly expanded Westhouse Farm and saw himself dressed like his father, giving instructions to his minions as to where they should be working, pointing to places with his smouldering pipe. Harry saw himself walking with Helen through a meadow festooned with wildflowers, holding her hand, lying down beside her on soft, warm hay.

'You'll be going ashore soon!' interrupted Midshipman Lawrence's voice. Bart and Harry wheeled around in surprise.

'Not normal,' the young man continued, 'but the surgeon's going to fumigate the ship. Says he's had a couple of cases of some disease or other. So, we'll all be off except for a few powder monkeys who'll be helping him. Won't do those boys any harm to be fumigated, either! No thoughts of running off, though. You'll all be under the guard of the marines, so watch your step. Deserters, what's caught, gets the rope!' His latter words were accompanied by a graphic enactment of a noose going around his neck and pulling tight on the imaginary rope above his head.

Richard Westhouse gave Enoch Hoskins a quizzical stare. 'Well? he demanded. The two of them began walking down the street.

'She's devastated, sir,' said Hoskins.

'Quite beside herself with grief. The letter made her a bit happier. She read it to me. Bart had written it for Smith. They had no idea, though, of how long they'd be away.'

The word "grief" had stunned Richard somewhat. Until now, he had been thinking of her as a wretched runaway. The foul abuse she had expounded on him. The venomous look in her eyes. The despicable fall into the gutter. He had not considered how she must be feeling.

'Grief, you say?' he uttered, and Hoskins realised that he had found the man's paternal instincts.

'Oh yes, sir, real grief. She thinks you'd kill her if she ventured home. She thinks Smith would kill her if he found what she'd become. She even thinks some "Stokes" fellow is out to get her. She's a real mess, sir, and no mistake. She hates what she's become. It was the only way out for her. Just imagine it. Running off to a new life with the man she wanted to share it with, only to get dumped on her own, alone in a strange place.'

Richard stared at the ground as he walked, deliberately slowing to let his companion keep up. Hoskins didn't like to stare too hard, but he thought he could detect a tear in the man's eyes.

'How the hell can I get her out of this? You know this town well enough, Hoskins. If she's determined to stay and wait for her confounded Harry Smith, there must be some way of getting her out of that dreadful tavern and into something respectable. That's the only way Smith would accept her. I've come into some money, Hoskins, from my brother's will. Is there some small, respectable business we could get her into? She needn't know it has anything to do with me. Think of something.'

Enoch Hoskins *was* thinking. Thinking hard, excited. The vision of Helen's eyes looking up at him. Her utterance of 'there must be more to life than this.' His heart was thumping. Things were falling beautifully into place.

***

'You wanna get out of this?' rasped a mysterious voice.

Harry and Bart turned around. A swarthy-looking fellow had crouched down behind their chairs, his breath stinking of tobacco.

'What?' uttered Bart.

'You heard. You wanna get out?'

'Out of this tavern?' said Harry.

'No, you, crazy man. Out of the bloody navy!'

Harry and Bart were stunned.

'What the hell are you talking about?' wheezed Bart.

'I'm talking about you getting out of the bloody navy! You wanna or not?'

The two sailors looked blankly at each other and then back at the intruder. His raised eyebrow stare demanded some kind of an answer. 'Look, we don't know what you're on about,' said Bart.

'Go away.'

'Hey! You no speaka to me like that,' said the man.

'I'm offering you a way out of this. Your freedom! You no want?'

'Look. You're going to get us a flogging or something!' said Harry. 'We've been told *no talking to the locals.* They meant local women, I think, but I reckon it means fellows like you, too. Just clear off, will you!'

'All right, but if you don't, someone else will. You missa your chance, yes?'

Bart and Harry answered by remaining silent. The man stood up straight and walked away.

'What the hell did he mean?' demanded Harry.

'God knows. Presumably, there are some kind of local crooks who can help you escape. If escape's the right word. Desertion's what the navy call it.' Bart adopted the local man's accent but repeated the words of Midshipman Lawrence.

'You getta the rope!' The companions laughed but noticed that the man was still watching them. Why was he so interested in Bart and Harry amongst a room full of revellers, relieved temporarily from their duties? Why did he not believe that he had received their final word? He stood in a corner, staring hard at the pair. He inhaled another cigarette.

Bart quaffed more ale. 'How do you suppose they do it?' he mused into the tankard.

'What? Help people to desert?' asked Harry.

'Yea. I mean, how can you possibly get away from these marines?' He nodded towards the door where three of the red-coated guards stood with bayonetted muskets.

'Don't know,' mused Harry. 'But what would become of the number three cannon without its rammer and sponger?'

'They'd find someone else.'

Both men sank more ale and then looked at each other, trying to read each other's minds. Two weeks ago, they'd have jumped at the chance to 'escape'. Now, they had mellowed into acceptance of their plight. The navy's enthusiasm for the fight had rubbed off on them. They even *looked* like sailors now in their issued clothes, *slops* as they called them, and tar-slicked hair. They were conditioned to play their part in defeating the enemy. *Then* they could think about going home. They glanced back at the man who was crushing the remains of his cigarette on the stone floor with a swivelling action of his boot. He caught their eye and moved back towards them.

'You giving it some thought, eh?' he asked.

'We were just wondering,' said Bart, 'how you do it.'

'It's easy, my friend. We distracta your guards. We whisk you out the back door. We hide you on my little barca de pesco. How you say? Fishing boat. You become Portuguese fishermen and you work for nothing till we put you ashore in England. That way, I don't hava to pay no crew and you gets home free as a bird.'

'Sounds crazy,' said Harry.

'I tell you, it works. A coupla days at sea. I sell my catch. I getta the money. You go free.'

'Have you done it before?'

'Many times. Donta you fret. It works easy. I betta you got a lovely missus at home, eh? She's just awaiting for you. Go on. You know you wanna go.'

Harry drank more ale. His head was beginning to buzz with the stuff. Bart was looking at him with an expression that seemed to say, 'I'm up for it if you are.' Visions of Helen were filling Harry's mind. He was chasing her through a field of wildflowers. She kept looking behind to make sure he was still there, her lovely hair streaming out behind her, then crossing her face as she turned. Her smile was enticing, inviting. She tumbled to the ground as she had done on that first occasion he had spoken to her. She gazed up at him, excited, alluring.

'Right,' he muttered on a deep breath. 'Let's do it.' The words were out. There could be no turning back.

The local man turned and nodded to the serving wench, who took her jug of ale to the marines at the door. She smiled her playful smile, giggled and admired their uniforms and weapons, ran her fingers up and down one of the phallic bayonets. When she returned to the back of the room, there were two empty chairs. Local men slipped onto them quickly to leave no noticeable gap. Two pressed British sailors were on their way out of the back door. To freedom. Or the hangman's noose.

Chapter 18

Could it really be him? Beatrice O'Malley's heart gave a thump of pure pleasure. The gate had swung open to allow a horse rider in and, yes! It must surely be him! The travel-wearied figure of Richard Westhouse clambered from the steaming mare and unbuckled his small bag of belongings from the saddle. His men were soon gathered around him, shaking his hand, fussing over the horse, asking the pertinent question, 'Did you find Bart and Hels?' Beatrice could see from his demeanour and sad shaking head that he had not.

He made for the front door and was about to ring when it opened. Beatrice's face could not have shown more delight. 'Oh, sir!' she gasped and flung her arms around him as emotion took over completely from protocol. Richard's stoic face could not help but break into a smile. He dropped the bag and hugged her hard. The men grinned and nodded knowingly to each other.

'Any sign?' managed Beatrice at last as they pulled apart. Both saw tears of emotion in each other's eyes. Richard had rehearsed this moment, but his voice croaked and wavered.

Beatrice intervened. 'Come on through and sit down,' she muttered and put a guiding hand on his back. 'You must be exhausted. Settle down and collect yourself. Then you can tell me all about it.'

It didn't take long. He smiled agreeably as he reacquainted himself with the welcoming armchair, lit his pipe and gazed up at the homely ceiling. He recounted his discovery that Bart and Harry had been coerced into the navy, drawing a horrified gasp from the attentive Beatrice, who had knelt at his side and leant against the leather arm of the chair. He said that he had written to Bart to let him know about the death of his poor Uncle Cedric.

Beatrice asked all the questions, 'What will become of them? How long will they be gone?' But Richard could only sadly confess that he didn't know. It was all in the lap of God. He went on to describe his search for Helen and stuttered somewhat as he lied. The girl was nowhere to be found. He said that he had hoped beyond hope that he would find her safely returned home. He felt that he had sounded convincing but couldn't see complete assurance in Beatrice's eyes.

'I'll go and get dinner,' she whispered and was gone.

The game pie was delicious and roundly filled the man's belly. He sipped on the wine that Matthew Stokes had brought him from his father's stock of imports. He offered some to Beatrice as she fussed around the table with used cutlery and plates. 'I shouldn't, really,' she replied but had never before had such an invitation. The ruby redness of the liquid was alluring as it poured from the bottle. She sipped away at it, loving the numbing sensation in her brain. Richard poured them both another glass. Before either of them knew it, they were sharing a warm embrace, eyes staring deep into eyes, faces flushed. Richard's hand wandered up from her waist to her breast, where it gently cupped and caressed.

'There now, sir,' Beatrice muttered. 'Sure, I told you I wouldn't scream.'

Both smiled. 'I've missed you,' managed Richard.

'Oh, sir, I've missed you too.' His hand continued its soft exploration of her bosom.

'What is it you're wanting?' she asked.

'I want you to call me Richard.'

'Yes?'

'And I want us to become lovers.'

There was a short gasp from Beatrice's mouth.

'Oh, it's making love you're proposing, is it, Richard?' she managed. 'Not marriage?'

Richard looked awkward, but she was smiling. 'I'll come to your bed, Richard,' she murmured, 'but then you must promise me something else.'

His heart thumped as she spoke and he felt his legs weaken. At that moment, he would promise her anything.

'What's that?' he enquired, trying to remain calm.

'You must tell me the truth about Miss Helen.'

It shocked him, but his mood was too mellow to react. He composed his thoughts.

'When once we are lovers,' he whispered, 'there won't be any secrets.'

Beatrice smiled a fully contented smile and although she burned to know the truth about Helen, she was burning even more passionately for her master. She took his hand and he led her up the stairs.

Chapter 19

The top stair creaked and there was a knock on the door. 'Hello!' shouted Helen.

'Come in. Don't be shy.'

The doorknob turned and the hinges creaked. She turned to see the well-known features of Enoch Hoskins in the widening gap. His serious expression broadened to a smile when he saw her. Hers, too, and she was glad that she was fully dressed.

'Mr Hoskins!' she gasped. 'What a surprise!' then 'Ooh! Have you brought me another letter?'

'No, dear, no. I'm not here as postman today, I'm afraid.' Her heart sank.

'Oh.' She breathed, disappointed. Then she saw him put coins into the box on the wall. She swallowed hard.

'Just for show,' he bumbled. 'I know the landlord requires me to pay for your time.'

She was still a little puzzled.

He began to speak in a serious tone. 'I've got a proposal to make to you. You don't have to answer right away. Just promise you'll give it some thought.'

She said nothing but adopted an attentive expression.

'I've come into some money. From a will. I've made some enquiries and have found that the Browns are willing to sell me their little baker's shop. They want to retire and they don't have any children to pass it on to, and I was wondering…'

'Yes, Mr Hoskins?'

'If I were to buy it…' She suddenly realised where this was going and felt a tingle in her spine.

'If I were to buy it, would you let me buy you out of this place and come and work at my bakers' shop?'

Her mouth gaped. This could save her life! A totally new identity! Nobody could have offered her such a wonderful opportunity to be a respectable woman again. Was this God's answer to her prayers? 'Oh, Mr Hoskins!' she yelped, drawing a roll-eyed expression from Susie, who was passing outside her door, 'that sounds wonderful!'

'Now, now, my dear,' said the would-be saviour, his hands outstretched, palms down in a calming gesture, 'I said you must give it some thought.'

'Oh, I have, Mr Hoskins!' Her hands were clasped together as though praying and she jigged excitedly, finding it difficult to breathe. 'That's the most wonderful idea! When can we do it?'

'And in the meantime…' He went on.

'What?'

'Well, you've got to get used to the idea of calling me Enoch.'

'Of course, *Enoch.*' She adopted a more serious look but still had to put a hand to her pounding heart.

'Is there living space above the shop?' she asked.

'Yes, there is, and you'll have your own bedroom, just in case you were worried.'

'Great! And when Harry comes home to me, I'll be a respectable baker lady and he won't need to kill me!'

'Wonderful,' said Enoch.

And if he doesn't come back, he thought to himself, *you might become respectable, Mrs Hoskins!* The thought was burning in his heart.

'Your father's gone home,' he added.

'Thank goodness!' she gasped. 'And he doesn't know about me being here?'

'No,' he lied but managed a sincere look. 'And when once you're established as a baker lady, I suggest you write to him and tell him how much you love him but that your life is devoted to your sailor man. He was worried sick about you and obviously loves you very much, in spite of everything.'

'All right... *Enoch.* I promise I will. I never wanted to hurt him. Life can be so cruel.'

'Oh, and one more thing,' he added as he turned towards the door.

'What's that?' she kept the words 'I'd do anything for you' inside, just in case he got the wrong idea.

'I suggest you buy a good cookery book. You'll need to learn the art of baking bread!'

Chapter 20

The rope swayed in the breeze in front of Harry's eyes. He swallowed hard. 'How could I have been so bloody stupid,' he pondered, past events resounding in his mind. The purple scarf was still around his neck; the blue john chip was back in his leather pouch. Blue eyes and green eyes pierced his darkness, but above all, the beautiful hazel eyes of Helen Westhouse. He wanted to see them smile. He needed their forgiveness and conjured a vision of them as he imagined the reunion. But she shocked him. 'Deserter!' she snapped, disgusted.

'For you, my darling,' he moaned. 'I risked everything for you!' but she closed those eyes and turned away. He felt empty and alone.

'For God's sake, hurry up!' The voice was a harsh whisper. The accent was Portuguese. Sandro Vargas was peering up at him. 'Are you coming or not?'

Harry shook the thoughts from his head and grabbed the rope. For the well-trained sailor, it was an easy descent and he found himself standing on a seaweed-slippery beam. Bart was ahead of him, ushered through the maze beneath the jetty by the expert who had done this many times before. They turned and beckoned urgently to Harry. He was probably the fittest of the three, physically, but his mind was holding him back. He picked his way carefully amongst the beams, watching the foaming brine rise and fall beneath his feet. 'Why the hell am I doing this?' he asked himself, but the thrilling vision of Miss Westhouse returned just in time. The wind swept her hair across her face and her smile returned. His pace quickened.

Sandro held his hands together to form a step. Bart put in a foot and clambered up into the tethered boat. Harry followed on. 'Get down below, quick!' came the Portuguese voice. If *Adventurer* had seemed claustrophobic, this was like a tomb. And the stench! This was a fishing boat and no mistake. Bart was nearly sick. Harry sank onto a wooden bench, grasping his gut.

'Don't shut that door!' groaned Bart, but Sandro did it anyway. 'You don't wanna be seen!' he returned.

'We want to *breathe*!' gasped Harry.

The fisherman responded, 'There's a, how you say? Vent thing up ahead. Go on through. It's less stinky in there!'

It was marginally better. A wisp of sea breeze wafted through.

'Hera, we sleep,' said Sandro. There were two sets of bunks, one on each side of the boat, angling in towards each other in the bows. 'I'll take the top,' said Harry.

'I suggest you get a good night's sleep,' said Sandro. 'I'll keep watch. We set off on the morning tide. Four bells of the morning watch, eh? Justa think! No more of that bloody navy nonsense. You're free, little birds, now. I hope you're very happy!'

'Oh, we are!' said Bart. 'Just get us home safely, Sandro. We're putting all our faith in you!'

***

'The master bedroom,' mused Beatrice. 'How many times have I cleaned and dusted it? How many times have I made this bed?' She let her hand explore the warm softness of the feather mattress and then the smooth, warm flesh of the man she loved. The sun's earliest rays were peering in, catching Richard's face. He turned towards her with a breath of contentment. He opened his eyes to her watchful smile.

'I love you so much,' he whispered. There were no barriers now. Their bodies moved together and merged once again, an encore of their splendid initiation the night before. Both lay contented, staring at the ceiling. 'That was so wonderful,' murmured Beatrice, but the late Sarah Westhouse was looming uncomfortably in her mind.

'Do you think she would be angry with me?' she uttered out loud.

'Who?'

'Sarah. Do you think she'd be angry?'

Richard imagined Sarah's face. She was smiling at him.

'No,' he replied. 'She'd be happy for us. She'd say life's too short to hold back.'

Beatrice nodded. 'Yes, she would,' she uttered. 'It *has* been a respectable four and a half years since she passed.' Both felt more comfortable and they hugged once again.

'I'll make us some breakfast,' she murmured and slowly extracted herself from the bed, leaving her man physically spent and exhausted, mentally content in those morning rays.

When he eventually came down, she had prepared his favourite kedgeree, which seemed to taste even better today. He was disappointed when it was finished. Thoughts were beginning to enter his emptied head. 'Lovers don't have secrets.'

He owed it to this dear lady. She had given him everything and more. She looked at him across the table, patiently, expectant. She could tell from Richard's fidgeting that he was preparing the words in his head.

'Miss Helen,' he mumbled at last. 'You want to know about Miss Helen... I saw her.'

Beatrice's look became quizzical. Was he going to say anything more?

Richard stuttered on. 'She... she has decided to stay in Norport. She is obsessed with this Smith fellow and thinks he'll come home to her.'

Beatrice stared hard at his worried face. 'She's in love with him, Richard. How could she do anything else? Why didn't you want to tell me this?'

'Because of what she's become,' he muttered, drawing a short Irish gasp of inquisitiveness. He gabbled the next few words. 'She is making her living and earning her keep as a whore.' Beatrice stared hard. Her eyes swam with tears. Her head was shaking as it sank into her hands.

'That poor, poor girl,' she muttered between sobs. 'And poor Sarah. She may be giving *us* her blessing but must be turning in her grave about Miss Helen.'

Both stared forlornly into space. Both feeling the guilt of their part in this awful mess.

'Is there anything we can do?' Beatrice managed at last.

'I don't know,' he replied. 'Maybe.'

She looked hard again at Richard, grasping at this small hint of hope.

'I've asked this Hoskins fellow. Port Admiral, they call him. Sounds rather grand, but he's some kind of organiser for everything that goes on in the harbour. Deals with the coming and going of ships, cargo, mail, everything.'

Beatrice was wondering how this could possibly help.

'He's taken a sort of uncle-like interest in Helen. He wants to help. He understands my fatherly disgust, guilt, horror… love. He'll help.'

Now, Richard would have to admit the truth. How he hoped he wouldn't give himself away by blushing or stuttering. He didn't want to relate that she had fooled him. 'I saw her,' he managed. 'But she doesn't know.' He stuttered a little, but Beatrice didn't seem to notice. 'She could still come home and pretend it hasn't happened.'

'But she won't, will she, Richard?'

'No. She'll wait for her man. God knows if he'll ever return. Same goes for Bart.'

Beatrice was trying to shake off her sobbing countenance, but she couldn't.

'How can this Admiral fellow help?' she uttered.

'I've promised him money from Cedric's will. He knows the ins and outs of that town. I've told him to set her up in some respectable business. Whether he can or not, I don't know. He said he'd get a message to me if he managed it. He wants to help; I know he does. He'll come up with something.'

'Oh, I do hope so, my darling. I do so hope so.'

Chapter 21

There were no bells that morning. No shrill boson's call to wake them up. No powder monkeys with their buckets of water ready to sluice down the deck, you too, if you weren't quick enough. They didn't have to untie hammocks from the hooks in the beams and roll them up, pass them through size-defining hoops and stow them in the nets on deck. There would be no physical exercises to the beat of the youngest marine's drum. Instead, they would simply clamber out of their bunks, stretch and yawn and wonder if they were utterly crazy to be running away.

'You boys awake?' came Sandro's voice.

'Kind of,' the muffled reply.

'Half hour we set sail,' went on Sandro. 'There's a nice stiff south-westerly.'

Bart and Harry emerged from their quarters, stooped and bleary-eyed. It had not been a night for sound sleeping. The bunks were hard and cramped. Their heads were full of contrasting thoughts. Somehow, they missed the rhythmic swaying of the body-hugging hammocks, the smell of damp canvass, the rattle of other men's snoring and grumbling.

'There's bread and cheese if you fellows are hungry,' announced Sandro. They both pulled faces but sat down to the only option available.

'Do we get grog at midday?' enquired Bart.

'Beer,' said Sandro. 'We only got beer, but plenty of it. No getting drunk, though, boys. You got plenty of work with the fishing nets.' Then he added with a grin, 'Anyone drunk gets a flogging, eh?' They all managed to laugh.

'And this is my other crew member,' announced the self-appointed skipper. They became aware of a fourth person on board, approaching the cabin door. He came in, smiling. 'He's gotta queer name. We call him "Poplar" for some reason.'

He shook hands with the new recruits, keeping a fixed grin on his face. To Harry, there was something sinister about those features, especially when the smile dropped into a more serious stare. When breakfast was over, Sandro gathered them all on deck. The single sail was hoisted and Poplar took hold of the tiller. The bows dipped and rose as the little craft left the harbour. Bart put his hand to his mouth. This was going to be a rough journey. Stomachs had to be braced.

'There she goes, sir!' shrilled a Midshipman's voice.

'Get on after her then!' replied the Fox cutter's master.

Sails were hurriedly raised, and marines grabbed their bayonetted muskets. The chase was on.

'Holy Mary!' gasped Sandro. It was a frightening vision. His Majesty's Britannic Navy had Sandro's illegal activities in their sights and had been lying in wait. Bart and Harry gaped in dismay as the smart little cutter swept into their wake. No sooner were they smelling freedom than they felt the oppressive power of the navy once again. Red-coated marines stood in the cutter's bows, white cross-belts gleaming, black shako hats, bayonets pointing skyward, all sails tightly trimmed to the wind. The fishing boat stood no chance. Her red and green Portuguese flag wavered defiantly in the stern, but she was doomed. The gazelle could run, but the cheetah would certainly catch her.

'Heave to!' came the demand from the pursuers. 'In the name of the king!'

Poplar let go of the tiller, fear etched on his craggy face, and in that split second, a flash of recognition appeared in Harry's brain. A blue-coated driver with a tricorn hat! 'His driver!' he gasped. 'You're bloody Stokes' driver!' Harry bashed his head with his right palm. 'Stupid, bloody fool!' he yelped out loud. Bart stared at him, astonished. 'Totally done in!' Harry croaked. 'Fooled completely!' He glared at Poplar Wainwright, then at the cutter in pursuit.

He groaned, 'We're done for!'

A voice in Harry's head yelled, 'Jump!' and for a split second, his brain was computing the distance he would have to swim. Sanity returned. He felt his fist clench hard and anger welled inside. He should have flattened the bastard that had led him into this trap, but he held it back.

Wainwright sneered at his accuser. The plan had so nearly worked. Sandro had been paid handsomely to lure the men away. They had been on their way home sure enough; to be delivered straight into the hands of the man who had sworn to have Harry Smith's guts for trinkets. The navy had been robbed, made to look stupid, and wanted their revenge. Death penalties would viciously ensue. Deserters unceremoniously hanged from the yardarm and left there to rot; an example to all. Harry and Bart cursed their stupidity. Was there any small chance of escape?

The cheetah was alongside the gazelle. Grappling irons were the big cat's claws. The cutter dropped all her sails and marines strode across to their helpless prey. Her sail was cut down and two boats bobbed silently on the choppy waves. The marines grabbed Poplar Wainwright and the cowering Sandro Vargas.

'Are you the master of this vessel?' demanded the marine captain.

'*Nao entendo*,' came Sandro's querulous reply. The marine captain ignored it.

'Where are the other two men?'

Sandro looked clueless and afraid.

'Search down below,' the captor ordered his men.

They dropped into the stinking cabin and made for the dividing door. They tried to shove the thing open, but something was stopping it. They looked knowingly at each other. They gave an extra shove and easily overcame the blanket that had been dumped beneath the door to trap it.

They poked bayonets into the room, but there was nobody there. They shoved blankets off bunks and wore quizzical looks. Where the hell were they? They stared around the tiny room till, at last, one of them spotted the dislodged panel. It was in the bows, in the gap between the two lower bunks. One man prodded the remaining toggle with his bayonet and the panel fell forward. He put his face to the black hole but could see nothing. Then, a scuffling sound. He pointed his weapon towards it and a terrified black rat ran out towards them.

The second marine instinctively thrust down with his musket and impaled the squealing creature to the floor. It was right in front of Harry's eyes as he lay peering through a crack from beneath the bunk. He shook discernibly, his phobia from boyhood rearing up in his head. Sweat oozed from his forehead, his mind filled with swirling visions of gnashing yellow teeth, staring eyes, twitching whiskers and horrible squirming tails. He shivered, heart thumping. It was all he could do to stop himself vomiting at the bloody sight. His despair overwhelmed him. He shoved his shoulder against the bunk base that hid them. It would give them away. He no longer cared.

'Fool!' screamed the first marine. 'Now, the fleas come straight onto us!' They both turned and scrambled out to their dismayed-looking captain. Harry gulped deep breaths. Bart thought his friend was about to die.

'Well?' enquired the captain.

'No sign of them, sir!'

'Don't be ridiculous! We saw them on deck. They haven't jumped off. They must be down there!'

Sandro and Wainwright looked equally puzzled.

'Watch these men,' the captain demanded. 'I'll look for myself.'

'Er, I should tell you, sir. There is a dead rat in there.' He started scratching at his leg. 'I think we're getting the fleas.'

The captain gave a disgusted look. 'All right then,' he went on. 'Perhaps we should just tow this tub back into the harbour. We can search her properly then.'

'Christ!' murmured Bart, who was squashed in right behind Harry. 'What the hell do we do now?'

Harry didn't answer. He was still breathing hard and couldn't wait to get out of that suffocating coffin. In any case, he didn't have a clue. He pushed the lid off their hiding place and clambered out. 'How bloody stupid!' he cursed at last. 'Thinking we could escape! That bloody Poplar fellow was taking us straight into Matthew Stokes' hands. He hates my guts, you know it! He would probably have tied me up and cut off a bit every day till I snuffed it. Bastard!'

Harry kicked the dead rat towards the door and covered it with the blanket. He tried to put it out of his mind and think logically about their plight. It wasn't easy. He eyed the removed panel and peered into the black hole. He slowly became accustomed to the darkness and dreaded the appearance of any more rats. He wondered if he could see more toggles in the roof. Yes! He could! He felt for them and twisted them around. There was a removable panel! Was it big enough to climb through?

'This might be our only chance,' muttered Harry. 'When once we're in harbour, we'll have to get out through this and hope somehow we can dodge the marines.'

'Then what?' groused Bart, drawing a sigh and haggard look from his companion.

'God, I don't know, Bart. Just pray and hope.'

Chapter 22

Matthew Stokes stared out of his office window at the lashing rain. He wondered how his trusted Poplar Wainwright was progressing with their plan. Would he really soon have that bloody peasant cowering before him? Begging for mercy? His hatred of that man would never diminish. His right hand formed into a fist and slammed into his left palm. 'You're going to wish you had never been born, Harry Smith!'

There was a knock on his door. 'Come in!' he yelled.

The clerk entered the room, cautious as ever, and could see from his master's flushed complexion that he was in a bitter mood. He held out the letter in front of him on a silver plate. Matthew snatched it and waved the man out of the room. 'This had better be good,' he muttered to himself.

It was not what he was expecting. He thought it would be from Wainwright, but it wasn't. It was from another spy who was still searching around Norport for the elusive Helen Westhouse. 'Possible sighting,' the letter read. 'A young woman of your description has been seen working at the Half Moon Tavern, Norport. They call her Helen of Troy. I think it would be worth your investigating. J J Roberts, Stokes Offices, Portsmouth.'

He put the paper down, and for the first time in a long time, he smiled.

Bart and Harry couldn't see out of that grim little craft but eventually felt it buffeting against the quay. Military voices rang out, some with instructions, some with obedience. Ropes were thrown and secured. All went quiet. Harry ducked into the dark and mouldy bow section and sought out the fixing toggles above his head. Once found and undone, he tried to push the panel upwards. It wouldn't shift. 'Probably got stuff on top of it,' remarked Bart, unhelpfully, 'or been painted over a dozen times.' Harry got angry with it. He knew it was the only chance of escape. He shoved his shoulder into it and heaved with all his might. Thoughts of the hangman's noose seemed to double his strength. An almighty crack! Dazzling light blazed in, along with a heap of old fishing nets. Harry pawed them out of the way and stuck his head up through the hatch. The marines were all standing around at the stern. None of them looked his way in spite of the noise he'd made, which must have been drowned out by the bustle on the quay. He beckoned to Bart. They both climbed out, hearts in their mouths, expecting to hear a shout. It didn't come. They climbed under the jetty, the same place as they had ventured the night before. They slipped and slithered on seaweed-slippery beams, watching foaming brine rise and fall beneath their feet and allowing themselves frightened glances over their shoulders. Still no shout. No glaring faces behind them. No cross-belted tunics or bayonetted muskets. Keep going.

Keep moving. Slip and slither on seaweed beams. Grab anything for support. The devils at your heels!

Harry was first to the rope. Could he grab it? He leapt at it awkwardly. It was slippery, but he held on tight. His feet gripped it, too. He heaved. He pulled. He felt himself rising. Bart was at the base of it now, holding the rope, looking upwards at Harry, fear and excitement in his eyes. Harry heaved and pulled again. He didn't know what he would see when he got up to the main quay, probably a bayonet at close quarters. He closed his eyes, not wanting to see. He stuck his head over the parapet and found the courage to look. What a crowd! Sailors milled about everywhere. Some carried their ditty bags, some odd bundles or wooden chests. Uniformed men had lists in their hands and inquisitive men gathering around. 'Quick!' gasped Harry. Bart clambered up the rope as well as he could and over the parapet. They both strode forward and into the throng. Chests heaving. Fear in their breath.

'What the hell's going on?' Bart stuttered to the nearest tar.

'Changing ship,' was the reply. 'Haven't you seen the notices?'

Bart looked blank and the sailor said, 'Ask *him*.' The man he was pointing to was Midshipman Lawrence. Harry looked back and saw red-coated marines on the front of the fishing boat. They were studying the open hatch, peering inside. One seemed to be looking his way. He ducked deeper into the crowd. He shook his head in disbelief at the sheer miracle of their escape. He followed Bart to the Midshipman's side.

'Where are we supposed to be going?' he heard Bart ask.

Lawrence rolled his eyes. 'For about the tenth time!' he groused. 'Odd number cannon crews of the larboard watch, transfer to the Captain!'

'Captain who?'

'Christ! I thought it was your mate Smith who was meant to be the thick one!' moaned Lawrence. *Captain* is the name of a ship! A very fine seventy-four gunner just like your beloved *Adventurer*. Get on board quickly. You're bloody late!'

There could be no more thoughts of escaping. They were back in His Majesty's Britannic bloody navy, whether they liked it or not. Their heads swam with incredulity. They looked back again and saw arguing marines pointing vehemently in different directions. They had to be quick.

Two navy ships were moored at the quay. They passed the first one, called "Culloden" and strode onto the gangplank of the second, named *Captain*.

'Odd name for a ship,' muttered Bart.

'Names?' rang out a youthful voice when they got to the top. It made them both jump.

'Westhouse and Smith,' replied Bart to the clerk who sat with quill and ledger.

'My God. We thought you'd deserted. Nobody's seen you for ages,' returned the boy. 'I've put you both down as *run*.'

'No. We're here all right,' confirmed Harry. 'We were on the wrong ship.'

'It's all my friend here's fault,' moaned Bart. 'He can't read.'

Harry adopted his worst rustic accent. 'That's right. The next ship along got a similar name. It begins with a "C" and ends with an "N" just the same, with a lot of confusing stuff in between. I thought that was the captain, and they were expecting two men with names like ours, so we just…'

'Oh my God. Spare me the bleedin' details,' moaned the lad. 'I'll change the entry from *run* to *late, confused*. That's all there's room for.'

'That'll do, I'm sure,' said Harry. 'Now we just need to find out where they want us.'

They gave each other the puffed cheek look of men who'd had the luck of the devil and went down to the lower gun deck. They found the Watch and Station Bill pinned to the wall along with the Quarter Bill, which told them exactly what they needed to know. Their cannon team had been transferred as a unit with Gun Captain Parker still in charge; they were still on larboard watch and were still designated 'B' for boarding. Cutlass and cannon were still their lot.

Poplar Wainwright protested and struggled. Marines held him tightly. They had only captured one of the three

Englishmen. They were embarrassed. They were not letting go of this one. Their captive wriggled one arm almost free, his elbow dislodging a marine's shako hat, but they held on grimly till the man's energy was spent. They marched him to their ship and presented him to Captain Miller.

'Name!' he demanded.

'I'm not one of yours! I'm a bloody civilian! Tell these dogs of yours to let go!'

Miller looked at him squarely. 'You were deserting! You were caught red-handed on some fishing boat!'

'No!' protested Wainwright and fell into his mother's Portuguese accent. 'I'm Pescador! Fisherman! Portuguese!'

'I don't believe you!' was Miller's retort, and went on, 'look. I don't have time for this. We're under orders to set sail. The penalty for desertion is hanging, but if I hang a bloody local fisherman, I'll be for it, so you get away with a flogging, all right? Twenty lashes. Take him away.'

'But I'm not even in the bloody navy!' yelled Wainwright.

'Sorry, my friend. Right now, we need every man we can get. You're in His Majesty's Britannic Navy whether you like it or not.' Miller broke into a forced smile and added, 'Welcome aboard!'

Chapter 23

Helen's eyes flickered open to another sunny morning. She still listened out for the cockerel but only heard gulls. She had taken Enoch's advice and purchased a book of recipes, which she now found open on her bed, obviously having lulled her to sleep the night before. Cooking seemed very straightforward. She had watched Beatrice at work in the kitchen. It always looked easy and fun being smothered in flour and singing some jolly ditty as you worked with rolling pins and scales. She had never offered to help. She wished now that she had.

She wondered if she might go down to Enoch's office and find out how he was progressing with his purchase of the baker's shop but then thought she may appear too eager. She turned over and concentrated her thoughts on Harry instead. 'I do hope you're all right, darling,' she whispered. 'And I do hope I become respectable Helen the Baker before you get back. You told me I should go home to be out of danger, but I just can't face Papa. I'm waiting for you here. I know! I should write to you again!'

She sat up at her dressing table and picked up paper and quill, her mind already picking out words that she wanted to use.

'My darling, Harry,' she began. 'Another sunny morning and I think straight away of you. I hope you are still well. I know that you advised me to go home and wait for you there, but I can never face Papa again. I am waiting for you here, in Norport. I am working at the baker's shop where I also have lodgings. I am perfectly safe there and have become quite an expert at baking bread and cake. Beaty would be proud of me, and so I think you should be. Fending for myself in such a strange place.'

God! she thought. *What a load of lies! If he only knew! Still, just hope and pray it all comes true and he'll come home to me, my brave sailor, having beaten this Bonaparte bastard, and I'll be his sweet, respectable wife!*

She put quill to paper once again. 'I hope you are looking after my little brother. I want you both to come home safely to me. This is all I can get on the page, so I'll say farewell. All my love as ever, Helen.'

She folded it and sealed it, scrawled "*Harry Smith, Adventurer*" on the outside. Now, she had a valid reason for visiting the Port Admiral. She would get properly dressed and do it right away. When she passed Brown's the Bakers, she saw that a man was busily painting out the name above the door.

Things are moving, she thought to herself and couldn't help thinking back to that fateful morning when she had gone into that shop asking for bread.

When she reached the office and knocked on the door, she was surprised to find it opened by Mark Williamson.

'Come in!' he said excitedly.

'I've brought a letter,' she explained, and Mark took it from her and deposited it in the sack. He still had such warm feelings for her even though he knew she had done the same for many other men.

'Mr Hoskins has gone to the bank,' he said. 'Exciting, isn't it?'

'Yes. I've just seen them painting out the old name. Has he told you that he wants to give me respectable employment there?'

'Oh yes. Me too! I'm to do the deliveries. And I'm to lodge there too.'

'Oh, I didn't know that.'

'Yes. Mr Hoskins is selling up his old place. Fact is, I'm like his adopted son, really. My real father got killed at sea and Mr Hoskins, who was his lieutenant then, promised he'd look out for me and my brother. That's how I come to lodge with him and I get this wonderful job.'

'Right,' she said. 'And what has become of your brother?'

'Andrew? Not seen him for a couple of years. He's older than me. He's an artist. Went off to Paris to learn from the masters,' he reckoned. 'Don't know how he's getting on. All I hear is that Paris is in a right mess. The aftermath of revolution and all that. Anyway, I expect he'll come home right as rain one day when he's made his fortune.'

'Let's hope so,' replied Helen. 'Let Mr Hoskins know that I was here with you and that I'm just living for the day I can start my new life at the shop.'

'Yes, I'll tell him, Mrs – I mean Miss... Oh, hell. What the heck do I call you?'

'Helen would do.'

'Not Helen of Troy?' he smirked.

'Definitely not! Forget that! It's just Helen.'

'Oh, I'll never forget,' he murmured, and both couldn't help but smile.

It seemed a long, dreary day at the Half Moon Tavern. Helen had dusted, polished and scrubbed, had changed her clothes for the evening and now sat in her little room just waiting to be some fellow's plaything, just longing for Enoch Hoskins to take her away. She was daydreaming when the knock on the door came. It startled her back to reality.

'Come in!' she shouted. What sort would it be? A drunken, rough type, stinking of ale, tobacco and stale sweat, his desires outstripping his capabilities. Some seasoned old brothel-dweller who would take her in his stride without a smile? Some coy young fellow like Williamson wanting to lose his virginity? Or maybe... the door creaked open; her musings were cut short. It was like a dagger to her heart. 'Oh God!' she gasped. Her hands moved involuntarily to her mouth. Her worst nightmare loomed in the doorway. The leering figure of Matthew Stokes!

Panic hit the girl hard. She backed away as he closed the door behind him. She climbed onto the bed and made for the window, heaving it open. He grabbed her arm.

'No, you don't.' He breathed. 'You're not getting away that easily!'

'Let go!' she demanded. 'I'll scream the place down!' He saw the venom in her eyes, determination. He loosed his grip but shoved her down onto the bed. As he did so, he reached out and closed the window and went to grab her again, but she felt his hand on her mouth and bit hard. The man winced, almost crying out with the pain but holding it back. He shook himself free and pinned her down.

'Now, you, miserable little bitch,' he spat, 'now, you can do some explaining! I've waited a long time for this, Miss Westhouse. After all my painful visits to you and your bloody chaperone! All my sucking up to your father! All my efforts to make you mine. Why the hell do you run off with some miserable, bloody peasant who leaves you to whore in some God-forsaken hole like this?' His voice was a passion-crazed bark; his eyes narrow slits of poisonous hate.

She spat. She spat hard. A wet smear appeared on his cheek and his expression changed from anger to deepest disgust. 'You bloody alley cat!' he snarled. 'You're not even human any more!' The back of his hand smashed across her face and she reeled. His hands grabbed the neckline of her dress and tore it down. The weight of his body on hers was too much. She tried to breathe. She tried to twist and turn. Anything but this! Of all the rough bastards she had dealt with in the last few weeks, this hate-filled man was the worst. Frustration and passion contorted his face, the humiliation of being ditched for some farm hand. He had nothing but contempt now for the girl he had once wanted to marry. He was strong. Fuelled by feelings of hate and revenge. He wanted to hurt this little whore just as she had hurt him. Her strength was fading beneath him. A sardonic smile creased his face. 'I expected a little more fight,' he muttered. She couldn't find breath enough to scream.

'Oh God!' she suddenly gasped. A loud thud had resounded on the back of his head and his eyes rolled upwards. He collapsed, a dead weight on top of her. He was being dragged away. She heard a boot kick hard into her assailant's head.

'Oh God!' she groaned again. 'What the hell's going on?'

'Are you all right?' wheezed a voice.

'What?'

'Are you all right?' It was a young man's voice. Mark Williamson was standing over her. Her head was spinning. She tried to focus her eyes. She didn't *know* how she felt. Half suffocated and breathless, she tried to speak without knowing what to say. Mark was pulling her dress back up to cover her semi-nakedness. She put her hand to her face. It was numb where Stokes had hit her.

'Who is he?' the young man was saying. She could only see the ceiling.

'He came to the office,' Mark went on, 'and asked where the Half Moon Tavern was. I didn't like the look of him. I told him and then felt all kind of worried, so I thought I'd follow him. He was up to no good; I knew it. The bastard!'

'Thank God you did!' Helen managed. 'He'd have killed me! Quick Mark! Get Yarker! Get this man thrown out before he comes round!'

Tom Yarker had already heard the commotion. He stood in the doorway, questions all over his face.

'This man attacked me!' Helen gabbled, pointing to the prostrate Matthew Stokes on the floor. 'And this young man saved me. Get him out!' she shrieked, 'before he comes round.'

Mark and Yarker dragged the unconscious fellow out and rather ignominiously down the stairs. They expected comments from the customers, but instead, everything went quiet. They stood aside and let them pass before exchanging looks and murmurs. Stokes was coming round.

'What the hell happened?' he croaked to two angry faces.

Tom Yarker upbraided him. 'That's what you get when you get rough with my girls!'

Stokes was regaining his senses. 'That bloody bitch!' he cursed but saw deepening anger in Tom Yarker's eyes.

'Don't you ever come near this place again,' threatened the landlord. 'Or you'll be dead meat!'

'You've not heard the end of this, you bastards!' yelled Stokes, but the two men were already walking away.

Chapter 24

'Just like old times, ain't it?' said Gun Captain Parker to his team. All the old faces were there. The cannon looked exactly the same, but they were no longer 'Adventurers.' The thinly populated *Captain* was in even greater need of men than their previous ship. The press gangs had been doing their best and had rounded up a few more petty offenders from jail, a few more crew members of honest trading ships, fishermen and drunks from the taverns, but it still wasn't enough. Admiral Jervis had requested more ships if he was to keep the Spanish at bay. Even more men.

'Ram!' came Parker's command. 'For God's sake, bloody ram!' Harry was startled back into action, his mind miles away in thoughts of the attempted escape, Wainwright, Stokes and Helen. He rammed. Parker glared.

'Two days! Two bloody days!' the Gun Captain exploded. 'That's all we've got at most! The Dons are on the move. It's down to us now! British guns are the fastest known to mankind. Or bloody well should be! Let's do it again!'

They did it again. This time, all minds concentrated hard. All bodies heaved and rammed as they should. They *were* the bloody fastest. Ready for those wine-swilling Dons!

'All hands on deck!' came a lieutenant's cry. 'Important visitor!'

The men moved away from their posts and assembled in neat ranks on deck. 'Who's the visitor?' men were asking, but nobody knew. The boson's call gave its shrill welcome and a barge party began to emerge at the top of the starboard ladder, smart blazers and straw boater hats emphasising the visitor's importance. At last, the man himself appeared and walked on board between the two neat rows that his barge party had formed. He was not tall. He was prematurely silver-haired. He smiled and shook hands with Captain Miller. He was Commodore Nelson.

'Who?' enquired Harry, but he was quickly hushed by the other tars. Captain and Commodore made their way to the great state cabin and were lost to sight, but the excitement was tangible amongst the men.

'It's Nelson!' they were muttering excitedly.

'He's back. Used to be captain here. There's never been a skipper like him. On his way up. Commodore now. Admiral, before long, you mark my words!'

'Where's his eye patch then?' someone was asking.

'Heard he'd lost an eye in some battle in Corsica.'

'Blinded in it, but he's never worn an eye patch. Didn't want to look like a pirate.' Harry and Bart stood and listened to the excited prattle. Some of the men had served under Nelson before in a ship called the Agamemnon. Had lots of stories to tell. What mattered now was that this ship with Nelson back aboard was going to be in the thick of the action. Men liked that idea. They slapped each other's backs and grinned. They cheered when they saw the Commodore's pendant hoisted up the mast. Excitement, enthusiasm, a thirst for action and the prize money they could share for capturing enemy ships. His Majesty's Britannic bloody navy was on the move.

'Get your things together. You're moving out.'

'What?' said Helen, somewhat stunned.

'Mr Enoch Hoskins has just paid your severance fee. You're his now.'

The voice was Tom Yarker's. The long-awaited event had occurred.

'I'm free to go?' said Helen, her heart leaping for joy.

'That's about the size of it,' mumbled Yarker.

She couldn't help herself. She flung her arms around the man and planted an excited kiss on his cheek. He shied away and she apologised. She wanted to thank him for saving her, but he and his tavern had also been her downfall. What a mixture of emotion! She grabbed her few belongings, shook his hand and walked out of the door. She had tears in her eyes when Enoch met her outside. 'Tears of joy,' she explained and linked her arm with his.

'Put your hood up over your head,' he whispered.

Together, they walked down the street. Helen felt as though she was floating. They reached the shop and stopped to look in the bottle glass window. She saw her reflection and smiled. The reflection smiled back.

A shadow drifted, purple, into Harry Smith's dream. He winced. He'd seen it before. The damned thing wouldn't leave him alone. It became a purple mist, then foaming brine. An agonised face broke through, a drowning man gasping for precious air. He saw his hands reach out to save the wretched fellow and felt icy fingers on the back of his neck dragging him down, down into freezing darkness. 'Wake up!' came the voice in his head. 'It's a dream. Wake up! You don't have to die!' His eyes flickered open, and he stared at the ceiling, twenty-four inches above his face. The hammock swung and spilt him out. Bare feet were thudding onto the floor all around, men grumbling at the inevitable start of another day, but no ordinary day. Hammocks were being unhitched from their hooks, rolled and passed through the limiting hoop, then carried up above and stashed into nets where they may well get wet but may well save your life from some vile musket shot.

There was to be no drill. 'What's happening?' The galley fire had been doused. The cook had been ordered to his station in the lantern room to illuminate the powder store. Something was afoot. The Gunner was already pouring water onto the woollen curtains of the powder magazine and flooding the inch-deep lead lining of the approach passageway. His steel buckles were removed, boots replaced with felt slippers; nothing was left that could remotely cause a spark. Officers stood on the forecastle, telescopes to eyes. Commodore Nelson was getting used to squinting with his left eye after losing the use of his right. He was focused on the messaging flags on Admiral Jervis's ship, the Victory. He knew it wouldn't be long. He'd seen the Spanish fleet in the Med only two days before. His frigate, La Minerve, captured previously from the French, had been the last British ship to leave those waters, now grudgingly referred to as the 'French Lake'.

Early morning mist was dispersing and the rocky cliffs of Portugal's west coast were appearing from the gloom. English frigates had been sent out to reconnoitre and were reporting back to Jervis. Yes! Six Spanish ships had emerged from the Strait of Gibraltar, known as "The Gut" to the navy, something far worse to the basic tars. Admiral Jervis felt a thud in his heart and knew that this was his moment. He had been bolstered by the fact that his squadron had been strengthened by six new ships from the busy shipyards of England. He now had fifteen ships of the line and five frigates. He knew he could beat the Dons. *They* had only six!

'Message to all ships!' Jervis called to his flag officer and felt the excited tingle of goosebumps as he spoke. 'Clear for action!'

All around the fleet, telescopes were slammed shut and animated readers of the signal repeated the words. 'Clear for action!'

'Yeaah! This is it!' mouthed excited tars. The hubbub spread around the ship. Harry and Bart knew their role, as did every well-drilled sailor. All lightweight partitions that divided up the decks were dismantled; all furniture was stowed away below the decks. The grand cabin was no exception. Its black and white chequered canvas flooring was rolled up, furniture taken apart and stowed, cannon untethered. Men moved methodically, silently, efficiently. Faces wore serious looks, and stomachs churned.

'Form line as most convenient,' came Nelson's voice as he read the Victory's signals. This was the tried and trusted way of conducting battle at sea. Two lines of ships ranged up alongside each other, blasting away with cannon fire until one was so badly damaged or depleted of the crew that they struck their colours and surrendered or succumbed to a cutlass-wielding boarding party. The *Captain* fitted neatly into the line, three from the back, with a strategic view of the scene.

'Beat to quarters!' yelled Captain Miller. The drummer boy, too nervous, dropped his sticks, earning a deserved glare from his captain. He soon recovered and rattled out his quick tempo beat. Pumps and the so-called "fire engine" appeared on deck with its hoses and nozzles. Water was sprayed onto decks. The powder monkey boys brought buckets of sand to sprinkle around the guns to aid barefooted sailors and maybe soak up spilt blood. Cannon crews gathered around their allotted weapon, grabbing rods and buckets they were going to need. Faces peered from the gun ports. 'Can you see the buggers yet?'

Bart pushed his way to the opening to vomit overboard. He was not the only one and a stench began to grow.

'There are more of them now, sir!' came a lookout's voice from the rigging. 'The frigates are signalling there's twenty!'

'Oh my God!' muttered Jervis. 'It's going to be more of a battle than we thought.'

'Looks like they've had a rough night, though, sir,' said his lieutenant. 'They're scattered around like rats from a cannon!'

'Let's get at them,' said Jervis. 'Before they can close into line.'

The Spanish Admiral Cordova had his telescope to his eye. He winced at the sight that filled his lens. The British line was in full battle order. Their gun crews were the best in the world. Majestic bows dipped and rose on white-crested waves. Sails were full-bellied, determined. Flags and pendants streamed proudly in the wind. He could even hear "Hearts of Oak" being drummed out on the leading ship, *Culloden*.

'Get into line!' he yelled. He'd been told that the British were light in numbers. Their tiny squadron wouldn't dare to challenge the might of Spain. His heart sank as he counted the sails. Spanish captains had pre-empted his order. They were doing their best to form some kind of battle line now.

'Tack in succession,' read Nelson from *Victory's* flags. He lowered his telescope and stared out to sea. The Spanish had good wind in their sails. Jervis's order was fair enough and should set the two fleets into fighting positions, but the foremost enemy ships were gaining speed and seemed set on escaping the British hold.

'We need to act,' said Nelson. 'Mr Jervis can't see what's happening at the back here. Wear ship, Captain Miller. Wear ship!'

Miller's face creased in astonishment. He stared at Nelson, his order conflicting with the flag ship's command, but the Commodore's face was set in steel. No more words were required.

Miller turned to his lieutenants. 'Wear ship!' he barked, and the men went about their task. The great wheel was hauled around. Men heaved on ropes to coax the sails. Below decks, gun crews stared, bewildered. The *Captain's* bows dipped and rose on the next foaming wave and began to slew off course, turning her back on the enemy.

'What the hell's going on?' demanded voices. Battle-ready men stared out of gun ports.

'We're turning away!'

'What?' demanded Harry to the "Old Agamemnon" gun crew. 'I thought your man Nelson was going to lead us into the thick of it!'

They all stared, bewildered, and the *Captain* continued to turn. She was now running in the opposite direction to the rest of the fleet and deriding voices cascaded from the *Diadem*, the next ship in the British line. 'She's running away!' men were shouting. 'The battle's *that* way!' Gun captains glared at lieutenants, puzzled, flustered. Lieutenants stared at each other. 'What the hell?' they muttered. Men threw down ramrods and sponges in disgust. The human chains conveying powder charges ground to a halt. The Gunner peered out through the wetted wool curtain of the magazine. 'What's happened?' he demanded. 'Why have you stopped?' Powder monkeys paddling in their wetted corridor shrugged their shoulders and made the same demand of people down the line.

Nelson could hear the incredulous voices and gritted his teeth. The *Captain* continued her turn. Far from running away, she was making the most of the wind! She cut through the line between the *Diadem* and *Excellent* and made for the foremost Spaniard. She was not picking a fight with just anyone; it was the mightiest ship of the fleet, the *Santissima Trinidad*. Fearsome in broad red and white horizontal stripes on her hull, black cannon mouths at every gun port, sails full-bellied in shades of cream and brown that towered above. She leant over the *Captain* with disdain.

'Christ!' gulped Harry as she filled his view. Men cheered as realisation set in. They picked up their jettisoned gear. Laughed and grinned in nervous celebration. 'Aha!' retorted the Old Agamemnons. 'Now, what have you got to say?' Harry was stunned by the sight.

'Make ready!' yelled Gun Captain Parker. The cannon was already loaded and primed. The men stood clear.

'Fire!' came the lieutenant's command. Gun Captains jerked their lanyards in succession. Flintlocks sparked, igniting powder, a classical rippling broadside. Ear-splitting explosions crashed out along the line. Harry held his head in pain. The mighty cannon flew back on its trolley to the extent of its restraining ropes, thumping to a halt, adding dust to the choking pall of yellow-grey smoke.

Harry's eyes felt as if they were burning in their sockets. They slammed shut. This was hell! Practice, practice, practice, could never prepare you for this. Each smoke-laden breath made his lungs burn; his head was still ringing from the deafening roar.

'Sponge out!' demanded Parker.

Bart was trembling. The noise, the fear. He shoved the sponging rod into the leather bucket, knocking it over but bringing the sodden sheep's skin dripping to the cannon's mouth. Outrageously hot, it hissed a mighty cloud of vapour into the foul air.

'Cartridge!' yelled Parker, and the powder man passed the canvas cartridge to the loader. The cannon begged like some crazed beast demanding food. The cartridge was shoved into its mouth. 'Ram!' Parker demanded. Harry, staggering, recovering, threaded the ramrod into the gaping muzzle and rammed. 'Shot! Ram! Wadding! Ram!' the orders kept coming. Harry was mechanical. For a moment, in his brain, the ramrod was a pitchfork and Helen Westhouse was giggling coyly behind her curtain. 'Run out the gun!' screamed Parker and all men heaved. The cannon was back at its port, staring at its prey. 'Fire!' came again and again, the wild explosion that numbed the ears and rocked the brains inside men's heads.

An attentive powder monkey had fetched another bucket of water. 'Sponge out!' demanded Parker again. Bart made a far better job of it this time in spite of the personal battle he was having with his rebellious stomach.

Harry hauled off his shirt and used it to wipe at his sweaty face, leaving it smeared in black. He pulled off the purple scarf and, as he had seen the Old Agamemnons doing, tied it around his head to cover his ears. Nelson may well have not wanted to look like a pirate, but right now, Harry felt like one.

At times like these, even the women showed their faces, times when it no longer seemed important to pretend they were not there. 'Christ!' muttered Harry as one girl took her place in the cartridge line. A freckly face, green eyes; could it possibly be? Rogue strands of red hair were escaping from her headscarf, soot-laden sweat her only disguise.

'Johnny Bloody Blue, John!' she managed through the din. 'I might have guessed you'd be a rammer! Give her one for me, eh!'

'Ram!' the command brought Harry back into action.

For all her firepower, the *Captain* did not seem to be inflicting much damage on her adversary. The Spaniard was pockmarked and some of her sails had developed holes, but she was like a farmyard bull swishing its tail with contempt at the flies. Red flames leapt from her gunnery, then the almighty crash of iron balls against the *Captain's* oaken walls. Huge, jagged splinters ripped away and speared at the men. Sailors were screaming, bleeding, dying. A decapitated body was hauled past Harry and ejected without ceremony into the sea. Blood boiled and baked on the seething cannon.

A powder monkey appeared with another bucket of sand. He shook the contents onto pools of blood to soak it up. How battle-hardened these lads seemed to be?

'Make ready!' Parker was shouting through the mayhem. Men got themselves as clear as possible from the weapon. The order, 'Fire!' rang out from the lieutenant somewhere ahead in the smoke and all gun captains followed through. As soon as the cannon ahead had fired, Parker followed, jerking the lanyard that sparked the powder and another mighty roar convulsed every sailor's body and brain. The cannon hurtled back in another dense pall of choking smoke, breeching ropes thumping it to a halt. Men shaken and reeling listened out for the next command.

Another mighty Spanish broadside crashed into the ship, this time higher. The whole place shuddered in a roar of destruction and everything went black.

Helen closed her eyes. Molly Elizabeth recoiled in pain. Something terrible had happened; both knew it. 'What's wrong?' demanded Enoch, but when Helen opened her eyes again, she could only stare, motionless, cold. She shuddered and Enoch wanted to take her in his arms but couldn't find the courage. He saw the beads of sweat stand out on her brow, the crinkled, furrowed lines across it.

'Christ!' she muttered. Don't let him die!' Molly held on tight to her purple scarf, the one cut from the same cloth as the one she'd given to Harry.

A voice of authority barked out orders. Men were chopping and hacking with hatchets on the upper gun deck. Musket fire from the Spanish rigging peppered the deck. Then there was cheering as sail, ropes and timber slumped into the water and dazzling light cascaded back into the lower gun deck. Harry winced and forced his eyes open. The blaze of light from the sea and sky was bewildering. Huge shapes, dark masses, mayhem! Other British ships, *Culloden* and *Excellent,* had joined in the fray. Spanish ships gathered around.

'Keep firing at will!' the lieutenant was shouting, but the *Captain* was drifting, her wheel housing shot away, her masts in a state of collapse.

Then, a horrendous flash of light, followed by the thud of explosion. Men looked across to where the *Adventurer* should have been. Instead, a black pall of smoke encompassed a shower of debris. Flames leapt up from the remains of her carcass. The deadly mass of gunpowder in her magazine had ignited with all its terrible force. Men signalled a cross on their chests or muttered a little prayer. 'There but for the grace of God, go I.'

'Men to steerage!' someone was shouting, and there was no shortage of volunteers. It was safer down there below the water line where cannon balls couldn't reach. In the absence of a wheel, the rudder would have to be operated by men hauling on ropes down there. It was tough but no worse than the hell of the gun decks.

Commodore Nelson surveyed the destruction, but alert as ever to all possibilities, he realised that two

Spanish ships, the *San Josef* and the *San Nicolas*, were in just as bad a state and had, in fact, collided, being totally out of control. 'We can still play a decisive part in this battle,' he uttered to Captain Miller. 'Get the boarding party ready!'

'Boarders!' yelled a lieutenant, and men began to move away from their guns. Harry loved the feel of a cutlass in his hands, not unlike a sickle, but wheat was an easy target. Would he be able to hack at a man? Bart hated it, but something drove him on. He saw Helen's red-faced fury. She was crying uncontrollably. 'Harry's dead and it's all your fault!' The men had christened him "Barnacle Bart" for the way he seemed to adhere himself to Harry. He didn't care.

The armourer was handing out the weapons as men got on deck. The *Captain* had managed to grind up alongside the *San Nicolas,* and marines were already leaping over the gap. Bayonetted muskets glinted in the sun, bright red tunics, white cross belts. The crowd moved forward, yelling abuse. Harry found himself leaping across, cutlass in his hand above him, seeking its prey. Euphoria, then pain; his head suddenly screeching agony, a load on his back. He twisted to see the snarling face of a hate-filled Spaniard yelling unknown profanity, breath reeking of mysterious spice. He heard the swish of steel, blood splattered, warm, onto his face. 'I'm sorry, Helen!' he heard himself say, expecting deliverance. It didn't come. The blood wasn't his. He saw a navy-issue cutlass deep in his assailant's throat. The hand on the handle was Barnacle Bart's.

Nelson, as ever, was at the front of the attack. His yell of "Death or glory" spurred men on. No wonder stalwarts like the Old Agamemnons idolised him. They would follow him into hell. They had broken into the upper gallery but found the doors locked. They were trapped! Spaniards with pistols saw their chance and eyed up their shots. Harry and Bart were onto them in a flash. Cutlasses swung. Swarthy necks were the targets. Navy training was ruthless and thorough. Flesh sliced: blood gushed. Wheat was harvested in scarlet. 'Those bastards won't murder our man,' rang in Englishmen's heads. Nelson and the marines broke free and made for the quarter-deck, where they saw the Spanish flag being hacked down. Captain Berry of the marines threw it away to loud cheering from the men. Then all was quiet, just the deep-throated laugh of a gull that seemed to find man's futile destruction of his fellow man amusing.

Musket shot ripped at the deck. Spaniards aboard the entangled *San Josef* were firing from the admiral's stern gallery. Nelson seized another chance. Men poured across to the stricken ship, but instead of mayhem, there was quiet. Marines and sailors stood on the deck; muskets, cutlasses and hatchets held firmly in determined hands, but there was no opposition. A door slowly opened and all British eyes turned towards it. Weapons stirred. A white flag fluttered from the widening crack, followed by a solemn-faced officer. 'Zis ship zurrenderz,' he managed, and the Captain followed him onto the deck. He held his sword by the blade, offering the hilt to Nelson. The Commodore accepted graciously and passed this and the swords of other surrendering officers to one of his barge crew. His men surrounded him, congratulating and patting their hero on the back. Harry could not resist the spreading idolisation of the man and held out a hand for shaking.

'Proud to have fought with you today, sir,' he managed. 'And what a brilliant idea to use one enemy ship as a bridge to get to another!' Nelson looked hard at the blood-splattered face and saw the dedication and pride. He shook the hand and rested his other hand on Harry's shoulder.

'Good to have men like you around,' he said in sincere tone. 'I think you saved my life today.'

'And this man saved mine,' said Harry, proudly pointing to Bart, equally blood-stained but beaming.

'Good man,' said Nelson. 'One way or another, we're all in this together. I think today we've robbed the French of a powerful ally. We're well on the way to making our homeland safe.'

Men all around nodded and murmured their agreement; then, some cheering broke out, rising to a full-throated release of emotion. 'Three cheers for Commodore Nelson!' one man exclaimed, a sentiment lustily carried out. They'd have picked up their leader and carried him off shoulder high if the protocol had allowed. It didn't. They settled for more beaming smiles and handshakes and an excited chorus of "Rule Britannia".

Chapter 25

It took a long time for a ship to recover from such a battle. Fallen sailors were solemnly buried at sea in their stitched-up hammocks weighed down with cannon balls, and the wounded lay groaning on makeshift beds of hay. The surgeon and his mates were blood-stained and exhausted. Amputated limbs were thrown overboard. There was little else that could be done for the unfortunate wounded ones except administer laudanum and rum and pray to God that their wounds would not be beset by gangrene. Decks were sluiced down and holy stoned, masts and sails re-rigged as much as possible, steering tackle mended. The carpenter was as exhausted as the surgeon. On board the *Captain*, the carpenter had several new helpers assigned, amongst them a surly, unwilling fellow who had only recently been pressed into service in Lisbon. His name was Poplar Wainwright.

'I still can't work you out, Wainwright,' said the lieutenant. 'Are you English or Portuguese?'

'I keep telling you,' he replied in his mother's accent. 'Portuguese! I'm a fisherman! Pescador! I'm not one of yours!'

'Sorry, my friend, but as Captain Miller clearly said, "you are now"!' Wainwright was shaking his head at the words. He dared not speak for getting into more trouble and maybe sentenced to more lashes.

'There were four men on that fishing boat,' went on the lieutenant. 'You and the skipper and two more. Who were the other two? We might be able to forget the flogging if you tell us.'

Wainwright thought hard. He would dearly like to escape the flogging, but his mind flickered back to his orders from Matthew Stokes. He'd been his faithful cohort for years, and unfortunately, not totally voluntarily. Stokes had a hold over him, which he couldn't ignore. His instructions were to bring "the peasant" back to him alive. If Smith was turned in for desertion, the navy would acquaint him with the hangman's noose. Failure for Wainwright. No, he must preserve Harry Smith for his master to reap his own revenge. Even turning in "Barnacle" Bart Westhouse would lead them straight to Harry. 'Hold your tongue, Poplar,' he told himself. 'Take the flogging like a man!'

'If you persist in saying nothing, Wainwright, you get the cat-o-nine tails at noon tomorrow! You've got until then to make up your mind. I'll get the boson's mate to show you how to make the dear cat. It'll keep you occupied while you think!'

Harry and Bart had just finished eating when an ominous shadow loomed from behind them. For a moment, the man didn't speak but then crouched behind them, putting a hand on Harry's shoulder. 'Was this it?' Harry wondered, a rush of guilt invading his mind. Had the attempted desertion been exposed? Caught up with us at last? At length, the man spoke, his voice a sinister whisper, 'See how clever we are at finding people in this navy?' he said. It was more a statement than a question. Guilt sent a shiver down their spines. They exchanged a worried look.

'Tracked you down,' said the lieutenant, and Harry started to stutter some kind of plea of innocence. Then the letter dropped onto his lap and he gave a puff-cheeked look of relief. He stared at the blob of red sealing wax and his name lovingly scrawled on the outside. The word *Adventurer* had been crossed out and *Captain* written in by some clerk.

'Thank God,' Harry muttered and turned to see the uniformed man walking away. *Is it going to be like this forever?* he wondered. 'Worrying about being caught. I daren't look an officer or marine in the eye. And that damned entry in the ship's ledger, *run* crossed out and *late confused* put in. Someone's going to get suspicious of that eventually.' He sat there staring at the letter, his mind elsewhere in turmoil.

Bart took it from him and broke the seal. He looked for some moments at his sister's loving scrawl, reminiscing on his childhood adventures with her. Eventually, he became aware of Harry's expectant stare and began to read out loud. It was like pouring life into a dead man's soul. Helen's words made Harry's pulse react. He imagined her lovely face, her hand undoing the buttons of that dress in the barn. 'Ah! Listen to this!' chirped Bart through Harry's haze. 'I am working at the baker's shop where I have lodgings. I am perfectly safe there and have become quite an expert at baking bread and cakes. What did I tell you? She's a resourceful girl, my sister! I could never have imagined her up to her elbows in flour and lard, though!' His face dropped a little when he read on and saw himself referred to as her 'little brother'. 'She still treats me with disdain,' he muttered to himself. 'She doesn't know that I saved her Harry's life or that one day I'll be lord and master of twice-as-big Westhouse Farm.'

Helen was loving her new life. She woke each morning to the welcoming cry of the gulls and opened her gaily coloured curtains. She would smile at nothing in particular then get dressed and sit at her mirror, brush in hand, giving her hair its daily ration of strokes. There would be no knock on her door. No drunks or serial brothel users. No young men wanting initiation. No, Matthew Stokes. Yes, he had returned to the Half Moon Tavern bent on revenge, but he'd been thrown out again by the landlord and his mates, told that Helen of Troy had left town. Her trail had gone cold. Nobody but Yarker knew that she was hidden away in Enoch's Kitchen. When she appeared in the shop, she was unrecognisably white-clad and hatted. There was no trace of auburn ringlets. No trace of Helen of Troy. She didn't know that Enoch had written a letter to her father saying that their plan had succeeded. She didn't know that every night, Enoch would pause at her bedroom door, look at the handle and wonder what would happen if he turned it and walked straight in. 'What do you want?' he imagined her saying. She would be sitting up in bed reading one of the new romantic novels that were all the rage. 'I want to share the pleasures of your bed,' he would reply. She would say nothing, but she would pull back the blanket to invite him in. He would smile to himself about what followed in his mind and continue to his own room. 'One night,' he mumbled to himself. 'One of these lovely, fine nights.'

'Have you heard the news?' said excited voices. 'What news?' It was spreading through the town like a fire. 'Great victory! The navy has beaten the hell out of the Spanish. Without them, the Frogs can't attack! Bonaparte can't invade!' The news swept into the baker's shop. Mark Williamson brought it in. He'd just finished his early deliveries and the word was on everyone's lips. The little cutter had brought the news from the fleet. It would soon be on the wonderful new semaphore system that passed it on from station to station till it reached the Admiralty in London. 'We're safe!' people were saying. 'The French can't invade!'

Helen could hardly believe it. 'Does that mean he'll be home soon? My Harry?' It was a rhetorical question. She was so excited that she gave Mark a big hug anyway and when she pulled away, there were tears making tracks through the flour on her face. Then another rumour spread to the customers. Words that changed her elation into groping despair.

'*Adventurer* blew up,' they were saying.

'Nobody survived!' She stared wide-eyed at the gossiping group. Fear was pounding in her heart. Enoch saw her plight and put a comforting hand on her shoulder.

'He'll be all right,' he murmured, his mind searching for words. 'He'll have been picked up by another ship.' Helen stared into his sincere eyes. He seemed so knowledgeable and experienced in such matters. She believed him, but he secretly hoped he was wrong. How splendid would be his comforting role?

The bell rang out eight times. It was noon. Bart and Harry joined the shambling queue to acquire their ration of grog. Not surprisingly, the stuff was getting more watery each day as levels ran low. They were also down to ship's biscuit and a brown slurry of stew, which reminded them of John Gun's stories about eating the ship's rats. 'Wonder if the poor lad got blown up with *Adventurer*?' mused Bart. 'Born there, died there?' The mood was solemn. The men were told to muster on deck. There was to be a flogging.

'Christ! It's that Poplar fellow,' Harry muttered. Bart gasped. They had not been aware he'd been brought aboard their ship. They hadn't seen his surly pursuit of the carpenter as he toiled to repair leaks and damages. His face was morose and furrowed, but his eyes were alert. They hunted around his audience and Harry almost melted with guilt when they settled on him, staring venom and hate. Vengeance would be his. One day.

'This man,' began Lieutenant Strater, 'was caught in the act of desertion.'

No, he wasn't, thought Harry. *He was sent by Stokes to kidnap me and Bart.*

'Two other men who were with him managed to elude our guards and their identities are yet to be discovered.' His words were slow and deliberate. His eyes roamed over everyone, making the whole company uncomfortable and fidgety. 'If anyone knows who they were, or, if here, would like to confess…' Bart glanced furtively at Harry. Thankfully, his face was reddened by the sun of recent days; otherwise, his blushes would have been unmistakable. Both men felt their heartbeats quicken. They were sweating but no more than their fellow men in the mid-day sun. The lieutenant had paused purposely to stare at the crew's reactions but, not seeing anything decisive, continued, 'You could save this man from his flogging. It could have been hanging!' he exclaimed, 'except that he claims to be a Portuguese citizen.'

Rubbish! thought Harry. *He's Stoke's bloody mate. Give him his bloody flogging. Pity it isn't Stokes himself!* All went silent. Only the pulse of waves on the ship's bows could be heard. The lieutenant turned to the boson's mate and nodded. He took the red canvas bag from the prisoner and pulled out the cat-o-nine tails that he had been compelled to make himself. The crowd gasped at the sight of it. Whether you'd seen one before or not, it was a vicious thing, a rope left thick at one end for a handle, then divided and plaited into individual strands with knotted ends. The boson's mate unrolled it and flexed it, giving a trial crack of the thing on the deck. Wainwright had stared at Harry until he was turned to face the upturned grating. To the other men, it just looked like a fixed glare at the crowd, but Harry knew. The prisoner's wrists were tied to the grate and the first stroke lashed in. Wainwright gritted his teeth in agony but told himself he mustn't cry out. A red streak showed exactly where on his back the whip had landed. It crashed in, again and again, rhythmic, methodical. Men winced. The muscular perpetrator had administered the dose many times in the past, some more deserved than others. He was particularly spiteful in cases of buggery or unnatural sex with animals. For attempted desertion, he eased back a little. Even so, the mess he made of the fellow's back was there for all to see. The whole ritual was designed to be as much a deterrent for would-be offenders as punishment.

The sound of the whip stopped. The agony continued. Wainwright's legs had ceased to support him and he hung by his tethered wrists against the grid. He had not made a sound, but the tears were rolling uncontrollably down his face. 'Take him away,' said the lieutenant. 'Dismiss!' he yelled to the crowd.

'Wonder who those bastards were that were with him,' men were saying. Bart and Harry said it, too, to cover their guilt. "Late confused".

At the first opportunity, as Wainwright lay groaning in the sick bay, Harry paid him a visit. 'Why the hell didn't you tell on us?' he whispered to the man.

'I swore I'd take you back,' managed Wainwright. 'I've taken one hell of a flogging for you two bastards. I thought I'd cope with a bit of pain, but it was bloody murder. Take you back for Stoke's pleasure and revenge? Split on you two as deserters? Nah! When I get out of this bed, I swear somehow, I'll do for you, Smith. And your bloody Barnacle Bart!'

Chapter 26

A French accent was still a suspicious sound to residents of the south coast of England. The new Port Admiral at Norport was no exception. 'Good efening,' the young man at his door had greeted him. Port Admiral Jenkins gave him a worried glare; the young man looked surprised to see the unfamiliar face, then asked, 'Is Mister Oskins around?'

'No. He's no longer here,' said the man, another ex-navy officer. 'Who's asking?'

'I'm a relative. Sort of. He's kind of my step farzer.'

'Kind of?' queried Jenkins.

'Yes. Me and my bruzzer. We were looked after by 'im when our real farzer died.'

The story was beginning to ring true. 'Are you Mark Williamson's bruzz... I mean, *brother*?' he asked.

'*Oui, monsieur*! Andrew! Do you know where I'll find zem?'

'At the baker's shop,' he replied. 'It's called Enoch's Kitchen.'

Andrew's surprised expression returned. 'Oh! Well. Sankyou!' he said and turned to follow the direction of the man's pointing finger. '*Au revoir*!'

He soon found the little shop and studied the inscription. 'Enoch's Kitchen! Quel surprise!'

He opened the door, causing a newly installed bell to jangle above his head. Mark looked hard at the visitor. He was silhouetted against the light from outside, but he was still recognisable. 'Andy?' he gasped. The two brothers laughed in delight. They fell into each other's arms and hugged for a full minute before Andy pulled away to study his brother's physique. 'You've grown!' he observed. 'Taller anyway. You still look just as weedy!'

'Ha! Thanks!' said Mark. 'What about you? A little *podgier,* I think!'

The two laughed and grinned, revelling in glorious reunion, ignoring Helen's curious look. Enoch walked in to investigate the din. There was instant recognition and again, this was followed by a hug. 'Are you well?' enquired Enoch. 'You look well! A little rounder, perhaps!'

'Oh, you people!' declared Andy. 'You're so quick with your insults! I might sound a bit Froggy, but I'm not ze bloody enemy!' They all laughed, and Enoch noticed Helen's concern. 'Mark's brother!' he added needlessly.

'Andy, this is my cook and assistant.' He hadn't needed to make up a false name for her yet and so had to think of one quickly. He could only think of the previous owners and said, 'Miss Brown!'

'Pleased to meet you, Miss Brown,' said Andy, his eyes enlarging even though he couldn't see much of her face. She smiled with her eyes and nodded her head.

'Look after the shop for a while, will you,' said Enoch to Miss Brown. 'We'll go through to the back. We've got a lot of catching up to do!'

They talked for a long time. Andy described his artistic tuition and some of the great artists he had seen at work. He had sat at their shoulder as they depicted scenes of the city in all weathers and moods, of beauty, serenity, death and revolution. It was not a good time to be English in Paris. While France's other neighbours were capitulating to Bonaparte's new regime, England, as always, stood its ground. Andy's teachers suggested in no uncertain terms that it would be a good time for him to return home. He packed his paintings into a square canvas bag, his other few belongings into a leather hold-all, and left via Belgium, glancing furtively back over his shoulder. 'And when I get here,' he went on, 'instead of feeling like a horrible English Rosbif in France, I feel like a horrible Frenchie Frog in England!'

Mark and Enoch laughed. 'That Froggy twang will soon wear off,' said Enoch. 'And we're all feeling a lot safer here now that the Spanish have been beaten. You'll be free to wander around painting whatever you like!'

'But what about you, Enoch? How come you've become a baker?'

Enoch stuttered a little. Of course, he had not even told Mark the full story. He had simply said that he was tired of the old job and wanted to try something different. He had noticed that the little baker's shop was up for sale and that he could purchase it with the proceeds of the sale of his own house plus savings he had put by. There was no mention of Richard Westhouse's involvement. He churned out the same tale to Andy, except that he said Helen was the orphaned daughter of a friend who had died at sea. Mark managed to keep a straight face.

'So you took her under your kind wing,' said Andy. 'The same as you did for me and Mark. That makes her our half-half-step-sister or something, doesn't it?'

'Something like that.' Laughed Enoch. Then Andy broached the more serious subject. 'Will you be able to accommodate me here?'

Enoch looked thoughtful, but Mark had already considered this. 'It's only small,' said the younger brother, 'but I reckon there'll be room for you in my little attic. Come on. I'll show you.'

Andy smiled. 'What a kind little *brother* I've got.'

Mark led the way up the stairs and opened the door. Enoch returned to the shop. '*Zut alors*!' gasped Andy. 'It's so small! And only a single bed!'

'There's one underneath,' returned Mark. 'You slide it out and it's like a camp bed.'

'Oh well. I suppose I can't be too fussy. Isn't there a bigger bedroom? Just over the shop?'

'There's two. One's Enoch's. One's Miss Brown's.'

'Oh, she lives here too?'

'Of yes.' Mark continued with Enoch's tale. 'He's promised to look after the girl and taking it seriously.'

The two of them sat down on the bed, reflective.

'Enoch seems to think we're all safe to carry on with life now we're not going to be invaded,' mused Mark.

'Ha! Well, I wouldn't be so sure,' replied Andy. 'That Spanish skirmish was just a distraction, I think. The French will rebuild. They'll be able to invade on their own given time. Then we get an Emperor instead of that crummy Hanoverian King we've got now.'

Mark looked a little puzzled. 'King George? Crummy? Why d'you say that?'

'You call him the "Farmer King", don't you? Don't sound very regal. Or the "mad Hanoverian". They say he's just a little crazy in the head.'

'I don't know. He's a good Protestant. That's all I know.'

'Does that make him a good king? Who's he ever defeated?'

'Nobody. You don't have to go around *defeating* people these days.'

'Bonaparte does. He's whipping the rest of Europe. If he comes here, there'll be no more kings and prime ministers. Just '*Vive l'Empereur*!' Andy's last remark was accompanied by a clenched fist.

Mark looked disgusted, saying. 'The Frogs will never get past our navy.'

Andy sensed that his brother was becoming emotionally patriotic and bit his lip.

'Anyway,' he continued. 'You're seventeen now, eh? Have you, er, been with a girl yet?'

Mark blushed. He didn't want to appear too unworldly. 'Of course,' he managed. 'How about you?'

'Ha! I left a few broken hearts behind in Paris,' he bragged. 'Those Paris girls! I tell you, when they find out you're an artist, they want to throw off their clothes and have you paint them in the nude.'

Mark gaped, impressed.

'And then,' the elder brother went on, 'if they haven't got the francs to pay for the painting, they do a little more posing. In my bed!'

'Wow,' said Mark. 'Now you've got me wishing I could paint.'

'Anyway,' said Andy. 'This girl of yours. What was she like?

'Oh, a bit older than me. She'd done it before. Taught me a lot, I can tell you.'

'That's the sort you want. For a start. So, where do we go around here? To pick up girls?'

'The tavern, I suppose. Just up the street.'

'Or,' said Andy, eyes twinkling, 'why go out when our lovely half-half-step-sister is just downstairs. That can't be illegal, can it?'

Again, Mark looked disgusted. 'Enoch's supposed to be protecting her from the evil fellows of this world, let alone her kindly half-brothers.'

'Nah! I reckon she'd be up for it. Tell you what, little brother, let's have a challenge like we used to do with other things. First to get her into bed!'

'Ha! That's not fair! One look at your paint brushes and she'll fall straight into your arms.' He'd wanted to say, 'I've already beaten you to it, along with half the navy,' but he held back.

'Sounds good to me! I reckon she's pretty good-looking under all that disguise. Gorgeous eyes, anyway. That's about all I could see! Hopefully, I'll get to see a lot more!'

Chapter 27

'Come on then, you lucky lads,' said the lieutenant. 'No more of this blockading bollocks for you!'

Harry and Bart glanced at each other. 'D'you mean we're going home, sir?' asked Bart, excited.

'Don't be silly, lad.' The officer smirked. 'You know us better than that! You're off on a little mission with Mr Nelson. That's *Rear Admiral Nelson* now.'

'Christ!' uttered Harry. 'The men all said he was on his way to the top. They'll follow him anywhere. Me too. Where are we off to, sir?'

'You'll find out. Now, get your things together and report to the "jolly boat" at three bells.'

'Aye aye, sir,' said Harry in his naval correctness, then, 'what the hell's going on?' he muttered to Bart.

The British were going to continue their blockade of Cadiz, where the escaped Spanish ships were skulking, but a squadron had been detailed to Tenerife, where the Dons were hiding their treasure ships bearing gold from the Americas. Nelson was in charge of the British squadron. They were to join him on the *Theseus*, a seventy-four gun, third-rate ship of the line, the same as *Adventurer* and *Captain*. She had barely been damaged in the recent battle and re-stocked in Gibraltar, so she was ready to go.

Nelson, in particular, tried to tempt the Spanish out of Cadiz, but there was no way they would oblige. In one skirmish, Harry heard that John Sykes, Nelson's constant protector and Old Agamemnon pal, had died protecting his hero, even taking a cutlass blow to the head to save the charismatic leader's life. He had followed him into hell once too often. 'I can quite understand him doing that,' mused Harry, 'Poor bastard!'

Helen flung the dough down on the table. Frustrated and weary, she scattered a liberal handful of flour and then flung the dough down again before attacking it with the rolling pin.

'Christ, I'm fed up with this!' she muttered. 'Why the hell can't Harry just walk in through that door and whisk me away to God knows where? They've beaten the bloody Spanish. Surely, they can do without him and Barty now! That's if they're still alive!'

'What are you muttering on about?' enquired Enoch, who had appeared at the door.

'Harry Smith!' replied the girl. 'Still no letter from him or from my brother. Do you really think they're still alive, Enoch, or are you just kidding me along?'

Enoch gave her a sincere look, almost apologetic. 'I just don't know,' he said at last. 'I don't know any more than you do. Just believe, eh? Pray and hope.'

He was standing quite close and it just happened naturally. They smiled into each other's eyes, and they hugged. Helen buried her head in his chest. He could tell she was sobbing and wiping her tears on his sweater. His hands gently caressed her back. She looked up at him, eyes wet and magnified. Both loved the feel of each other's bodies. Neither knew what to say.

'Those deliveries ready yet?' shouted Mark as he strode into the room. He stopped dead in his tracks, embarrassed. The two pulled away from their embrace.

'Yes,' said Helen in a matter-of-fact tone. 'On the shelf.' All three felt awkward. Mark took the basket and carried it to the back door. 'See you later,' he said as he disappeared, thinking, I knew all the time he fancied her. But not half as much as I do!

Harry and Bart climbed into the little boat that was ferrying men around the fleet. Bart looked a bit sickly. 'You'll enjoy this,' said the bargeman. 'Up and down like a whore's knickers!' They all laughed. Oars plunged and pulled. Men strained. Bart braced his stomach against the pitch and roll. It was hard work. They were all relieved to pull up alongside the *Theseus* and clamber aboard on the slippery rope ladders.

'Another new home,' breathed Harry.

'Just wish we knew where the hell we're going,' said Bart.

'Welcome aboard, men,' came a voice, a voice they seemed to recognise. It was midshipman Lawrence, only now in the uniform of a lieutenant. 'Christ! I mean, thank you, sir!'

'Surprised to see me a lieutenant, eh, Smith?'

'Yes, sir. I mean, I'm very pleased for you, sir. All that studying and stuff you were always doing.'

'Hard work pays off in the end, Smith, and of course, it helps when a couple of other offices get despatched in battle. You move up the list! I'm the most junior, of course, Fourth Lieutenant, but still, it's a start. Look at the Watch and Station Bill; see where you're wanted.'

'Well. Nice to *know* we're wanted, I suppose,' said Bart. 'Can you tell us where we're going yet, sir?'

'Not yet, Westhouse. You'll find out in good time.'

***

The letter that landed on Matthew Stokes' desk was a mysterious affair. Obviously censored by the navy, it was a mess of part obliterated sentences and ink blots; Wainwright's usually immaculate writing had become a pathetic scrawl. The gist of what remained was as follows:

'My dear Matthew. Whilst carrying out my occupation as a fisherman, I was mistaken for a deserting British sailor. I am now, by fate, in the British Navy and have been given permission to write to you to request evidence vouching for my Portuguese nationality. This, I trust, will secure my release. In the meantime, I am serving as a carpenter's mate and have played my part in a great battle, but I am somewhat injured and incapacitated, which is the reason for my poor handwriting. Please send the document as soon as possible so that I can resume my lawful occupation. Kind regards, Poplar Wainwright.'

Matthew sighed. 'Bloody fool. Bloody, bloody, incompetent fool! What bloody document? There isn't any! You're the illegitimate product of a drunken British sailor and a Lisbon whore. As long as you want me to keep that secret, you do all the dirty work I ask. You think you've got a wonderful certification of birth, like some royal prince or other? You know damn well you've not! There's nothing I can do, my friend. You're just making a show of all this for the benefit of the navy. You're stuck with them just like Smith, till such time as they throw you out. What's happened to Smith and Westhouse, anyway? That's what I want to know. You were supposed to be on your way back with them by now. Did they escape or what? That's probably what all this blacked-out stuff is about. What a mess, Wainwright. What a total bloody mess. Good God, Helen Westhouse, the trouble you've caused me! I wish I'd never seen your bloody face! And when I do catch up with you again, my dear, which I'm sure I will, I'm going to wring your bloody neck!'

Chapter 28

'It's Tenerife.'

'Where the hell's that?' muttered Harry, attracting a stare from Lieutenant Lawrence, who wasn't supposed to hear.

'Which, as some of you will know,' Lawrence continued pointedly, 'is just a little way down the African coast. About a day's sailing should do it. We have a wonderful plan to bring honour and glory to our country, not to mention considerable wealth. Due to our brave and magnificent victory over the Spanish fleet, the remnants of which are blockaded in Cadiz, Spanish treasure ships from the New World have had to divert to Tenerife, a Spanish possession, for shelter. Our plan is to bring utter devastation to the Dons following our victory by raiding the main harbour, Santa Cruz, and taking their damned treasure ships as prizes, cargo and all!'

A loud cheer went up amongst the men. Lawrence knew how to deliver a speech. Even the weariest amongst them looked bright-eyed at the news. Prizes meant money shared by everyone, and these sounded like big prizes. They went back to their duties with a new sense of purpose, their strength and enthusiasm re-found. Lawrence walked over to Harry and Bart, who had not shared the celebration. They would so much prefer to be going home.

'The good news for you fellows is that after this little skirmish, you pressed men will be allowed home if that's what you want.' A smile creased their lips at last. 'Thank you, sir,' muttered Harry with professional sincerity. Inside, his heart did somersaults.

'No more letters for a while, though,' said Lawrence.

'This is a secret mission. We'll be out of touch with the main fleet for some time.' 'Christ Bart!' groaned Harry. 'We should have written back to Helen before now.'

'Don't worry,' said Bart. 'You heard what the man said. We'll be home soon. You'll be able to tell her in person!'

Poplar Wainwright groaned every time he moved. Sometimes, tears would come to his eyes. In spite of the surgeon's best efforts of administering lotions and dressings, his wounded back kept searing; it was a reminder of the flogging. His mind was tormented by conflict. 'Do I preserve Smith for Stokes' pleasure as I'm expected to do, or do I kill the bastard for causing me all this pain? Him and that bloody Bart Westhouse!' One way or the other, he'd keep sight of his quarry. He volunteered for the Tenerife squadron, quelling surprise by saying, 'I'd rather die as cannon fodder than of boredom hanging around here.'

'One blasted ship!' moaned Nelson, accompanying the words with a thump of his fist on the table. 'One blasted ship, and that most probably unloaded and its cargo stashed away in some harbour stronghold. When Blake attacked Santa Cruz, he captured a whole fleet. What will the history books make of Nelson when he takes one measly ship?'

Captains Troubridge, Hood and Freemantle looked shocked. Nelson had written to Admiral Jervis outlining his plan, describing the wealth that could be won by taking the treasure ships. The Spanish had pre-empted the attack by diverting these ships to other ports in Africa. They had also put artillery on the high grounds overlooking Santa Cruz. They were determined not to be disgraced by the British again. Nelson was determined not to fail.

'We take the whole damned island!' he expounded. 'We're not to be blessed by the backing of our land army, but we have marines plenty and our brave navy boys. We just need some favourable winds and currents to get our fleet close in, then we go ashore in boats. They won't resist.

'We're with you, Horatio,' said Troubridge after some discussion amongst the other captains. Let's really ram home our victory over their fleet. Let's teach those Dons that they don't side up against the British. We can have the landing force ready in a couple of days. Let's do it!'

Nelson smiled.

Harry winced. 'More cutlass practice?' he groused when he was given the news. He and Bart went through the motions again. It had stood them in good stead on the

San Nicolas. 'Just keep thinking of it as a sickle,' he told himself. 'Harvest that wheat!'

There would be no cannon drill for the time being. The heavy artillery was not going to be used, just guile and courage and a show of strength. Tenerife would fall easily into their hands.

In the two days promised, the landing force was ready. 'After this skirmish, we're off home,' muttered Bart. Harry nodded contentedly. He was proud to have been selected for Nelson's barge crew. There were Old Agamemnons and a couple each from the *Captain* and the *Theseus*. They were joined by Nelson's stepson, Lieutenant Josiah Nisbet, although Nelson had told him to stay behind to take charge of the *Theseus* should anything happen to him.

The lad refused, saying, 'I'm sure this dear ship can look after itself. I'm coming with you now even if I never do again.' Nelson couldn't refuse. Nisbet may not have had Nelson's blood in his veins, but he had certainly acquired his spirit.

The hour was come. It was dark and bitter. Eleven o'clock at night. Men climbed into boats quietly and calmly. Marines had bayonets fixed, solemn glares. Sailors had hatchets and cutlass. Hearts beat hard. Stomachs churned.

Harry dipped and pulled on his oar, timely with his colleagues, although choppy sea and surf made conditions hard. The shoreline slept. Each stroke of the oars brought them closer through the waves. "Up and down like a whore's knickers" came back into his mind, and he chuckled, bringing an inquisitive stare from Lieutenant Nisbet. Men dipped and pulled on the oars. Dipped, pulled and dipped again, guiding the boat into shallow, raging surf. Then, a grating sound of sand underneath them. Men leapt out. Nelson leapt out as he always would. First in line. Glory or death. His stare was set firmly on the alluring coast. He drew his sword with the words 'Follow me!' Men followed. Then a crack! An awful sound and a splattering of blood and flesh as Nelson's elbow appeared to explode right in front of Harry's face. The sword span from Nelson's right hand as the musket ball hit home. He twisted around and incredibly caught it in his left. He treasured that sword with his life. It belonged to his uncle Maurice Suckling; he would never let it go. Blood had splattered, warm, onto Harry's face. He closed his eyes and reeled. Had the ball not hit Nelson's arm, it would have hit Harry between the eyes. *I should be the one protecting you*, thought Harry. *Not the other way round.*

Cannon and musket opened up from the shore, cracking and flashing, reflected in the sea. Nisbet got Nelson down into the boat, blood spilling freely. 'Get us afloat!' he yelled to men standing in the sea, shocked and static, faces afraid. They shoved, cursed and battled with the waves, got her afloat and leapt back in. 'Under the cliff where the batteries can't reach us!' yelled Nisbet over the din. 'Give me cloth!' he went on, anxious eyes glaring, 'Anything!'

One man hauled off his shirt and tore it into strips. Nisbet tied it tight to stop the bleeding. Harry gave him his purple scarf, saying, 'Use this as a sling!' Even at a time like this, the scarf caused a picture of Molly Elizabeth to flash into his mind, her beautiful naked body against that rough old door. Nelson's eyes were rolling, seeing angels and death. One fair-skinned angel stared straight at him and began to beckon. He had never seen such a beautiful face or been lured by such a curvaceous form. She was smiling, glowing, warm. It would be so easy to let go of worldly cares and fall into her arms, that soft, devouring bosom. She reminded him of someone he once knew, a reminder of the distant past when times were tranquil and life serene. Her hand reached out to stroke his troubled brow. 'Sir! Sir! Stay with us!' a stern voice was yelling, interrupting his peaceful surrender. His eyes focussed on the worried face of a sailor. 'Come on, sir! Stay with us!' repeated Harry Smith.

Nelson was wincing with pain and staring disbelievingly at the blood-soaked bandages on his arm. He struggled up to peer out of the boat. Cannon raged and ravaged all along the sea wall. Boats were slewing sideways in the surf. Some spilt their occupants overboard. Men were swimming, wading, protecting their muskets. It was very clear to Nelson that things were not going well. Then it got worse. Much worse. The *Fox* cutter was ripped open as a cannonball hit her on the rise. When she dipped again, she dipped for good. Dozens of men screamed in unison, in terror. Arms flailed on the surface. Faces gasped and spat. 'Get to them!' yelled Nelson. Nisbet hauled the tiller across. Men strained on the oars.

Harry stared at the scene. It was somehow becoming familiar. The sea seethed in purple and white. It was the dream. The horrible dream that disturbed his nights. Purple mist and shadows, and the face, the face! Yes! It was there! The terrified features of a drowning man were right alongside him. He let go of the oar and grabbed the head, pulling, heaving. The man gasped at the precious air.

'Oh God!' surged through Harry's brain. He stared at the man's features. It was a man he knew well. A man who had sworn to kill him. Poplar Wainwright! He wanted to let him go. He couldn't be blamed for failing in such difficult circumstances.

'Let him go!' said the voice in his head. But he couldn't. Icy fingers reached up and grabbed the back of Harry's head, pulling him down, down into the freezing darkness. 'Wake up!' shrieked the voice. 'You don't have to die! It's a dream!' but it wasn't. He would sink into oblivion. Then, another sensation. Something was pulling at his back. His head re-emerged from the foam and his lungs filled with air. The hand on his back was Horatio Nelson's remaining good one. The leader had saved his life once again. Other men joined in, heaving, straining, pulling. First, Harry and then Wainwright were hauled into the boat. Wainwright lay unconscious, breathing shallowly, in a strange state, somewhere between life and death. Others were being rescued, hauled half-drowned from icy graves.

'Back to the ships!' yelled Nisbet, and the men pulled the oars, needing more effort against the heavier load. The nearest ship was the *Seahorse,* but Nelson refused to go aboard it, saying, 'I'd rather suffer death than have poor Mrs Freemantle see me in this state when I can give her no tidings whatever of her husband!'

They rowed on to the *Theseus,* where Nelson said that he knew the arm would have to be amputated, and 'the sooner the better!' He turned down the offer of help to get aboard, saying, 'Throw me down a rope! I've still got one good arm and two legs!' They threw him the rope and he astonished everyone by twisting it around his left wrist and clambering up the side of the ship.

'Christ!' marvelled Harry. 'For a little fellow, he hasn't half got some strength!'

'It's all from the heart,' said Nisbet, staring upwards. 'All heart.'

'Unload these poor wounded souls,' grumbled Nelson. 'Then get back and rescue more!'

Chapter 29

Sunlight streamed in through the huge stern windows of *Theseus'* state cabin. The ship bobbed at anchor. Nelson sat in a reflective mood, glancing down from time to time at the empty sleeve as if needing to convince himself that it had really happened. Not just his own ignominy but that of the British Navy and the nation it represented. 'Could we ever really claim superiority over bloody Spain?' he pondered, 'especially combined with the blasted French, who're unstoppable on land.' He peered with his one good eye at the sad scene outside the window. Boats and barges still rowed solemnly around the fleet, trying to return the retreating sailors and marines to their respective ships. There were far fewer than set out on that fateful night. The retreat had been honourable enough. In fact, plenty of the British had managed to land their barges safely and storm the town square, but there they had discovered a kind of stalemate. The Spanish had far more land forces than expected, but wouldn't risk an attack against the bayonet, pike and cutlass of the British. Neither could they use their heavy artillery, which would have destroyed their beautiful town. Captain Hood was sent into the governor's office, where he was told he should surrender his people as prisoners of war. Hood's terms, however, were that the

British would not "molest" the Spanish at the point of the bayonet if they were allowed to return peacefully to their fleet. This was the amicable agreement made; the Spanish even offered assistance with boats and the sale of supplies. Nelson shook his head sadly and glanced down again at the empty sleeve.

'I suppose I should try to manage the quill in my left hand,' he murmured. 'The admiral will be waiting for news.' He picked up the quill, fingering it awkwardly before settling on the best possible grip, dipped it in ink and began the difficult task.

'My dear sir,' he scrawled, 'I become a burden to my friends and useless to my country.' A teardrop splashed onto the page. He screwed it up and began to write the same thing again.

'Still no news?' enquired Enoch. Helen just shot a disgusted look and threw more dough onto the table. 'He's dead!' she croaked. So's Bart! I know it!' She kneaded at the shapeless lump with unnecessary vigour, throwing on more flour. 'They know I'm worried sick that they were blown up with their ship. They'd have written by now if they were still alive!'

'No, no. Not necessarily.' Enoch's voice was calm and soothing. 'The navy can be real funny about letters, especially just after a battle. They don't want information leaking out until they've given their own full account of it. Then there's a matter of priorities. Things have to be put back into shape, mended and fixed. Writing and sending letters? Well, that kind of gets pushed down the list.'

Helen had stopped kneading and looked up at Enoch. She wiped the tear away just before it dropped onto her work. 'You're such a darling, Enoch,' she muttered. 'I don't know where I'd be without you. Oh, actually, I do. Still at that knocking shop with the memory of Matthew Stokes on top of me. The fear it might happen again.'

'No, you're safe here, my dear. No one has the faintest idea who you are. Helen of Troy has disappeared off the face of the Earth.'

'But what if Harry never comes back, Enoch? What if he really is dead?'

'Well, we'll just have to cross that bridge when we come to it, I mean "if".'

Enoch expected some kind of rebuke for his slip. It didn't come. The dough became the recipient of a long and weary kneading as Helen tried to put her fears out of her head. Her thoughts turned over and over. Something else was troubling her, something more commonplace. It was Mark's brother who had drawn her into conversation the night before.

'How good an artist is Andy?' she asked, apparently out of the blue.

'I don't know, my dear. Why do you ask?'

'He said he could paint my portrait if I wanted, that's all. Only I asked if I could see some of his work, and he said 'no'. There wasn't anything suitable. Yet I know he's got a bagful of his work upstairs.'

'Well, let's go and sneak a look,' said Enoch with almost childlike secrecy. 'He'll be out for the rest of the day with those new friends of his. Let's see what he's been up to with his Paris masters.'

The two of them went upstairs, then further up to the attic. Yes, his canvas bag of paintings stood in one corner. Enoch picked it up and laid it on the bed. The top picture was a beautiful array of flowers. The two observers nodded and smiled with approval. Then, more "still life". Fruit, wine bottles, then trees in a park and some beautiful buildings. Andy certainly had a talent.

'Oh!' said Enoch, a little surprised and embarrassed as he turned over the next painting.

A naked lady stared out seductively at him. 'Well,' said Helen. 'I hope he doesn't expect to paint me like that!' Enoch turned hurriedly to the next and the next, but they had the same theme. At last, something more decent. Scenes of Paris, but some of them were a little gruesome. A guillotine, severed heads and blood. Again, Enoch turned them quickly. The last painting was very odd. Undoubtedly, Emperor Napoleon Bonaparte stood in a triumphant pose in front of a castle-like building. There was no mistaking the famous ramparts of the Tower of London! Even Helen recognised them from pictures in her father's books. Both looked aghast. In an attempt to be diplomatic, Enoch interpreted the title "Notre Reve" as being 'Our Nightmare'. He knew very well that it meant 'Our Dream'.

At last, Harry and Bart met up again. Bart was full of his adventure, having been one of those fortunate enough to have landed on the beach and followed the thorough marines over the defended lines and batteries. He had only had to wield the cutlass once when a Spanish defender rose from his wounded position to swing a sword at him. Bart had parried the weapon before delivering a mighty blow to the assailant's head. He didn't see the outcome. He just kept on going, but he heard the continuing clamour behind him as the opponent finally succumbed to the following sailors. Harry told his far more gripping tale of how he had saved Nelson from bleeding to death and been saved by him in return. 'Bloody shame we couldn't take the island, though!' concluded Bart. 'We could have told everyone back home that we helped take Tenerife for Britain!'

'Yep,' said Harry. 'Also, a shame about poor Nelson. One eye, and now only one arm. He's going to have to retire now. There's no way he can carry on like that.'

'Knowing him, he's probably got other ideas!' said Bart.

'Oh, bloody hell!' cursed Harry, remembering another vital part of the story. You'll never guess who I saved from drowning.'

'Who?'

'That bloody "Poplar" fellow!'

'No! Oh, Christ! What was he doing here?'

'Same as us, I suppose. Doing one last job to get his freedom to go back home.'

'And you saved him? I doubt if *he'd* have saved *you!* He wants your blood! *Our* blood!'

'I know. Can you imagine how I felt when I realised it was *him*? I wanted to drop him back in the sea, but there were too many others involved. We had to save the bastard. Saved a lot more fellows, too. That *Fox* must have lost half her men—'

'Right, you lot,' interrupted a lieutenant. 'As you know, Mr Nelson has suffered an awful injury. Right arm amputated. Very nasty.'

The tars nodded solemnly. The lieutenant saw that he had attracted a sizable group and waited for them to assemble more closely before continuing.

'He's to go back to England immediately to have it properly seen to. You pressed men who are fit enough to form the crew of the *Seahorse,* along with a few more experienced fellows. Pressed men will then be at liberty to leave if you so desire, or of course, you could volunteer to become regular sailors in His Majesty's Britannic Navy!' He didn't mind the few expected cat calls that greeted his comment.

Bart and Harry grinned heartily at each other. 'We're on our way home, Harry!' said Bart. Harry just nodded, his eyes beginning to glaze, thoughts of Helen looming large and filling his head.

***

That night, Enoch stopped outside Helen's bedroom door. He wondered what kind of courage it would take to turn the handle and walk in as he yearned to do. 'You're such a darling,' her words came back to him. 'I don't know where I'd be without you.'

'She really likes you,' he told himself. 'She sees you as her saviour. That hug before Mark came in and interrupted us felt so good. Can you really go on wanting her like this? For God's sake, Enoch, do something about it!'

He saw his hand on the handle. It turned. The door swung open. He heard her gasp. She was sitting up in bed, reading a romantic novel. 'Enoch.' She breathed. 'What do you want?'

He heard himself say, 'To share the pleasures of your bed with you.'

There was another short gasp and a few moments of silence. She saw the hope and expectancy in his eyes. It had taken all his courage. He had been so kind to her. So gentle, reassuring. He had been her salvation. Her heart was melting. 'Was Harry ever going to come home?' she asked herself. There wasn't an answer. She looked into his eyes and saw silent desire. She put down the book and pushed the blanket away.

Chapter 30

The makeshift crew of the *Seahorse* cheered as they hoisted Nelson's pendent on the mast. He would always be their hero no matter what the history books made of him. As well as the fit and able seamen, there were the "walking wounded" bandaged and lotioned, limping on crutches, arms in slings. The worst cases had beds of straw in the hospital room, where they lay in rows under the surgeon's watchful eye. He had laudanum to administer to ease their pain, or rum or wine or beer. He couldn't offer them much hope. They were slowly succumbing to gangrene or tetanus. He fed them and bathed them with the help of a few orderlies and stitched a few into hammocks for burial at sea. Bart was one of those who "volunteered" to assist and was sent to get cannon balls for the weighing down of the bodies. He watched the surgeon stitch them in at the deceased's feet and then proceed up the hammock with the needle and thread, finally administering the last stitch, as tradition demanded, through the man's nose to ensure and demonstrate that he was, in fact, dead. He helped to remove the "good luck" trinkets from around the corpse's necks and wrists, although traditional tokens such as wren's tail feathers had demonstrably failed.

'Is it Johnny Sapphire?' whispered a voice behind Harry.

'Or Johnny Bloody Blue John?' He wheeled around and could hardly believe it. The melancholy of the sickly surroundings disappeared. It was the ever-smiling Jelzina! She couldn't help herself. She planted a meaningful kiss on his cheek, adding to his surprised expression.

'What the hell are you doing here?' he gasped.

'I'm following you,' she replied calmly. '*Adventurer, Captain, Theseus, Seahorse.* You may not always have known it, but I was on them all!'

'My God,' he replied, still trying to master his astonishment. 'And are you still plying your usual trade?'

'Oh, yes. I'm also a nice, respectable nurse, though, sometimes.'

'Ha! I've heard there's no such thing as a respectable nurse!'

They smiled deeply into each other's eyes. They had been through a lot. Battles, boredom, the small matter of the blue john stone that he had so wanted back. 'Did you ever get it made into a ring?' she asked.

'Yes.' He pulled out his leather pouch and produced the ring. The carpenter had entwined the stone in copper for him. It was quite a sight.

'Wow!' said Jelzina. 'Can I try it on?'

'Of course,' said Harry. 'But there's no way you get to keep it.'

'Not even if I make your toes curl like last time?'

'No way.'

'I know. You're saving it for that lucky girlie of yours back home. That's if she hasn't given up on you thinking you were blown up with poor *Adventurer*.'

Harry's face furrowed into worry. 'She wouldn't have heard about that, would she?'

''Course she would. Oh God, don't tell me you never let her know you'd changed ship, you bloody fool!'

'I don't know. I mean, oh Christ. I can't remember!'

'Hoo, hoo,' said Jelzina meaningfully.

Harry responded with, 'We weren't allowed, were we, to send letters while we were on the Santa Cruz thing?'

'No. But don't tell me you didn't have a chance before that. I reckon she thinks you're dead.'

'Ah, don't say that,' said Harry. 'You've got me really worried now.'

A bell rang out eight times. It was the end of the second dog watch.

'I'll have to go!' said Jelzina. 'I'm back on duty as "Nurse Janet".'

'Hey! Give me the ring back first!'

'Spoilsport!' she moaned and pulled it off her finger. 'Come down and see me sometime, eh? I've got a cosy little place down on the orlop. Get you back in practice for that girlie of yours if you ever find her again. What's her name, by the way?'

'It's Helen. She's Bart's sister. He's as worried about her as I am, but we think she's all right from her last letter.'

'Don't worry, my love,' breathed Jelzina. 'I'm sure she'll be there waiting for you!'

Harry's head was tinged with doubt.

He couldn't help himself. Later that evening, he found himself wandering down to the orlop deck. Her green eyes lit up when she saw him there. He smiled, they caressed, the dress tumbled from her shoulders and she loved the weakening glaze in his eyes as they took in the splendour of her breasts. He was lost but as powerful as ever. Jelzina groaned and sighed with delight. She didn't have to pretend. They lay on the straw, exhausted and spent. She nuzzled up against his chest, his arm around her, his hand curling onto her breast. Her fingers played in the hair on his chest.

'You *are* the best I ever "'ad",' she muttered and he had to believe her.

'Just tell me one thing,' she went on in a more serious tone.

'What's that?' enquired Harry, curious.

'You weren't the ones who tried to desert with that man who was flogged.'

Harry sat up, shocked. 'No!' he lied. 'Whatever made you think that?'

'Just the ship's log,' she said calmly. 'On the *Captain*. It said "run" next to you and Westhouse. Then it was crossed out and changed to "late confused". You were the only ones late. It made me think.'

'Well, don't think so bloody hard!' groused Harry. 'We had got on *Culloden* by mistake! There were similar names to mine and Bart's. When it was sorted out, we got ourselves onto the *Captain*, quick as we could!'

'Fine!' said Jelzina. 'I'm sorry. I had to ask. I'm surprised nobody else has seen it, though, and suspected something.'

'Well, nobody else has,' groaned Harry.

'Good,' went on Jelzina. 'Let's just hope they don't.'

Chapter 31

'He's in the sick bay,' muttered Bart.

'Who?'

'The man you saved. The man who tried to fool us into deserting straight into the hands of Matthew Stokes. The man we know as "Poplar". Poplar Wainwright's his full name. He's lying there moaning and groaning. God only knows where his mind is. His body's barely hanging on to life.'

'Good,' returned Harry. 'The world will be a better place without that bastard. I still can't believe I saved him from drowning! Should have just let him go!'

'Well, something's keeping him alive. Probably still thinks he can get you back to Stokes or get some kind of revenge for the flogging that he took for us.'

'Bloody ungrateful bastard!' spat Harry. 'I saved his life!'

'Yeah, well, he probably doesn't realise that. He was pretty far gone when they fished him out of that boat.'

'Perhaps I should go and see him,' mused Harry. 'Put him straight.'

'You'd better make it quick,' said Bart. 'Before he departs this world!'

Harry opened the hospital door. The stench was terrible. He put his hand to his face to shield his mouth and nose but couldn't stop the awful penetration. The lighting was dim from odd lanterns that swung with the motion of the ship. Cries and moans came spasmodically from the dying souls. 'This is hell!' muttered Harry to no one in particular and walked along the first row of unfortunates, then the second. The last man he came to in one corner was the white, emaciated Wainwright. Lying on his back, eyes closed, the skin stretched thinly over his nose, his mouth gaped in its fight for shallow breaths. 'Christ,' muttered Harry. 'You're all but gone.' Then he stepped back, just a little alarmed, as Wainwright's eyes flickered open. They stared at Harry, full of hate. This was what kept him alive! Wainwright was trying to speak, but it was incomprehensible. If Harry could have discerned the man's words, he'd have understood.

'That's the man!' the words boomed in from the doorway. Harry swung around to see a lieutenant pointing in his direction. The other man who appeared from behind him was slightly shorter. His hair was a blaze of silver in the sunlight, his right sleeve pinned empty against his side.

'Late confused,' the words sprang guiltily into Harry's mind, and he suddenly realised the implications of being seen as an associate of the supposed deserter, but they weren't the next words he heard. 'The one in the corner,' went on the lieutenant.

'Does he mean me?' muttered Harry. 'I'm done for! A bloody deserter! I'll get the rope!' Harry held his breath, heart thumping hard. "Wainwright, his name is" were the next words Harry heard and he allowed himself the luxury of breathing out a slow, controlled sigh of relief. 'Claims to be Portuguese, but nobody really knows. He sent a letter to his employer asking him to vouch for him, but there's been no reply. Anyway, I reckon he'd pass for you with a bit of sprucing up!' The words were a mystery to Harry, but thank God! He wasn't being accused.

The two men approached and Harry stood back to accommodate their closer inspection of the recumbent man. 'You must be joking,' said Nelson. 'This man's at death's door. This is the fellow Smith here and I saved from drowning.'

'With a bit of care from our surgeon, sir, he'll be fit enough to sit in a carriage and wave to his adoring crowd, er, that is, *your* adoring crowd, sir. We'll strap one arm to his chest to give him an empty sleeve and an eye patch.'

'An eye patch?' complained Nelson. 'I've never worn an eye patch!'

'No sir, I know,' the lieutenant stuttered. 'But people will have heard you've lost an eye. It's what they'd expect to see.'

'Hmm, well, I'll leave it to you, lieutenant,' said Nelson, who then turned and looked squarely at Harry.

'So, Smith,' he began.

'Yes sir,' said Harry, surprised that his hero would engage him in conversation.

'I hope I thanked you properly for saving my life again the other day.'

'Oh, well, I was *one* of those who helped, sir.'

'Hmm. Modesty, eh? I like that in a man.'

The dim light made it impossible to see that Harry was blushing. Far from the harsh accusation he had feared about being Wainwright's co-deserter, he was being praised.

'I've got something of yours in my cabin,' went on Nelson. 'Report to me there and I'll give it back. Oh, and bring that pal of yours, Westhouse. I've got a task that I think will be right up your street.'

'Yes, sir,' said Harry, curious, confused. He watched the officers leave and turned again towards Wainwright. 'Seems like you're not allowed to die yet, Poplar Wainwright. More's the pity!'

***

'So, how do you want me?' said Helen.

Naked in my bed, thought Andy, but over by the window, came out instead.

'I've never done this before,' she went on. 'You'll have to excuse my naivety.'

'I'll excuse my half-half-step-sister anything,' said Andy, oozing charm. 'Just sit there very still and look at that crack in the wall.'

'Oh God. That's not very interesting,' she complained. 'Can't I read or something?'

'No, no. Now, come on. You have to be a good girl and keep still for me. It won't be for too long. You are a very interesting subject,' he went on, studying her face and, for the first time, making her feel a little uncomfortable. 'Lovely cheekbones,' he muttered. 'Beautiful hair.'

She blushed slightly and straightened her back. 'That's lovely,' said Andy. 'Now chin up a bit and just a semblance of a smile.' She did her best to oblige and the artist began to scrawl loosely with the charcoal. He stood back a little from the easel, half closed his eyes and scowled.

'Hmm. That dress,' he said. 'It's spoiling the line of your neck and jaw. Could you just undo it a little?'

'Certainly not,' said Helen.

Oh, Mon Dieu, thought Andy. *This is going to be harder than I thought!*

***

'The *Seahorse*?' mumbled Matthew Stokes. He put the letter down again on his desk. 'What wonderful spies I've got! Heading back to Portsmouth under crippled Mr Nelson's pendent, are you Harry Smith? Well, perhaps I should arrange a little homecoming party for you, you bloody peasant!'

***

'What's your business?' demanded the stern marine guard.

'We're to report to the Rear Admiral,' said Harry.

A demeaning grunt was the only response as the man knocked on the state cabin door. It opened about an inch and a curious eye appeared at the crack. 'What is it?' demanded the aide.

'Two men out here say they're to report to the Rear Admiral.'

'Names?' said the aide. 'Names?' repeated the marine.

'Smith and Westhouse,' said Harry. The door opened wider.

The visitors strode inside and stopped dead in their tracks. They had never seen such opulence on a ship. The light from the broad stern window was dazzling and reflected into their eyes from the polished oak table. Oak panels and paintings adorned the walls; the floor a chequered canvas of black and white. Everywhere, brass ornaments glinted and shone.

Nelson stood up from his chair and smiled. He held something out in his left hand, saying, 'This, I think, is yours.' A purple scarf.

Harry pushed the immediate image of Molly Elizabeth out of his mind. 'It is, sir. Thank you.'

'A bit blood-stained, I'm afraid. My aide says he's done his best to remove it but still the marks remain. Perhaps the blood of Nelson will make it an even more valuable relic.'

'I'm sure it will, sir. Thank you.' Harry took the scarf and held it tight. Something Molly Elizabeth had said sparked in his mind. 'It'll save the blood of your hero.'

Harry's head swam. That girl! She seemed to know everything! He felt numb, but the words of his hero pierced through.

'I understand that you were both pressed into the navy. I know it seems a bit harsh at the time, but it's hard to get volunteers these days. What with the Spanish and the French all against us. Anyway, you have both served with honour and courage, and I reiterate what has already been conveyed to you. You will be free to leave, but I have just one small task for you before you go.'

Bart and Harry were glowing with pride, but those last few words cast a curious look over their faces.

Nelson went on, 'I understand that there may be French spies about in Portsmouth. I am, therefore, planning a little deceit. There will, I'm told, be adoring crowds turn out to welcome me in the belief that I brought honour and victory at the battle against the Spanish, now known as The Battle of Cape St Vincent. The Nelson they see will not be me. It will be the unfortunate Wainwright who, the surgeon assures me, will be made up to look how people imagine me to look. In the meantime, I shall remove myself from the ship in the guise of a common sailor. I shall then make my way to Bath, where my dear wife resides, while Wainwright makes his way to the hospital at Greenwich, as Nelson would be expected to do. Am I making myself clear?'

'Perfectly, sir,' said Harry, tempted to ask where they fitted into the plan.

'I expect you are wondering where you fit into this scheme?'

'Yes, sir.'

'Well, I want you smartly dressed as footmen, one as a driver, one as escort to the supposed Nelson. I understand that the poor fellow's brain is completely addled and he will, therefore, need guidance and keeping in check so that no one suspects him to be other than the Rear Admiral. Do you understand?'

'Yes, sir, perfectly.'

'It should only take you a couple of days. Bring the coach back to Portsmouth and then go on about your normal lives; all the better, I trust, for your experiences at sea. Now, we dock tomorrow morning, so report here to my aide, who will help you with the necessary attire. Happy?'

'Yes, sir.'

'Dismiss.'

The two of them strode out of the cabin, their minds a jumble of mixed emotions, but uppermost in Harry's mind was returning to Helen. It would only be a couple of days!

Chapter 32

'It's the *Seahorse,* sir!' an excited voice declared.

All along the coast, Nelson's pendent was looming large in telescope lenses. It was a crisp September morning and the Solent was shimmering blue. Portsmouth was waking up to the welcome news. Any ship approaching was good news for all those who could provide the goods and services for the sailors' needs. Inns and taverns prepared themselves, and merchants and shopkeepers boosted their displays. Women known as "Norport Nonnies", and "Portsmouth Polls" would prepare to go aboard the ship to be "sailors' wives" for the day.

'Did you hear that?' said Mark Williamson. 'A ship! Nelson's ship!'

Helen looked up from her dough and flour. Her eyes looked bright but then suddenly afraid. As the thought pulsed in her brain, *He could be on it!*

'I must go to the docks. I must see Nelson!' gabbled Mark. 'What a hero!'

'That's up to Enoch,' said Helen, trying to compose herself. 'If he'll let you take the time off.'

Mark didn't care. He'd done his early morning rounds. Enoch was nowhere to be seen. He turned and was gone.

Helen left the kitchen and went upstairs. Enoch was still in her bed. 'Wake up, darling,' she muttered, gently shaking his shoulder. His eyes opened slowly, taking in the beauty of her concerned-looking face.

'What is it?' he murmured sleepily.

'There's a ship,' she went on. 'Mark is all excited 'cos they say Nelson's on it. He's run off to try and see him.'

'So, I'm needed in the shop,' he said groggily.

'Yes.'

He could sense her discomfort. It would be like this every time a ship came in. 'What if he's alive? He could have been picked up by another ship, as Enoch had suggested. This could be it. What if he'd tried to get a letter to her and it's been lost at sea? What if he comes in bold as brass, expecting her to be his?' It didn't bear thinking about. She had played her part. She had survived. She had become respectable Miss Brown, the baker, but now a new chapter. Instead of quietly waiting for him, she had lapsed again. She had become Enoch's lover. She felt suddenly ashamed.

There was mayhem at the quay. Mark tried hopelessly to push through the crowd. He could hear horses neighing and hooves scraping, alarmed by the din. 'Make way! Make way!' a blue-coated driver was shouting. Bart was unrecognisable; his collar turned up, tricorn hat shadowing his face. He cracked the whip on a horse's rump.

Mark managed to avoid the slithering hooves and peered into the carriage window. What a spectacle! Shining medals adorned the smart uniform. One sleeve was empty, pinned to his side. The face bore a smile but was partly obscured by the eye patch. The hat covered most of his hair. The good left hand waved regally, mainly thanks to the man beside him, the smart, unrecognisable Harry Smith.

'Well done, sir!' shouted Mark uncontrollably. 'We showed those damned Spanish!' He had to dodge back quickly to avoid the following rear wheel but took off his hat to wave as many others were doing and was somewhat engulfed by the happy crowd. Back at the ship's gangplank, nobody took notice of a one-armed, silver-haired tar, stooped under the heavy load of the bag upon his back, making his way to a waiting carriage that would take him to the city of Bath, to his long-suffering wife.

At the back of the crowd, across the street, stood a man neither cheering nor smiling. Black-hatted and solemn, he peered at the disembarking sailors, seeking out one particular face. He was getting impatient. Surely, his information was correct.

'Good morning, Matthew Stokes,' came a small voice beside him. He wheeled around to see a green-eyed smiling face, more vividly freckled than he remembered. 'Janet!' he croaked. 'It's been a long time!' She smiled.

'*Nurse* Janet,' she corrected him, 'when it's not Jelzina.'

He held her hands lightly and looked into her face. 'Lovelier than ever,' he mused, 'I bet you gave those sailor boys a good time.' She just giggled.

'But what of Harry Smith?' he asked. 'I got your letter, of course. Can't see hide nor hair of him.'

'You will. He's here somewhere. And there's no way he'll be staying on board to revel with these Norport and Portsmouth girls. He'll be off to that girlie of his. He never stopped talking about her. I'm imagining some kind of explosion when they meet up!'

'Oh, yes. He'll go straight to her, no doubt,' said Matthew. 'I'm banking on it.' Janet scowled, not liking his tone of voice. He had said all along that he was a friend of Smith's and that he was planning a secret celebration, but she was detecting something else. She saw him make a signal to another man and another. There were several of them, grim-faced in the crowd. She felt a little scared.

The carriage stumbled across cobbles and stone. Wainwright was still sitting upright thanks to cushions and the man at his side. 'Have you any idea what's going on?' asked Harry, but the man's silence prevailed. His hand still wavered at the window. The crowd was thinning. Some stalwarts followed the carriage out of the town, flags waving, still cheering, but eventually, they were left alone. Harry looked at Wainwright's one visible eye. It was misting and glazed. He couldn't feel a pulse.

The beauty of Sir George Murray's wonderful semaphore system was that a message could flash from station to station, from Portsmouth to the Admiralty in London, in a matter of minutes. Its downfall was that anyone who understood the coded signals could decipher its messages. To a group of black-cloaked riders in the

Hampshire countryside, its message was wonderful news. Their target was on his way. They didn't know how many guards. They would find that out. There were only six in their group. Four French men, two English. All wished success to Napoleon Bonaparte. They would be forever in his favour if their mission was a success.

The carriage lurched and Wainwright winced. 'You *are* still alive,' said Harry, and the one good eye shot its hate at his escort. In his normal state of health, Wainwright would have attacked the bastard, but right now, he had no strength left in his body, and his right arm was trussed up against his chest. 'This is all your own bloody fault,' moaned Harry. You took Stokes' shilling to come after us. It was a clever plan, only the navy was just that little bit cleverer, and me and Bart were cleverer still. The one thing we've got to be thankful for is that you never told on us. Otherwise, we'd have got the noose. That would have been too good for us, eh?'

Harry thought he heard a derisive grunt in response. Then, a sound from outside. A faint drumming noise from somewhere behind. He twisted his neck to peer out of the back window. Bart had heard it, too. He cracked on the reins. The drumming got louder and the vision of flowing black cloaks and horses in pursuit got clearer. Determined masked faces were set to their target; dust billowed out behind. The coach was no match for the free-running horses. They galloped on past and then slewed and stumbled to a halt in a cloud of cloaks and masks and dust. The coach had slithered helplessly towards the shallow ditch and canted at an angle, the two outer wheels still spinning. When they stopped, the only sound was a whinnying horse. Bart already had his hands up in surrender. He was ordered down from his lofty seat.

'Get out!' came a voice at the carriage door. It was not so easy. Wainwright had landed on top of Harry and he had to push and shove his way past him. 'I think he's dead,' he said to the horsemen. He heard muttering amongst them, '*Il est mort*? Your grand admiral? Mort?'

'He had terrible injuries,' said Harry. 'Been at death's door for days. We're taking him to hospital, but I don't think he's survived.'

They pulled the carriage straight and a dead body slumped partway out of the door, the man's head tilted back on the step, mouth gaping, one visible eye glazed and staring. Bart and Harry made a show of forlornly lifting him back into the carriage. Somehow, Bart even managed to shed a tear.

'Then our work is done, Messieurs,' said one of the men. 'You two had better continue your journey, but not to the hospital, eh? To the morgue!'

There was some cheering amongst the men. 'So, no more Nelson!' they were saying. 'What will England's navy be without him?'

'Ze French will beat you at sea yet. Then what will you do, eh? *Vive l'Empereur*! Ha ha!'

Horses were reined in and turned. '*Au revoir*!' they shouted and put their horses to the gallop. How delighted would Bonaparte be when he heard the news! Shouts of glee and victory could be heard as they raced away.

Harry and Bart couldn't help but laugh. Their villain Wainwright dead. The French believing that the threat of Nelson was over. 'Let's get this to Greenwich, then head back to Norport,' said Harry, his heart pounding fast. They clasped hands and grinned deep into each other's eyes.

'I've got a better idea,' said Bart. 'You know, the bloody navy must have suspected this would happen. Nobody really cared if we got killed defending the supposed Nelson. Let's rough ourselves up a bit, act all distraught, and say these bloody Frenchies murdered him and dumped him in the river. We can go back right now!'

'Bloody good idea, Bart! We can weigh his body down with rocks like a burial at sea. He'll never be found. I doubt if anyone would even bother looking for him. Let's just bloody well do it!'

Harry and Bart rubbed the smart coats in the dirt. They threw the hats away, snagged and smeared the trousers. They hauled Wainwright's body to the river bank, weighed it down and dropped it into the water. It was surprisingly deep. He disappeared from view. They even hacked a few sword marks into the side of the carriage, stood back and admired their work.

Bart cracked the reins on the horses' rumps and turned them around. 'Was this really happening?' they asked themselves. 'Was their scheme really going to work? They went over it again in their minds. 'There were six of them. Mostly French, but a couple of English. They really thought it was Nelson. They did him in, shouting, '*Vive l'Empereur*!'

'We're free, Helen!' yelped Harry. 'Free at last! And I'm coming home for you!'

Chapter 33

'So, where the hell is he?' demanded Stokes.

Nurse Janet stared at the stream of departing sailors, her eyes dancing from face to face. She recognised some, but there was no Harry Smith. They stood and they watched until the last man was gone. Janet was puzzled and somewhat embarrassed. 'I thought he would have been one of the first to get away,' she mumbled. Stokes was clearly agitated. His associates in the crowd kept glancing in his direction, concerned, askance. Janet didn't like it.

'Are you sure it was him?' groused Stokes.

'Of course, I'm sure!' she shot back. 'I'm not bloody stupid! He told me his name. He matched the description perfectly. There's no doubt. I had tabs on him through thick and thin. Ship after ship. Right up until this morning. Now he's just vanished into thin air!'

Stokes said nothing. He turned his back on the girl and wandered away.

Janet's stare remained fixed on the gangplank. Her head was a mass of confusion. Why was Stokes so angry about this? And what had become of her blue-eyed lover?

The bell above the bakery door jangled, and Enoch looked up. The silhouette in the doorway had a military bearing, a lieutenant, if he wasn't mistaken, hat tucked under one arm. He strode into the shop, giving Enoch an inquisitive stare.

'Can I help you, sir?' was Enoch's polite greeting.

'I'm looking for Miss Westhouse,' said the man.

Enoch was somewhat taken aback. He thought that trail had gone cold weeks ago.

'What? Why?' he began, stuttering.

'I've got something for her, from a Mr Harry Smith. Is she here? I've been asked to deliver it in person.'

Helen peered nervously from the kitchen door. She had heard the voice. It was not one that she knew. Lieutenant Lawrence saw her there. 'Miss Westhouse?' he enquired.

Enoch looked angry. She was supposed to stay hidden on such occasions. She started to tremble. She knew what the man was going to say. Harry and Bart were brave men. They gave their lives fighting for our freedom. They should never be forgotten. We should all be proud.

'Is he dead?' she asked shakily.

Lawrence looked surprised. 'No, my dear!' he responded, 'far from it!'

Her heart went from sinking to elation. She couldn't help her gasp. 'He's alive? Are they both alive? My brother, too?'

'Yes, ma'am,' he replied, trying to remain stoic. 'Smith has asked me to deliver something to you, said I'd find you at the baker's shop. I wasn't sure if this was the right place. But it obviously is.'

'Yes, yes,' she managed and watched as he pulled a familiar leather pouch from his pocket and handed it to her.

The excited gasp echoed all around the tiny shop! She couldn't believe it! Her sapphire! She pulled it from the pouch, entwined now in copper. It was a beautiful sight. She couldn't help but slip it onto her finger. It fitted exactly. Her heart pounded hard. 'How wonderful!' she cried, 'where is he?' She went on, excited, 'Where's my man?'

She wanted to fling her arms around the lieutenant but would only have covered him in flour and embarrassment. She stretched her hand up towards the ceiling and stared at the lovely blue stone as it sparkled in the light. She spun around and beamed in delight. 'Where is he?' she demanded again.

'He's on his way,' he said a little guardedly. 'He was on the ship that just came in, but he's on a final mission. Bit of a secret thing really, for the navy, but he'll be here in a day or two. He's free to leave. He just asked me to give you that and to say he'd be home soon.'

'That's wonderful, wonderful news, Mr, er?'

'Lawrence, ma'am,' he advised her. 'Lieutenant Lawrence.'

'Thank you so much, lieutenant,' she said, 'but what's this mission?'

'I can't say, ma'am,' he replied. 'But I'm sure he'll tell you all about it when he returns.'

The lieutenant said his goodbyes and backed out of the shop. Helen raised her bejewelled hand and admired it once again. 'It's so beautiful!' she mused. 'He promised to have it made into a ring for me! And I said I'd be so proud to wear it! What a wonderful idea,' she gabbled on, 'to have someone deliver it here today. To let me know he was alive and well, and that he'd soon be home! I can't wait to see you, Harry Smith! You lovely, lovely man!'

She turned around to show it once again to Enoch, but he wasn't there. He'd seen enough and a dull ache had hit him hard. He had gone out through the kitchen, out of the back door and kept going. There were tears in his eyes, a dreadful buzzing in his head. She was *his*! For a few days, maybe, but he had dared to believe. He had known the ecstasy of her body. Her loving warmth and gratitude. He had given himself to her completely, and she had done the same. Their lives and their bodies are forever intertwined. Gone! All gone! In one fell swoop. The appearance of a mighty ring. It was finished. The end!

People stared at Enoch, his limp becoming more pronounced as he went. They tried to greet him, but his eyes were fixed ahead, blurred by tears. He walked and walked, his heart pounding, broken. They watched, amazed, as the determined man staggered onto the quay. 'What the hell's he doing?' they muttered, but it was all too late. He bent and wrapped the heavy chain around his ankle. He knew exactly what he was doing.

'Enoch!' men were shouting. 'Stop, you fool!' Too late. He dropped the chain and went with it. Green water, weed and bubbles raced up past him. His mind blackened. The pain was gone.

Chapter 34

Janet was feeling stupid. She had been used in different ways all her life. She had sold her body as "Jelzina". She looked at her reflection in the baker's shop window.

'What the hell was Matthew Stokes up to?' she pondered. 'I kept Harry Smith in my sights for him all that time, though I must admit, it was very pleasant. One slip up at the end and he was gone. Now he doesn't want to know me, the bastard. Been used again, Janet Charnley. Used again.' Her reflection stared back at her. She was looking older. She didn't want to turn into one of those fat old slags who still worked the harbours and taverns because they were no good for anything else. She always thought she would get lucky someday. Make some kind of fortune; she didn't know how. She looked in her purse and was hit by a terrible truth.

'Oh drat!' she said out loud, attracting a disgusted stare from a bonneted lady passing by. She had accumulated food and drink plenty and bottles of French perfume but didn't have any money. Not even a farthing for a bread roll. She didn't know why she did the next thing. She opened the shop door and went in. The bell jangled. There was nobody there.

'Shop!' she shouted, and Helen peered in from the kitchen. She was looking for Enoch. The realisation had hit her that her elation had meant heartache for the man who had virtually taken over her life. The man who had given her back respectability, who had become her lover, had lost himself entirely in his love for her.

Janet didn't know what to say. Then, a thought. A little deceit. 'My, er, little boy wants to feed the seagulls,' she muttered. 'Have you got any scraps of bread I could give him?'

Helen's mind came out of its worried state and tried to focus on the young woman's words. She had heard them before. A lifetime ago.

'I'm sorry,' she heard herself say. 'All the scraps and bits go straight to the orphanage. You could buy some nice fresh rolls. Only a farthing.'

'Oh, I'm sorry,' said Janet. 'I seem to have forgotten my purse.'

The words reverberated in Helen's mind. *I know your plight,* she thought. I *know just how you feel.*

She grabbed a couple of rolls from the shelf and put them into a paper bag. 'That's all right,' she said. 'Pay me when you're next passing by.'

The gasp from Janet wasn't for the act of trust. It was for the sight of something glistening on the shop girl's hand. A sparkle of light. Sapphire blue!

'My God!' she couldn't help but say. Both looked inquisitively for several heartbeats into each other's eyes; then one of them breathed. 'You're Helen!'

Silence. Both minds juggled, trying to put words into mouths. Helen was suspicious of everyone, terrified of Matthew Stokes' spies, her mind still horrified by Enoch's disappearance. She wanted to find him. She could feel the man's desperation. Now, this woman was butting into her life! Who was she? 'How does she know my name?'

'The ring,' said Janet at last. 'I've seen it before.' She wasn't going to admit to having it on her finger just a couple of days ago. 'One of the sailors had it made. I saw the carpenter's work. I was on the ship that just came in. I'm a nurse.' Her words were stuttered and nervous. She didn't want to say the wrong things. 'The carpenter told me afterwards that the sailor's name was Harry Smith and that he'd wanted it engraved "for Helen", but he couldn't do it.'

Helen eyed her quizzically, her story taking over in her mind from Enoch's plight. The voice continued. 'There can't be more than one ring like that in the whole world. You're a very lucky girl!'

It all seemed innocent enough. 'Thank you,' muttered Helen, but she could see a worried look now in her customer's eyes. 'What's wrong?' she asked.

'Your sailor, Mr Smith,' she began. 'I take it he's here somewhere, is he?'

'Not yet, no. He's on some mission or other. He got someone to deliver this to me. Said he'd be home in a couple of days.'

'Oh right,' said Janet. 'Well, you might just say that Nurse Janet was here. Recognised the ring. Wished you both every happiness for the future.'

'Yes, yes, I will,' replied Helen. 'Thank you.'

'Thank *you*,' said Janet and gestured to the paper bag. 'I'll pay you tomorrow.'

Once outside, she made a puff-cheeked gesture of relief and began to turn things over in her mind. 'On some mission or other?' she pondered and began to walk, nibbling on one of the rolls. 'If he's on some mission, that's why I never saw him leave the ship, nor his mate Westhouse for that matter. Oh Christ!' It dawned on her. She had only had eyes for Nelson as he drove away. Two blue-coated men, one driving, one in the carriage, tricorn hats hiding much of their faces. 'Bloody hell, Harry Smith. You don't know how lucky you've been!'

Chapter 35

'So,' said Lieutenant Lawrence. 'You say they killed the poor bastard and dumped him in the river?'

'That's right, sir,' Bart responded. 'And they really thought it was Nelson?'

'Yes, sir.'

'Bloody fools!' he yelped. 'Didn't they even count how many arms he had?'

'No, sir!' said Harry, and all three men couldn't help but laugh.

'They really think Nelson is dead?'

'They really do, sir, but even more important, sir, did you find *her*? Did you deliver the ring?'

'Yes, of course I did. To say she was shocked and thrilled would be an understatement! She danced around the place, just staring at the thing. She couldn't believe it. Kept asking, where is he? Where is he?'

The scene degenerated into one of back-slapping merriment. 'I'm so glad things are working out for you.' Chortled Lawrence, but he barely got the words out when his face dropped at the sight of two serious-looking marines approaching. Bart and Harry wheeled around to see the cause of his distress. The "red coats" had bayonetted muskets. 'Westhouse and Smith!' one of them growled. 'You're to come with us!'

There could be no argument. The marines grabbed them by the arm and directed them in the direction of the ship. Their astonished protests of 'what the...?' and 'why?' were ignored. Lawrence looked on in disbelief. They stumbled and grumbled their way ahead of the pushing marines, up the gangplank and towards the great cabin where more marines were waiting, guarding the door.

'These two are to see Lieutenant Strater,' announced one of the arresting pair. The name struck fear into their captives' minds. The cabin door opened and they were bundled in. 'Westhouse and Smith!' said the marine, with a tone of pride in his achievement. Strater was sitting at the polished oak table, looking far more important than his status deserved. He didn't look up until the armed guard had left. When he did, it was slowly and with a withering stare. They had expected praise and congratulation on their accomplishment. They looked quizzically at Strater's officious stare. They shifted their feet about, anxious, anticipating his words. They were to be shocked.

'You two are under arrest,' Strater murmured. 'Suspected of attempted desertion.'

'But.'

'What?' they stuttered in response.

'We've just been part of a brilliant scheme to fool the French,' said Bart, gathering composure. 'They think Nelson is dead. It had nothing to do with desertion.'

'I'm not talking about that ridiculous escapade,' grouched the lieutenant. 'I'm talking about you two on that fishing boat with Wainwright and that damned Portuguese fisherman. You were running away. Deserting!' He added the last word for clarity when he saw the gaping expressions on the two men's faces. They didn't know what to say. They swallowed hard, minds reeling at the sudden plunge from heroes to villains. They thought all that was behind them. They thought they were free!

'Admiral Nelson said…' Bart's words were cut short by an angry thump of Strater's fist on the table, and the accuser, at last, stood up to glare into their eyes. 'Admiral Nelson has nothing to do with this!' he barked, and the two men cowered away. 'This was before he even re-joined the fleet. I've seen the entry in the muster book,' he went on. 'Late confused,' it says. 'Late confused!' The word "run" is crossed out underneath it! 'You were the only two not accounted for when that damned fishing boat was taken into custody. Four men were on her. Only two were arrested. Two men, very cleverly, somehow evaded us. If they hadn't, they would be sunken corpses now at the bottom of the sea with the hangman's noose still around their necks! Late confused? It was you two, wasn't it? Wasn't it?'

Bart and Harry struggled for words. They struggled for breath. So close to freedom. After all, they'd been through. The praise they'd had from Nelson himself. Harry had even saved the revered commander's life! Harry shook his head. He couldn't believe it.

'It wasn't us,' Bart managed.

'Ha!' Laughed Strater. 'Can you prove it?' He gave the men perhaps ten seconds of silence in which to respond. They didn't. 'You're both under arrest till we can muster a trial. Guard!' he yelled, and the two arresting marines appeared at the doorway. 'Take these men below. They're prisoners of His Majesty's Britannic Navy! Dismiss!'

Chapter 36

'Andy!' yelled Mark as his brother opened the tavern door. 'Come and join us!' The elder brother was met by a wall of merry voices, clanking pewter and a haze of tobacco smoke.

'You're all as drunk as lords!' He laughed. 'What's going on?'

'We're just celebrating!' cheered Mark. 'Just seen the great Admiral Nelson. He looked great! Great victory! Great man!'

Andy's grin could not have been wider. If only the foolish little brother knew that his hero was dead! Andy and his cohorts knew. The thoughts were there in Andy's head. Victory was not so very far away. Celebrate now while your freedom lasts, crazy Englishmen. It won't be long. *Vive l'empereur*! Absorption into this jolly little party would be the perfect cover for his crimes. 'Rule Britannia!' he cried and joined the group with his tankard held aloft. 'Let's drink to our wonderful navy!'

Mark was astounded by his brother's apparent change of heart, but their tankards clanked and the contents were swallowed. 'More ale over here!' he yelled to a struggling wench, already surrounded by empty tankards begging to be refilled.

***

Janet Charnley stood at the quayside. She had swallowed the last mouthful of Helen's bread roll and was watching the seagulls wheel around in their eternal search for sustenance.

I'm just like you, she thought to herself. *Just grabbing what I can here and there.* She felt a certain envy for Helen Westhouse. Not just because she had won the heart of a dynamic sailor but because she had settled in one place with a job and a roof over her head. She seemed so "in control" of her life.

'Me? I just go where the wind blows me,' she mused. 'I don't belong anywhere or to anyone. I suppose I could go back on the ship. I need to earn some money. See if any stray fellows are in want of a wife for an hour or so.' She dawdled along and noticed a young officer at the foot of the gangplank. She knew him well how he'd progressed. A smart lieutenant now. She'd entertained him below decks when he'd been a playful midshipman. Both smiled in recognition as she drew near. He raised his hat slightly in polite greeting and she gave a little mock curtsey.

'Nurse Janet,' he muttered. 'How nice to see you again.'

'Likewise, I'm sure, lieutenant,' responded the girl. 'Are there many left on board?'

Lawrence made a thoughtful face. 'A few, I think. Want to take a look?'

She nodded and gave a coquettish smile as she reassumed the demeanour of Jelzina.

'If not,' said Lawrence. 'I'll come back in myself.'

'I look forward to it,' she muttered and ventured onto the gangplank.

On board, she caught the faint whiff of vinegar where the surgeon had been fumigating the ship. She saw marines guarding the great cabin door and gave them her professional smile, but their eyes remained stoically glazed. She ventured down the first companionway to the gun deck, usually alive and vibrant, now silent, ghostly. A giggle and a groan broke the silence to her right and told her that a romantic assignment was taking place. She hurried on down to the dingy orlop deck. It would always be her station in life. The lowest of the low.

More marines! 'What's going on?' she said out loud.

'No use you coming down here, love,' the nearest responded. 'Guards on duty, that's all. Got men under arrest down here.'

'What? Enemy sailors, d'you mean?'

'Nah. Deserters, that's all.'

She gave a quizzical look. 'Who is it?' she ventured.

'Those two who went off on that Portuguese fishing boat,' he replied. 'Caught up with them at last. At least, old Strater thinks so. Don't know whether he can prove it.'

Jelzina looked thoughtful. She had had her suspicions about Harry, what with that strange entry in the muster book. She had even warned him that it looked a bit damning.

'What's their names?' she persisted, but the marine was shaking his head.

'Can't tell you that, now can I, miss,' he replied with correctness, and she shrugged.

'Just that I know quite a few of them,' she said with a pout. She was worried. She couldn't press it, though, without sounding as if she had some knowledge of the affair. *It can't be Harry,* she thought. *He's off on some mission. I need to find him, though, and let him know that Stokes is lying in wait for him.*

She turned around and went back up to the gun deck. The cavorting couple had disappeared, leaving an eerie silence. Lieutenant Lawrence was coming down towards her.

'Nobody there?' he queried.

'Only marines. All on guard duty.'

'Oh, yes. Your poor Harry Smith...' said Lawrence. She gasped, interrupting. In one loose-tongued moment, he had confirmed what she feared. 'Harry Smith? Harry Smith? They think he's a deserter? That's rubbish! He's a brave, brave man! He saved Nelson's life, goddamn it! How on earth can they accuse him of that?'

Lawrence was agog. He knew that she cared for the man, but not to the extent she had just shown. 'I was shocked too,' he continued. 'They just got back from their decoy mission and bang! There was an armed guard marching them off to see Strater! God knows why he's landing this on them after they'd done such good work.'

Her face had crumpled into desperation, anger and disgust. 'I need to see Strater!' she growled. 'This can't be happening, the bastard!'

'Oh, now. Hold on a minute!' he gasped, but she was determined. He tried to grab her arm. She wriggled it free. 'Don't you dare tell him it was me who told you who it was!' he yelled after her. She was out of sight. He didn't see the hand gesture, which was her response.

The marine guard blocked her way. They held out muskets as she tried to burst between them. 'Come off it, miss!' one of them groaned. 'You can't just burst in there!'

'I want to see Strater!' she demanded, but the guard gave her a withering look and held the musket across her chest.

'Tell him I want to see him!' she growled. The guard laughed.

'He's a busy man. He's in charge of the ship for the time being. He's got no time to fool around with the likes of you.'

'I'm not here to fool around, as you put it. I've got serious business to discuss. Now, tell Strater I need to see him. I've got evidence about those prisoners you've got downstairs!'

The guards looked thoughtfully at each other, then nodded. One of them knocked on the door.

'Enter!' came a voice from within.

'A young lady here to see you, sir,' said the marine. 'Says it's to do with your prisoners.'

Strater looked interested. 'Better show her in.'

Jelzina walked past them with a look of acquired disdain. Strater stood up.

'So, miss,' he murmured. 'What's so important that you just can't wait to say it?'

***

Andy put his arm around his younger brother and spoke into his ear. 'There's something else I might be celebrating soon, little brother; I'm almost there!'

'Where?'

'I have shown her my brushes!'

'Ha! And don't tell me. She threw off all her clothes and begged for the pleasures of your body!'

'Not quite. Almost there,' is what I said. Andy took down another large gulp of the beer and pulled a grim face. 'You and your bloody beer,' he moaned. 'Wine is so much more sophisticated.'

'You and your bloody French ways!' returned Mark. 'You've got to remember you're English now you're back here. You could get yourself into trouble!'

'Bah!'

'So, have you painted her, you know, naked?' Mark's words were getting a little slurred. Andy signalled to the serving wench to refill their mugs.

'Not exactly. Just a portrait. But it's a start. She's sitting for me again tomorrow, then, who knows?'

'Ah, so for all your fine words, you couldn't get her into bed?'

'Not *yet*, bro, but it's only a matter of time.'

The buxom girl replenished their drinks. 'That would be a fine subject for you,' observed Mark as she walked away. They both laughed. The Half Moon Tavern was as lively as ever. Mark couldn't help thinking about that evening when Helen of Troy had ravished him, leaving him breathless, spent. A man.

'Anyway, if you do get her into bed.' Mark's head was fuzzy and he wasn't going to put up with his brother's bragging. 'If you do get her into bed,' he repeated.

'What?' said Andy, amused at Mark's drunkenness.

'You won't win the bet.'

'What?'

'You won't win the bet 'cos I've already beaten you to it!'

Andy looked astonished at his brother. His face was red, eyes swivelling about in their sockets.

'I had her here when she worked here.'

'I'd better get you home,' said Andy.

'No, no. I'm fine. I need more beer! I had her here before dear Enoch took her in. Before she became our lovely kitchen person, she worked here. She was Helen of Troy. She did me good and proper and wouldn't let me pay her. So, I win the bet, dear brother! I win!'

A man sitting behind them couldn't help but hear. He smiled, stood up and left.

***

'Innocent?' said Strater. 'Innocent?'

'Yes, sir,' Jelzina replied. She had calmed down significantly, her thoughts becoming clearer. 'I know those men, sir. They're brave sailors. Press gang recruits. They gave their all for the navy. Smith even saved Nelson's life when he was bleeding to death.'

Strater was shaking his head. 'I know all this,' he grumbled. 'But the evidence all points to them. They were unaccounted for when a desertion took place. "Late confused" it says against their names with "run" crossed out. They say they went on *Culloden* by mistake, but nobody saw them there.'

'Yes, they did, sir,' she muttered. 'I saw them.'

Strater's eyes widened. Jelzina felt her heart pounding hard. There were moments of silence as the words sank in.

'You saw them?' he managed at last.

'Yes, sir.' Her brain was working hard. She wished she had rehearsed this before making her hot-headed approach.

'Fact is, sir, I'm a nurse. I was called on *Culloden* to tend to a fellow who'd collapsed. Your two men were there then. The clerk was arguing with them, saying their names weren't in the book, so they must be on the wrong ship. They insisted they were right.'

'Rubbish!' said Strater. 'Do you think I'm stupid? I've already asked the clerk on duty in Culloden that day. He has no recollection of these two men.'

'Then he must have forgotten!' she said, indignant. 'I remember it clearly.'

'They're as guilty as hell and you know it! You've come here with a pack of lies to try to get them off. It'll land you in trouble, too, you fool! Now get out and count yourself lucky I'm not putting you under arrest too!'

She stared at the man. Her efforts had failed. Tears began to well in her eyes, accentuating their emerald green hue. 'I do remember it. I do,' she stammered.

He watched the tears overflow and dribble down her cheeks.

'Don't be angry with me, sir,' she managed. 'They're good, brave men. They deserve to go home. Back to the lives the navy robbed them of so cruelly.'

For probably the first time in his life, Strater was disarmed. Her eyes were appealing now, soft and seductive, full of promises. Her words were hitting home, melting his iciness. He turned and stared out of the huge stern window, seeing gulls wheeling, screeching, free.

He turned back into the room. Jelzina had pushed her dress off of one shoulder. She pushed it off the other and let it slip to where only her bosom held it up. Strater felt emotions that he hadn't known for far too long. He put his hands on the soft, warm flesh of her shoulders, then helped the dress tumble to the floor. She told herself it would soon be over. Her head filled with thoughts of her blue-eyed Harry Smith. She imagined it was him. The first time for a shilling, then his precious Blue John stone. They sank onto the chaise longue. Strater groaned, he moaned, he shuddered and gasped. It was all so familiar to Jelzina. It was soon over. She even managed to mutter, 'You're the best I ever had.' His mind was a blur. They lay in recovery for several minutes.

How can I deny this woman her simple wish? went through his brain.

'I believe you,' he whispered at last. 'If you say you saw them on Culloden, then I suppose they were telling the truth.' Jelzina stared at the man and smiled.

He stood up, adjusted his clothing and waited until the newly found witness had done the same. He went to the door and spoke to the guards. 'This woman has convinced me of their innocence,' he muttered. 'Let the prisoners go and dismiss the guards.'

'You're free,' said the guard to Bart and Harry. 'Better get lost quick before he changes his mind.'

Chapter 37

The bell clanged above the door of the baker's shop and two young men staggered in, red-faced and sweating.

'You two are a disgrace!' shrieked Helen. 'Drunk as lords at this time of day!'

'We've been celebrating!' slurred Mark. 'I saw Nelson! Great, great man!'

'That's no reason to get so drunk!' she retorted.

'Get lost, little sister!' groused Andy. Helen was incensed. She felt strength amassing in her right arm and slapped him indignantly across the face. It was a heartfelt blow, numbing his cheek. 'You bitch!' yelled Andy. 'You bloody whore!'

Silence. Angry faces. Then realisation. This wasn't just a mindless insult; it was an accusation. She glared at Mark, who reddened even more. He steadied himself against the counter, reading her mind, preparing for the onslaught. 'I'm sorry,' he tried to say but hardly got the words out when her hand smashed into his cheek, too.

'Bloody fool!' she yelled. 'You promised me! You bloody, bloody fool!'

'So, it's true!' said Andy, recovering from the slap, sneering. 'You *were* Helen of Troy! Biggest whore in town! And Enoch bought you out to be his respectable

Miss Brown, the baker! His own personal plaything more likely!' Helen was seething. She picked up a rolling pin and went to hit him again, but he was ready this time. He grabbed her wrist and twisted her arm behind her back. 'Where's your saviour Enoch Hoskins now, little sister?'

'Let go, you bastard!' she yelled and stamped down hard on his foot. Andy screeched but wouldn't let go. He picked her up and began to shove her up the stairs. She kicked, she punched, she bit and scratched, but the young man was powerful, strengthened by his anger, his ignominy, his alcohol. He hurled her onto the bed.

***

Two bewildered ex-sailors trod carefully towards the gangplank, their eyes becoming accustomed to the daylight. In the doorway was the familiar figure of Nurse Janet Charnley, Jelzina.

'Be bloody careful,' she said. Harry looked shocked. 'Jelzina! What the hell's wrong?'

'It's Stokes! He's got spies everywhere! He's just waiting for you to lead him to your Helen, and then he'll move in on both of you!'

'My God,' muttered Harry. 'I can't move for people wanting to do me in. How do you know about Stokes?'

'Oh Christ, Harry! It's a long, long story and one I'm not about to bore you with now. Just believe me, eh?'

Harry stared at her earnestly.

'I met her, your Helen,' she said at last. 'She's a lovely young woman.'

'You met her? You didn't tell her…?'

'No, of course not,' then after a pause, 'she's got my ring on.'

'It's not your ring, Jay. I told you. I promised it to *her*.'

'I know. I still think I deserve it. You would too if you knew what I've just done.'

Harry stared harder, more quizzically. What had she done? He couldn't help but remember the wonderful moments he had with her. But it had all been professional. Hadn't it?

'You can't walk straight in through the front door of that damned bakery,' Jelzina went on. 'His men will see you. You'll have to sneak in around the back.'

***

'Andy, don't!' yelled Mark.

'Get out!' returned Andy. 'Unless you want to help! I'm about to win our little wager, dear brother. Yours doesn't count. Not when she was still a whore!'

Mark dithered. Helen spat. She spat hard into Andy's face. Venom and lust were in her assailant's eyes. His hand smashed across her face, numbing it, drawing blood.

Bart and Harry followed Jelzina's advice. Secretly, furtive, they moved like alley cats, eyes scanning everywhere: behind, above, ahead. When they saw a cloaked figure someway behind them, they realised it was Jelzina covering their backs. What a saviour she had turned out to be, what unknown sacrifices she had made. They reached the back door of the bakery. Harry ventured inside. He imagined the thrill, the ecstasy on Helen's face, the hug, the wild embrace.

'You bastard!' Helen's voice shrieking from upstairs shocked Harry to the core. 'Shut up, you bitch!' came a man's coarse roar. A girl's scream. The sound of a slap, yelps of pain. Harry leapt up the stairs. Mark, on the landing, was flattened by the power of the man's charge. This was no longer Harry Smith, the reticent farmer boy; this was the battle-hardened sailor with Nelson's cry of "death or glory" ringing in his ears. Andy spun around to see the horrendous approach. He climbed off the girl and felt her knee take full advantage of its freedom, slamming up hard into his groin. He barely had time to feel the pain. Harry's fist crashed down on his jaw, smashing him onto the pillow. Helen still kicked at the bastard. Harry hauled him up by the collar and smashed his fist into his already bloodied face. He pulled him up again and hurled him across the room, sending him crashing into his easel and canvas, splattering blood on his precious work. He lay there, spent and defeated, in a whimpering heap.

Bart arrived in time to see Mark kneel, distraught, beside his battered brother. Peering further into the room, he saw Helen and Harry standing, staring at each other, a thousand questions and answers befuddling their minds, but mainly disbelief that this was real. The faces had changed. No longer fresh and innocent. No longer reflecting the joys of life. They had gathered worldly experience, maturity and pain. Harry's face was bronzed and roughened, his hair bleached and long with its sailor's slick of tar. Helen's eyes were fierce as though hardened by the cruelty of life. They continued to stare and gradually, slowly, the dim, questioning look grew warmer. Hazel and blue eyes regained their shimmer, their shine, their sparkle. The embrace was robust. The pent-up emotion was expressed in a flurry of wordless moans and sighs. Images of their lives rampaged through their minds: ecstasy and disbelief that they were back in each other's arms.

'Remember me?' enquired Bart, and his sister released one arm from her hold on Harry to include him in their heart-thumping reunion. Then Bart pulled away from them. He knew this moment belonged to lovers. He could see the urgency in their eyes. He looked over to where Mark still knelt over his stricken brother. Andy could only see dim, smeary images. His only other sensation was the taste of blood in his mouth.

Then a scream! A terrified scream from a woman downstairs.

Chapter 38

Matthew Stokes sent two men to the front of the shop while he and two others went around the back. One of them was the spy who had overheard Mark's drunken bragging in the tavern. Hiding, they had seen Jelzina's furtive movements, and ahead of her, the two jacktars. Matthew's eyes narrowed. Almost a year's disgust was thumping inside of him. They had seen the two sailors go into the baker's yard. The red-haired pursuer span around, but they were invisible to her in the deep shadows of the walls. As they entered the yard, they could hear the commotion from the upstairs window: crashes and yelps of pain. Then, in the doorway, loomed the defiant figure, green eyes glaring, hands gripping the frame.

'You bastard, Matthew Stokes!' croaked Jelzina, stopping the man in his tracks. 'Your letters said you were a friend of his! I was the only bloody spy clever enough not to be discovered! That's what you told me. What's this all about, Matthew? Why do you really want him?'

'Just get out of the way!' he growled back. 'You don't need to know!'

The rumpus upstairs had subsided. Matthew was so close now to his quarry, that lousy peasant who had taken his girl. He could still picture his mumbling face. 'She doesn't want you,' he was mouthing How he'd wanted to hit that insolent cur. He remembered how he'd reined it in for the sake of appearances, uttered the curse that he should consider himself "already dead". Now was his moment. The failed schemes that had gone ahead were no longer of any consequence. Poor Poplar Wainwright had given his all, his life. The anger thumped on in Matthew's heart and brain.

'Move!' he yelled at the obstinate girl, but she held on tighter to the frame of the door, green eyes flaring, defiant. She shivered as she heard the awful scrape of steel withdrawn from the scabbard. The blade shone in front of her, but she still wouldn't move. He didn't want to use it. He shoved her with his free hand. He felt her weaken and shoved once again. She fell but grabbed his leg as he staggered past and wouldn't let go. A resigned look of anguish engulfed his face. He lunged with the sword. She screeched out in terrified pain!

'What the hell was that?' croaked Bart, and a moment later, peered down the stairs as Matthew withdrew the sword from the girl's awful wound. In the same movement, he began to bound up the stairs. 'Out of my way!' he yelled, but Bart was too shaken, too shocked to move. Matthew shoved him in the belly with his elbow as he strode past, his followers pushing him to the floor. Matthew burst into the room and then stopped, chest heaving, eyes glaring. There before him stood the objects of his hate, Harry Smith and Helen Westhouse, tracked down at last. Still holding both hands, their faces had turned in the last split second away from each other's deep stare to the horrendous din of the scream and the man's approach. Now they gaped, shocked, paralysed. Matthew's accusing sword pointed at them. They were defenceless, at his mercy. He smirked. He leered. He laughed. He played with the sword, pointing it at him and then at her how he'd dreamt of this moment. He loved the terror in their eyes.

His cohorts had tied Bart's hands behind his back and Mark's for good measure, though they didn't know who he was. Both were dumped with the stricken Andy in the corner. Matthew diverted the point of his sword towards Harry's throat.

'I told you to consider yourself already dead,' he growled, 'and you can be sure you won't be leaving this room alive. But first.' He turned towards Helen. 'We're going to be entertained by Miss Westhouse, or is it Helen of Troy, whore of all whores at the *Half Moon Tavern!*'

Her face visibly crumpled. 'You bastard!' she managed as she reddened, tears welling and spilling from her eyes.

Harry was stunned and joined her verbal assault of their assailant. 'You bloody liar!' spat Harry. 'How can you be such a lying bastard?'

'Oh, it's true,' sneered Matthew. 'I almost delivered her the pleasures of my body there myself, didn't I, my sweet? Except for that crazy boy!' He pointed disdainfully at the cowering Mark Williamson. 'And the bloody landlord!' He was grabbing Mark by the shoulder now, although keeping the sword watchfully towards the two would-be lovers. 'Tell the sailor all about it,' he went on in Mark's ear, 'and tell him all about your own initiation into manhood with her.'

Harry didn't look at Helen. He didn't have to. She was doubling up in tears, the sobs coming loud and clear. His heart was sinking fast. It all seemed so believable. Unbelievably believable! There were tears in Harry's eyes, too. She had fallen from grace but he was far from innocent himself. He couldn't judge her. He couldn't be the one to cast the first stone.

'So, Miss Troy,' Matthew sneered on. 'Perhaps you would entertain us with a little dancing. Get undressed!'

'For God's sake, Stokes!' growled Harry. 'What the hell's wrong with you?'

'You know damn well! You humiliated me by running off together when I'm about to propose marriage to this woman! Look at her! A snivelling wreck! How could I ever have imagined that I could make a respectable wife out of her? Bloody farm girl! Whore!'

Helen was crumpled completely on the floor, withered and destroyed by Stokes' words, crying uncontrollably.

'Stand up!' yelled Matthew. 'And dance for us!'

Harry took a step towards the despicable man, but a shake of the sword in his direction was deterrent enough.

In the corner, Bart was picking at the knot behind his back. He had come across better knots in the navy. His fingers had become quite nimble and strong. Helen somehow got to her feet, hands to her eyes. She daren't look at Harry. She felt Matthew's hand on her bodice. He ripped at it. 'Bastard!' she muttered, but it all seemed in vain. Then a glimmer of hope. She looked again, not daring to believe. Harry had seen it, too. Bart had got his hands free.

'Dance, pretty lady!' yelled Matthew. She put her hands above her head in mock obedience and began to gently gyrate; then, shocking everyone, she pushed down the torn bodice, revealing her naked breasts. The men gasped. The men gaped. Bart leapt. The two cohorts crashed down face-first with the weight of the ex-sailor on their backs. Matthew staggered back, and Harry seized his moment. His right fist swung into Matthew's face; the sound of the jawbone breaking was obvious. He dropped the sword as he fell. Shock and fury were on his face and filling his mind. It was agony, but he wasn't finished. He stood up and ran manically at Harry. The two toppled and Matthew's pent-up hatred gave strength to his hands. They were around Harry's throat, throttling, squeezing. Harry's eyes dimmed. He couldn't move. *I'm sorry, Helen,* went through his mind. He waited for deliverance, but it didn't come. Blood splattered, warm, onto his face. It wasn't his. He opened his eyes to see a sword digging deep into Matthew's throat. The hand on the hilt was slender white-knuckled. The courageous right hand of Helen Westhouse.

Chapter 39

Harry felt something cold, wiping his face. His eyes flickered open, groggily working out where he was. He was on a soft bed. Helen was sitting, leaning over him. She dipped the cloth into a bowl of reddened water. 'It's not your blood,' she mouthed reassuringly. 'It's *his*.' She accompanied the last words with a glance in the direction of Matthew Stokes, who lay face down in his wide crimson pool.

'I saved your life, Sailor. You owe me one.'

Harry couldn't help but stare at her lovely eyes. The eyes he had yearned for through thick and thin.

'It's all true, Harry,' she bumbled on. 'What he said about me. It's all true. You can hate me for it if you like, but I can't change it. Can't hide it from you. I was going to try. I said in my letter to you that I worked and lodged at the bakers. I hoped you'd think that was from the start. Fact is, the people who saved me that night, the owners of the inn, were the only ones who'd take me in, but then they expected me to work there for my living, and now you know how.'

She kept mopping at Harry's face as she spoke, even though the blood had all disappeared from it. He noticed that she was wearing a shawl. His last memories were the sight of her lovely naked bosom, Bart crashing onto two men's backs, his own fist smashing into Matthew Stokes' jaw.

'So, what happened after I hit him?'

'He dropped the sword, leapt on you and got his hands around your throat. You were turning blue. I grabbed the sword, but I didn't know what to do. I had the sudden flash of a memory. The bloody sight of a pig being slaughtered on the farm. I thought, *Go for the throat! I sliced it in, and, God, I feel sick.*'

Harry held her hand while she composed herself. 'What happened to the others?' he muttered as she took deep breaths.

'The two fellows Bart jumped on got up and started laying into him. He took quite a battering, but he'll be all right. They turned and looked at me. I was up on my feet. I must have looked grotesque, half-naked, blood all over the place, dripping off the sword. I shook it at them a bit. They gaped at Matthew's bleedin' body, and they ran off.'

'Well done,' returned Harry. 'They could do with you in the navy!'

Both sniggered at the thought.

'The two brothers?' she went on. 'The younger one, Mark, has taken Andy to get some treatment. I don't know where. Again, he'll recover, but you certainly sorted him out.'

'What was that all about?' asked Harry, his mind clearing. 'Who the hell was he?'

'They live here. Enoch Hoskins has sort of adopted them since their parents died. Andy thinks that because he's an artist, women should throw themselves at his feet. When he found that I wouldn't, he got grouchy with me. It turned into a silly argument, and then it got more and more out of hand. That's where you stepped in. My knight in shining armour!'

'See! So, I saved your life, too! We're even!'

There was a pause, both reflecting heavily on the events.

'So,' said Helen at last. 'Do you hate me or love me?'

The ex-sailor's head juggled with the jumble of messages. He hated her for selling her body, but she had been through hell for him, longed and waited for his return. Now, she had saved him from certain death. He owed everything to her. He had not been perfect himself. The images of Molly and Jelzina flickered in his mind. His hand went instinctively to the purple scarf, and Helen saw how important it was to him.

'I can't hate you.' He sighed. 'And look, I've got confessions to make myself.'

She gave him a puzzled glance but then cocked her head to one side as she heard a groan from downstairs.

'Who's that?' demanded Harry.

'It's that Nurse Janet!'

Harry startled Helen by sitting up rather abruptly, anxiety in his face.

'What's she doing here?' he croaked, his memory blurred and confused.

'Bart said she followed you two here; some kind of guilt about giving you away to Matthew. Anyway, it seems she tried to stop him'—gesturing again at the blood-soaked body—'and got stabbed for her trouble.'

'How bad is she?'

Helen now felt that he was showing far too much concern. 'Could this be one of the confessions he was talking about?'

He climbed off the bed and made for the door.

Earlier, Jelzina had struggled to her feet and made her way to the front of the shop, blood seeping freely from her wounded chest. She saw the two spies outside and managed to bolt the door. They barged at it, but it wouldn't give. The other two then came charging down the stairs, terrified witnesses of Matthew Stokes' demise, ran out of the back door and around to the front. There was urgent discussion, the gesturing of a finger across the throat, and frightened looks. They turned and made off down the street. She had leant against the counter for support, but it was getting more and more painful to breathe. She slumped to the floor with a loud groan.

Harry rushed down the stairs, Helen right at his heels. He stared at Jelzina's heaving bosom, the blood-soaked dress. Her eyes were rolling, looking dim. Harry knelt beside her, fear and horror on his face. Helen knelt down, too and stroked at her forehead. The green eyes followed her hand.

'My ring,' Jelzina muttered. 'You're wearing my ring.'

Harry was shocked by her words. He gasped and dithered.

'It's not yours,' he mumbled at last. 'I told you. It's Helen's.'

Helen no longer had to guess.

'I'm going,' mouthed Jelzina and heaved more painful breaths. 'At least let me die wearing it.'

Helen slipped the ring from her finger and onto Jelzina's.

'I deserve it,' came Jelzina's voice, now barely a whisper.

'Did I tell you, Johny Sapphire?' she managed. 'You're the best I ever... had.'

The green eyes stared vacantly at the ceiling and Harry's tears splashed down onto her waxen face. He pushed her eyes closed and slowly took the ring from her finger, offered it to Helen. She stretched out her hand for him to slide it on.

'I assume this is your confession,' she muttered, collecting her thoughts, and Harry nodded.

'She was very pretty,' said Helen sincerely. 'And very brave.'

Bart had come down from the attic where he had been bathing his wounds. 'Christ!' both men said in unison, Harry because of Bart's battered appearance, Bart because of the body laid out on the floor. The three living souls stared at each other. So much had happened in such short a time. Emotions and thoughts ran riot in their heads. There were two dead bodies. Enemies had fled but would return. Enoch Hoskins had simply disappeared.

Chapter 40

The sun had dipped low in the western sky, casting long shadows, and a cool breeze was wafting in from the sea. Harry peered out of the back door of the bakery. All was quiet.

He bent down to pick up one end of the rolled-up carpet. Bart lifted the other end. It was a struggle. The dead weight of Matthew's body made them stagger as they carried it to the cart. Blood oozed through the carpet and onto their clothes. They shoved it into place without much respect and returned for the second, lighter body, the much more revered and respected body of the brave, red-headed Jelzina.

Bart slapped the reigns and the old delivery cart wobbled gently out of the yard with its awful cargo. Harry sat next to Bart on the driver's bench, both men staring ahead, hardly comprehending the events that had led to this moment. The elation they had felt on attaining their freedom, dreams of the magical reunion with Helen, all was now shattered. Their spirit couldn't have been lower. The dear horse could not be rushed. She was used to the easy trek around the town with its many stops, its nosebag and a simple cartload of bread. Bart's constant reminder of gently slapping reigns kept her moving, the damp cobbles proving difficult for hooves and for the wheels.

Nevertheless, and slow though it was, relentless progress was being made. Cobbles gave way to hardened mud as they cleared the town, the same familiar track they had returned on, the one they had been adored on by the crowd as they took the supposed Nelson on his victorious way. They knew the ideal spot to head for: the deep bend in the river where Poplar Wainwright was submerged. He would soon be joined by his master, Matthew Stokes, and poor Jelzina. It was not a time for conversation; the only sounds were the horse's plodding hooves, her occasional whinnied complaint and the creaks and groans of the cart.

At last, they reached the familiar spot. The horse came gladly to a halt, sweating and snorting as she scraped a hoof at the grass. It was dusk by now, an eerie mist hovering over the water, the sound of the ripples on the nearby bank. Harry clambered down, and so did Bart, not bothering to tether the horse as she would obviously be going no further without encouragement. They hauled the larger of the two carpet-shrouded bodies from the cart, leaving a smear of blood on the boards. They struggled, they staggered, and they hauled the detested body through shrubbery and long grass. They stopped and looked around for the rocks that would act as cannon balls and weigh the whole thing down to the river bed. Harry stopped dead in his tracks, his face distorting into shock. He held an arm out to stop Bart from moving any further. He had realised they were not alone.

***

For all her best efforts, Helen was having great difficulty in scrubbing and mopping the floor. Congealed blood clung to the crevices on the floorboards where it had soaked through the carpet. 'What the hell will Enoch say when he comes home to find this lot?' she muttered to herself. 'That's if he comes home at all. He must be damned fed up with me going on about Harry coming back, my beautiful sapphire ring. He thought I was his. God, I should never have let him into my bed.' She dabbed at her brow with the back of her hand and pushed damp auburn strands back into place. 'God, I hate all this,' she mumbled on. 'Why the hell didn't I just stay at bloody Westhouse Farm?'

''Cos then you wouldn't have met me!' came a voice from the door. Helen gasped, heart thumping, and she turned towards it. 'Christ, Mark! You gave me a scare!'

'Ha! A scare? Count yourself lucky! After all that's gone on here tonight, a scare is the least you could hope for.' Helen scowled and went back to her scrubbing. Mark watched.

'You could bloody well help, you know!' moaned Helen, but as usual, he was too besotted by her body, the overwhelming memories of their encounter, and now, the more recent images of her half-naked dance. He just stood and watched.

'What's happened to Andy?' she asked at last, giving up on her request for help.

Mark sneered and said, 'He'll mend, looks worse than it is. I bloody hate him for what he did to you, and I love the way your feller sorted him out. He deserved it, didn't he? Where is he now?'

'On body disposal duty.' The comment made it sound like an everyday occurrence. Mark winced. Helen kept on scrubbing.

'Have you seen Enoch?' she ventured at last.

'No. Why? Where was he when all this was going on?'

'I don't know.' There was anxiety in her voice, then some hesitation before she felt the compulsion to explain. 'He disappeared soon after we learned that Harry was alive and on his way back. It must have been quite a shock. I mean, we both thought that Harry was dead.'

Mark felt a glimmer of understanding, remembering the embrace between her and Enoch that he had walked in on and disturbed.

'There aren't many places he might have gone,' said Mark. 'I'll go and see if I can find the old codger.'

***

Two unknown men stood on the river bank, little more than silhouettes, pointing, gesticulating downwards. Two others were waist-deep in the icy water, grovelling and struggling with an immovable object. 'Christ!' muttered Bart, on a gasp. He and Harry turned instinctively, their first thought to get out of there. 'How the hell could this have happened?'

'Nobody knew except for us!' But they turned straight into the burley figures of two more strangers, anger and questions on their haggard faces. 'Who the hell are you?' one demanded gruffly. Neither Harry nor Bart had breath to answer.

The two men at the water's edge heard the commotion and turned away from their task, looking inquisitively instead at the two interlopers.

'Who are they?' one demanded. Bewilderment was on all six faces.

'I know,' came a small voice from the side of them. All turned to face the diminutive lady, black-veiled, black cloak, a serious look on her swarthy face.

'These are the men who brought him here,' she went on. 'I recognise them, even without their smart uniforms and hats.'

Bart and Harry gaped. Her accent was familiar, like Sandro, the fisherman who got them to escape the navy, unmistakable Portuguese.

'They're not to blame,' she went on. There was a pause while all the men puzzled over her words.

'You must surely have realised who I am,' she directed the comment at Harry and Bart. 'I'm Poplar Wainwright's mother.'

Helen paced the floor. She'd tired of scrubbing and was feeling scared and alone. She had bolted the door when Mark left. Now it was dark and the window only offered a reflection of herself with her flickering candle. 'Where the hell is Enoch?' she pondered again. 'And where the hell are Harry and Bart?'

At that moment, Harry and Bart were staring incredulously at the black-adorned woman, now lit by a flickering lantern in her hand.

'His mother?' managed Harry. 'But how on earth? I mean…'

'How did I know where to find him? I followed you on horseback. I'd had a letter from the navy telling me he was badly injured. I went to the quay expecting to see him on some stretcher or other. Imagine my shock when I saw him dressed up in that uniform in a smart carriage with you two, his escorts. Everyone was cheering. They thought, as they were supposed to, that it was Nelson, their hero. I must have been the only one there who knew that it wasn't. I'd recognise my son anywhere. A mother always can, you know, no matter how good the disguise.'

There was silence, pity for the bereaved mother, and incredulity of the circumstance. It was her voice that arose again. 'You laid him respectfully to rest,' she said. 'I saw you do it, but I was too scared and grief-stricken to intervene. Those other brutes who overtook me and stopped you would have killed him if he'd still been alive. The plan worked perfectly, didn't it? They all think that Nelson is dead?'

'As far as we know,' offered Bart.

'I watched your stupid antics, roughing yourselves up and gashing the carriage. I assume you told your commanders what a brave fight you'd put up?'

The woman gazed intently at the bulging rolled-up carpet at their feet. Her eyes asked the question. She didn't need to speak.

'Another unfortunate sailor,' invented Bart. 'Died in port, so no burial at sea. Nobody knows who he is. We've been detailed in dealing with it.'

'Same watery grave as my son?' she enquired. Bart nodded.

The men in the river were shouting for help. 'Where the hell have you gone?' came their voices, left struggling in the darkness and freezing cold water. The first two men returned and were ordered to haul on some ropes. Bart and Harry even helped as men strained on the impossible weight. 'There's rocks in there,' said Harry. 'It was never meant to move. It's how we did burials at sea; only then it was cannon balls.'

'I want to give him a proper funeral,' said the mother. 'And a proper grave.'

Men were nodding, expressions sombre and pained, as they struggled to get the shrouded body onto their cart. There it lay, water streaming out of it onto the floor. One of them spread a black sheet over it. The mother mumbled a little prayer and climbed up alongside the driver.

There was a crack of the reigns and a shout of, 'Get on!' from the driver and the cart began to move. 'Goodbye,' said the mother.

'Goodbye,' returned Harry and Bart.

The two men returned to their dreadful task, silent and bewildered by such weird events. They wondered if they had used too many rocks. The body of Matthew Stokes was impossible to carry. They resorted to dragging it through the undergrowth. They heaved and groaned, muscles straining to the limit till they reached the water's edge. The river had cut a steep bank there, a vertical drop of about four feet. They rolled the body over the edge and, in the darkness, simply hoped it had disappeared. Harry couldn't resist spitting hatefully into the rippling flow of water and muttering, 'Enjoy hell, you bastard!'

The burial of Jelzina was a far more sombre affair. Harry remembered her cheerful, freckly face, her colourful little phrases, the splendour of her body, her bravery at the end. 'And she really wanted to wear my sapphire ring,' he mused. They laid her at the top of the bank. 'Unto thee, we commend this spirit,' Bart muttered. 'Will she make it to heaven?' he mumbled. They rolled her into her dark, watery resting place. Harry smiled and said, 'I think her sins will be forgiven.'

***

Helen turned, startled, towards the sound of knuckles rapping urgently at the back door.

'Who is it?' she demanded, striding towards it.

'Mark! Let me in!' was the loud whisper.

She pulled back the bolts and hauled on the door to see a tearstained face, reddened with the exertion of running, eyes pained by an awful truth.

'What the hell…?' she managed as he strode past her into the room.

'Enoch!' he groaned. 'He's dead!'

Helen couldn't breathe. Mark watched her crumple to the ground. He didn't know what to do. He had never seen anyone faint before. He tried to sit her up. He tried patting her face. Thank God! At last! He saw her lungs fill up and heard a grinding in her throat. Her eyes opened and rolled around; her hands pressed the floor for stability.

'Where am I?' she croaked. Mark handed her a mug of water. She gulped it and then sat up, rubbing at her head.

'Christ, you scared me,' said Mark. 'I thought you had died!'

'What happened?' she grumbled, still unable to grasp reality.

'I think you fainted. I don't know.'

'Why did I faint?'

''Cos of what I told you. Don't do it again. I'm sorry, there's no easy way of saying this. I told you that Enoch was dead.'

Helen gasped. She gasped hard. Her eyes rolled again, but she managed to fight it, shaking her head in disbelief and biting manically at the back of her hand.

'How? What?' she uttered, trying to mouth the words that her shocked brain was screaming.

'Drowned in the harbour,' said Mark. 'Did himself in, they said. No one could stop him!'

Helen's mouth gaped in horror as he spoke. Mark recoiled.

'God. It's my fault!' she gasped. 'Me and my fancy ring!'

Mark looked bewildered. She thrust her hand towards him; the "sapphire" sparkled its reflections of the candle. 'This!'

'What d'you mean?' he demanded.

'A lieutenant brought it to me from Harry. Told me he was alive! I couldn't believe it! I waved the thing in the air. Can't remember exactly. Said something about how thrilled I was that he was coming home to me! Poor Enoch! I can't believe he's done that!'

They both breathed hard. Both had tears in their eyes. 'I know how fond he was of you,' whispered Mark, not knowing the full extent of the growing relationship. 'What a mess!' he groaned at last, and he put his arms around her, hugging her tight. 'What a God damned bloody mess!'

The journey back to town was an arduous affair. The horse shied and whinnied at every little noise. She hated the dark. She stumbled and stopped several times. Bart coaxed her on with the reigns but eventually gave up and got out of the cart, taking hold of her bridle and leading her along the uncertain track. Both men were exhausted and it was a weary knock at the door that eventually heralded their arrival at the shop. Mark asked who was there and recognised the voices as they grumbled their reply.

'What are *you* doing here?' demanded Harry. 'Where's Helen?'

'I live here,' responded the young man. 'At least, I *did.* God knows what's going to happen now.'

Harry was too tired and ill-tempered to ask what the hell he was talking about. 'Where's Helen?' he repeated.

'Upstairs, asleep as far as I know. She made me stay on guard and let you two in. Nobody else.'

Harry couldn't help a slight sneer as he cast a disdainful look at the young man's slight physique. 'Going to fight off all those evil bastards yourself, were you, if they came back?'

'Fight them off? No. But I could give 'em hell with this.' He picked up the blunderbuss from the table, a fearsome-looking weapon that made Harry wince and believe that he might well have slaughtered the attackers if the need had arisen.

Harry made his way upstairs and knocked on Helen's door. There was no response. He saw his hand take hold of the handle, turn it and push the door open. She was deeply asleep. He listened to her heavy breathing and maybe, just maybe, between the breaths, a little sob. He bent over her and placed a light kiss on her forehead, then retreated, closed the door quietly and went back downstairs.

'You live here, you say?' he asked. Mark nodded.

'Yes. I seem to remember Helen telling me that.'

'I've got a room in the attic.'

'Well, if you want to turn in, you can. Me and Bart will take over guarding. Morning Watch by now, eh, Bart?' The two ex-sailors exchanged a grin, and Mark went wearily up the stairs.

Chapter 41

It was a morning like any other in Norport. Shopkeepers were making ready for the onset of their earliest customers; innkeepers were cleaning floors and testing the quality of their ale. The harbour was busy with goods being moved in and out. Seagulls wheeled around, scavenging, squawking. Dogs barked. Horses champed at the bit and scraped hooves on the cobbles. It was a day like any other except for one thing. There would be no deliveries of bread today from Hoskins Kitchen.

Bart was the man on watch. He'd positioned himself in the middle of the shop where he could see both doors and windows. He'd perched on the most uncomfortable stool he could find to prevent himself from falling asleep. He had two huge kitchen knives at his side in case "cutlass was required to repel boarders". He certainly didn't trust himself to use the mighty blunderbuss gun. His mind was wandering around Westhouse Farm, the letter he'd received from his father, wondering how he was coping with all that extra land. Dear Beatrice. How he missed that lady with her kind words, game pie and freshly baked bread.

Seagulls were massing around the backyard. They could usually rely on stale scraps being thrown out at about this time. Not this morning. Helen woke when she heard their protesting commotion. She buried her head in the pillow, but they wouldn't go away. Awful realities started creeping into her mind. 'Was Enoch really dead? Did Harry and Bart ever come back from disposing of those bodies?' She slithered out of bed, got dressed in a hurry and pulled the brush painfully through her knotted hair. She hated her mirror that morning. She had dark rings sagging under her eyes.

At last, she ventured down. Harry was asleep and snoring loudly on some sacking on the kitchen floor. Bart sat upright on his stool, slowly rotating one of the knives in his hand. He looked up at her and smiled. They both remembered those evenings by the fire, moaning, 'There must be more to life than this.'

'What a pickle we're in, eh, sis!' were his words of greeting. He didn't seem like her "little brother" any more. His chest and shoulders had broadened. There was black stubble on his thickening jaw; his hair was long and sailor-fashioned, slicked down with tar.

She sighed. She looked out of the window. 'People will be expecting their bread,' she mumbled. Both smiled resignedly. Both had so many questions in their heads. Harry stopped snoring. He sighed deeply and turned over. Uncomfortable, his eyes flickered open. He stared hard at the tiles around him, wondering where the hell he was. Why was the floor so still? Not rocking. He sat up and saw Helen and Bart looking his way, the truth of the situation slowly coming into his brain.

'So,' he ventured amidst a sleepy yawn, 'What the hell do we all do now?'

The question hung in the air. Harry clambered from his sacking, stretched and yawned again. He was staring out of the window when he next spoke. 'You two *have* got a home to go to.'

It was Helen who responded. 'You have too, Harry. If you want to, that is.'

He turned and looked at her. It was the same enthralling face that had been in his mind, his dreams, his hopes, as he battled and fought his way home. 'Is it what you want?' she asked, but he didn't have time to answer. Mark was running down the stairs. 'You need to get out!' he yelled urgently. 'It's my brother! I've seen him in the street getting his gang together. He's after your blood!'

Bart and Harry didn't waste any time. They dashed into the yard. 'Quick! Harry was saying, 'Get the cart harnessed up! We need to get out of here!'

They *were* quick about their business and Bart was soon up in the driver's seat, slapping the reins on the complaining horse's rump. They turned out of the yard and onto the road, hoping and praying that they'd have enough time to escape.

The cart trundled on. Bart continued to urge the beloved mare into faster steps, but she would not be bossed around. Harry and Helen sat behind the driver's seat, facing backwards. It was every bit as uncomfortable as the contraption that had brought them to Norport almost a year ago. They remembered that first glimpse of the place, the awful stink of the sea. Funny, but now they couldn't smell it at all.

'You two comfortable?' asked Bart with a smirk.

'Bloody awful!' moaned Harry. Helen added, 'Good job, we've got this sacking to sit on, or we'd be black and blue!'

'Ha!' grumbled her brother. 'Take another look at my face! I already am!'

Norport continued to slither away behind them. The cart swayed and lurched over cobbles and stone.

'So,' said Harry, a little apprehensively to Helen, 'Are you going to tell us all about Enoch Hoskins?'

'It's simple enough.' She sighed. 'He saved me. Saved me from that dreadful life I was living at the tavern. He gave me back some respectability. Hid me away in his kitchen. I just wanted you to come back to me. Spent my days at that table, that oven. It wasn't great, but it wasn't bloody whoring. I heard about your ship blowing up! I thought you two were dead! I didn't get any more letters. Enoch kept saying things like you'd be kept too busy or letters get lost at sea, but I really reckoned you were both dead! Anyway.' She took a deep breath. 'He came to me one night, less than a week ago. He'd been such a gentleman with me, so considerate and kind. He was so polite. He said, 'Can I share the pleasures of your bed?' I was astounded, of course. He looked so pitiful, so sincere. I couldn't refuse. I just pushed back the blanket and invited him in. He was really gentle with me. Not like some of the bastards I had to put up with. So, there we were. I thought

I was safe and secure. He thought all his dreams had come true. Got his shop, his customers, and me sharing a bed, then *wham!* In comes a lieutenant with your beautiful ring, who says you're still alive. I go into raptures of delight, and his world falls apart. Poor bastard. It's the end of the world for him. He throws himself in the harbour.' She had to stop talking. Her throat was croaking with anguish. There were tears in those beautiful eyes.

Harry had listened to her tale. His heart was sinking. Being forced into whoring was one thing. Going willingly with another man was different. He knew he wasn't perfect himself, but then, both Molly and Jelzina had taken the lead on him. He realised that Jelzina's death was bearing heavily on his soul. He was finding this all hard to take.

Helen was drying her eyes on the sacking. She said gently, 'I told you you'd hate me. I understand.'

'Oh Christ!' was Harry's unexpected response, but it was nothing to do with Helen's confession. He'd been keeping an eye on the road behind and was the first to see them. Then came the sound of their hooves. Bart twisted around; his battered face contorted even more. He and Harry had seen this before. Black cloaks spread out like raven's wings, followed by a curtain of dust, hooves drumming hard. There was no contest. Their pursuers were gobbling up the ground. The cart was soon surrounded. Horses were reined in, snorting, sweating. The leading man loomed above them. His pistol wavered around his quarry as though ready to pick off the first to offer a threat. There was none. Harry stared at the man; his eye mask covered much of his face, but recognition was immediate. It was no surprise, just self-disgust, that he had not realised that Andy was one of the gang that had waylaid the supposed Horatio Nelson. Even so, he was proud of the way he had dealt with the bastard. Those knuckle-stinging blows had demolished him. The sight of him sent sickening memories through Helen's head. 'Bloody rapist,' she couldn't help but mutter. His jaw was black and blue and so was one eye when he pulled off the mask.

'I thought you'd like to admire your handiwork!' snarled Andy. He winced as he spoke and held his painful ribs with his spare hand, groaning, 'Get out of the cart!'

'We're not going anywhere!' was Harry's shocking retort. 'Now Mark!'

The command staggered the assailants. They gasped and gaped as the sacking was thrown back to reveal Mark Williamson lying prone with the blunderbuss. The huge weapon pointed straight at the group; its splayed end ready to blast lead shot into all of them. How Mark hoped the sight of it would be deterrent enough. He didn't want to use it. Horses whinnied and reared. Men hauled on the reins. Some men were thrown off; others galloped away expecting the boom and peppering of deadly shots. Only Andy remained, and he had hardly spat out the words, 'Stupid, stupid, little brother!' when Bart leapt at him from the driver's seat, sending them both crashing down to the ground. There was a sickening crack as the pistol went off.

Agonising moments went by as both men lay motionless on the ground. Andy's group had steadied themselves; some were remounting. They all kept their distance, wary of the weapon that still pointed their way, even though their supposed executioner was distracted now by his brother's distress. Harry got down from the cart and went to Bart, who was lying face down. He turned him to see his bruised and swollen face. 'Thank God!' he muttered; his friend was still breathing. The blood on his shirt was Andy's. Mark deserted his gun and ran to his brother. He was a crazy, half-French bastard, but he *was* his brother. There were a few shallow breaths still left in his body and he tried to breathe a few words. Nobody was quite sure what he said, but it sounded rather like "*Vive l'Empereur*".

Helen had grabbed the gun as Mark deserted it. She looked fearsome even though she had no idea how to use it. The group kept their distance. They watched forlornly as their leader was hoisted onto his horse, face down across the saddle. Mark was streaming tears. Andy's horse made its way back to the group. They were wrecked. They doffed hats and crossed their chests. They turned away and wandered off.

Mark was devastated. Even a hug from Helen was not enough to bring him around. They all clambered back into the cart and Bart cracked the reins.

'He was a bloody fool!' uttered Mark at last. 'And I'm so sorry for what he did to you, Helen. All that time he spent in Paris. It just ruined him.'

The others could only nod with sincerity. Helen gritted her teeth as last night's awful attack on her reared its ugly head in her brain. She continued to hold Mark close and felt that it was almost as comforting for her as it was for him. 'Would you like to come and stay on the farm with us?' she mumbled.

Mark thought about poor Enoch and poor, poor Andy. His family was destroyed. He almost smiled in the security of Helen's arms and mumbled, 'I've got nowhere else to go.'

Chapter 42

Beatrice blinked hard.

The bedraggled mare looked ready to collapse. The cart it pulled through the gate of Westhouse Farm was faded and worn. The man at the reins was darker skinned than she remembered him, his features distorted, swollen and bruised. His shoulders and chest looked broader, but it was *him* all right. She had told him not to try too hard. 'Bart?' She breathed. Then just shouted, 'Richard, Richard! It's them!'

She ran to the door and glared in amazement. Bart beamed a huge smile at her. So did Helen. Poor Beatrice almost fainted. 'Richard!' she called out again.

Four people climbed from the cart and came towards her. It was like a dream. The first to hug her was Helen. 'You're so thin!' muttered Beatrice.

Richard, at last, appeared in the doorway. His shock and surprise were obvious to all as tears rolled uncontrollably on his face and he steadied himself against the frame.

Then Bart was enveloped by Beatrice's next embrace. 'God, you've grown!' she said and gave one of his biceps an admiring squeeze. 'But what on earth happened to your face?'

'It's a long story,' he replied. 'A long, long story.'

Richard and Helen hugged almost tentatively. Helen's head was full of guilt about having run away from home. Richard was full of regret for driving her away. Neither quite knew how the other would react, but the underlying love was enough for the moment. Then Richard held out his hand for his son to shake. 'I told you I'd bring them home, Papa,' he muttered and they both smiled.

'We've prayed for this moment,' said Richard. 'God, how we've prayed.'

The chatter went deep into the night. Tales of Bart and Harry's heroism dominated with perhaps a little enhancement here and there. Beer and wine were quaffed heartily, which helped colour their reminiscences. Mark chipped in with his description of the hero Nelson's departure in his carriage. Bart and Harry just cast each other a knowing glance. Nobody needed to know of the plot to kill him and his remarkable survival. Helen described her rescue from the press gang, how she went off and found work and lodgings at the baker's shop. Everyone knew she'd blotted out the months of debauchery at the Half Moon Tavern; everyone was trying to expunge it from *their* minds, too.

The next morning found everyone waking and wondering, 'Was it all a dream?'

Helen smiled when she heard the cockerel instead of the gulls. Harry and Mark were in the outhouse with the other men. Their appearance had, of course, caused mayhem the night before. Drunk and noisy, they had staggered in, disturbing everyone's sleep. Harry had to recount the stories again, but what all of the farmhands wanted to know was. 'What was Miss Helen like in bed?' Harry blushed. His worldliness would have to plummet with this confession. 'I never got to find out.'

The room fell silent with disbelief and disappointment. 'I was nabbed by that bloody press gang before I had a chance,' he muttered. 'When I finally got back to her, we had to run for our lives and landed up here!' Mark squirmed a little. He could have told them what she was like. He had burning memories of Helen. Memories he had to keep to himself that warmed him every night.

'So why aren't you in bed with her now?' someone asked.

'It just wouldn't be right, would it? Back in her family home. Her father lords over us all. He still hates me for taking her away, though he did his best not to show it. I could hardly say, 'Goodnight then. I'm off to bed with your daughter!'

Men grimaced and nodded or shook their heads. They settled again onto the pillow and mattress. Harry closed his eyes and saw Helen, but she was cavorting with other men, pushing back that blanket for Enoch. He couldn't help the tear that escaped from his eye.

When dawn broke, Helen peered from her window and gazed down through dazzling morning light at the barn. She remembered that first glimpse of Harry with his pitchfork, muscular, happy. She remembered sitting by the fire with Bart, saying, 'There must be more to life than this.' She shook her head, hoping for some clarity of thought, washed her face in the cold water from the jug, and looked ruefully at the empty bed. 'Oh, Harry.' She sighed and went downstairs.

Beatrice was the only one there. They hugged again, heads full of whirling thoughts, images and regrets. 'It's so good to have you home,' managed Beatrice at last. 'But it might have been even better had you and Harry got away together and started a whole new life of your own.' Helen smiled. Then she saw the basket of morsels for the chickens and her smile broadened even more.

'Can I?' She giggled.

'Be my guest,' lilted the maid.

Helen loved it. The birds came swarming around as though she'd never been away. She stepped around the yard, casting handfuls of the stuff and watching them squabble. *They're like men,* she thought to herself. *Fighting over this and that. Pecking hatefully at the one that gets the prize in the hope they'll drop it.*

She tipped the basket upside-down and tapped away the last crumbs. She wondered if Harry was hiding somewhere watching her as he had before, not daring to speak until that fateful tumble brought him dashing to her aid. She smiled again. She was getting used to smiling. She liked it. Her life should be full of smiles. Someone *was* watching her smile. Someone skulking in the hay loft. It wasn't Harry. It was Mark.

Richard Westhouse stood by his wife's grave. He'd brought flowers for the first time since her funeral. He knelt down beside the tombstone and laid them across her chest. 'They're back,' he murmured. 'You knew I would get them back.' Sarah's face smiled from the engraved stone.

'Yes,' she nodded. 'I knew you would.'

'I'll always love you, Sarah,' he whispered. 'I want to ask your blessing, though. For me and Beatrice.' There was silence, but he saw the merest hint of a nod as she faded from view.

Then her voice whispered in the breeze, 'I love you too.'

When he returned to the farm, he found Bart ready and waiting for him. His bruises had subsided somewhat; a blackened eye and a healing cut on his lip were the remaining reminders of what he'd been through.

'We need to survey all this land we've got now,' said the gentleman farmer, trying not to stare at his son's wounds. 'All of your Uncle Cedric's as well as dear Westhouse Farm. We need to work out how to manage it between us.'

Bart nodded. 'Shall we saddle up the horses and take a trip around?'

'Yes, we should,' said Richard. He liked the keen attitude that his son had found. It gave him a new outlook on what had seemed an impossible task.

'Can we take Harry?' went on Bart.

Richard grimaced. He had no enthusiasm for this idea. He had played along with the euphoria of the homecoming last night, but deep down, he couldn't forgive Harry for stealing his daughter away.

Bart could see the clouds in the man's eyes. 'He's my greatest friend now,' he felt the need to add. 'We've been through so much.'

There was a reluctant smile from his father and a nod, which Bart took as acceptance, saying, 'I'll go and saddle up the horses.'

Mark wasn't sure what he was supposed to do. As the three men rode off, he was left high and dry, somewhat ignored. He finished his exploration of the barn and stables, talked for a while to the geese and the cockerel, then went into the kitchen.

'Something to eat, young man?' offered Beatrice.

'Yes, please. That bread smells lovely.'

'I hear you were a baker,' said Beatrice. 'Hope mine's as good as yours.'

'Oh, I never actually baked any,' replied Mark. 'Just delivered it. Helen did all the baking.'

'I'll have to get her baking here,' she went on. 'She never did any cooking before she left. God knows how she learned so fast. Hidden talents; that's what she's got.'

Mark just smiled and chewed on the bread.

'Beatrice says you've got hidden talents,' were the young man's words as Helen walked in. She looked a little surprised. 'Learning to cook so quickly, she meant. She says she'll get you cooking here!'

'Well. Perhaps in a day or two,' said Beatrice. 'That's if you want to, of course. Anyway, I must take this tray up for your father. He'll be wondering where I've got to.'

Helen looked across the table at Mark, who couldn't hide the smirk on his face.

'I don't want any of that cheek from you,' she said. 'I know what you were thinking with those "hidden talents". Those days are behind me now.'

'It must be difficult,' said Mark, but Helen just pulled a rueful face. 'Where are the others?' she went on.

'Gone off riding around the estate,' said Mark. 'Something about working out how to manage it.'

'So, what are you going to do with yourself?'

'Don't know. I guess someday someone will find a use for me. Ledger clerk. Deliveries. Anything. Don't have any real talents. Not like my brother.'

'Oh, come on! You don't want to be like him. All those crazy ideas from France!'

'I know, I know, but he did have a talent. He was a really good artist.'

'God, don't I know it. An eye for all the ladies he painted too.'

'I've never tried, though,' said Mark, overlooking her comment.

'You should,' insisted Helen. 'You did all that beautiful writing. I reckon you'd have as much talent as him. Tell you what. Mother had a whole lot of painting stuff, easels, brushes and the lot. She used to love it. Landscapes, flowers, all sorts of things she painted. I'll look it out for you, and you can give it a go!'

Chapter 43

'Is Harry all right?'

'As far as I know. Yes. He seems fine to me. Why?'

Helen stared into the fire. 'I haven't seen him today,' she said. 'That's all.'

'He came out riding with me and Papa,' replied Bart. 'We had a look all over the farm. I hadn't realised how much land there was when you put this one together with Uncle Cedric's.'

'No. I'm sure,' she agreed and continued staring at the flames. 'So, where do you think he is now?'

'I don't know. I left him in the stables dealing with the horses, at least, learning how to take off the harness, I think, from one of the men.'

'Did he say much? I mean, about me or anything?'

'Not really. He was a bit quiet, I suppose. Me and Papa did most of the chatting about what crops we should grow where. You know. All that kind of thing.'

He stared with her at the fire. 'No more Matthew Stokes, eh?' mused Helen. Bart smiled and she went on, 'Saw him off good and proper, didn't I?'

'You sure did. You saved Harry's life at the same time, that's for sure.'

'Has he lost interest in me?' she asked, her eyes looking a little moister.

'Of course not. I guess it's just taking time for him to adjust. This is a different world, you know, to being in the navy. It's so regimented out there. Bells sounding off and you know where you've got to be. Get a bit out of line and you get a flogging.'

Helen nodded. 'Being home feels odd to me too.'

***

It was the next day when the knock came at the front door. Beatrice opened up to see a smartly dressed, official-looking man with a leather case in one hand. 'Is there a Miss Westhouse here?' he asked.

'And you are?' she asked a little brusquely.

'I deal with legal matters,' the man said. 'It's concerning a will. Is Mr Richard Westhouse here too?'

'You'd better come in,' she said, opening the door further. 'I'll go and get them.'

The man was ushered into the drawing room, where he stood admiring the view of the garden until they arrived: Richard and Helen, inquisitive.

'Good day, sir,' uttered Richard. 'It's concerning a will, you say?'

'That's right, sir. Goddard's the name. I deal with most of the navy wills. This one's to do with Mr Enoch Hoskins.'

Richard gasped. This was the first he'd heard of the fellow's death. Helen grimaced and both felt uneasy. 'Died in a drowning incident two days ago,' went on Goddard. 'He didn't have any family, but the last owners of the bakery are keen to buy it back. Say they've never been so bored since they sold up. Thought it would be nice and restful, but no. Mind you, it will take a lot of clearing up.'

Father and daughter still looked somewhat quizzically at the man, who realised he was rambling on unnecessarily. He opened his case and produced some papers.

'I have here the written will of the said Enoch Hoskins, bachelor of the parish of Norport. It says that the quarter share of the bakery which he owned, he bequeaths to Miss Helen Westhouse, late of Westhouse Farm, Fernhills.'

'Oh my God!' gulped Helen, her hands going instinctively to her mouth. There was nothing she could do about the reddening of her cheeks. She knew what her father would think, but in Richard's mind, it was another concern that she would find out who owned the major share. *Oh Christ,* thought Richard. *What a dreadful, dreadful mess!*

'The remainder, of course, remains in your ownership, Mr Westhouse,' said Goddard.

Richard closed his eyes. Helen's head swam. She had to sit down. 'You own it?' she demanded. 'You?'

Richard had to sit down, too, head in hand.

Goddard carried on. 'If you wish to keep the bakery, well that of course is up to you. Should you wish to sell to the Browns, I will of course distribute the proceeds to you in the same proportion.'

'You bought it from the Browns? You?' Helen went on, ignoring Goddard. 'You knew all about me!' She was reddening with anger and disbelief. 'You helped Enoch set up as a baker on the condition that he got me out of the tavern and into respectable employment! Oh my God! I should have known it was all too good to be true!'

The two stared at each other for several heartbeats. Helen flustered and furrowed, Richard resigned, forlorn. Goddard was the next to speak.

'I'm quite used to opening cans of worms within families over wills,' he muttered. 'This seems to be an exceptionally large can.'

Richard replied, 'I think you had better leave, Mr Goddard; we have a lot to discuss.'

Father and daughter simply sat and stared at each other as the man departed. Beatrice did the work of seeing him out, full of apologies and promised to make contact again when things became clearer. 'I hope you weren't rude to that fellow,' were her words as she entered the room. 'He's left a calling card for when you want to contact him again.'

'How did you find out about me?' asked Helen, a little calmer now.

'I came looking for you,' he replied. 'You and Bart. I found out about the press gang from Hoskins; God rest his soul, but I couldn't find you. Then, on the day I decided to give up and come home, he told me he had a letter to deliver to you and knew where you were. I couldn't believe it. I had to see for myself. I almost fell for your little ruse, someone else masquerading as Helen of Troy. I would have, too, if I hadn't heard someone behind me open a door. Just had to take a peek, didn't you, to make sure I'd been fooled?'

'I just wanted to protect you, Papa, from knowing what your daughter had become.'

'And, don't you see that by helping Hoskins buy that place, I was just trying to help *you*. I wanted to pretend that I knew nothing about it.'

They both stared at each other. All those mistakes, the good intentions, the exceptionally large can of worms.

'What on earth would your mother have made of all this?' mumbled Richard.

'Oh, I'm sure that mother would have quoted the bible. 'Let he who is without sin cast the first stone!' I suppose that would have been you, Papa. Paragon of virtue. Saint of all saints. Never let the slightest thought of sin enter your mind.'

He looked uncomfortable. Beatrice did, too. She blushed.

'Oh, wait a minute! Have I hit a raw nerve?' Helen demanded. 'While we've been away…' the words trailed off. Helen just nodded, realising the truth. 'You two have been acting as a married couple! Bedding out of wedlock! Well, that's a sin if ever there was one!'

'That's nothing to do with you, Helen,' groused her father. 'I've had just about enough of this.'

'Me too!' moaned Helen. 'Looks like we're all a lot of dreadful sinners, doesn't it? Can't see any of us making it to heaven, can you? What on earth must Mama be making of all this? Sitting patiently waiting for us up there. Never going to see us again, is she?' She was quickly up on her feet and out of the room. She was angry, let down, confused. She caught sight of her reflection in the mirror, dishevelled red, but she didn't care. She pounded on every stair as she escaped to her room. 'What a bloody, bloody mess!' she cursed as she went. 'Life! It's just a bloody mess!' She threw herself on the bed and sobbed deeply into the pillow.

'All of this because me and Harry ran off together!' she cursed. 'People dead! Enoch, Stokes, Andy, Nurse Janet! Countless others, I expect. Harry miserable, doesn't want to know me any more. Papa was disgusted but every bit as much a sinner. Beatrice too! What a mess! What a bloody, bloody mess!'

There was a tentative knock on her door. She was surprised. Who on earth would want to speak to her now?'

'Who is it?' she demanded, but there was no reply. 'Come in!' she croaked through her tears.

The handle turned and the door creaked open. 'Beaty, most likely,' she supposed. 'Come with another consoling hug.' She was totally wrong. She had seen that wide-brimmed hat and upturned collar before in a different life.

The fraction of his face that she could see was smiling. 'Mark!' she exclaimed. 'What are you playing at?'

'I have come to paint your picture,' he said in an attempted French accent. She wiped at her tears and even forced back a giggle.

'You reckon you're an artist now, do you?' she managed.

'Ah, *mais oui*!' he replied. 'Take a look at some of my work.'

He held two canvasses. One was a good representation of the farm with its background of rolling hills; she nodded politely; the other looked as though it might be a view from the hay loft. In the centre was a young woman with a basket, feeding the chickens.

'Is that me?' she chuckled.

'*Mais oui*,' Mark replied.

'I suppose I've just never seen myself from that angle before. I look happy.'

'That's the only time I see you looking truly happy,' he replied. 'With your adoring flock.'

She continued to study the image and asked. 'Are my breasts really that large?'

'Ah, *mais oui*,' he went on. 'In my eyes, anyway.'

'You are very naughty,' was her intentionally weak reprimand.

'Are you going to sit for me?'

'What? I'm such a mess! Well, if you're sure you are ready to take on such a difficult subject! I'll have to wash and do my hair.'

She splattered cold water onto her face, then sat at her mirror and brushed her hair. Mark watched. 'Where do you want me?' she asked at last.

Naked in bed, he thought, but it came out, sitting over there. With the sun on your face.

She obliged. 'Just stare at that crack in the wall,' he instructed. 'I'll try not to take too long.'

He began to scrawl with the charcoal. It was so amusing. He was a perfect parody of his late brother. 'Ah, *zut alors*!' he cursed, rubbed out, retried.

'I can't seem to get the line of your jaw and neck. It's that dress,' he grumbled.

'Should I undo it?' she asked.

'Yes. Just a little,' he swallowed hard as the top two buttons came undone, and seeing her willingness, suggested, 'And just a little bit more.'

The dress was slipping down off her shoulders, revealing substantial cleavage. It was difficult to continue with his heart beating so hard, his mind incapable of logical thought. He tried to concentrate and scribbled some more, but the charcoal was becoming slippery with sweat.

'I think perhaps I should call it a day.' He sighed. 'It doesn't seem to be working very well.'

'Oh well,' she said, disappointed. 'We should try again tomorrow.'

'Yes. That's a good idea.'

Harry was in the yard. He held the pitchfork firmly and began shifting the hay. He loved it. Silent, uncomplicated, the dear thing swung, picked up hay and let it fly. It seemed easier than he remembered, his muscles having increased in power due to navy life. *Hard to believe,* he thought. *Just a few weeks ago, this was a ramrod in my hands. Helping to blast those Spanish bastards to pieces!*

He continued to swing, the heat of the day causing him to abandon his shirt. He felt the weight of somebody's stare from the house. He looked up to see auburn hair, a white smile and bare shoulders turning away.

God, Helen, he thought. *If we could only turn back time!*

He bent to his task once again but couldn't resist another peek. Perhaps she was trying to invite him to her room. Yes! There was a face at the window! But, bloody hell! It wasn't Helen. It was Mark! The young man smirked and then turned back into the room. 'Same time tomorrow then,' he confirmed to his model.

Helen laughed.

It was more than Harry could take. He could never stop loving Helen, but it was never going to be the same. Mark could amuse her, but Harry couldn't. He was dour and confused. The thought of all those customers she'd had. Even Enoch Hoskins. He couldn't go on. Ramrod and cutlass loomed large in his mind. Full-bellied sales, the wind tugging at his hair, the smell of tar and brine. He couldn't help it. He could even see Jelzina in the heat of that battle. 'Give her a ram for me,' she said. At last, the crease of a smile came to his lips.

That night, he lay in his bed, thoughts churning endlessly in his head until they transformed into a dream and sleep engulfed him. He winced. He saw a shapeless purple shadow drifting as it had before, swirling, teasing, making him wonder what shape it would adopt. It wouldn't be the drowning man. That had come to reality and gone. The new shadow never made itself clear. It looked oddly like a smoking chimney, but he couldn't be sure.

The trusty cockerel crowed and he was startled awake. He pushed the strange dream out of his thoughts and pictured instead the buffeting cannon, the swing of the cutlass. Nelson's face looked close to death. 'Stay with us, sir!' he heard himself saying. Molly tied the scarf around his neck. 'It'll save the blood of your hero.' His mind was made up. He made for the stables and, with his new-found skills, hitched the baker's mare to the cart. He went back to the outhouse and gathered his few belongings. With the load slung over his shoulder, he passed the house. His eyes were cast down on the ground, heavy, blurred, but he saw it. He saw it land in front of him. A blue tooth of stone made into a ring. There was an audible sob above him. A tearful voice. 'Give it to someone who deserves it, Harry.'

He didn't look up. He trod the ring into the ground. He tried to pretend that his heart wasn't breaking. It was.

Chapter 44

The cart trundled on. The poor mare stumbled over stones and mud in Fernhills Lane. They passed the Plough and Horses. Harry wondered briefly if he should stop and give Molly Elizabeth back her scarf. He didn't stop. It would only cause more pain.

At the crossroads came another thought. Smith Farm! He hadn't given it any consideration since he left, erasing it completely from his mind. 'I wonder if their graves are still there,' he mused. 'I should go and pay them my last respects.'

He steered the horse towards the farm, memories of his childhood invading now and that fateful day of the fire. He stopped at the gate and got down from the cart. He could see the graves, the wooden crosses still there and, *Weird,* he thought. There were fresh flowers lying there. He opened the gate and went in, his eyes fixed on the two graves. He stood there and crossed his chest as he had seen other sailors do. It seemed appropriate. He mumbled a little prayer and then told his parents that he was going back to sea. They should be proud of him. He turned away. Then, 'My God!' he gasped. 'The House!' It stood there bold and real, just as it had been. White painted walls, thatched roof, little oak door. He stood. He stared. 'But the fire!' He breathed. 'How the hell?'

Smoke was coming from the chimney. 'My God!' he muttered again. 'That's what I saw in the dream! Who on earth could have done all this?' Just a minute. Wasn't this rightfully his? Hadn't he inherited it? The thoughts churned through his mind. Why had he never thought of this before? He went to the door and raised the knocker. It was exactly the same as it was before. A tentative knock. No response. He knocked again, but nobody came, so he pushed the door. It wasn't locked. 'Good morning!' he shouted into the void.

It was gloomy in there and smelled a little damp, but it was obviously lived in. His eyes were drawn to a flickering light. On the table was a cake with a burning candle. He couldn't help it. He was drawn to the mystery. There were words inscribed on the top. He couldn't read the first two, but the third was easily recognisable. 'Harry.' He stared, his mouth uncontrollably agape. He heard someone moving in the other room. Footsteps. The door opened and a young woman peered out. She had blonde hair and a joyous smile. 'Good morning,' she replied, giggling. He gazed into the "forget-me-not" blue eyes of the girl they called Molly Elizabeth.

'Have you come to return my purple scarf?' she asked coyly.

For several seconds, there was astonished silence in the room.

'I've no idea,' said befuddled Harry Smith. 'What on earth's going on?'

'I knew you'd be back,' she went on. 'That's what the cake says; 'welcome home Harry.'

He stared in disbelief. 'How? All this?' he stuttered. The room was exactly how it had been. 'Are you some kind of witch or something?'

Her eyes flared bluer than ever. 'Some people call me that,' she muttered. 'They want me to tell their fortunes, read their palms. Some who really connect with me say they have purple dreams that give them glimpses of the future.'

Harry swallowed hard. Molly saw it and her voice became a sincere whisper.

'I have the same sort of dreams,' she went on. 'That's how I knew you'd be back; how I knew it was time to make the cake. I had this all rebuilt,' she said, with an expansive gesture of the arms. 'I just somehow knew what it looked like.'

'What about Hugo?' he managed. 'Is he here?'

'Hugo died,' she replied, adopting a serious look. 'He had an awful accident. Soon after, you left; it was a silly quarrel. It became an even sillier fight. I'd never seen him so angry. He came at me with a stool and tried to hit me. I dodged it. He fell. He hit his head on the floor and bled to death. I couldn't stop it. He died in my arms.'

Many people wouldn't have seen it, but Harry did. It only took a fraction of a second, but he saw it. As she reached the words, 'He died in my arms,' it was there. Her eyes flashed guiltily to her right, to the heavy candle stick in the hearth. The one that she cleaned and polished every day.

'I was left all alone,' she went on. 'I couldn't cope. I sold the inn and used the money for all this.' There were tears in her eyes now. Harry untied the purple scarf from around his neck and handed it to her to mop her face. She looked at it and the smile returned. 'Look at the state of it,' she said. 'It looks as if it's been to hell and back.'

'It has,' replied Harry. 'But it kept me going somehow. Whenever I touched it, I could see you clearly against that rough old door.'

'That must have inspired you,'

'It did. I was quite the hero. Saved Nelson's life. That's his blood on there!'

Molly nodded sagely. 'The blood of your hero.'

Harry swallowed hard. 'You knew,' he stuttered. 'Somehow, you knew. You just seem to be guiding every part of my life.' Molly just smiled.

Harry struggled for words again. 'I'm on my way to rejoin, going back to the navy.'

'Oh, Harry,' she said. 'You have already done your share of duty. Now you deserve a more peaceful life.'

At the same moment came another sound. A sound from the other room. A baby's cry. Harry looked astonished as Molly left the room. The crying stopped and she returned with the suckling child adhered to her breast.

'The day you were hot pressed into the navy, Harry Smith, you had me "hot pressed" against an outhouse door. You left me with this lovely present. Her name's Harriet.'

'You mean?'

'That's right, my love. You're her daddy. And she's going to need her daddy growing up in this grim old world. A few brothers and sisters, too.'

Harriet fell asleep at her mother's breast and was put on the big, safe armchair.

Molly sat there, her breast unashamedly exposed, looking beautiful, irresistible. 'And this place definitely needs a big strapping fellow to run the farm,' she said. Harry couldn't help it. He looked deep into those eyes. Her lips parted slightly and seductively. He sat beside her and felt his heart pound. Their lips met tentatively, then firmly. His hand cupped the milk gorged breast and then wandered down to the hem of her skirt. He reached inside, stroking her knee and soft, warm thigh. If he could have read her mind, he would have found the words, 'Got you at last, Harry Smith. I've got you at last.'

Chapter 45

Right. Where were we?' asked Helen.

'I've barely started,' groaned Mark, and he stared hard at the charcoal smears on the canvas. 'Turn to your left a bit.'

She swivelled a little on the stool.

'That dress,' said the artist and Helen nodded, knowing exactly what he meant. She began undoing buttons. She waited for his stream of pseudo-French chatter, but it wasn't there today. He looked serious as he sketched away. For all his apparent light-heartedness, he was hurting inside, and today, he couldn't hide it. Yes, his brother had been stupid, and he couldn't forgive the way he had molested Helen or the way he had pursued the trundling old cart with his gang of thugs. As usual with Andy, things got out of hand. The resulting fight with Bart. The pistol shot that could have gone anywhere but chose to rip into Andy's chest. Mark wondered where his grave would be. Would it even be in England? The thoughts were filling his mind. His brush strokes were mechanical.

Helen stared hard. He was filling the background of his creation with black paint even though the walls were white, a touch of anger in his staring eyes. Then the anger turned to concentration as he dealt with the detail of her eyes, her nose, her full, slightly smiling lips. He began to perspire as his brush caressed the curve he had created in her luxurious cleavage.

'I'm getting a little bit tired, Mark,' said Helen.

'Oh, that's all right. You can move now if you want. I've got the finishing touches in my head.'

She gave a sigh of relief and went to sit down on the bed. Mark was still concentrating, mopping his brow now with his sleeve.

'Can I see it?' said the model.

'No. Of course not. You should never see a portrait till the artist is content with it.'

She frowned. He was being so serious with her.

At last, he declared that he could do no more that day. He would have to rest; then, out of the blue, he smiled his boyish smile and whispered the words they were both aching to hear. 'Can I share the pleasures of your bed with you?'

Helen looked into Mark's eyes and wished to hell that it was Harry. Harry looked into Molly's dazzling blue eyes and wished to heaven that it was Helen. The lovers rose and fell together, both feeling the ecstasy of each other's embrace, the powerful climax bringing a fusion of their minds. Both were lost in each other's souls. Both lay spent and exhausted, gasping on the precious air.

***

Days and nights slipped idyllically by for Mark and Helen and for Harry and Molly Elizabeth, but as the ladies' monthly cycle came around, both Molly and Helen shook their heads, Helen relieved, Molly disappointed. How she hoped and prayed for a brother or sister for Harriet, but nature was not playing her part. They tried every way possible to make the dream come true, even re-enacting their first encounter against an outhouse door, in case it held some kind of magic. It didn't.

Chapter 46

A ringing of the front doorbell disturbed the tranquillity of Westhouse Farm. Beatrice had not seen the visitor's approach. She looked up, surprised from her knitting, then made her way to the door. The face that greeted her was one she knew. She took a sharp intake of breath. 'Good morning, ma'am,' he uttered.

'Mister Stokes!' she responded. 'Not seen you for a while!'

He smiled. 'No. It's been a long time. I wonder if I could see, Richard?'

She ushered him into the drawing room, where he stood admiring the view from the window. When he turned back into the room, his eye caught sight of a new painting on the wall: a portrait of the beautiful Helen Westhouse. He cringed a little.

Richard gave a puzzled grimace when Beatrice told him his visitor's identity but walked in to meet the fellow with a smile on his face.

'Walter!' he enthused. 'How nice to see you again!'

The man responded, 'Likewise, Richard,' but the smiles didn't last for long.

'I'm afraid I'm a worried man, Richard. I don't know if you can help or not.'

The master of the house gestured his visitor to a comfortable chair. The two had known each other for several years. This was how the "pairing" of Helen and the man's son, Matthew Stokes, had been spawned. The visitor looked somewhat greyer and furrowed than Richard remembered. There was a slight croak in his voice as he continued to speak.

'I'll come straight to the point, Richard. Matthew has gone missing. It's not like him to go off without contacting anybody. He's been away for several weeks. My wife, of course, is beside herself with grief. She thinks something dreadful must have happened to him. You know what mothers are like; they always fear the worst.'

Richard's brow crumpled as the man spoke. 'You thought he might be here?'

'Well, maybe. I don't know, really. I suppose I thought he might have somehow got back with Helen. I've been trying everywhere. The thing is, his associate, Poplar Wainwright, has tragically died. I've got an invitation to his funeral next week. Maybe Matthew will be there. I don't know. I just can't work it out. He was terribly upset, I know, as I was, about his break up with Helen. Almost suicidal, in fact. I just hope he hasn't done anything stupid.'

Walter's gaze fixed itself on Helen's portrait as he spoke. Richard's expression grew more worried. He felt somewhat responsible. He should never have tried to make that match. He was only trying to do what was best for his daughter and, so he thought, for the apparently reticent

Matthew Stokes. He had not been told the full story by his returning family, certainly not the episode of Matthew's intended vengeance and grim and dreadful end. He could only offer sympathy and understanding of parental worry after the trauma he had been through himself.

'I know how you must feel, Walter,' he managed in response, 'I went through hell worrying about Helen and Bart when they disappeared.'

'Oh, I didn't know Bart had disappeared too!'

'Ah, yes. He went off looking for her. Took a long time. He got hauled into the navy by one of those dreadful press gangs. Went through all sorts. They both did. Brought her back eventually, though.'

'She's back? Oh my God. You mean she parted with the farm hand too?'

'No, no. Well, not at first. She brought him back here with her, but it didn't last. She took up with this artist fellow. He painted the picture you're admiring. No. Harry Smith no longer works here. We've no idea where he's gone.'

'Hmm. A complicated life your daughter's having.'

'I've learned my lesson with her, Walter. She's her own person.'

'I know what you mean. I've a daughter of my own, as you know.'

The visitor refused Richard's kind offers of beer or wine or refreshment of any kind.

'No, my dear fellow. I must be on my way. There's other places I must go. Somebody must know what's become of him. Just hope and pray that it's not as tragic as I'm beginning to fear.'

The man donned his smart top hat as he left the building and strode off towards his waiting carriage: polished oak, two immaculate black horses and a blue-coated driver with a tricorn hat.

The extended family were assembled in the drawing room. Mark was becoming accepted even though he was younger than Helen, which didn't seem to matter to anybody. Richard's cohabitation with Beatrice had also become accepted as the norm. Bart had immersed himself in the running of the farm which he now took an even more active role in than his father. They enjoyed their evenings: the roaring fire, piano playing, the idle chatter. There was rarely anything contentious to discuss, perhaps not until now. The visit of a worried father, the implication that perhaps the missing son still had contact with this family. The subject had to be broached. Richard cleared his throat and began to speak.

'I had a visitor this morning.' All eyes turned towards him.

'It was Walter Stokes, Matthew's father. Matthew has gone missing. He wondered if we'd any knowledge of his whereabouts.'

Helen's heart thudded down into her stomach. She could feel a reddening of her face. How she had hoped that this subject was as dead and buried as the man she had killed. Visions of that awful day invaded her mind, just as they did in her nightmares every night. Those visions wouldn't go away no matter how she tried to expunge them: the sword, the blood. She had found the courage from somewhere to plunge that weapon deep into Matthew's throat. He was strangling poor Harry to death! She swallowed hard; so did Mark; so did Bart. Nobody knew what to say. At last, something came to Helen's lips.

'What makes Mister Stokes think that *we'd* know anything about him?' she managed.

Richard stared at her obvious discomfort. His expression slipped from mildly enquiring to deep concern. 'I'm sorry,' Helen went on. 'I find this subject far too upsetting to discuss!' She was on her feet now, and as she quickly left the room, her audible sobs alarmed everyone, especially Beatrice, who was quickly on her feet to follow. The others were left to exchange anguished looks, Richard thumping the arm of his chair in disgust at himself for upsetting the girl, the darling daughter he had vowed never to upset again. 'Damn, damn, damn!' he grouched. 'Why do I have to open my great stupid mouth?'

Walter Stokes was at the Plough and Horses Inn. He ground his teeth in angry frustration. 'Somebody must know something about Matthew!' he cursed. 'Nobody just disappears like that, especially my son. He always gets in touch somehow. Somebody must be hiding something. I wish to God I knew who.' Blank faces. He gave up. He got back into his carriage and journeyed on. His earlier conversation with Richard Westhouse turned over and over in his mind. 'Ran off with the farm hand. Now she's back home with some artist fellow? Matthew must be really hurting about all this, wherever he is. Something's weird about all this. Where the hell can he be?'

Helen had locked herself in her room. The best efforts of Beatrice, Mark and Bart had failed to bring her out. The only sound from inside the room was a soft, muffled sobbing.

Richard was mulling over Walter Stokes' words. A name was ringing a bell in his mind: the peculiar name of Poplar Wainwright. 'Haven't I heard that name somewhere before?' he eventually asked his son. 'Somewhere in the tales of your adventures. Wasn't he the one Smith said that he'd rescued at the time when Nelson had his arm shattered?'

'That's right, Papa,' agreed Bart. He swallowed hard. He didn't want to discuss this. He knew that his father had a way of dragging things out of him.

'Did you know he was an associate of Matthew Stokes?'

The question stabbed deep. 'How much of this story should he reveal?' Bart stammered as he tried to reply.

Harry recognised him. 'He was Matthew's coach driver, and he brought him here several times. I must say I never paid him much attention, but apparently Harry did. He'd been sent on a mission by Matthew. He tried to get us to abscond from the navy and tried to lead us straight back to him. He was really out for Harry's blood, Papa, and I was caught up in the middle.'

Richard was absorbing Bart's words and, at the same time, trying to piece this all together.

'How did this Wainwright die?' Richard's words hung in the air, a shocked silence.

'How did you know he was dead?' muttered Bart.

'Walter told me. He's going to his funeral next week. He's hoping Matthew will be there. He's worried sick about him.'

Bart's involuntary gasp surprised Richard. 'What's wrong?' he demanded. Bart was imagining a conversation between Wainwright's mother and Walter Stokes. He took too long trying to conjure up words.

'Look, Bart, if you're mixed up in something, you might as well tell me now.'

Several seconds passed as the son grappled with his thoughts, reddening as he did so, heart thumping hard. It was much too difficult for him to keep hedging around the truth.

'It's no use Walter Stokes searching for his son,' he managed at last. 'He's dead too!'

Richard felt faint. He sat down quickly in his leather chair. 'What? How?' he stuttered, trying to mouth the words that his brain was screaming.

'A fight,' said Bart. 'He was so obsessed with getting revenge on Harry for stealing Helen away.' Bart watched his father's face contort into a dozen questions. He started to pre-empt them. 'When me and Harry finally got out of the navy, we went straight to where we'd find Helen. Matthew followed us with some cronies. Then he attacked us. I got tied up, and Helen and Harry were held at the point of the sword. He wanted to humiliate them, but I got myself free. I leapt at a couple of them, causing enough mayhem for Harry to have a go at Matthew. Next thing I knew, I was coming around on the floor and Matthew was dead.'

It took some time for Bart to convince his father that was the extent of his knowledge. He left him muttering, 'What the hell do I tell Walter if he comes around here again?'

Knuckles rapped urgently on Helen's bedroom door. She span towards it with a scowl.

'Who is it?' she demanded.

'It's me. Bart! We have to talk!'

'What about? I don't want to talk to anyone!'

'Papa has made me tell him things. We have to get our stories straight!'

A key turned in a lock and Helen cracked the door open. One curious eye peered out, checked that he was all alone and scrutinised his face for sincerity. Satisfied, she opened it wider, revealing a tear-stained face and a scramble of unkempt hair.

'God, you look a mess,' were his words of greeting. She sneered.

'Can't sleep. Can't eat or drink. Do you think I give a damn how I look?'

'Everybody's worried sick about you. You're going to have to pull yourself together. Papa is going to want a word. I've told him Matthew's dead.'

Helen's mouth gaped open. Her eyes glared in anger. 'What?' she almost shrieked the word.

'Why the hell?' words failed her.

'I had to. You know what Papa is like when he's intent on dragging the truth out of you. Questions, questions about what happened. I couldn't keep lying! I told him Matthew had followed us with his bunch of cronies, tied me up and threatened you and Harry with the sword. I said I managed to get free and leapt on two of the men. It caused enough mayhem for Harry to have a go at Matthew. The next thing I knew, I regained consciousness on the floor and Matthew was dead. So, I'm claiming I never saw how he died. You should do the same.'

'But that'll leave the suggestion that it must have been Harry.'

'Well? So long as it's only a suggestion, what does it matter? Nobody knows where Harry is now. We'll probably never see him again. No one will ever suspect that it might have been you. It'll all blow over and be forgotten. Now, come on. Get yourself together and come downstairs. Everyone's worried sick about you.'

'What about Mark? Where's he?'

'Mark? He's taken himself off to Fernhills. He's really fed up that you wouldn't even talk to him. Thinks he can make his fortune painting portraits.'

'Oh my. I really mess up, don't I, with the men in my life?' She turned away and sat at her dressing table, threatening her hair with the brush. 'I'll be down in a bit,' she mumbled, 'with my tale of innocence. Don't like making people think it was Harry that killed the bastard, but so long as that puts an end to it, I suppose it's the only way. Matthew, Harry, Mark.' She growled the words at her dreadful reflection. 'Bloody men!'

At that moment, the young artist walked into the Plough and Horses Inn. He surveyed the scene, mostly men sitting quietly on their own, but in one corner, there was a small group, lively in their chatter, some slapping of backs.

'Good to have you back, Harry!' he heard one of them say. 'That spell in the navy's really done you good!'

'Yeah, you know it was a bit strange, but when I looked at the scoreboard and saw I'd scored eleven runs, I thought of my hero, Nelson. You know, two ones. One eye, one arm. It sort of spurred me on.'

'Well, my friend, perhaps if he lost one of something else, you might just go on to score a hundred and eleven!' The laughter increased. 'Or get yourself out dreaming about it!'

Surely it couldn't be! Mark moved a little closer. 'Never seen anyone hit a cricket ball so hard,' said one of the group. 'We really gave those townies a whacking!'

Mark stared harder. 'Christ!' the word tumbled from his lips. Harry heard it and span around. He looked past his chattering team mates into the face of Mark Williamson. His eyes widened in disbelief. 'Mark!' he expounded, shocked.

The two stared at each other, searching for their emotions. This was the bastard who'd worked his way into Helen's life. He pictured his appearance at her bedroom window. The smirk that had made up his mind to leave

Westhouse Farm. There was anger and disgust. Harry breathed hard to keep control.

Mark almost trembled under the withering stare but held his courage. 'We all thought you'd gone back to the navy,' he managed.

'Are you going to introduce us to your friend?' asked one of the cricketers.

'Sorry. Yes. Of course,' said Harry. 'This is Mark who helped me get straight again after the navy.'

They all looked a little puzzled, but it seemed amicable enough. The same team member introduced all the players, names Mark forgot as soon as he heard them.

'I'm an artist now,' Mark stumbled on. 'I do portraits. I was hoping to drum up some trade.'

'Well, here's a fine-looking bunch of men,' returned Harry, keeping his emotions hidden. 'I'm sure you could make some pretty pictures out of them!' General laughter and merriment ensued, the pulling of supposedly handsome faces. Mark blushed somewhat and grimaced at Harry.

'So, how is the lady Helen?' asked Harry as the raucousness died down.

'She's well,' replied Mark, with a tiredness Harry could detect. 'And you? Are they finding a use for you on the farm?'

'Not really. That's why I've taken up painting. It's what my brother used to do, you know? They all say I'm pretty good. I'm not so sure.'

'Well, I've got a lovely lady at home. I think she'd make a beautiful subject for a painting.'

'Home? Where's that? Like I said, we all thought you'd gone back to the navy.'

'I was going,' mused Harry. 'But went back to take a look at Smith Farm, where I grew up. Got the shock of my life. It had all been rebuilt. I live there now.'

'Yeah. With the witch!' said one of his mates. They all laughed, but it struck a sour note with Harry. They saw the grimace as he tried to hide the hurt.

'Why do you call her that?' he grumbled but was met with silence.

'Why do you call her a witch?' he went on, his eyes wandering around the group, but no eyes met his.

'You should have seen her,' one of them ventured. 'Crazy, some people called her. Heroic, others said. No one could quite believe that the cottage could be rebuilt. We never dreamt you'd ever be back, Harry. Thought you'd made off forever with that Westhouse girl. Somehow, you must know that it's your destiny. Some said...' and the voice hesitated here, 'that she knew... how the fire started.'

Other fellows were searching for the right words. 'Nobody knows, really, but she seemed so obsessed. She got everyone working on the place,' one went on. 'Seemed to have a gift for getting people at it. We all did a bit, one way or another.'

Mark felt there was a need to lift the spirits a little here. He put on a grin and laid a hand on Harry's shoulder.

'I've got the pony and trap outside with all my gear in it. If you're serious about the painting, we can head off there now.'

Harry forced himself back into semi jovial mood.

'Ooh no!' he responded. 'There's just a bit more celebrating to do first. We've just beaten the townies by fifty runs. Let's have another refill, eh boys!

Chapter 47

Black plumes nodded on horses' heads as they hauled the coffin into the churchyard. The waiting men doffed black top hats; the women sobbed beneath their veils. Maria Fortuna gave an audible moan. She had given her son the name Poplar after the tree she told him he was born under, although, as he suspected, it was where he had been conceived. In a former life, a Lisbon whore had cavorted with a drunken British sailor. The mistake of a lifetime. The product was this Anglo-Portuguese fellow who they now mourned, called Wainwright after the occupation of his adoptive father. He was there too, equally morose, standing next to Maria. Walter Stokes stood respectfully back.

The wake was held at the Wainwright's house.

'So good of you to come, Mister Stokes,' said Maria. 'Poplar always spoke highly of you and your son, Matthew. He enjoyed his work at the Stokes Shipping Company.'

'Yes, I'm sure. It was always a pleasure to speak to him; such a hard-working fellow. Of course, he was much closer associated with Matthew than myself. Such a pity my son is away on business.'

'Yes. He sounds like a very interesting man to work for. Poplar came to see me, you know, in Lisbon, just before all this unfortunate affair with the navy. Said he was there on a mission for Matthew. He was very proud.'

'I'm afraid I'm not familiar with these events, Maria. What happened with the navy?'

'Oh. Well, apparently, while going about his mission, he was on a small boat and mistaken for a British deserter. He pleaded his innocence, of course, but the British Navy needs little excuse to force men into its ranks. Before he knew it, he was serving on board a ship, got involved in some battle or other and got badly injured. I got letters telling me how bravely he had served, but he was critically hurt. He died soon after being brought back to England.'

'I'm so sorry, Maria,' uttered Walter. 'I'm sure you can be very proud of him. Strangely enough, I was only talking to somebody the other day who said that *his* son had been coerced into the navy, along with one of his farm hands. Awful business. Still, the navy seems to be doing a sterling job of protecting us from the damned French. You have to admire what they do.'

'Indeed, Mister Stokes,' came the reply, but with it came a change in her eyes. They went from politeness and charm to a serious stare.

'You say your son is away on business?' she asked, her tone slightly cynical. Walter felt uncomfortable. 'Yes,' he responded but without much conviction.

'Mister Stokes. I have other guests to speak to,' Maria said with a return to a hostess's charm. 'But I would like to talk to you again before you leave. Would you mind staying behind for a short while when the other guests have gone?'

'Not at all, Maria. I hope I can be of some assistance.'

She smiled politely and turned away, leaving Walter standing alone, a ponderous look on his face, a glass of whisky in his hand. His thoughts roamed around the situation. 'She didn't seem to believe that Matthew was away on business. Why not? Is there more to all this than meets the eye? What on earth has she got to say to me that needs to be said alone?' He took another sip of the whisky, realised that he had emptied the glass and, poured himself another, then waited.

It was a good half hour before the other guests had slithered away, uttering final condolences and empty offers of 'if there's ever anything we can do to help.' At last, there was only Maria and her husband left in the room with Walter. He looked at the stern expressions on the other faces and began to feel trapped. He poured another drink.

'We had rather hoped that Matthew would be here,' said Maria, and before Walter could repeat his assertion, the adoptive father spoke out. 'Maria has told us all about Poplar's visit to her when he was sent to Lisbon by your son.'

Walter's expression turned inquisitive, saying, 'I don't know much about it.'

'Let me enlighten you,' said Maria, and there was an expectant pause as she took a sip of wine. 'Poplar said that he had been sent to Lisbon on a mission. Matthew was bent on avenging himself on this Harry Smith fellow who had stolen his intended wife, and he was to somehow prize this rascal out of the navy back to England where Matthew could deal with him.'

Walter's face crumpled with a tinge of disbelief, but Maria went on. 'He didn't have a clue how to do it. He was terribly distressed. I knew how much it meant to him to be Matthew's hero. I helped him all I could,' she said. 'Told him about a local fisherman I knew, who'd been known to do a little "people smuggling" in his time. Introduced them.' She took another sip of wine and watched Walter's discomfort increase.

The adoptive mother was beginning to sob and dabbed at her face with a lacy handkerchief. Her husband put a comforting arm around her shoulder.

'Anyway,' continued Maria. 'He put the plan into action, but it failed. British marines were wise to it and intercepted their boat. Poor Poplar was arrested, flogged and all sorts, but this Smith fellow and Westhouse got away scot-free.'

The name "Westhouse" hit home like a knife, stabbing Walter's brain. 'Westhouse?' he couldn't help repeating. 'The Westhouse boy was mixed up in this?'

'He and Smith were inseparable,' said Maria. 'Wherever one went, so did the other. Barnacle Bart they used to call him, apparently. Poplar had to get our fisherman friend to convince them both that they could safely abscond together.'

Walter swallowed hard, began to feel the effects of the whisky in his head and sat down. There was silence except for Mrs Wainwright's sniffling.

Maria's voice inevitably broke in again. 'Poplar was forced to serve in the navy and was nearly drowned when a landing craft he was in got sunk. Nelson himself saved his life. In return, as we understand it, he offered to act as a decoy for Nelson when they got back to England so that any French spies would be led the wrong way while Nelson slid off to his wife and, hopefully, to get his amputation properly seen to. The decoy plan worked, but it worked so well that Poplar was waylaid and died in the fray. Now, the French believe that Nelson is dead and that the British Navy will be far poorer as a result. A very brave last act by my son, don't you think?'

Walter was nodding and could see where all this was leading; glorification of Poplar Wainwright and the vilification of poor Matthew. He didn't know how accurate the story was, but it all seemed so plausible.

'So, as you see, my dear Walter, we are not surprised that your son has not turned up today. His jealousy and hate led directly to Poplar's heroic death. He should be here now, on his knees, begging for our forgiveness!'

'I don't know where he is,' confessed Walter at last. 'He's been missing ever since that day of Nelson's return. I've searched everywhere.' He looked up at the stern faces and thought he could feel a tear welling in his eye. He stuttered on. 'If what you say is true, well, God only knows what's happened to him, but I must say, I feel nothing but sympathy for you and your dear son. I swear I'll get to the bottom of all this, and in some way, Matthew will get his just deserts.'

'Oh, and what will that mean, Walter?' Maria's voice was charged with cynicism. 'Put across your knee for a good hiding? It's not good enough, Walter!' There was anger there now, spite and venom. 'We want him to pay severely for what he did, Walter. Very severely indeed!'

Chapter 48

'Look what I've brought you!' yelled Harry as he walked in through the front door.

Molly looked up in anticipation. She would never have guessed at a young fellow carrying an easel and artist's palette. She didn't have time to respond before Harry was planting an ale-laden kiss on her lips, then muttering, 'God, I love you.' She smiled. 'Been celebrating?' she asked. 'I guess you won.'

'Oh yes!' said Harry. 'And H Smith hit seven boundaries, scored forty altogether and bowled two of their best men out!'

'Well. That sounds terrific!' she enthused. She could never forget that first time she saw him. He made that great catch to win the game. So much had happened since then.

'Who's this?' she said, nodding towards his companion.

'This is Mark,' he replied. 'People tell me he's a wonderful artist. I said he could paint a portrait of a beautiful lady at Smith Farm, so here he is. I knew him before. We met when I got out of the navy.'

'Oh?' said Molly with a curious glance. 'I guess that's another of your stories you're yet to tell me about.'

'That's right,' said Harry, then, turning to Mark, 'how long will it take you?'

'Two or three days,' was the eye-twinkling reply. 'It depends how still she'll sit.'

'Oh my God,' giggled Molly. 'I'm going to have to pose for this?'

'Just for a while, till I get the idea of it. Then I can just finish by memory.'

'We've got a spare room you can have,' said Harry. 'You can start in the morning, can you?'

'That'll be fine,' said the young man. 'Just one problem, I think.'

'What's that?' said Molly.

'I don't think I'll have a good enough colour to paint those bright blue eyes!'

They all laughed as Mark left the room, but as soon as he was gone, Harry's expression sank into an accusing glare. It frightened Molly. 'What's wrong?' she stuttered. Harry was pacing around the room, eyes fixed on the floor, shaking his head, sighing the sighs of a man battling with something that he couldn't possibly believe.

'The fellows in the cricket team,' he said calmly. 'They say you know how the fire started.'

Molly sighed and rolled her eyes, her pale face reddening. She fought against the flustered feeling she had inside and struggled with the threatening tears.

'What the hell do you know?' he demanded, and she was losing her usual calm countenance. Her face sank deep into her hands among audible sobs. He wanted to shake her but held it back.

'What the hell do you know?'

At last, her face lifted a mess of tears and redness. She could hardly speak and her first words escaped as a pitiful croak. 'Some ladies,' she managed. 'Some ladies I know. They experiment a lot.' She didn't know how much to tell him. 'They try to make medicines and things, you know, from herbs and anything really.'

Harry's face was furrowed with questions and anger. His fists were clenched as he struggled with his feelings of aggression. Her eyes were wider and bluer than ever behind the pools of tears. Her lips quivered again as she tried to speak.

'They were boiling things together,' she went on, wiping at her wetted cheeks. 'They threw a lot of stuff on the fire, like chaff or something. It all flared up. Sparks flew everywhere. Some blew onto the roof. It was all so dry. Flames just ripped through the place.'

Harry squirmed as he relived the awful sight. The heat, the dazzling fury of the flames, but something wasn't making sense. 'And you?' he stuttered. 'Where were you? Were you with them?'

'Yes.'

'You're one of them?'

'Yes. Don't be angry, Harry. I'm so, so sorry. There was nothing I could do. I ran back to the inn. I told Hugo. I told him to get over here and see you were all right. I told him to bring you back to the inn. I just,' she swallowed hard as the words formed in her head. 'I just wanted to be close to you.'

Harry stared at her hard. It seemed more than ever that she was orchestrating his life. The baby she had tricked him into fathering. The power of the purple scarf. The fire. The miraculous rebuilding of the cottage. His head swam. He pulled her to her feet, picked her up in his arms and carried her to bed.

Chapter 49

'Oh no,' grumbled Richard Westhouse. His heart sank as Beatrice delivered the news. 'Walter Stokes is here to see you, and he's brought Samuel Stevens with him, the Parish Constable.'

'Good God, this is real trouble,' muttered Richard, pulling himself reluctantly to his feet. 'You'd better get one of the men to find Bart and warn him. There's going to be some awkward questions asked.'

'Good morning, Walter!' enthused Richard with a forced grin, but his visitors wore grim expressions.

'Good morning,' muttered Walter. 'I take it you know Mister Stevens and his official capacity.'

'I do indeed,' said Richard and held out a hand for shaking, which the Parish Constable accepted.

'A serious matter,' said Stevens. 'Mister Stokes here has some questions to ask of your son, Bartholomew.'

'He's out in the fields, sir,' said Richard. 'Tending to farming matters.'

'We'll wait,' returned Stevens. 'While you send for him.'

'Yes, yes, of course. Sit down, gentlemen. I'll get Beatrice to make you some tea.'

It was about twenty minutes and two cups of tea later when Bart arrived, brushing scraps of plant life from his shirt.

'I'm so sorry to keep you waiting,' were his opening words. 'I was in a far corner of the fields.'

'That's all right, Master Westhouse,' said the constable. 'But I'm afraid there's some serious business to be discussed.'

Bart looked at Walter, whose stare made his insides squirm.

'Mister Stokes here is extremely concerned about the whereabouts of his son, Matthew. You may not know this, but Matthew's close associate, Poplar Wainwright, was killed in action and his bereaved mother told Mister Stokes that he was on some mission to get you and your farm hand friend back to England.'

He paused, expecting a reaction from Bart. There wasn't any.

'The upshot of this,' went on Stevens, 'is that Wainwright's family blames Matthew rather vehemently for their son's death. They're out for his blood. Walter thinks he may have gone into hiding somewhere or probably even met some terrible end. He's a very worried man. His wife, I understand, is virtually paralysed with grief. The only names we keep hearing about in all this are "Harry Smith", who was involved with your sister's disappearance, and yourself, Master Westhouse. So, if you can shed any light on Matthew's whereabouts, we would be pleased to hear about it.'

This was going to be the hardest thing Bart had ever done. He even wished he could be back on that damned ship of the line, cutlass in hand, wading into the snarling mob of Spanish sailors intent on ending his life.

He looked at his father, whose stare was one of expectancy. He had to repeat the story. He started with the words that he knew would destroy Walter Wainwright and bring a barrage of questions from Samuel Stevens.

'I'm very sorry,' he started, then hesitated before almost whispering, 'I'm afraid I know that he's dead.'

Chapter 50

It was a morning like any other for a farmer's wife when Molly Elizabeth woke up. The cockerel was crowing its welcome to the sun; the curtain was flickering in the morning breeze. She turned towards her man with more confirmation of their love on her mind, but the bed was cold and the expected warm body wasn't there.

'Oh Christ,' she muttered and donned her clothes quickly to venture downstairs. No sign. Harriet was crying in the other room. She peered in and gathered up the whimpering child, joggling her for comfort, but knew that the child would sense her anxiety. Everything had ended so well last night. Her body uniting with Harry's in exquisite harmony, her sleep so deep and unblemished. Then she remembered. The harvest! 'Oh my God! He'll be out there with his sickle!' Sure enough. She looked in the usual place and it was gone. Then, another thought hit her. 'That damned artist fellow! Mark, or whatever his name was. He'll be wanting me to do all that posing business! What a stupid idea, Harry Smith. What a bore!'

Mark was not an early riser any more. Those days as a clerk or baker's delivery lad were well and truly behind him. He believed in his talent as an artist now. He had Helen to thank for that. He had Helen to thank for many things. He lay dreaming about her in his semi-conscious state but slowly succumbed to reality and thoughts of the task ahead. He had to paint a portrait of a complete stranger, albeit a beautiful one. He was nervous, perhaps even a little bit scared of what Harry would think of his ability. He persuaded himself to get out of his bed and readied himself for the task. He plucked an air of confidence from somewhere and descended the stairs.

'What a bore,' were the first words he heard.

'Oh, dear,' he muttered. 'I hope you don't mean me.'

Molly wheeled around, startled, Harriet at her breast. 'Christ!' both she and Mark gasped together. She hurried out of the room, leaving Mark in embarrassed isolation. He fidgeted and paced around till she reappeared, Harriet having finally settled in the other room and Molly's dress re-buttoned to the neck.

'I'm very sorry,' were her opening words. 'I hope I didn't embarrass you too much.'

'Oh no, no,' said Mark. 'It takes more than that to embarrass a painter.'

'Oh yes, of course, you artists seem to think it quite normal to paint people devoid of any clothing whatsoever.' She giggled as she spoke. 'I suppose we should get down to the business of producing this portrait. Where do you want me?'

Mark stared at her. God, she was beautiful. Her eyes were even more radiantly blue this morning. He swallowed hard.

Naked in my bed ran through his head, but it came out differently. 'Over there. By the window.' She sat obediently, looking straight ahead.

'That's fine,' said the artist, taking charcoal to the canvas and beginning to scrawl.

'Do you want your hair up like that?' he queried.

'Why? Do you think it looks better down?'

'Yes,' he murmured and she removed a pin, letting her blonde tresses tumble to her shoulders. Stunning. Mark felt his pulse quicken and his hand trembled a little, breaking the charcoal stick. '*Zut alors!*' he cursed, drawing a giggle from his model, followed by the query.

'Is that French?'

'*Mais oui,*' he went on. 'My brother's influence. He studied in Paris.'

There was silence as he continued to scribble. Molly was amused by his studious look, his intermittent stare, his pulling at his collar showing his rising body heat.

At last, he stood back and squinted slightly disapprovingly at his work.

'That dress,' he mumbled. 'It's spoiling the line of your neck and chin. Could you undo it a little?'

***

A shadow drifted, purple, into Harry Smith's dream. An onlooker, had there been one, would have seen his quizzical frown. He was almost afraid of it. 'What sort of message would it convey?' He stared hard as it drifted, shapeless, mysterious. He hoped it would form itself into a nubile young woman. It never had in the past, but he felt his heart quicken as a long, slender female back began to appear, pale flesh and a head of long flowing hair. A bead of sweat formed itself on Harry's brow. The woman stirred and moved, bringing a reprimand from someone in front of her. An artist's palette loomed large, an easel, white canvas. The man was moving towards her now, a look in his eye that smouldered deep. His hand rested on the flesh of her bare shoulder. Harry woke with a start. He stared madly at the overhanging branches, the chasing white clouds. 'Was it her? And was that Mark? These bloody dreams have never been wrong.' His heart thumped a warning. He climbed to his feet. 'Don't panic,' he told himself, stretched and rubbed at his back where the tree that had shaded his post-lunch nap had dug into it. He rubbed his bleary eyes and began to walk, not quickly, not slowly, but directly back to the house. He opened the back door. The giggling sound of a womanly voice drifted out. Harry's eyes narrowed. 'Surely not! Surely, I could trust dear Molly. Surely Mark wouldn't do this to me again.'

'Do you want me to undo some more?' her voice wavered on.

'Just a couple,' said the man's voice. 'Just give me a hint of cleavage. Look, I'll show you where I mean.' He strode towards her and boldly touched the target button. At that moment, the door opened and revealed Harry Smith, red mist in front of his eyes.

'You bastard!' he croaked. 'Get your hands off her!'

Two pairs of startled eyes darted at him. 'Oh, Harry!' gasped Molly. 'Don't be silly!' But the intruder was unstoppable. Three strides took him across the room. His venomous fist smashed straight into Mark's smirking face, sending him reeling into his easel, his palette smearing paint on the wall as he fell.

'Christ, Harry!' cried Molly. 'He wasn't doing anything! We were just discussing the portrait!'

Mark was clambering to his feet. He held out his hands, palms facing Harry to beg for the violence to end. Molly's words were sinking into Harry's brain. He managed to hold back the battle-hardened fist that his instincts demanded, and he threatened it once again at the cowering weasel in front of him. 'Get out!' he growled. 'Just get the hell out of this house!'

'Harry!' Molly was still gasping in shock. 'You're crazy!' But Harry had got hold of Mark and stared at his swelling face and frightened eyes.

'That's the second time you've messed with a woman of mine!' He snarled the words. 'I should smash you into kingdom come!'

Mark twisted away from the onslaught and made for the door, a trail of devastated paints, portraits and easel in his wake. The front door slammed and he was gone.

'You stupid, stupid man!' Molly was yelling between heaving breaths, her face streaming with tears. 'The *second* time, eh?' Harry span towards her, eyes blazing. She knew what he meant. He had never really got over Mark's seduction of the lovely Helen Westhouse. 'Why the hell did you ever trust him again?' she spluttered. Her hands clutched at her hair as she sank into the chair.

Chapter 51

Helen peered from her bedroom window as she heard the pony and trap pull up. Mark climbed down. She couldn't see very clearly, but it looked as though he had blood on his face.

She had been keeping out of the way since the appearance of Walter Stokes and the constable but was so shocked by Mark's appearance that she ran downstairs.

'What the hell happened to you?' she demanded. He was staggering and holding his swirling head. He couldn't answer. She grabbed his arm and led him towards the kitchen, where the horrified Beatrice had also seen his arrival. She grimaced at the sight of his swollen face, black and blue with a nasty scarlet split across his cheek. They sat him down and began dabbing at the wound with a wet cloth. He winced and pushed them away.

In the drawing room, Walter Stokes was in tears. Bart had described the fight Matthew's terrible obsession with seeking revenge. Constable Stevens had taken it all down, scribbling madly into his notebook, a look of true anguish on his face. Walter accepted the brandy that Richard Westhouse proffered. Stevens squinted back through his notes.

'So,' he said at last. 'It's been a very complicated business, hasn't it?' They all nodded silently, sadly. 'Would it be possible to get your daughter Helen to join us?' he asked. Richard knew that Stevens could insist. He left the room to find her. She knew the moment would come. Guilt and embarrassment. Such a mixture of thoughts and emotions. How on earth could she bumble her way through this? All eyes were upon her. She tried to remember what Bart had told her to say. She stuttered and sobbed but somehow found the words, the words that Constable Stevens struggled to write down; the same story that she had told her father the night before, described the fight exactly as Bart had done, told of the mayhem that followed Bart's surprise attack. 'Had she seen how Matthew had died?' In spite of the vivid memory of sinking that damned sword into his throat, she managed to answer, 'No. I'd been bundled out of the room somehow. I remember falling at the bottom of the stairs, people pushing past me. I might have passed out. Then Bart said something about Matthew, Something like, 'Oh my God. He's dead!'

Stevens kept scribbling his notes and eventually looked up at the sullen faces. 'So,' he went on. 'Does anyone know the whereabouts of this Harry Smith?'

'Not been seen for a couple of months,' said Richard. 'Just wandered off one day. Everyone thinks he missed the action and danger of life in the navy. We assume he's gone back to join up again.'

There was silence in the room. Walter had managed to staunch his sobbing. Helen and Bart felt the horror of knowing exactly how Matthew had met his end, the guilt of inferring that Harry had been the killer. 'I can make enquiries,' Stevens broke in. 'With the navy. See if he's re-joined.'

Helen shuffled nervously. *Could he really? Could he really find Harry and question him? Would Harry confess to save her? No! He hated her. That's why he really left. Because I was a lousy whore. Went with other men. Even paid Mark more attention than I paid to him. He'll say it was me that killed Matthew, even though it was to save his rotten life. Oh God. If you're ever going to speak to me, God, speak to me now. Should I just say, 'For God's sake, it was me?''*

The words were forming on her lips; she had even cleared her throat with a grunt when a young man staggered into the doorway and supported himself against the frame. Everyone turned to stare. A frightful sight. Bandages across his battered face. 'I know where he is,' came his words, then, through gritted teeth. 'I know exactly where he is.'

'Mark,' muttered Richard. 'What on earth happened to you?'

'He thought I'd got a bit too friendly with his woman,' grumbled the intruder. 'I was only getting her set up for her portrait.' The words "his woman" caused a thump of curiosity in Helen's heart.

Blood was oozing, scarlet, through his bandage. His blackened, swollen eye completed the picture of his despair. Inside, his mind was still staggering, raging at the ignominy of the attack.

Constable Stevens was eying the fellow's state and asked, 'Are you saying that Smith did this to you?'

'He did, sir,' came Mark's reply. 'Smashed my equipment. Threw me out. The man's a maniac. Seemed so friendly at first, then just snapped just because I was discussing my model's appearance. Her clothing. Getting too close, I suppose, but not enough to deserve this lot.' Helen smirked a little, knowing only too well the artist's patter, the clever, seductive words that would lead to the pleasures of the flesh. She also understood the reaction of Harry Smith when he'd heard what was going on.

'So, where is he?' asked Stevens.

'Smith Farm,' said Mark, drawing a gasp from the others in the room. Richard groused, 'He's been on our doorstep ever since he left?'

'Seems like it.'

'Me and Walter need to pay him a visit,' said Stevens. 'Richard, you'd better come too for identification purposes.'

The three of them left the room, leaving Mark, Bart and Helen to stare at each other and wonder just where and when all this would end.

***

Molly stared up at Harry, his face reddened and anguished. She managed to dry her tears and grouched. 'You've never really got over her, have you?'

Harry glared. His anger still raged in his head and this was a jibe too many.

'Of course, I have! It's you I love, Molly. I always will. I can't bear other men messing with you. It... it...'

'Reminds you of how other men messed with your dear Helen?'

Anger flared again on his face. 'You bitch!' he yelled. 'People in the village call you a witch! They're right! You think you know everything about everyone. They say you killed Hugo to get possession of the Plough and Horses. They say you rebuilt this place to lure me back into your life. I tried to ignore all they said, but last night you told me you're one of that band of women. Are you all witches? Is this all bloody witchcraft?'

'No, it's bloody not!' she cursed, but Harry was moving towards her as he spoke, menacing, venom in his eyes. She picked up a broom to defend herself and pushed him away. He stumbled and fell into the hearth, hitting his head on a solid stone. His rage surged higher. He would kill her with his next deadly blow. He staggered. She saw her chance of survival. She reached madly for the heavy candle stick, the one that she cleaned and polished every day.

***

'Should I have just confessed to it?' mumbled Helen.

'Of course not!' said Bart. His heart went out to his sister. She'd been through so much. He could see the madness in her eyes. 'Don't torture yourself,' he went on. 'Harry will come up with some tale about self-defence. It's obvious Matthew was out to get him from everything that's been said. Harry will get out of it, you'll see.'

Helen's worried expression did not improve. 'They'd hang him, wouldn't they? If they found him guilty of murder?'

Bart's head filled with visions of the hangman's noose suspended from the yardarm, blowing in the breeze. Then visions of poor Wainwright taking that flogging. Mark jolted him back to reality. 'Honestly, the man's gone crazy,' he groused. Bart stared at him and stuttered, 'Something's happened to him. Something very odd. I went through lots with that man. He was such a hero in the navy. He's so different now—'

'I think we should go too,' Helen interrupted. 'If he tries to take the blame, I'll confess it was me.'

Bart was shaking his head, but she'd made up her mind. 'Come on!' she insisted. 'Or do I just go on my own?'

There was no point in arguing with her. Bart and Mark followed her out of the door. Beatrice's worried face drew back from the scullery window.

***

The candle stick was in Molly's fearsome grasp. It bore down towards Harry's head. His hand shot up instinctively in the preservation of his life. 'How dare you say I'm a witch!' Molly shouted as the weapon was parried away.

'If you're not a witch, you're just plain crazy!' retorted Harry. 'You could have killed me then like you did, Hugo!'

Her anger flared higher. She kicked the man hard in the ribs. He struggled to his feet and caught her as she turned away. They fell onto the table, sending an oil lamp toppling across the floor in a streak of dazzling flames. Curtains and furniture caught alight. Smoke billowed out at them, choking, blinding. Harry clambered to his feet, looking for Molly. He couldn't see her in the thickening blackness of smoke. Then a sound. A sound that made his heart thump in horror. An innocent baby cried. He must get her out!

He fumbled his way to the door. He choked; he staggered. 'Harriet!' he shouted. Her cry became an agonised scream. The disorienting smoke filled the room. He followed the sound of her cry till he found the cot. He grovelled inside. Never mind that he had her by the feet. At least he had hold of her. He clasped her upside-down to his chest and fought his way back towards the door. She screamed; she choked. Flames were engulfing the place. Heat hit Harry's face. The voice of Horatio Nelson echoed in his head. 'Death or glory!' was the cry. He was in the thick of a battle. 'Follow me!' his hero shouted. Harry ran by instinct to where the front door should be. He couldn't find it. Then, by some miracle, a voice. A man. 'Give it to me!' he was saying. Harry saw outstretched hands through the smoke. The red sleeves of a lieutenant's jacket. He pushed Harriet into the imploring hands. He saw the ceiling spin around and everything went black.

Stevens, Richard and Walter had seen the smoke. The constable in the driver's seat gave the reins a sharp crack on the horse's rump. She quickened and then whinnied and shied away as she smelled it. Stevens had to keep coaxing her on. At the gate of Smith Farm, Richard leapt out of the carriage. As he opened the gate, a man staggered away from the blazing house, babe in arms. He stumbled and fell to the ground in front of them, the baby still screaming with unknown terror.

'My God!' gasped Richard. 'What the hell?'

Lieutenant Lawrence was trying to speak, but his throat felt as though he'd inhaled on a discharged cannon. No voice came out. He pointed in horror at the inferno. 'Smith!' he managed at last, but the whole place was caving in, sending showers of sparks skywards.

Helen, Bart and Mark arrived at the gate; Helen's face was a distorted caricature of her usual beauty. The heat of the devastation drove them all further back. Lawrence shoved Harriet into Richard's arms, took off his jacket and held it over his face, then ran heroically back towards the flames. Neighbouring farmers were appearing.

'Not again!' some were muttering, remembering the time when Harry's parents had died. There was no chance of fighting the fire. They stood and watched it burn. The air filled with odd, purplish smoke.

Helen strode towards her father. 'Give her to me,' she said firmly, and Richard passed the crying infant into Helen's arms. Harriet nuzzled into Helen's bosom, looked up at her with Harry's eyes, and went quiet.

The flames were subsiding into a smouldering wreck of ash and vapour. A strange green light began to penetrate Harry's mind, and voices, muttering voices all around. Blades of grass came slowly into focus. 'He's coming round!' someone was saying.

'Is this Harry Smith?' asked Stevens, and Richard nodded his response, adding, 'Right now, it's probably a miracle he's alive.'

Constable Stevens surveyed Walter Stokes, whose face was a picture of misery, saying, 'This is obviously not the time to be discussing the death of your son.'

'Will discussing it ever bring him back?' he asked sincerely. 'I doubt if we'll ever get at the truth.'

He looked at Harry's agonised face. 'This man will deny any knowledge of Matthew's death, won't he? Nobody else seems to have witnessed it. I'll be left pondering, suspecting. Such a terrible thing, jealousy. That's what killed poor Matthew when all's said and done.' Walter was shaking his head, his world in ruins. 'My poor, poor Matthew.'

'I know how he died,' croaked a voice. Faces wheeled around to the perpetrator. Mark stood there, trembling slightly.

'What?' asked Stevens. 'What do you know?'

There was a silence. What would he say? That it was Harry? Helen? Mark relived the scene. Matthew brandished that sword, drooling over the look of terror in the lover's eyes. Helen's gyrating dance. The sudden shock of her pushing down the torn dress. Bart's crazy leap and the horrendous fight that followed.

'What an idiot I've been!' His head was a mess of memories. 'I deserved that beating. Playing the amorous artist with his woman. Stealing Helen's attention. Why the hell did I get mixed up in all this? Now everyone's looking at me. Their lives in my hands.'

He looked at the inquisitive faces and shivered and spoke, 'I saw a man grab the sword and drive it into Matthew's throat!'

The listeners gasped. Those who knew the truth squirmed inside. A man grabbed the sword? What on earth was he going to say?

'He saved Harry's life,' went on Mark. 'Matthew was strangling him to death!'

'Who killed him?' demanded Stevens.

'A hero,' said Mark. Then silence, except for his heaving breaths. A lie was forming in his head. A lie that could save their souls, their lives. Lives he had messed up with his stupid behaviour. A chance. A chance to relieve them all of their burden. 'A really brave hero,' he said and filled his lungs with chest-swelling pride. 'My brother, Andrew!'

They all stared agog, unable to believe what he'd said. Now, all of their stories fell into place. Mark's inventive mind had wrapped it all up so neatly, and Andrew was the untouchable hero in his premature grave.

Bart stared at Harry sprawled on the ground and at his sister. She clutched the child as if it was her own. Harry was groaning. A vision of worried faces in front of him and a blackened lieutenant's jacket. The man it belonged to had saved his life. He, too, lay gasping, groaning, his past life passing before his eyes.

The next time Harry woke up, he saw a fluttering curtain and heard a baby cry. He was lying on a comfortable bed, the sun streaming into his eyes. He winced. He tried to sit up, but his head felt like an enormous weight. He rolled it from side to side on the pillow. 'Are you alive?' asked a voice he knew well. He focussed on the worried face of Helen Westhouse. He tried to speak, but only a groan came from his throat. 'I'll take that as yes,' she confirmed. He found himself being propped up in the bed, Beatrice and Helen pushing pillows behind him. He wanted to collapse, but there was a compelling smell of meaty stew.

'You've got to eat!' came an Irish lilt, and a spoon was forcing the hot liquid into his mouth. It hurt, but he swallowed. It felt good. He opened his mouth again like a child wanting more.

More sleep, more food, more sleep. The sequence continued. Then, a cold, wet cloth was dabbing at his brow. 'Are you sure you're alive?' the voice questioned.

He wasn't sure, but he was feeling stronger. His eyes stayed open a little longer, taking in Helen's look of concern. The baby cried again.

'Harriet,' the name tumbled from his lips. The last thing he remembered was pushing her into the red-sleeved arms. 'Is she all right?'

'She's fine,' replied Helen. 'Got a good pair of lungs. Got her daddy's good looks.'

'And Molly?' croaked Harry.

Helen just closed her eyes.

There was silence as Harry reeled through the memory of those last moments before the fire. What a bastard he'd been. He hated himself. Then, the image of those hands reaching out to take Harriet at the moment when he thought all hope was gone. 'Who saved us?' he managed before passing out again.

A hand was shaking his shoulder now. A firm hand, masculine but youthful. There was a smell of burned cloth. Harry's eyes flickered open to the face of Lieutenant Lawrence, his scorched and torn jacket undone, revealing a bandaged chest.

'Christ!' muttered Harry. 'What a mess!'

Lawrence smirked a little. 'I reckon I'll have to get a new one.'

'You saved us, didn't you?' asked Harry, and Lawrence just nodded.

'Brave man,' went on Harry. 'Brave, brave man.'

'Lucky I was there, eh?' added the lieutenant. 'Have you started to ask yourself yet, why the hell I was there?'

Harry shook his head. Very little had engaged his thoughts except being lucky to be alive and what a bastard he'd been to poor Molly. Now she was dead and he hated himself.

'Are you ready to ask yourself now, what the hell I was doing there?'

'I suppose I am,' muttered Harry, although his glazed eyes said otherwise.

'I had an invitation in my pocket. I say *had* because it got lost in the fire, so you'll have to take my word for it.'

Harry was looking puzzled, but Lawrence continued.

'It took me a long time to track you down, but eventually, someone at the local inn said you were to be found at Smith Farm. It was a hell of a shock, I can tell you, to find the place going up in smoke and flames! Anyway, having saved your skin, I have to tell you that I was to deliver to you personally an invitation from none other than Rear Admiral Horatio Nelson. He loves having men like you around him. Men who share their loyalty to the nation and pride in doing one's duty. He remembers how you saved his life. He wants you to continue in his special barge crew.'

Harry could not have looked more shocked. That statement would take some time to sink in. He couldn't find words. So many images rampaging through his mind.

'I expect you're surprised he's going back to sea at all,' said Lawrence. 'One eye, one arm and all that, but he's the one man trusted with the mission of seeking out the damned French Fleet, skulking somewhere in the Med.

Anyway, he's getting his trusted men together for it and that includes you.'

Harry didn't know what to say. 'Think about it,' said Lawrence. 'But don't take too long. I've already used up too much time finding you and I don't know if you know, but it's four days now since that fire.'

'Christ! Is it really?' groaned Harry.

The next morning, Harry clambered out of bed to the sound of the cockerel. He washed and dressed and made his way somewhat lightheadedly downstairs. In the kitchen, he startled poor Beatrice with his sudden appearance, but she quickly recovered and produced an abundance of bread, jam and scrambled eggs, which Harry scoffed away at till he couldn't eat another thing. Helen appeared at the doorway. She didn't speak. She had Harriet in one arm, picked up the basket of chicken feed and took it out into the yard. The youngster laughed and giggled happily at the adoring flock as Helen distributed the morsels, just as she had done in her own mother's arms so many years ago. When the task was over, Helen returned to the kitchen, sat Harriet in her chair with a bowl of breakfast and came to sit at the table with Harry. Beatrice slipped out of the room.

'So,' she said in a meaningful tone. 'I hear Lieutenant Lawrence has given you a message from high places.'

'Yes,' muttered Harry. 'Did he tell you all about it?'

'He did, yes. He told me exactly what the message said. Called it an invitation.'

'Lawrence saved my life,' Harry mused. 'Harriet's too.' He didn't look Helen in the eye. He could tell she was giving him a furious glare.

'It doesn't take much working out, Harry,' she said at last. Your daughter was conceived just before we ran away.' Harry hated himself even more.

'And that lovely purple scarf that mysteriously appeared and you told me belonged to your mother? It was your lover's memento, wasn't it? She gave it to you the night we stayed at the Plough and Horses and you gave her this lovely baby!'

Silence. Just the throbbing of hearts, heaving of breaths. Harry was shaking his head slowly, sadly.

'It's all true,' said Harry. 'None of it was my idea. You can hate me if you want. I can't change it.'

'And I thought I was the guilty one,' went on Helen. 'Miserable little whore that I was. Then Enoch, then Mark. Even *that* little rat has left me now. Says it was wonderful, but I seem to bring him nothing but trouble.'

Both sat silently, exploring their emotions, realising how much they had hurt each other. Realising that it mattered. Then he saw it. He hadn't noticed it before. Something on her hand, on her finger. A tangle of copper that housed something precious. A glistening little chip of blue john stone. So proud to wear it. 'Give it to someone who deserves it,' she had said, then found it trodden into the ground under her window some days later.

'Are you going to accept the invitation to serve your country once again?' she asked.

'And leave you to look after my daughter?'

'I will if you want me to. We've become quite attached over the last few days.'

'What if I never get back?'

'You will, Harry Smith. Somehow, I know that you will, and what would poor Nelson do without you to protect him? You know you have unfinished work. .They looked earnestly into each other's eyes and, after several heartbeats, Helen took the necklace from around her neck and handed it to Harry. 'I'm going to wear your ring while you're away. I want you to keep this as a symbol of our love. Look at it every day and think of me. I've no doubt you will wear that awful purple scarf as you think it has some magical powers, but don't let it remind you of Molly Elizabeth, let it remind you of your beautiful daughter, and your mission in the navy. Be proud that it's stained with the blood of your hero.'

End.

The sequel.

Join me in the further adventures of Harry Smith. He re-enlists into the navy with Bart hoping to continue his loyal service to the charismatic leader who has invited hm to return. There are more sea battles to be won but he must also tussle with enemies within the navy, who still believe he attempted desertion and want justice. A new witness has been found and things look bad.

It's not plain sailing for Helen either. She is terrified that Harriet is in poor health and that Harry will despise her if she is lost. She puts her faith in disreputable people who do not have the child's best interests at heart. Could her sordid past return to haunt her?

What would await Harry if he overcame all the struggles and difficulties to return? There are far more twists and turns in his tormented relationship with Helen. Will this bring an end to their saga? It's difficult to believe that it will.